FROM THE AWARD-WINNING AUTHOR OF THE ZOMBIE WEST SERIES

ANYONE?

ANGELA SCOTT

Anyone?
Copyright © 2014 by Angela Scott
Cover Art Copyright © 2014 by Mallory Rock

FIRST EDITION SOFTCOVER

ISBN: 1622538633
ISBN-13: 9781622538638

Editor: Stevie Mikayne

Interior Layout & Formatting: Mallory Rock

Printed in the U.S.A.

www.EvolvedPub.com
Evolved Publishing LLC
Cartersville, Georgia

Anyone? is a work of fiction. All names, characters, places, and incidents are the product of the author's imagination, or are used fictitiously. Any resemblance to actual events or persons, living or dead, is entirely coincidental.

Printed in Book Antiqua font.

OTHER BOOKS BY ANGELA SCOTT

THE DESERT SERIES
BOOK 1 - DESERT RICE
BOOK 2 - DESERT FLOWER

THE ZOMBIE WEST SERIES
BOOK 1 - WANTED: DEAD OR UNDEAD
BOOK 2 - SURVIVOR ROUNDUP
BOOK 3 - DEAD PLAINS
OMNIBUS EDITION - THE ZOMBIE WEST TRILOGY

WHAT OTHERS ARE SAYING ABOUT ANGELA SCOTT'S BOOKS:

WANTED: DEAD OR UNDEAD

"IT WAS WELL WRITTEN, WELL PLOTTED AND VERY ENTERTAINING (EVEN THE LOVEY DOVEY ASPECTS OF IT!). IF YOU LIKE A GOOD SHOOT OUT, AND ZOMBIES TRYING TO EAT YOUR BRAINS FOR BRUNCH, PICK IT UP... YOU WON'T BE SORRY."

- KINDLEOBSESSED REVIEWS

"I GAVE THIS BOOK FIVE STARS, BECAUSE IT WAS A TOTAL SURPRISE. I THOUGHT - ZOMBIES - WILD WEST - WHERE CAN SHE GO WITH THIS. AND SHE TOOK ME ON A RIDE THROUGH TOWNS, PRAIRIES, HOT AND COLD AND EVERYTHING YOU CAN THINK THE WILD WEST WOULD INCLUDE. EXCEPT FOR THE ZOMBIES. A UNIQUE READ AND I AM ALWAYS HAPPY TO COME ACROSS A BOOK THAT SURPRISES ME AND TAKES ME OFF ON A NEW AND DIFFERENT ADVENTURE. THIS WAS A QUICK READ. GRIPPING FROM THE FIRST PAGES. ONCE I STARTED IT, I COULDN'T PUT IT DOWN."

- SHERRI FUNDIN, AMAZON REVIEWER

DESERT RICE

"I SERIOUSLY STILL HAVE CHILLS ON MY ARMS!! ANGELA SCOTT HAS SOME OF THE BEST FIRST CHAPTERS AND MID BOOK TWISTS THAT I HAVE EVER READ."

- BOOKLOVER BLOGGER

"TO SEE THE LOVE OF A BIG BROTHER, JACOB, FOR HIS LITTLE SISTER, SAM, UNFOLD AS THEY TRY TO SURVIVE AFTER A HORRIBLE ORDEAL WAS MESMERIZING. THIS IS A MYSTERY, A THRILLER, BUT ABOVE ALL, FOR ME, A STORY OF LOVE AND HOW FAR SOMEONE WILL GO TO PROTECT THAT LOVE. SCOTT'S CHARACTERIZATION AND PACING IS SENSATIONAL"

- MICHAELREVIEWS, AMAZON REVIEWER

"I'M A VERY DIFFICULT READER TO PLEASE AND THIS ISN'T A BOOK I WOULD TYPICALLY READ, BUT I READ IT AND BOY WAS I BLOWN AWAY. THIS NOVEL CAPTIVATED ME, NOT FROM THE FIRST PAGE BUT FROM THE VERY FIRST SENTENCE, WHERE WE ARE BROUGHT SMACK IN THE MIDDLE OF THE ACTION."

- MOSLIMAH

For my husband and three children.
I dedicate this book to you, despite knowing you will most likely never see this dedication.
Especially, since not one of you has read ANY of my previous books.
I expect this will be the same.

This is book number seven after all.
I will say this, though: whether they read this dedication or not, I still appreciate their unwavering support and oodles of love.
I know they think having an author for a wife and mother is pretty darn cool — except for the times they go without being fed so I can reach a deadline.

CHAPTER 1

The blast rocked the house on its foundation, imploding the windows. I covered my face with my arms and dove onto my mattress as tiny shards of glass pricked my skin and sprinkled through my hair. A loud rumble washed over me, almost deafening. I didn't dare raise my head, but when the shaking subsided a minute later, I peeked between my arms. *What in the world is that?*

Pictures had fallen and now lay broken on my carpet. The wall shelf dangled by one hook and swung side to side like a pendulum, with all my trophies and souvenirs lying scattered below. My desk chair had tumbled over and large snowflakes flittered in through the broken windows to melt to death on my warm floor. My curtains danced with the winter breeze.

Dad came to a skidding halt at my open door, his hands gripping the frame. "You okay?"

Unsure, I took a moment to examine the cuts on my arms and legs — mostly scratches, nothing serious — before nodding.

"Then grab your bag, Tess! Grab it now!"

"What's going on? What was that?"

"Just do it!" He disappeared down the hall.

Maybe I didn't need to know what was happening or maybe he didn't know either, but either way, being told to grab my seventy-two hour kit was enough.

I wasted no time sliding to my knees next to my bed and reaching underneath to pull out the emergency duffle bag — clothes, toiletries, blanket, MREs, my own compact Smith & Wesson I'd been given almost seven years ago for my tenth birthday — a gift I remembered being quite pissed about. I'd wanted an American Girl Doll and was given a gun instead. Every little girl's dream.

I tugged my winter boots over my bare feet and threw a jacket over my nightgown just as Dad stopped in front of my door again. Instead of looking at me, he stared off down the hallway, looking both ways, then waved me toward him. "Let's go!"

I hitched my bag onto my shoulders, but a tiny *meow* stopped me before I took Dad's outstretched hand. The orange and white ball of fluff trembled in the corner of my closet amid the large pile of dirty laundry I kept swearing I'd wash but never seemed to get around to.

"Come here, Callie. Come here girl!"

"Leave her, we've got to go!" Dad still wouldn't look at me.

I took a step toward the closet, ignoring him. "Come on, Callie. It's okay. Come on now."

"Leave the damn cat! We don't have time for this."

"She's scared. I can't leave her!" *How could I leave her to fend for herself when she could hardly remember to use the litter box on her own?*

Dad released his breath and pushed me aside, then reached for the four-month-old kitten and grabbed her by the scruff of her neck. He shoved her into my arms as she fought against his rough hands, squirming to get away. "Can we go now?"

I nodded, and he slipped his own bag onto his shoulder and darted down the hall.

I wrapped my coat around my terrified cat, doing my best to ignore her frantic clawing as she wriggled around, seeming to find safety in the pit of my arm—a very sensitive place to keep a cat.

Dad had already taken off for the front of the house, but when I stepped into the hallway, my breath caught in my throat and my feet rooted me in place. Down the far end of the hall, the outside wall lay in a crumbled mess, covering Dad's bed in sheetrock and aluminum siding. Snow blew in through the giant hole and dusted his overturned dresser. The ceiling lamp dangled from an electrical cord.

"Tess!"

I found my feet, turned in the opposite direction, away from the destruction, and followed after his voice. Most of the windows in the living room and kitchen were shattered, and my boots crunched the glass into the wooden floor as I passed. The microwave had fallen from the counter and crashed onto the dishes and food that had been dumped from the cupboards. Family pictures had slipped from their nails.

Mom's treasured curio cabinet, with all the knickknacks she'd collected before her death, lay face down—bits of broken ceramics and blown glass figures mixed together. I fought the urge to right the curio and save what I could—save her memories—but Dad called me to follow him.

He climbed out the sliding door toward the backyard. "Watch yourself!"

I angled my body sideways and avoided the jagged edges. I'd barely stepped onto the patio when he grabbed my hand and yanked me across the snow-covered grass.

Callie dug her claws into my side and hung on to my ribs.

A yelp escaped my lips, but Dad didn't stop dragging me away from the house, and Callie adjusted herself again, her sharp nails tearing even further into my cold flesh.

Maybe trying to save her had been a huge mistake.

Another *boom* caused the ground to tremble, and I nearly lost my footing, but Dad held me upright and dragged me after him. Dark clouds mushroomed a few blocks away and rose into the sky. The crackling of fire and the smell of smoke rattled my senses as wisps of snow twirled around me, licking my lashes and stinging my eyes. Gray ash mixed with the falling snow.

He didn't have to tell me where we were headed. When he knelt over the square metal door, partially hidden by shrubs and wild trees, a great sense of gratitude flooded over me for my doomsday father and his insane need to prepare for every possible end-of-the-world disaster. Only now, he didn't seem so insane.

He brushed the snow aside, popped the hatch, and lifted the door that led down into the darkened shelter. He tossed his bag inside and it landed with a resounding thump against the metal floor. "Go on!" He urged me forward. "The generator switches are on the left." He grabbed my bag and tossed it into the hole too.

I tried to shift Callie, but she wouldn't retract her claws, so I ignored her the best I could and climbed down the ladder into the dark metal tube.

"Can you find the switch?"

I ran my hands over the cool interior of the bomb shelter, searching for the elusive switches that would bring the whole thing to life. The metal reminded me of a green bean can with all its rolling bumps—life in a giant vegetable can.

My fingers ran over the switches and I flipped them both upright. The florescent lights flickered, and it took a moment for my eyes to adapt to the harsh light.

"I got it!"

The air system started to whirl, bringing fresh air from the outside into the underground bunker.

Callie finally released her mad grip on me and ran down my side to disappear under the couch. I couldn't have been more pleased.

Dad knelt near the opening and looked down at me. "Don't open this door for anyone, do you understand? Not anyone."

"Wait! What? You're leaving me?" Panic gripped my chest and crushed my lungs. I reached for the ladder, determined to climb back out. I'd rather fight against whatever was happening outside than be left alone down here.

"I've got to go for Toby, and once I find him, we'll be back."

How could I have forgotten my brother? Maybe because he was a giant asshole to me and an even bigger one to Dad, but whatever, he was still my brother—even if the idea of spending any amount of time with him in an underground bunker sounded torturous.

I let go of the ladder. Of course, Dad needed to find him, wherever he was. At his girlfriend Kenzie's? Behind the MoviePlex smoking with his stoner friends? Or maybe hustling pool at Parker and James's bar? It shouldn't be that hard to find the loser.

"We'll be back, I promise. It won't take long. Don't open the door unless you hear this." He gave the metal door a rap with his knuckles—my name in Morse Code. "Don't you come out, Tess. You stay put and we'll be back. Promise me you won't open this door."

I nodded.

"Promise me!"

"I promise."

He paused, his hand on the square hatch. "Lock it from the inside. Every latch."

Panic began to rise in my chest again. "I will."

"I love you, Tess."

"I love you too." Tears welled in my eyes. "Please hurry."

With that, he lowered the door into place.

CHAPTER 2

I stood there for the longest time staring up at the square door, the latches unattached. Part of me hoped Dad would change his mind and come back. Screw Toby. He didn't seem to care much for Dad or me, not after Mom died, so why should Dad risk his life for him? He should stay with me, here, where it was safe.

It was selfish, but I didn't care. I needed my dad.

But the door didn't open. The realization Dad wasn't coming back anytime soon finally settled in, so I shimmied up the ladder and snapped each latch into place like he'd told me to. It took a little muscle, but I got them closed. No one was getting inside— not by trying to pull it open, not by pounding on it, not even by gunfire. The bunker was built to withstand almost everything tossed at it.

But when the earth trembled, I slid down the ladder and stood at the bottom with my heart thumping like crazy and my arms wrapped around my middle. I waited for the whole contraption to come squeezing in on me; for the dirt to fall in and crush the entire thing like stepping on an aluminum can. Yes, the

Atlas Survival Shelter was supposed to protect against all sorts of horrible things, but would it really? *Really?*

Callie meowed from her safe place under the couch, and I wished I could squeeze under there with her.

"Hey, baby! Come here. It's okay." I knelt beside the couch and tried to reach her. She'd scratched the heck out of me, but for some reason the idea of holding onto her, holding onto *something*, was better than the alternative—alone and afraid twenty feet below the ground. "Come on, Callie!"

She was outside my reach, so I lowered myself to my belly and tried again. The earth began to shake and I froze, as if freezing in place could stop everything bad from happening. *Please, no, please no, please no.*

Nothing happened, so freezing must have worked. The shelter remained intact, but I couldn't move. I didn't dare.

Dad always had these wild ideas of possible wars with other countries, or a giant earthquake which would destroy half the planet, or medical mishaps which would render a person brainless but alive. Zombies. Toby and I had teased him about that.

"You can't possibly be serious about the walking dead? That's just plain jackassery." Toby had smiled at me then and used his finger to make a swirling motion near his ear—cuckoo. Perhaps it was the only time the two of us ever agreed on anything.

Dad *was* losing it. We joked, but there was also something behind Toby's eyes I recognized. I felt it too. Ever since Mom's death, Dad had gone to the extreme—seventy two hour kits, guns, food storage, practice drills, the bunker—but neither of us knew what to do about it.

I brushed it off as harmless. What did it matter if Dad installed a forty-five foot bomb shelter in our suburban backyard? Who did it hurt? Nobody. Plus, it seemed to make him happy. How could I fault him for that?

But kids at school kidded around. Some even nicknamed my dad the Militia Man, and would ask me if I slept with an AK-47 under my bed. The idiots. I'd looked them dead in the eye, all serious, and leaned in close. I told them no; I slept with a Smith & Wesson instead. That usually shut them up.

Who was laughing now? I bet they were all running around up above, wetting themselves. Dad had been right and he'd been prepared unlike their parents who spent money on fancy vacations or in-ground swimming pools and hot tubs. Nothing lasting. Not like this.

I chuckled at the thought of Dad being right and their parents being wrong, and my maniacal laughter echoed off the metal. Fear and mirth—two emotions on the opposite ends of the emotional spectrum, but I felt them both, plus everything else in between. I shouldn't be laughing at anyone else's possible misfortunes. Here I was in the middle of a giant tin can below the earth and I was terrified too.

I chuckled again.

Get a hold of yourself, for Pete's sake! It's gonna be okay. It will.

Callie inched toward my outstretched hand. My laughter must have eased her fears, even though it only exacerbated mine. It didn't matter. I grabbed onto her and drew her into my arms, nearly squeezing the life out of her.

The florescent lights flickered, and even though it made no sense, like running down the aisle of a plane falling from the sky, I climbed into one of the bottom bunks and pressed my back to the far corner. The bit of darkness felt more natural than the harsh light and having the upper bunk above me made me feel the same way Callie must have felt under the couch.

The kitten snuggled into me, her claws gripping my shirt. I didn't care. I needed her as much as she seemed to need to me. I curled myself around her and drew into a tight ball as far away from the edge of the bed as I could manage.

"It's going to be okay." I whispered. "It's going to be just fine."

Callie meowed in response as if she understood me.

Funny, because I wasn't even talking to her.

My eyes blinked open, and I flew upright, nearly cracking my skull on the bed above me. I didn't realize it was possible to sleep while the world ended all around me, yet somehow I'd done just that.

The clock on the shelf blinked. Ten-thirty. Six hours since Dad had left me down here. Six hours. He should've been back by now. *Did I miss his knocking? Did I sleep right through it?*

Panicked, I left Callie asleep on the bed and went to wait beneath the door.

If he knocked and I missed it, he'll come back, right? Of course he would. There was no way he'd leave me. No way at all. Still I waited and listened as if at any moment the Morse Code knock would happen. *What's taking Dad so long?*

I glanced at the clock again. It had to be wrong because finding Toby shouldn't take six hours. I climbed the ladder and pressed the side of my head against the door, listening for any clue as to what was happening outside. Whatever had caused the earth to rumble and make mushroom clouds burst in the sky seemed to have stopped. That had to be a good sign, but I couldn't hear a thing.

"Dad, you out there?"

Come on, knock. Please!

Silence.

Callie stood at the edge of the bed and stretched, arching her back. She stared at me and began a string of non-stop *meows*.

"Shush, I can't hear." She needed to be quiet, just in case, but she kept right on at it.

A part of me wanted to unlatch the door and fling it open, check everything out and see for myself, but I'd promised I wouldn't.

The darn cat wouldn't shut up.

"Okay, okay." I climbed back down the ladder. She was still a baby after all and probably hungry. As for using the litter box, I hadn't thought of that when I'd brought her down here, but I'd need to figure something out quick or I'd have quite the mess on my hands.

As for Dad and Toby, I'd have to stay awake and make sure to really listen. If they'd come and I had missed it, I knew Dad would wait and try again.

I scooped up the kitten in my arms. "I guess it's time to figure out what we've got down here to eat, huh?"

She nuzzled against me, but kept on with her incessant howling.

"Okay, we'll find something for you." *And maybe a little something for me while we're at it.*

There were MREs in both mine and Dad's bags, but the very idea of cracking any of them open seemed appalling. There had to be something better. Dad had installed several shelves, and lined them with various sized cans, along with toilet paper, hygiene products, medicine, and vitamins. The endless supply of cans overwhelmed me, but I grabbed a small tin can I recognized.

"How about some tuna for you?" I put Callie down and she followed at my feet as I searched through the various cupboards and drawers for a can opener. Dad had thought of it all, and to see his preparedness not only gave me even more admiration for him, but scared me a little too. He'd seemed to have planned for everything, and that couldn't have been a happy way to live—fearful of the worst.

He'd supplied the place with food, a small fridge, a stove, a sink, a toilet, a trash compactor, and a television with shelves of DVDs and board games. There was even a CD player and dozens of CDs to choose from. In one drawer lay crayons and coloring books—princess and Barbie. He'd been putting things down here for years. He must have forgotten I wasn't ten anymore and didn't color, but it was nice of him to consider my boredom.

I opened the can and sat it in the middle of the floor. Callie dipped her face right into it and the *meowing* stopped as she started eating.

A sigh escaped my lips as I took in my new surroundings, trying to figure everything out. I turned on the sink faucet and water poured out. *It works.* I quickly shut it off, not wanting to waste a drop.

I took more time looking through every drawer and cupboard, and opening every storage bin to see what supplies there were, though I didn't intend on staying down here long enough to use most of them.

Each of the mattresses hung over the edge of the beds and when I lifted them, saw a good three inch deep storage area under them, the entire size of the bed. Dad's clothes filled one, Toby's filled another, and a third bed held my clothes—underwear, socks, sweatshirts, and pants. Remembering the coloring books, I suspiciously plucked out a pair of jeans, shocked to find they were my exact size. So what was with the coloring books then? It didn't matter. I tossed the jeans back inside and lifted the fourth mattress.

Thick winter coats, several sleeping bags and blankets, hats, and gloves, and to top off the stash, a huge stack of porn magazines in the corner. *Seriously?* The very idea of my dad or Toby looking at them gave me the creeps. *Yuck.* They looked brand new, but still.

Well, if they didn't come back soon, I'd put the dirty magazines to use and let Callie do her business on them. I mean, my bed was right across from theirs—what were they thinking?

I lowered the mattress and noticed the latches all along the floor boards, so I bent and lifted one. Underneath the entire floor, lined from one end of the bunker to the other, stood fifty gallon barrel drums, presumably filled with water. There had to be thirty of them. *Good to know.*

After exploring the toilet and figuring out how to use the darn thing, and checking the emergency hatch on the opposite side of the shelter, I grabbed a can of peaches from the shelf, opened it, and flopped down on the couch to eat.

What's going on up above?

CHAPTER 3

Thirty-six hours.

I paced from one end of the shelter to the other. They should've been back by now and since they weren't, I had no idea what to do. Dad had said to stay put, but a large part of me wondered if they were in some kind of trouble—hurt or injured—and needed my help.

Go? Stay? I didn't know which option was right, or even where I would begin to start looking for them. *What's happening out there?*

I picked up Callie, cradled her in my arms, and sat on the edge of my bed. "Should we go?" I asked the wiggling kitten. "We could pack a bag and some food, and go look for them. We could always come back if we had to. This place will still be here." I stroked her fur, which seemed to please her and she purred and settled in my lap. Going seemed the best choice, because staying made me feel helpless and afraid. Not knowing what was going on caused my mind to imagine the worst scenarios.

"After lunch we'll leave." I included the little cat in my plans, because I couldn't leave her alone in case I found my brother and dad and couldn't get back to her. It would make things tricky, carrying a kitten around, but she was my responsibility. I'd begged for a cat until Dad had finally given in. It only took a few tears and threatening to pierce my tongue to get him to cave. If it came down to it, piercing my tongue was never an option. Hangnails hurt so I couldn't even imagine deliberately forcing a piece of metal through the floppy muscle I used to eat with. And besides, I liked food. I wouldn't want anything to get in the way of that.

At first, taking care of the defiant little creature had taken a lot of work and patience, and I'd even planned to give her back to the animal shelter at one point, but now I was so grateful to have her. Especially down here in the belly of the earth.

I would make sure to leave a note for Dad in case he came for me and found me gone.

"Yep." I continued to pet the kitten. "We'll leave after lunch." Perhaps the more I said it out loud, the braver I'd become. Hopeful thinking.

Callie swiped at my hand, her sign she'd had enough, so I stopped, and she jumped down from my lap. I sighed. *We'll leave after lunch.*

While an individual serving of macaroni and cheese warmed in the microwave, I grabbed my bag and added more supplies to the already bulky thing—food for Callie and extra water for the both of us. I included an extra wool blanket and a few winter items to keep the weather from kicking my butt.

I couldn't find any paper or pens anywhere, so I used the crayons and ripped a page out of the coloring book to write on, drawing all over Sleeping Beauty's face.

WEDNESDAY 10:00am

Dad,
You said to wait, and I stayed as long as I could, but I started to get worried. I left to go looking for you since you took forever to come for me, but I will be back on

Friday, in case you came back while I'm gone. Stay here. I WILL be back. Unless I find you, then ignore this.
  Love, Tess

P.S. Don't be mad at me. You were supposed to be here by now, so technically this is your fault.

I placed the note on the counter, propped against the microwave so it could easily be seen. After giving Callie some condensed milk, I sat down on the couch to eat my lunch.

The idea of leaving scared the crap out of me, but the idea of not knowing what was going on scared me even worse. I ate my lunch slowly.

The kitten started with her incessant meowing. She had food. She had milk. She'd already used the litter box.

"What do you want?" I lowered my fork to my bowl.

She arched her back and stared at the open door between the decontamination area of the shelter and the living room, then kept *meowing*, which was strange for her. She hadn't behaved like this before.

"You want to play? Is that it?" I waved around a pair of balled up socks, a homemade toy I'd made out of Toby's supplies—the jerk—but even when I threw it for her, she didn't bother to go after it like she normally did. It rolled across the floor and came to a stop in the far corner.

I placed my bowl to the side, scooped up the cat in my arms, and started petting her, trying to calm her. "You okay? What's going on, huh? You nervous too?"

She twisted away from me—giving me two fresh scratches on my arms for my effort—and disappeared under the couch. She kept right on meowing.

"You know, sometimes you remind me of my brother." *Weird cat. Whatever.*

I held my empty bowl under the sink spigot and pumped a little water to rinse it out.

Banging on the square metal hatch caused me to drop the bowl in the sink. It clattered and I spun around.

Slam! Slam! Slam!

Muffled yelling and even more banging followed, then the sound of a shovel scraping against metal, like nails scratching a black board.

I stiffened, didn't move, and hardly breathed.

Dad?

A large part of me hoped it was him, but a greater part of me knew he would have used the code.

Callie's meowing grew louder.

Voices, definitely male, were forceful, frantic, but their words were indecipherable. Chills ran down my spine and the hairs on my neck and arms stood erect.

When rapid fire bullets ricocheted against the door, I dove for my bed. Lost in the shadows, I covered my head with my arms, trying to block out the machine gun sounds. Not the bravest thing to do, but the *only* thing I knew to do.

My heart thrummed and my chest heaved with frightened breaths. *What do I do? What do I do?*

The gunfire ceased briefly, replaced by more banging. In a moment of courage, I managed to run from my safe place and slam the door shut, separating the decontamination area from the living area. My hands shook, but I latched the lock into place. Even if they managed to break through the metal square door—highly unlikely—they'd never get through the bomb door. Still, fear continued to hold me in its grip.

I ran to the opposite side of the shelter and crawled up the tube toward the escape door and found relief at seeing it secure. No one banged on it or fired bullets at it. Perhaps they had no idea it even existed. Dad had hid it quite well.

The crazy noise, now muffled by the bomb door, seemed to carry on forever. Dad should have stayed with me. He shouldn't have left me alone here. What would happen if they got inside? What did they want? Would they take everything I had? The supplies? The food?

Would they kill me?

I wanted to cover my ears with my hands and refuse to listen to the men's crazy efforts as I'd done before, but I forced myself to slide to my knees in front of my bed and reach for my duffle bag. My fingers shook as I fumbled around inside, wrenching out all the things I'd packed earlier, scattering the contents around, until I found what I was looking for.

My gun.

I planted myself square in the middle of the bunker, aiming toward the door. My arms shook and my breathing quickened. I pulled back the hammer and the gun seemed to weigh a ton, heavier than it had ever felt before.

My training had only been at the local firing range and with black and white paper targets. Nothing threatening. Nothing real. Could I shoot a person if I had to? I didn't know. I wasn't the violent type— more like a wallflower when it came to other people and to confrontation. I was more likely to walk away than throw a punch.

But this was different.

I'd become so used to the on-and-off-again machine gun fire that when it ended for good, the surrounding silence felt loud in my ears. The voices fell away to nothingness. The quiet of it all engulfed me, but I refused to lower my gun. My courage had budded to the surface just moments before the silence, a burst of adrenaline, and now it wouldn't fade so easily, even though the threat appeared to be over.

I don't know how long I continued to stand there with my arms straight, the gun pointed at the door and my head swimming with horrible images of what might be happening above me.

Was this it? Was this the end of the world Dad had prepared for?

Maybe it was better not to know. At least that way, I still had some hope.

Callie rubbed herself against my leg, purring like a completely different cat than the maniac animal she'd been earlier. I ignored her until her tiny claws pierced the material of my pants and pricked my skin.

I pushed the hammer back into the safety position and tucked the gun in my waistband. My heart still thrummed, but I picked up Callie and held her tight.

"So what do we do now?"

She purred a response, and I buried my face in her soft fur and cried. After several minutes of my holding her, she wriggled free and went back to exploring our tiny home, walking along the counters and the back of the couch as though nothing had ever happened.

I grabbed my crayon scribbled note and read it over several times.

Please be okay and please come back for me. Please.

I closed my eyes, angry for being left alone and not being strong enough or brave enough to go after them or to simply be on my own either. I sank my teeth into my trembling lip in an effort to stop more tears sliding down my cheeks, then crumpled the paper into a tight ball and tossed it away.

Callie bounded after it and proceeded to rip it to shreds.

CHAPTER 4

"This city is headed for a disaster of biblical proportions."

"What do you mean, 'biblical'?"

"What he means is Old Testament, Mr. Mayor, real wrath-of-God type stuff."

"Exactly."

"Fire and brimstone coming down from the skies! Rivers and seas boiling!"

"Forty years of darkness! Earthquakes, volcanoes...."

"The dead rising from the grave!"

"Human sacrifice, dogs and cats living together... mass hysteria!"

"All right, all right! I get the point!"

I pressed the rewind on the remote; the video skimmed backward and the scene and words repeated themselves. At the end, I pressed pause and watched the stilled actors on the television, their mouths contorted, their eyes half blinking. *Thanks a lot, Ghostbusters. Thanks a bunch.*

Was that going on above? Fire and brimstone, boiling seas? I'd been down in this tin box for eight *long* days, crossing each one off on the calendar with the hope that Dad would finally show up. The stupid movie was supposed to take my mind off my troubles, but instead it got me wondering and thinking again—not a good pastime for an idle person. And I thought I was safe with *Ghostbusters*.

Dad supplied the bunker with a shelf of movies, but the majority of them leaned more toward Toby and his tastes, not mine—*Resident Evil, The Shining, The Ring, Silence of the Lambs, etc.*... There were also some Disney princess movies to go along with my coloring books—something I may have enjoyed when I was three—and nestled between *Snow White* and *Ariel,* he had tucked the movie *Black Swan.* He obviously had no idea that movie had no Disney qualities to it whatsoever. At least he'd installed a TV and movies. It would be a whole lot worse down here if he hadn't.

I continued to hold the remote as I rolled over flat on my back and stared at the ceiling above me.

Callie napped on the back of the couch, curled in a little ball, content. She didn't care what movie we watched. She had come to accept our new surroundings, adjusting to life living in a twenty-by-eight-foot space a lot easier than I thought she would.

I ran my hand lightly over her fur, not waking her, but needing to feel her to remind myself I wasn't truly alone.

I hit the play button and the silence fell away to the sounds of ghosts and men trying to capture them without getting slimed, but looked away from the screen. For all I knew there could very well be a real life giant marshmallow man stomping around above me right now, crushing houses and causing destruction with his inflated body. Not knowing allowed me to think about all sorts of strange possibilities, but a giant marshmallow man didn't sound half as bad as some of my other thoughts—earthquake, war, aliens from another planet.

Screw this.

I tossed the remote aside, leaving the movie on, and rolled

over with my back facing the television. I didn't want to watch anymore, but couldn't face listening to silence either.

Thirteen days.

I held up my princess coloring page—outlined in darker colors and shaded for effect. It had taken me three hours to add the details and the appearance of texture to give the manufactured coloring page a bit of needed flare. "Whatcha think?"

Callie stopped licking herself, glanced at me for a brief second then went back to grooming.

"Well, I think it's pretty darn good." I ripped off a piece of duct tape and hung my masterpiece on the only flat surface in the bunker—the bombproof door. If only I'd taken my time like this on my school art projects, maybe I would've produced something worthy of a grade higher than a C. Oh, well. But one thing was clear: I had talent, even if Mrs. Dillagre didn't think so. No one looking at my shading and texturing of Cinderella could think otherwise.

I stared at the door with my crooked coloring page dangling from it. I hadn't opened the door since the day the men tried to break in. I hadn't dared. That also meant I hadn't taken a full-fledged shower since then either. The only shower was in the decontamination area, and with the door shut I had no access to it. Sponge baths helped, but barely hid my stink, not like it mattered.

Who did I have to impress? Callie? I actually think she preferred my malodor.

The earth no longer rumbled, and no one had banged on the square door in an effort to get in—not since that day anyway—but having one extra door between me and the world gave me comfort.

"Should I open it? Huh?"

Callie arched her back and stretched. She jumped down from the couch, came to me, and rubbed herself against my ankles. That seemed like a yes.

"You want more space to explore? Is that it?" The decontamination area was only four feet long, if that, but cramped in our tiny space it may as well have been a football field. More room. More possibilities. And I could really use a shower.

I refused to open it without being prepared. No way. So I grabbed my gun off the top bunk—close, if I needed it, but not in the way—and reached out my hand to open one of the latches. If someone had managed to blast a hole through the square door, then I'd shut the bomb door once more. Simple. Who needed a shower anyway?

One latch clicked open, then another. I really could have used both hands free, but I had no plans to set the gun down at all. One handed, I removed each latch and opened the door, a crack at first, then a little more.

Callie shot past my feet and ran into the new area. *Damn it.* I should have realized that would happen. Now I didn't have a choice but to open the door the entire way if I wanted my cat back.

Cautious, I continued to hold the gun and pushed the door all the way open. My heart pounded, but seeing the square door above me secured and undamaged from this side brought me a lot of relief. I lowered my gun and stepped into the dark area.

There wasn't much to it. The door, which led to the world above, the ladder to climb up or down, and the shower area. Not much at all. It was kind of a disappointment, like waiting all of December to open the biggest present under the tree to only find out it was a stupid desk for studying and not the stereo system Santa was supposed to have brought.

It wasn't as though I hadn't seen the area when I'd first come into the shelter, but after nearly two weeks of not seeing it, I guess I'd hoped for more. Even Callie seemed a bit put-off by it. She wandered around, rubbing herself against the walls before returning to her favorite napping spot on the couch.

In that moment, I kind of wanted to do the same. Sleeping at least made the time go by quicker.

I made sure the safety was on my gun and tucked it into the waistband of my pants, then scaled the ladder, a bit afraid, but not nearly as much as before, to listen for any sound—anyone talking, screams, gunfire, anything. Nothing but silence greeted me.

It would be so easy to unlatch the door and step out, breathe in fresh air and take in my surroundings. I could finally figure out what was happening. Only three latches separated me from leaving the shelter. Dad had said to wait, and I had for two long weeks. He wasn't coming back; I knew that now.

But I climbed down the ladder and stared at the door. My mind wondered endlessly about what might be happening above, but opening the door would bring reality crashing down around me. What if I didn't like what reality had to offer? What if it was terrifying and awful?

Nope. I would leave another day, when I felt more ready.

I turned the knob on and a fine stream flowed out of the detachable shower head. Not cold, but not hot either. Lukewarm at best.

Letting it run didn't help, but I gathered a towel and some soap. Even though it wasn't a steamy hot shower as I would have liked, it did the job and I stood under the stream for a long, long time.

Twenty-six days.

I was getting lazy and fat, which didn't make a ton of sense, especially since much of the food down here sucked—processed and canned, *yum*—but with so little to do, I kept finding myself camped out on the couch, watching movies over and over while snacking on anything I could get my hands on. Sometimes salty. Sometimes sweet. Whatever it took to match my mood. I actually tried sardines once out of salty desperation. Yeah, sardines. I could only stomach one, but Callie sure seemed to enjoy them, so I gave her the rest. She could have them all.

Some days I ate mashed potatoes—well, a form of mashed potatoes—add hot water and mix together. The mac and cheese I'd polished off the week before—the only thing tasting half decent. Dried fruit. Canned veggies. Beef jerky. I ate a whole bottle of peanut butter in one sitting once by dipping my fingers inside the jar like an animal. I didn't care and at the time it tasted wonderful, but now, the very idea of anything peanut-related made my stomach curl in on itself.

The food was gross, but I ate it anyway, and had become a big underground couch potato blob.

Twelve days ago, I'd told myself I would leave this place after thirty days. I would pack up, get brave, and head out of here. But four days didn't seem like nearly enough time. I shouldn't have screwed around, doing nothing, watching movies all day.

I pinched my belly fat, holding my skin between my thumb and forefinger. I hadn't gotten obese yet, but I needed to make some serious changes. Who knew how far I might have to walk once I headed outside or if I might have to be physical with someone, heaven forbid.

I'd lived twenty-six days down here, on my own, and to poke my head outside only to have someone knock it off would really blow.

I couldn't exactly go for a walk anytime I wanted. The shelter wasn't equipped for exercise, just surviving, so I had to make do with whatever came to hand—not much.

I grabbed a mattress off one of the beds and tossed it on the floor in front of the couch to give me a little cushioning, then put on a little music—oldies my dad listened to—and slipped my feet under the couch for leverage. Ten sit-ups sounded like a good place to begin.

But in reality, ten sit-ups felt like hell.

I couldn't believe how out of shape I'd become. I wasn't a super athletic person, but I did P.E. every other day at school, which should count for something—all those laps and dodging balls. Twenty-six days shouldn't have erased all that. Though apparently, it had.

I lay on the mattress and took a little rest before attempting another set of sit-ups. By the time I reached twenty my gut burned. No good.

No way I'd be ready in four days.

CHAPTER 5

Forty-two days.

The only type of candle available was one of those thick emergency ones, white and ugly, but I decided to make it work for my purposes. It would have been nice to have seventeen smaller candles, but no such luck. One big fat candle would have to do.

I shoved it in the middle of the ready-to-eat vanilla pound cake—something I'd been saving, but never thought I would actually need. The fat candle destroyed half the cake, turning it into crumbs, but it didn't matter. Every birthday cake needed a candle.

I lit it and watched the flame fan to its full potential, then turned off the lights to enjoy the shadows that danced across the curved walls, so beautiful. Wax dripped and melted, making a mess, but the tiny light intrigued me. It provided something different in my stagnant little world of repeat DVDs and playing *Call of Duty* on the X-Box. Who knew a candle could be so entertaining?

It burned to the halfway mark, dripping and smoking, before I leaned over the table and began to sing *Happy Birthday* to myself. I started softly, but by the last chorus I sang at the top of my lungs, my own words bouncing back at me as they echoed off the walls. In my lunacy, it almost sounded as though a group of people were singing to me and I wasn't celebrating my birthday on my own.

Callie scrammed to the opposite side of the bunker, her nails scraping on the floor as she crawled between crates and boxes to hide from the racket.

I sang to myself once more from the top, determined to get the most out of a crappy situation, and ignored Callie's irritated meows in the process.

Finished, I drew in a large breath and held it as I made my wish. *Please let Dad and Toby be alive.* Then I blew out the candle.

I pretty much wasted my wish, but I didn't want anything else in the world but that. If dad or Toby were alive, they would've come for me by now. No other explanation made sense. I didn't want to believe they might be dead, but with each ticking day, it became more and more clear they could be. Dad would have never left me here like this. Not for this long. But it was my birthday and I could wish for whatever I wanted.

Complete darkness encompassed me now that the little flame had died, but I wasn't afraid. Nothing could get me, not even in the dark. Without my sight, the only sound was my breathing. Callie had gone quiet once I'd stopped singing. She obviously hadn't been a fan of my vocal abilities, but captive audiences don't get to have opinions.

I held my hands in front of me and couldn't see my own fingers. I wiggled them. Still nothing. The darkness was powerful and amazing. Not even a hint of light showed anywhere.

Carefully, I made my way down the center of the bunker, my hands out as a guide. Ten steps to my destination and I recognized the open door to the decontamination area. I ran my fingers over the wall to the right, searching the metal for the switches to turn everything back on.

I flipped the two main switches upward, but the bunker remained in darkness. I tried again. Nothing. The blackness around me no longer felt powerful and amazing, but stifling and heavy. Panicked, I flipped the switches up and down several more times. *Come on, come on!*

They controlled the generator, which controlled the lights, the heater, and the intake of air. *Please, please!*

Nothing happened.

My chest tightened and my hands shook. *What do I do?* I had no idea. *Is there a backup? A control panel somewhere? Another switch or button to push? What?*

I turned in a circle, wracking my petrified brain for the full layout of the bunker in the pitch dark. Every nook and cranny had been explored, but nothing stood out as the answer.

Shelves of food. Beds. Toilet. Water storage. Disposal. If I had ever found a hidden box with wires to twist to bring everything back to life, I would have run right to it, because bored people explore and touch everything, and I *had* done both those things!

Yes, there was a crank for the air unit. I could manually bring in fresh air from the outside by continually turning the lever, but for how long? That wouldn't bring back the lights, the electricity, everything else I *needed* to survive.

I managed to get myself turned around in my tiny hole in the earth, and as my hands brushed over the walls in a frenzy to grab onto something, my chest squeezed tighter and breathing became more difficult.

I tried to reorient myself and couldn't. Was I facing the front or the back? The bunker was only so big, but it seemed to have increased and decrease in size at the same time. One second, it was huge. The next it felt like a coffin.

How much air did I have? Five minutes? Ten? An hour?

Questions swirled inside my head, blurring my thoughts, but one thing was for certain: I had to get out of there.

Frantic, I grabbed the wall to use as my guide, refusing to let go for even a second. When I came to the open door, I nearly tumbled through it, but caught myself in time, finally realizing where I was. With my arms stretched out in front of me, I managed to find my way along the bunk beds, past the couch, and to the kitchen area.

The candle remained in the cake with the lighter at its side, and when I relit it and the tiny light began to glow, I took in a great big lungful of air, just noticing I'd been holding it the entire time.

"Okay, okay, okay." I scanned the layout of the bunker while holding the edge of the table to remain upright and steady my wobbling knees. "Think."

I forced myself to move and grabbed a lantern off the shelf, which I fumbled with it until it switched on. A huge sigh of relief escaped my throat as the presence of light eased my panic somewhat.

Whether I was ready to go outside and face the world — or whatever remained of it — was no longer relevant. The air would eventually run out and living in the dark didn't seem all that appealing.

I gave the crank to the air intake several twists, buying more time, and easing my worry that I just might pass out from lack of air before I could move.

Callie crept out from her hiding place, looking at me cautiously, as if I might break out singing again—even though any thoughts of birthday celebration had long passed.

Thoughts crashed around inside my brain, but I managed to haul out my duffle bag, organize my supplies, and add more things that would come in handy—matches, water bottles, air mask, first aid supplies, medicine, knives, lightweight food, and extra clothing.

The bag would be heavy, but I didn't want to leave anything behind in case I might need it later. As long as I kept busy, there wasn't time to think about my situation, so I didn't stop gathering items until Callie jumped onto the bed and walked along the edge.

"What am I going to do with you, huh?"

The kitten rubbed against the side of the bag then jumped on top of it as if saying, "Enough."

At the rate I was going, the entire bunker would be shoved inside my duffle bag.

I stared at Callie, and she stared at me. Carrying her in my arms was out of the question—she might bolt once we stepped outside and end up scratching the crap out of me in the process.

Shove her in my bag? She'd hate that, and I wasn't sure I wanted my cat curling up next to my food and clean underwear.

I flipped open my pocket knife and ran my thumb over the small blade. *Ouch! Jeez!* A small trickle of blood formed on my skin. Though small, the knife sliced my thumb clean. I grabbed the bag and slid it closer while keeping an eye on my unreliable cat, but Callie rode the thing like a queen perched on a float. She looked up at me with her green eyes, unafraid.

I took the knife and leaned closer. "You're not going to like this, but it's for your own good."

Quickly, I jabbed several holes in the pocket of the duffle bag—air holes—then scooped her up and shoved her inside before she could protest.

She meowed and wiggled around, scratching the fabric in an effort to get out.

"It's only temporary." I patted the bulging pocket, trying to calm her. "I promise."

I'd have to come up with something better soon, but for now it would have to do.

My breath caught in my throat as I looked around the tiny space that had been my home for nearly two months. This was it. Time to go. The number of jumping jacks, stomach crunches, and push-ups I'd done over the past weeks would have to do. I could build muscle and I could build stamina, but bravery was something entirely different—I couldn't build that. Some things had to be seized.

I shoved the gun in my waistband and tucked the small knife in my pocket before slipping my arms through the straps of the duffle bag and situating the heavy sucker on my back—cat side up. Callie meowed near my ear, but I ignored her, grabbed the lantern, and made my way to the ladder.

Fifteen rungs high, the ladder may as well have been a thousand.

I climbed, reached the top, and placed my hand on one of the latches, but hesitated as Dad's voice played over inside my head, *"Don't you come out, Tess. You stay put and we'll be back. Promise me you won't open this door."*

For how long, Dad? Until I die in here, waiting for you? You should've come back for me.

I flipped open one latch and then another, but with the third, my fingers trembled and I struggled to hold onto the ladder as I removed the final barrier to the outside.

This wasn't right. I shouldn't have been celebrating my birthday like this. There would have been a big cake — Dad would have bought me one from Costco — and all my friends would have been at my house, dancing, playing games, and watching movies. Maybe Landon would have been there too, and Toby would have stood in the kitchen doorway making kissy faces at me while making a loser sign with his thumb and forefinger — the dork.

There would have been balloons, streamers, and music. The table would have been piled with presents too — probably a new iPod or concert tickets to *One Direction* — but instead I stared at the square door over my head, terrified of what waited for me outside.

All of those things — the balloons, the presents, the cake — seemed so dumb now.

I wanted my friends, my dad, and even my stupid brother and his idiotic ways. "Please let them be okay," I prayed. "Let this be some horrible mistake."

The last latch unlocked, I used all my strength to push the heavy metal door all the way open.

CHAPTER 6

I lifted my hand to shield my eyes from the intense glare of the sun. The darkness of the bunker plus living without natural light for so long made my sight like a newborn's emerging from the womb.

Feeling vulnerable, I grabbed my knife from my pocket and held it in front of me, waving it around in the air, though I doubt I would have sliced anyone, even if they were stupid enough to walk into my flailing knife. This was the perfect time for someone to shoot me, stab me, or even eat me because I couldn't see a damn thing!

Callie screeched her high-pitched panicked meow, and since she sat near my head, I couldn't hear anything either. Blind and deaf, I had a great urge to jump back inside the hole and forget the whole thing. Being brave would have to wait for another day....

But nothing grabbed me, no one shot me, and as Callie settled down and my eyes got used to the mid-day sun, everything became a little clearer.

I didn't know what to expect exactly, but the sheer silence settling over me definitely wasn't on the list. Except for the slight breeze rustling the leaves overhead, profound quietness engulfed me, and nearly sent me to my knees.

Something wasn't right, but I remained upright, trying to figure it out. No cars, no sounds of vehicles rumbling in the distance. No planes—which normally filled the sky since we lived only a handful of miles away from the airport and a military base. Not even the sound of a bird broke the extreme calm.

I lowered the knife, but continued to hold it firmly in my grip.

The bunker door had taken quite a beating. Bullets left large divots and pockmarks in the surface, and most of the paint had been either blown off or scraped away. Someone had even attempted to dig around the door as if trying to find a way to pry it open. Whoever it was had put a lot of effort into trying to get inside before giving up—thank goodness.

I dropped the door into place, but knew if I locked it, there would be no way to get back inside if I needed to. Unlocked, others could raid it, but locked would make it useless to everyone including myself. The choice was an easy one.

The snow that had covered the ground in a thick layer of fluff only two months before had long since melted, and now tall grass, several inches high, needed to be mowed. I had packed my duffle bag anticipating the snow and cold, remembering everything the same way I'd last seen it, but flower buds escaped their dirt beds and hinted at an early spring. Yellows and pinks pushed upward—Mom's flowers—tulips and crocuses she'd planted several years ago right before she had started chemo. They kept returning year after year.

Everything looked normal, except for the back of the house, which crumbled in on itself, and the family car in the driveway covered in dust with all of its windows shattered.

I didn't know what to do, where to even begin, but my feet dragged me forward one step at a time until I reached the open wall that led into my father's bedroom. Curtains fluttered and electrical wires hung from the beams. Dirt covered everything and large puddles of water sat stagnant in the middle of the bed, and a large section of the floor.

My boots crushed the glass as I stepped inside Dad's room, and the sound of it seemed louder than normal. Nothing looked safe to touch, so I kept my hands to myself, but I took in everything—the way the bed sagged from all the debris, the wedding picture of my parents still hanging on the dilapidated wall, and all the clothes on hangers in the closet.

I entered the hall, afraid to look at the rest of the house, but needing to.

Toby's room looked like a tornado had hit it, but I had no idea if the mess had occurred before or after the night I went into the bunker. He wasn't known for his cleanliness. His windows were blown out, like the rest of the house, and several of his treasured posters hung limp and crinkled on the walls, ruined by the weather.

At the door to my room, I stood in the hall and stared in at my broken bed, shattered windows, and all the things I'd loved at one time, destroyed by almost two months of winter snow and spring rain. None of this seemed real, almost as though I was looking at someone else's life.

But this *had* been my life, my home, my *everything*.

Now my home had been wiped away as though no one had ever really lived here at all. Like a set in a bad horror movie—vacant, eerie, disturbing.

I swallowed and moved quickly through the other rooms, not wanting to spend any more time thinking about a life that was no longer an option for me or my family.

"Dad?" I eased open the bathroom door, the den door, the kitchen door.

Of course he wasn't here, but as long as the possibility remained, and as long as I didn't see his body in the rubble, I would call for him—I'd always call for him.

The front door fell onto the porch floor, leaving the house wide open to the neighborhood, so I climbed over it and walked down the cement steps toward the middle of my front yard in search of someone, *anyone,* who could help me make sense of what had happened.

Cars with broken windows lined the streets. Several large trees had fallen across the road and a house three doors down from mine was nothing but a pile of wood and bricks. In an ironic twist, the house's mailbox stood with its red flag upright.

Electric poles had tumbled like a row of dominos and the wires snaked into the streets, falling over cars and trees in their path. Leaves blew across the sidewalks with the breeze and the faint smell of charred wood encircled my senses.

"Hello?" I cupped my mouth as I glanced from one direction to another, searching.

"Hello?" My own voice echoed back.

"Anyone?" I called again.

Abandoned homes and cars stared back at me. Something moved in one window, and hope filled my chest, but it soon deflated as only a set of broken window blinds clinked and moved with the wind.

Several minutes ticked by without a response, and my arms dropped to my sides. *Where did everyone go?*

The world spun around me, turning with increased speed, though my feet remained grounded to one spot. The stillness grew larger, almost deafening, until Callie gave a soft meow. Her single protest brought the spinning world to halt, and I took a deep breath to calm myself. I wasn't really alone—I had Callie.

If people weren't here, they had to be somewhere, because whole cities didn't disappear. They just didn't. They *couldn't.*

I shifted the enormous bag on my shoulders, distributing the weight evenly, then looked left and right and left again before stepping into the street. Habit. I felt a small smile curve my lips and I closed my eyes briefly as I realized the absurdity of what I'd done. A speeding car would have been welcomed at that moment.

I hoped all the sit-ups and jumping jacks over the past several weeks had made me a physically stronger, tougher person, because there wasn't anything left to do but start walking.

A ragged U.S. flag hung from the pole in front of my high school. Half the building had crumbled in on itself while the windows along the rest had sprayed glass across the yard below. Several cars in the parking lot were crushed, leaving only flat tires on bowed rims, and a couple of other cars lay on their sides as though an invisible hand had picked them up and set them down that way.

Papers littered the ground while others continued to flutter out of open windows whenever the breeze took hold of them. They floated in the sky for a moment then drifted to the ground like a paper snowstorm.

School had never been my thing, but to see the building in such a shamble didn't fill me with the relief I'd always figured it would. I mean, all kids joked at one time or another, myself included, about hoping the school would burn down or be whisked away by some unseen force, but now that it had actually happened, it didn't feel like a celebratory moment at all. It seemed sadder than anything.

I walked up the unstable cement steps, avoiding the ones with the most damage, and pushed against the partially opened door. Debris on the other side made it difficult, but I shoved my shoulder against it and managed to squeeze inside.

Doors on many lockers hung from their hinges. Others were blown off and lay scattered on the linoleum floor. Text books, backpacks, and papers added to the mess, and I made sure to be careful as I stepped over them.

Air whirled from the open windows and caused ghost-like sounds to come from under several of the closed doors. I drew the straps of the duffle bag tighter and quickly moved past them. A musty smell drifted from several corners where the roof had caved in. It mixed with the cafeteria smells—*how is that even possible?*—and churned my stomach. *So gross.*

I passed Mr. Stanger's science classroom. The door remained shut—one of the few—but the tiny rectangular glass window was gone. Tiny shards of glass lined the frame. I never did care much for science, but Mr. Stanger had prided himself in being a good teacher and to see his classroom wrecked—the periodic table shredded and hanging from only one tack and thick science books spread out over the floor in between turned over desks—almost brought tears to my eyes. He was one of the few teachers I had actually liked, even if my grade didn't reflect it.

I'd never liked school before, not really, so I didn't know how to process these bizarre feelings. Instead of trying to understand them, I moved past classrooms, and made my way down the junior hall, refusing to look inside any more rooms.

The further I went into the middle of school, the darker the hall became, but enough light filtered in from under doors to pick out the larger objects to avoid. My locker, near the end of the hall, was one of the few with a door intact—strange how things can be so random—and I turned the lock, following my combination, until the door popped open.

A jacket, a brush, several books, notepads and pencils, in no organizational order, came spilling out. I didn't need any of those things and I kicked them aside as I reached up and ran my fingers over the top shelf.

My phone.

Our school had a strict policy of no phones in class, so I'd stored mine in my locker, like everyone else did, but I'd forgotten it in my hurry to get home and enjoy my weekend away from quizzes, reports, and stupid assignments.

It had been nearly two months, long enough for it to lose its charge, but I held the power button down, hopeful that maybe, just maybe, it still had a little bit of life in it.

The screen lit up, illuminating the entire hall and took me by such surprise that I almost dropped the phone.

Holy crap, it works!

No bars, no signal, but seventeen messages flashed at me. The battery icon was in the red zone, so I didn't press play even though I really *really* wanted to. Finding a signal and calling my dad outweighed the need to hear any of the two-month-old messages. Those would have to wait.

I turned to leave with the idea I'd find a signal once outside, but before I could press the power button to save what was left of it, my glowing screen highlighted Mr. Stanger's face, staring right at me.

CHAPTER 7

I stumbled backward and crashed into my open locker, cutting my arm on the jagged frame and causing Callie to start screeching. Blood pounded in my ears like a base drum over her meows while warm blood dripped down my elbow. My stomach tightened into a ball as though I'd done a hundred crunches in less than ten seconds. Breathing... *how do I even do that?*

People shouldn't appear out of nowhere, not with everything so insanely crazy outside. He should know better. Even though I was only seventeen—*happy freaking birthday to me*—I was pretty sure heart attacks didn't care about age. "Jeez, you scared me."

His eyes stayed transfixed on me, open, wide, unblinking. He didn't say a word in response. He didn't move. He didn't *do* anything.

"Mr. Stanger?" My words squeaked out as I tried to understand his hesitance.

The strange cocking of his neck caused me to cock my own, and I managed to take a step toward him. "You okay?"

One step and no more.

I couldn't move.

Foam oozed from his gaping mouth. His eyes, the color of chalky clouds, stared at nothing. Half his skull was crushed in, like an optical allusion. Brain matter, dried and chunky, clung to his left ear, cheek, and covered the wall behind him. A large teacher's desk, pressed into his middle, pinned him to the wall and kept him upright but he had slumped awkwardly to one side. A bloodied bat marked THE PROPERTY OF WESTLAND HIGH, lay near his feet.

My hands shook as I took in his lifeless form—broken, beaten. The sight and smell of death rolled my stomach and I retched my morning's breakfast on the floor, adding to the already gruesome scene.

I'd never seen a dead body before. Not like this. It took me several minutes of bending over and holding my knees to settle my stomach.

His death wasn't an accident, but *why?* Who would want to kill him? Kill Mr. Hoffman, the biology teacher, sure, but Mr. Stanger? Everyone loved Mr. Stanger!

Poor Mr. Stanger. Someone should really do something with his body, something proper, but that someone would *not* be me. I hoped he would forgive me for leaving him. The idea of him being here, dead, for all this time, bothered me. No one, not even the government, had hauled his body away. That had to mean something.

I wiped my mouth and scanned the hallway, looking both directions, not sure for what. Only the sound of wind whistling through the halls, nothing else. Whoever had done this wasn't here. Even in the near darkness I could tell Mr. Stanger had been dead for a while, but the very idea of someone using a bat to kill him put me on edge.

The world had gone to hell and people were killing one another? Why? *Why?* Were these the kind of people who had tried to get inside the bunker? My stomach coiled in on itself again, but this time I didn't vomit.

I had to get out of there. Every dark hall and hidden corner freaked me out. With my cell phone now in my possession, there was no reason to stay.

Callie kept right on meowing and had someone been in the building they would have heard her and killed the both of us by now. I needed to do something about my cat, and when she started hissing and clawing at the duffle bag, I realized it needed to be sooner rather than later.

I tucked the cell phone in my pocket and made sure my knife was accessible if it came down to it.

My arm stung and would need to be taken care of, but with a dead guy in the hallway, half the school blown apart, and a cat screeching in my ear, it would have to wait.

I stumbled over broken desks and chairs, and pushed a banner announcing the winter formal aside as I made my way toward fresh air and daylight.

The fading sun had never felt so good—visually and physically. The outside air may have been tinged with the smell of burnt wood, but I took in a huge lungful and held it before releasing it slowly.

Were *all* the buildings like my school? Were there more dead bodies inside them and if so, how many? From where I stood on the crumbled sidewalk in front of my once historical high school, every abandoned building seemed to hold horrendous possibilities. What would I find in the post office on the corner? Or the mini-mart down the street? How about Julia's house? Or Nathan's?

I swallowed hard, gulping down my rising emotions as I thought of my friends, and started walking. Maybe it was best I didn't know.

Callie howled in my bag like a lamb being led to slaughter. I needed to remedy the situation before attempting to call Dad.

I'd never hear him answer with the way she carried on.

The strip mall with its rows and rows of stores looked terrifying but not in the usual way. Nothing appeared misplaced or out of line. All the windows were intact and only a handful of cars sat in the parking lot where their owners had left them. It actually looked much the way I'd expect it would on Christmas morning—vacant, but ready for business on the twenty-sixth.

I'd kind of hoped I'd find sections of it in rubble like the high school so getting inside wouldn't require me breaking and entering. I hadn't seen a soul—well, a living soul—but the idea of smashing in one of the windows didn't seem right.

I passed by the nail salon, the tax store, and a chiropractor's office without looking in the windows, avoiding the possibility of dead bodies.

In front of the pet store, I cupped my eyes and peered in the window. No human legs stuck out in the aisles and the space behind the cash register appeared empty.

Callie kept right on clawing at the bag, and her ruckus annoyed me. I placed the duffle bag on the ground at my feet. "I know, I know! You'll be out of there in a second." *Freaking impatient cat!*

The door was locked, of course, and except for a metal garbage can, I couldn't find anything to break the large glass window. I tried using the metal lid off the trash can, but it only came bouncing back at me when I threw it against the glass. Not even a crack. *Seriously?*

The one time I could have used some debris to smash the window happened to be the one time I was standing outside a building unaffected by whatever had caused some of the others to crumble. *Damn my luck.*

I knelt beside the bag, ignored Callie, unzipped the main compartment, and dug out my gun. That should do it.

It had been quite some time since I'd last shot the thing— maybe a year or more—but I concentrated on the steps my dad had taught me. Feet apart. Shoulders level. Both hands on the gun. I aimed and steeled myself for the impact as my finger squeezed the trigger.

Glass sprayed out in all directions, and I turned in time to avoid being pelted by flying pieces. My ears rang as the blast rocked off the brick walls surrounding me on three sides. The security alarm blared and added to the high pitched humming in my ears.

I scanned the parking lot, worried all the noise would bring unwanted people. Strange how Mr. Stanger's death had changed my desire to find people into fear that I might find them. I continued to hold the gun in front of me and Callie continued her crazed hissing.

Several minutes ticked by, enough for someone to come at me, but no one came. I stood there, aiming the gun first one way and then another, but saw nothing.

The alarm slowly faded to silence as whatever backup system it used wore down. With the ringing in my ears settled, I assessed the damage.

One bullet had caused quite a bit of destruction to the window, enough for me to crawl in if I knocked some of the larger pieces from the frame. A fish tank had taken the brunt of the bullet and shattered, splashing green murky water all over the floor. Dead fish and slimy gravel bits littered the ground.

The smell hit me, and I pinched my nose. Pet stores usually smelled bad, but this smell was worse than Mr. Stanger's dead body. The odor caused my eyes to water, and I gagged several times. *I hate this day!* Had I not thrown-up earlier, I probably would have right then.

Dead birds lay in piles on the bottom of their cages. Some bodies had been picked clean, eaten by the birds that had outlived them before they, too, had succumbed to the lack of food and water. The rodent and reptile cages looked even worse—hamster skulls, bloated rats, and bloody bedding. The fish tanks were so murky, I could hardly see inside them. Nasty.

Get in, and then get the hell out. That was the plan. I held my nose with one hand, shoved the gun in my waistband, and grabbed a basket with the other. I ran up and down aisles, careful not to step in the slippery water or broken glass, until I found something I'd come for—a harness and a leash.

Callie was bound to love that, but what else could I do with her? City folks sometimes walked their cats—weird, but doable—

so why couldn't my stubborn cat learn to do the same? Even if she hated it, she'd have to get over it. It was this or the bag.

Holding my breath, I grabbed a pink leash with the letters SASS spelled out in rhinestones, and a matching harness from the hooks on the peg wall. I used my arm to swipe all the cans of cat food into the basket—fancy stuff too—and then got out of there before I started dry heaving.

I grabbed the duffle bag, the basket, and moved as far away from the pet store as possible. At this rate, going inside buildings would suck something royal.

Callie had fallen silent—whether that was a good sign or not, I didn't have a clue, but opening the bag right there in the middle of an open space didn't seem like the best idea. If she was dead, she was dead. I wouldn't be able to change it. But if she wasn't, I was certain she'd sink some teeth and claws into me before sprinting off.

The sun cast an orange haze over everything and reflected its beauty in the unbroken windows—the perfect hour, Dad had called it, for taking pictures. That meant I only had about an hour before everything fell into complete darkness. The idea of that terrified me, and as much as I didn't want to go back inside any building, staying outside sounded even worse.

Maybe the third time would be the charm—no dead things, fingers crossed—and I decided the apartment complex across the road would be as good as any place to spend the night.

At least one apartment was bound to be dead-free.

Dad could pick me up from there once I called him, but first things first: I needed to let my cat out of the bag.

CHAPTER 8

The second floor studio apartment faced west and continued to receive light from the setting sun. I only had a few minutes before the sun set, so I hunted for candles, lanterns, anything to provide light. The place was clear of dead bodies—I'd already done a quick search for anything horrific or nasty smelling—but now I tossed open cabinets, drawers, and closets in hopes of finding something useful before it was too late and the place became shrouded in shadows, leaving me with only my flashlight to go by.

Two scented candles would have to do. Once lit, the place began to smell like a mixture of clean sheets and cherry blossoms. Not too bad, especially after the kind of day I'd been through.

"Okay, Callie. Time to come out." I unzipped the side pocket of the bag then scooted as far away as I could and waited for the hellcat to emerge.

It took a minute, but her orange and white head peeked out over the top. *Thank goodness.* She hadn't died and she wasn't any worse for wear, having existed in a duffle bag for nearly two hours. The guilt I'd been carrying lifted from my shoulders.

She hesitated for a moment, which seemed odd since she had scratched the crap out of the bag in an effort to escape only minutes before. Now, she perched there, her front paws on the edge of the bag, the remainder of her body tucked inside.

She wasn't as pissed as I'd imagined she'd be. Somehow, I'd figured she'd look right at me, hiss and arch her back, and then attempt to claw my eyes out for having shoved her in the side pocket like a pair of dirty gym socks, but she actually looked rather cute and innocent. All appeared forgiven.

"You hungry?"

She meowed — adorable.

"Here you go." I twisted off the lid to a can of food and placed it near her, but slid myself out of the way once more. Just because she was cute and didn't look as though she'd tear my face apart didn't meant I trusted her — not yet.

She took to the food and while she ate, I poured some water from a bottle into a small bowl and placed that near her too.

Feed her, water her, let her explore the place, and then I'd wrestle her into the harness. It sounded like a good plan to me — butter her up before torturing her once more. She'd need to get used to the leash soon, so she would be safe and I could grab her if I needed to.

With my cat occupied for the moment, I snatched my phone from my pocket and pressed the power button, turning it on. The battery flashed red, not a good sign, and indicated only twenty percent of the battery remained, which sucked since I had no connecting bars. Not even one. *Damn it.*

I stepped out onto the fire escape and made sure to shut the sliding door behind me. All I needed was for Callie to get out after all the effort I'd put into keeping her safe.

I raised the cell phone over my head and turned in several circles, even hanging myself over the edge of the railing, but still got no reception. Maybe getting higher and more open would be better.

Callie had climbed on the kitchen table then made a leap for the counter, barely making it. Apparently, she was attempting to get higher too as she explored her new surroundings. She'd be okay for a moment, so I tucked the phone back in my pocket, grabbed hold of the ladder, and climbed two stories to the roof of the building.

Heights, along with school, were on my list of hated items but the need to call Dad outweighed my fear. I stepped away from the edge of the roof, lessening my chances of falling to my death, and did my best not to look down.

Still no bars and my battery slipped to ten percent. No cell service? Really? What had the world come to? The message icon with seventeen voicemails was too tempting, and though I should have saved the battery until I could find a way to use it, I pressed play.

"Tess, it's insane out here! Oh, my gosh! People are looting stores and everyone's trying to get out of town. I'm stuck in traffic. This is so scary. Call me and let me know you're okay. Okay?" *Julia.*

"Where the hell is everyone? Dad's not answering his cell and you're not either. Tell me you didn't leave it at school again. Damn it, Tess! Half the town is on fire and the other half is bolting for the hills. Where are you? Shit. I gotta go. Call me when you get this." *Toby.*

"Tess, this is Grandma. I can't get a hold of your dad and I'm worried about all of you. I've been watching the news and... and I need to know you're all fine. Please have your dad call me as soon as you get this message, okay sweetheart. I love you. Be careful."

I swallowed hard and wiped my eyes. How I missed hearing their voices.

"Tess, it's me, Dad. I don't know if you have your phone or not or even if you can get cell service in the bunker, but honey, I'm not going to be able to get back to you as soon as I thought. I'm sending someone for you though. They don't know Morse Code, Tess, so open the door for them, okay baby. Just open the door. They will find me and your brother and bring you to us. Right now we're staying—"

The phone died.

Where? I shook my phone, willing it back to life, and it tumbled from my fingers onto the gravel roof. The battery fell out, slid several feet away from me, and the face of the phone shattered. *Stupid.*

I dropped to my knees, ignoring the bite of the tiny pebbles digging into my flesh, and scooped up my broken phone and dead battery. I pressed them to my chest — my life line — and knew I needed to somehow find a way to figure out where Dad and Toby were.

When I climbed to my feet after several moments of trying to convince myself not to fall apart, the devastation of what had happened to my city almost caused me to fall to my knees again.

No.

This couldn't be real. No way.

My chest grew heavy as if a Sumo wrestler sat on it, squeezing the life out of me. My breath came in small spurts when I happened to breathe at all and my hands shook, the rest of my body slowly following suit. I wrapped my arms around myself to steady the unrelenting tremors. *Don't cry, don't cry, don't cry.*

Cars sat stationary along the roads, lining both directions, some lying on their roofs, some on their sides. The scene looked normal like a movie put on pause. Trees had tumbled over, uprooted from the spots in which they had lived for decades. Power lines, street signs, billboards — scattered like a box of Legos. It looked much the way my neighborhood had, but on a much larger scale. Garbage, debris, and dirt covered everything.

A large section of the city no longer existed, gone, replaced by a large crater several football fields long. Skyscrapers, businesses, homes — wiped away. Shells of buildings, burned to only their frames, lined the circumference. More smoking craters dented the landscape to my left, my right, and behind me. The normally busy freeway in the distance, taking people to and from destinations, remained stationary.

Miles and miles of stillness stared back at me. No movement anywhere except for downy clouds floating overhead and the occasional piece of trash rolling across the street. The lack of noise, *any* noise, seemed surreal.

This is not my life.

It had been nearly two months since.... Jeez, I didn't even know *what* had happened. The city and the cities next to ours had all apparently been evacuated, but this was insane! Why weren't the people back already? What was going on? Where were the people who fixed everything after a disaster?

Red Cross where are you?

My brain could hardly process what my eyes were taking in—a nightmare of epic proportions—but the one thing that seemed certain was that, whatever happened, I was on my own.

A thick coating of dust covered the futon couch. I smacked the mattress several times with my hand, the cloud of yuck swirling in the air nearly choking me before I spread my sleeping bag on top.

The candles burned down to liquid and one began to sputter out.

Callie situated herself out in front of the sliding glass door and began her grooming, completely content to be in this new environment. I kind of wished I was a cat—self-absorbed and unaware of my surroundings. Unfortunately for me, that wasn't the case. I was quite aware. *Too* aware.

I didn't bother changing clothes or brushing my teeth or doing anything normal. Nothing was normal. Not anymore. So I climbed into my sleeping bag and pulled it up over my head. Screw this. Screw *all* of this.

Today was the worst birthday ever, and as much as I willed myself not to, I ended up crying myself to sleep.

Puffy red eyes stared back at me in the bathroom mirror as I leaned in closer to inspect myself. Gnarly hair, knotted and crazy, stuck out from the sides of my head. I felt the same way I looked.

Somehow, in the midst of everything, I had managed to fall asleep. Weird, since the apartment didn't belong to me and the world had become a scene reminiscent of every apocalyptic movie I'd ever watched. Minus the walking dead or terrifying aliens—at least to this point I had yet to lay eyes on any.

Please don't let me lay eyes on them. That's all I need.

Callie purred and rubbed against my ankles.

"You want to know what the plan is, huh?" She probably wanted to be fed again, but I scooped her up so she could look in the mirror too. "I wish I knew, but we need to figure it out soon. First, breakfast."

My hair and face could wait. Maybe I wouldn't even brush my hair. Or my teeth. Who would know if I did or didn't?

I was hungry, and though the idea of eating canned or MRE meals made me nauseous, they were better than nothing.

A can of food and some more water and Callie became an affectionate cat, purring and following me around. The rest of the time she had very little to do with me unless I forced her to snuggle. She didn't have a choice. I needed snuggles.

I was about to open a can of peaches, but stopped before turning the crank of the hand-operated can opener. A box of rainbow deliciousness peeked out from one of the opened cupboards. *Poptarts.*

No friggin' way!

Poptarts lasted forever. All the artificial flavors and additives meant they could survive nearly anything, which, as I'd found myself in the middle of a nightmare apocalypse, came in handy.

It didn't take much to open the box and pluck out one of four silver packages. A brand new box—such joy. Eight pop tarts for me!

I slid to the floor right there with my back against the counter and shoved almost half a pop tart in my mouth. Strawberry. Sprinkles. Gooey goodness. It had been forever since I'd tasted something so sweet. It nearly caused my eyes to roll into the back of my head and I almost forgot my troubles for a moment.

Four pop tarts later, I stood up and dusted off my butt. Yes, life still sucked. Yes, I was still alone without a clue as to what had happened to make it that way. But one thing was for certain: staying in the apartment forever, as I had planned to do the night before, would not change my situation. Maybe I wasn't a brave or strong person—physically or mentally—but I could do something. What other choice was there really?

I needed a battery. I may need a new phone.

Because finding out where Dad went had become priority number one.

CHAPTER 9

A few unscathed cars remained in the apartment complex parking lot and somewhere there had to be keys. The apartment I had spent the night in turned up nothing, not even in Marin Peterson's purse, though the unused chapstick, roll of lifesavers, and sunglasses might be useful. Her cell phone had some battery life in it, but no bars. It also had a pass code to open it, and after spending several minutes punching in random numbers, it died and became a useless piece of junk. Go figure.

She also had a pair of really nice Doc Martens boots in my size—new and in the original box. I would have preferred black, but the dark red would do. It sure beat my pair of worn out Toms—not practical for walking long distances even if they were extremely comfortable.

Stealing wasn't my thing, along with school and heights, but leaving perfectly good items to gather dust seemed wasteful. Recycle and reuse was a pretty good practice to adopt, especially now. Besides, these were Doc Martens. Anyone with a sense of wicked-cool style would have done the same thing. This was a smart move. Even Marin Peterson would have to agree with me.

But I needed keys! I left Callie, made sure the door remained unlocked, and went hunting in the adjoining apartments. Every time I stood outside an unlocked apartment, I gave a mental chant *no dead bodies, no dead bodies,* before pushing open the door. So far, the chant had seemed to work.

I rummaged through purses, backpacks, and drawers and searched closets and boxes. A set of keys hung on a hook in one guy's kitchen, but none of the keys looked like they belonged to a vehicle—more like house keys. I pocketed them in case I happened to be wrong. How did one person come to have so many random keys? Either he was the super, or he was a freak. By the looks of the apartment—a 1980's Chucky poster on the wall, several Betty Boop figurines on a shelf, a boat load of Star Trek Enterprise toys, still in their packaging, and hand-me-down furniture—I would have to go with freak. But to each his own.

Several bags of unexpired chips sat in the cupboard of the weirdo's apartment, plus some individually packaged cookies and an unopened bottle of Mountain Dew. *Sweet happiness.* I saved all of it for later.

Rule number one when searching an apartment, which I learned the hard way, was never to open the fridge. Horrible, horrible, horrible, such a big mistake. Nasty things are left to rot and die in there, and after several months with no electricity, it becomes vomit inducing.

But after searching five apartments, I had the keys to a Ford vehicle. Not my first choice, but being picky had no place in an apocalypse. Now, I had to hope the Ford wasn't lying on its roof.

"You little bugger!"

Callie wiggled in my arms, and as I shoved one of her legs in the harness, she'd yank out the other. She dug her claws into my thigh and a string of profanities escaped my lips.

"I'm this close" — I pinched my fingers together and placed them in front of her nose — "to shoving you back inside the bag. Is that what you want, huh? Really?"

A dog wouldn't be this difficult. A dog would love the idea of a leash. A dog would bathe me in kisses and think I was God. It would look up at me while it skipped at my side. But cats, *arrgh*... they thought *they* were Gods, which probably stemmed from the Egyptians treating them that way. *Damn Ancient Egyptians.*

"You're an animal! I'm human. If times get tough, I could eat you, you know?" Okay, that was creepy. "I won't though, because that would be weird and you'd probably taste horrible, but come on. This is for your own good."

I managed to finagle the pink glittery harness onto Callie's stubborn body and attach the leash. Once free from my grasp, she bolted, but as the leash tightened she came up short. The jolt flipped her onto her side, and when she righted herself, she gave me an "I will kill you in your sleep" kind of look.

"It's for your own good! Get used to it."

She took a few steps, trying out the strange contraption attached to her back, and I couldn't help but giggle at her antics. The harness weighed only a few ounces, but the way Callie behaved it may as well have weighed a hundred pounds or more. Each step she took was calculated and precise, not to mention hilarious.

She tried shaking it off.

She tried turning herself in a circle to get a better look at it.

After several minutes, she simply fell over on her side and lay there defeated.

"You're being dramatic. It's not that bad." I scratched her between the ears. "Think of it this way: not only are you safe, but now you're the coolest looking cat around. Very hip." Most likely, she was the only cat around, but she didn't need to know that.

She stared up at me and gave a pitiful meow.

I left her lying there on the floor and proceeded to repack my bag. It already weighed a ton, but since I had the keys to a Ford, I figured I might as well pack it. I shoved in a jacket from Marin's closet, a Beatles' tee from the apartment on the bottom floor, and a pair of jeans from a girl's dresser in the apartment directly above.

People had left a lot of great things behind, so wherever they went they left in a hurry. No one leaves Doc Martens and Beatles' tees behind. No one.

The cut on my arm had stopped bleeding the day before, but ached whenever I moved my arm. The budding scab, every once in awhile, would snag on my shirt and remind me of its presence, so I decided to take a look at it since I'd ignored it since yesterday.

It stung a little but for the most part wasn't nearly as bad as I'd first imagined: three inches long, but more a deep scratch than a full-blown cut.

After using some rubbing alcohol from the medicine cabinet, biting my lip as I dabbed the cut with cotton balls, I slapped a Band-Aid on it and went back to ignoring it.

The outside world awaited, so I slipped the duffle bag over my shoulders and jerked on Callie's leash to get her up and moving.

She didn't budge.

"Come on." I tugged the leash, dragging the obstinate cat a foot or so across the floor. *Are all cats this stubborn?* "Fine."

I picked her up and perched her on top of the duffle bag next to my shoulder. I had hoped she would walk and reduce the weight I already carried, but since she seemed pretty determined not to, she could ride. At least she wasn't shoved back inside the bag, and with the strap of the leash wrapped around my wrist, if she took off, she wouldn't get too far.

I let out a huge sigh and placed my hand on the doorknob. "Time to go."

I had wasted several morning hours searching for keys and wrestling my cat into the harness, so the orange sun hung high overhead, bathing everything in its warmth and causing shadows to hide. The day still offered plenty of daylight, but I really should have gotten a much earlier start, except that getting up early wasn't my thing and I had no interest in changing my bad habits. Not today anyway.

The parking lot was of average size, but finding the vehicle that matched the set of keys proved a lot harder than I had first anticipated. The number of Fords in the lot surprised me, but I inserted that key into every upright and undamaged one until, finally, a door opened.

As would be my luck, both side mirrors hung like broken bodies and dangled by only a few cords. The back windshield was blown out and tiny shards of glass and dried leaves covered the entire back seat. A giant spider web crisscrossed over the opening—beautiful and somewhat uplifting—but I didn't see the spider anywhere, which was a good thing. I would have probably killed it had I seen it. Spiders gave me the creeps. Good for the spider to survive the initial blast and craziness, but it sure as hell needed to have moved on.

I placed Callie in the car and attached her leash to the gearshift—another unlucky thing for me. Of course, I would have to find the keys to a standard. She turned herself around in the passenger seat and curled up into a ball. I tossed the duffle bag on top of the leaves in the back seat and slid in behind the wheel.

I gave the key a quick turn while pumping the gas and pressing down the clutch. I may not have had a lot of experience with driving a standard—okay, I had very little—but I was doing my best to make lemonade out of the massive lemon life had handed me.

The beat-up car came to life, but jerked and sputtered, surprising me so much that my foot slipped off the clutch. I bounced around inside the car as it stalled and settled.

Callie freaked out and jumped into the back seat nearly hanging herself in the process. I unraveled her, gave her several comforting strokes, and placed her on the seat next to me once more.

"Okay, car. Work with me here. It's the end of life as I know it and you're all I've got." I glanced at Callie. "Well, besides a temperamental cat, but I could really use a break."

One foot on the clutch, the other on the gas, I turned the key once more. It chugged to life, and as long as I kept my feet balanced on the pedals, the car didn't bounce around like it was having a spasm.

"I did it!"

Callie didn't appear too impressed.

Now came the tricky part—putting it in reverse and backing out of its covered spot. Had the cement barrier not been placed in front, I would have driven forward, up and over the sidewalk and grass, but the barrier nullified that plan.

Six attempts to put the car in reverse, and I still hadn't moved more than a foot, but I had succeeded in scaring the crap out of my cat. She'd gone as far under the seat as her taut leash allowed. This wasn't working, but the idea of leaving a car with half a tank of gas didn't feel right either, especially when carrying a cat and a huge bag on my back seemed like the only alternative. Why couldn't things work out for me? Just once? But the car did run, it had half a tank of gas, and a cigarette lighter. If I could only get my hands on a car charger for my phone, I could find out where my family had gone.

And if walking was my only option, then I guess I would start pounding the pavement in my new Doc Marten boots.

CHAPTER 10

What I would have given to hear an airplane fly overhead or even the annoying blast of a train's horn. The heavy silence of nothingness was slowly killing me, bit by bit.

I had never experienced this kind of quiet before. Even in the stillest times — a library, a hospital, a funeral, the middle of the night — there had always been some background noise to fill the void.

But not now. Not here.

My boots pounding against the concrete and the occasional hiss from my frightened cat were the only sounds. No traffic drone or white noise.

Absolutely nothing.

The normalcy of day to day existence — the buzz, the chatter, the hum of the living — swiped clean like an eraser over a blackboard, leaving only faint signs of what had once been. Each empty building I passed made the reality of my situation that much more deafening, and lonelier.

I shifted the bag, lowering the straps to my upper arms to give my aching shoulders a break. The need for a phone charger kept me moving forward one step at a time. My small town didn't boast any large chain stores, so I had my walk cut out for me.

I tried each car I passed, looking for a miracle among the abandoned vehicles—unlocked doors, keys, a charger that would work for my particular phone—but nothing. A car would have been nice, but the roads were such a mess, I doubted I'd have gotten very far anyway.

When the sun slipped further in the sky, I stopped looking. It marked my time, gave my only real light, and forced me to hurry along.

I'd walked miles and yet, the large city, my destination, seemed to grow farther and farther away the more I traveled toward it. From the apartment roof top, it seemed so close, and since Dad and I had driven into the city several times, taking only fifteen minutes to get there, I hadn't expected walking to take *this* long.

I had definitely underestimated this trip.

My shoulders ached from carrying the heavy bag, my boots rubbed against my ankles, and I wasn't even halfway yet. Another hour and I'd have to start looking for a place to stay the night. Then, to top off this whole trip, if I was successful in finding a charger, I'd have the joy of turning around and walking back to the apartment where the car waited-the only car I had access to.

There had to be a better way, because this way totally sucked.

"I'm not cut out for this survival crap!" Maybe I had to walk, but that didn't mean I had to do it with a pleasant attitude. Complaining about it was the only thing that gave me some relief. I tipped my head to the sky and voiced my displeasure, "This sucks *so* bad!"

Callie meowed near my ear, nearly deafening me—at least it wasn't silence—but when she quieted down, I could have sworn the slight breeze in the air carried a deep, but faint laugh.

I whipped around, knife in hand, and searched behind me, all the while unsure whether to be excited, weary, or afraid I had lost my mind.

Everything appeared the same as it always had: empty, barren, abandoned, and more than a little depressing. I scanned the side streets, the desolate homes, and stationary cars. My eyes jumped from one spot to another like a hyperactive child's. If there was movement anywhere, I was going to find it.

But I didn't see a thing. Nothing stood out as different. Nothing appeared hopeful at all. Just me, myself, and I... plus an ornery cat.

Had someone been there, I had no idea what I would have done—cried, wet myself, fainted, thrown myself in their arms—but knowing I was still alone, a deep sadness gripped my heart and wouldn't let go.

Even though there was still a good couple hours of daylight left, I no longer had the desire to keep going. Not today.

I couldn't.

I'm not sure where I had pictured myself sleeping when nightfall came, but camping in a gas station certainly hadn't occurred to me. The door had been left ajar, and seeing the candy bars and bottles of soda made my decision easy, despite the automotive and stale coffee smells.

I pushed the rack of greeting cards away from the big glass window and spread out my sleeping bag on the linoleum floor beneath it. That way the moonlight would brighten up my dark existence once the sun completely disappeared from the sky.

Callie tested her boundaries, walking with a little more ease as she got used to the harness and leash. I had tied one end to the bottom of a magazine shelf so she couldn't get too far, and watching her coming around to being a bound animal instead of a completely free one lifted my heart a little, as weird as it sounded.

I placed my back against the wall and popped a handful of Skittles into my mouth before taking a big swig of warm Sprite. It didn't taste as great as it had before all the end of the world nonsense, but I finished both of them. No need to be wasteful.

Besides Poptarts, soda, and Skittles, I hadn't eaten much of anything — nothing substantial anyway. The freedom to eat what I wanted without anyone to harass me or wag their finger in my direction began to take its toll. The sugar rush was awesome. The coming down part, not so much. My stomach ached and my head hurt a little, so I slid a little further down the wall and rested my cheek against my knees.

I would try to eat something more nutritious later, like a bag of pretzels or some stale nacho chips — both available for a limited time at the local convenience store. *Yay, me.* I should have busted open a Ready Meal right then, but that required being in the mood to eat the dried mix with warm bottled water. And with a belly filled up with Skittles and Sprite, the very idea of eating an MRE didn't sound appetizing at all. Spewing seemed most likely.

Callie meowed, and I managed to slide an open tin of cat food in her direction, which shut her up. I had no energy to do anything more, so slipped off my boots and crawled into the sleeping bag. It wasn't quite time for bed, but the desire to disappear in sleep outweighed the desire to keep my eyes open.

Suddenly, I felt really, really tired.

The hard linoleum of the floor cooled my cheek and felt amazing against my hot skin. Part of me wanted to strip to nothing and spread my entire body over the dirty floor to absorb the coldness, but the rational part, the lazy part, stayed in the sleeping bag and shifted back and forth between sweating and shivering.

The sun poured in through the large window, and had actually done so for hours, but I couldn't manage to rise from the uncomfortable spot on the floor. My head hurt. My body ached. I wanted to keep sleeping.

Callie licked my face and meowed over and over, refusing to be ignored, until I finally pushed myself up on my arms. My left arm hurt, and warmth radiated from my elbow to my shoulder. I managed to sit upright with my back against the wall. Callie rubbed against my legs as I removed the nasty Band-Aid on my arm. Yellow pus oozed from the cut and a deep redness surrounded the entire thing. It felt warm to the touch and it looked worse than it ever had.

The cut hadn't seemed like a big deal two days ago, nothing a Band-Aid couldn't handle, but now as I inspected it a little more, I wondered if it hadn't actually needed stitches. *Stupid high school locker.* Thankfully, I remembered having received a tetanus shot with my immunizations before starting tenth grade, so I wasn't going to die a painful death, though my arm hurt like hell and made me think otherwise.

I poured some bottled water in a little dish for Callie, then poured some more on a clean shirt from my bag and dabbed at the messy cut, wincing when the fabric touched my sensitive skin. The dried scab fell away and a trickle of blood mixed with puss dribbled down my arm. *Beautiful.*

The first-aid kit in my bag held more bandages and some antiseptic cream, but with the redness, the inflammation, and soreness, not to mention my growing fever, I needed antibiotics. Something I didn't have.

I rubbed a little bit of the cream on the wound and did my best to close the deep cut with butterfly bandages before wrapping the entire thing with a roll of gauze to hold it all in place. Two ibuprofens and a bottle of water later, I shoved everything back in my bag, hooked it over my good arm, and took hold of Callie's leash.

She needed to walk, and no longer fought the harness, though she made walking a slow-going process. I didn't mind. Slow-going sounded good to me.

The bright sun caused me to squint, and I dug out my confiscated sunglasses from the bag, finding relief from the glaring rays and giving my budding headache a break.

"Now what? Where do we go?" I directed my questions to Callie, but she was too busy trying to capture her own shadow, jumping on it before turning to see where it had disappeared to. Not that she would have answered, but it would have been nice not to be in charge for once.

The big city was out of the question. Another nine or ten miles would do me in. I doubted I would even be able to walk to the opposite corner as tired and as feverish as I was. But the need to keep moving forced my feet to take step after step. I weaved down the middle of the street, around abandoned cars, trash cans, and garbage that covered the old highway.

The local hospital was miles off, at the edge of the city. I wracked my brain to remember the nearest pharmacy and figured it would be a good three or four mile walk. At my current pace, I could plan on it taking most of the day to get there.

Tears trickled down my cheeks, but I kept moving. Bravery and guts in the face of disaster was obviously not my strong suit. Tears and whining were more like it. Toby and Dad would know what to do, where to go, and how to make the best of this situation. They would have got a car running. They would have found a phone. They would have been saved by now.

Even Mom—sweet, caring, Mom—would have managed to figure out how to live this kind of existence with a smile on her lips. She had faced some pretty extreme situations in her shortened life and I had no doubt she would have kicked butt during this one.

But not me.

I couldn't stop crying.

I wanted Dad to swoop in and whisk me away to my home, to my comfortable bed, and make me soup. Soup sounded *wonderful*. I really wanted my dad, but since he didn't show, I dragged myself down the road unsure of where I was going or what I planned to do once I got there.

CHAPTER 11

I dropped the duffle on the pavement, and it fell with a resounding thump. My shoulders couldn't handle the weight any longer. Somehow, by the grace of God, I had managed to walk the four exhausting miles to the neighboring town. Dazed, feverish, and a bit wobbly on my feet, I had done it, but instead of celebrating the fact that I now stood in front of Rite-Aid's sliding glass doors, all I wanted to do was fall onto my bag and not move. Taking care of myself was a lot of work.

A few blocks over, a large crater had replaced the Five Points Mall and the surrounding areas. Buildings large and small seemed to have evaporated—*poof*—not even a hint of framework left behind. But here, right in front of Rite-Aid and the grocery store next door, everything appeared normal. Except, of course, for the ghost town feel. A giant tumbleweed rolling down the middle of the street would have completed the picture. Only tumbleweeds didn't grow around here.

I tied Callie's leash to the handle of the duffle bag, and gave her and myself some water, then cupped my hands around my eyes and pressed my face against the glass window. Even though I had only seen Mr. Stanger's dead body and no others, *knock on wood,* I didn't want to take any chances. I doubted I could become desensitized to death and decay, and wasn't in the mood to find out.

Dim rays from the late afternoon sun penetrated the interior of the building, lighting it enough to see that, for the most part, the store looked intact: the Photo Center to the right, the perfume section to the left, the seasonal supplies—Christmas decorations—in the middle. Easter decorations should have been on display now that Christmas, New Year's, and Valentine's had passed. Those holidays had slipped by and no one had been back. A shiver crept up my spine. My stomach turned to lead, and I forced myself to breathe and swallow my rising emotions.

One step at a time, Tess. One step at a time.

The intensity of looking at my situation as a whole would drown me and right now, I needed to focus on getting my hands on some antibiotics. I couldn't think too far ahead to phone chargers, to keys and cars, to calling for help, to any of the hundred other things needing my attention or I would have given up right then.

Callie had curled into a ball on my bag, so I did my best not to disturb her and reached inside for my gun.

It had worked for the pet store, and since my mind was a sick mess, I didn't have it in me to find a different way.

Lift. Point. Aim. Prepare for loud noise. Fire.

The glass shattered into tiny diamond shapes that glittered in the sun as they came raining down, covering the ground.

Callie bolted, but her leash kept her tied in place.

Sorry, kitty. So much for not disturbing the cat.

The human shadow popping up from behind a display case sent me scrambling backward, and I forgot all about my screeching cat. I nearly stumbled over, but managed to keep upright with the gun pointed straight at him. *What? No. What?*

His wide eyes locked onto mine. "Why in the hell did you do that?"

A person. A living person. Why couldn't I move? Speak? Say anything?

He motioned behind him with his thumb as he stepped into the aisle. "Before you go around shooting at things, you should really check out all the entrances first. The back door was open, you know?" He shook his dark shaggy head. His shoulders rose and fell. "Just a suggestion."

I couldn't say anything. Not a word, though my lips trembled.

"You think you can put that down for a second?" He nodded to the gun. "You're making me nervous."

I couldn't quite figure out what he was making me.

"Do you speak English? *Habla ingles?*" He made some quick motions with his fingers—sign language. "*Parlez-vous Anglais?* Anything?"

I lowered my arm, aiming the gun at the ground. "I'm sick." There was so much I should have asked, should have said, should have done, but I chose, in that pivotal moment, to announce my illness to the only other living person around. *Great.*

"Sick, huh?" He took a few more steps toward me, crunching the glass beneath his worn cowboy boots as he drew closer. "How sick?" Before I could answer, Callie's tugging and fighting against her harness drew the stranger's attention and he gave a low chuckle. "Well, a'righty then. Just when you think you've seen it all, a cat on a leash."

His deep laugh caused my shoulders to go rigid. I kept my finger on the trigger, but the gun pointed down. "Are you following me?"

He returned his attention my way. "Following you?" He shook his head. "Kid, I was here first, remember? If anything, you're following me."

"But I heard you, yesterday. Your laugh. You were laughing at me."

He shrugged. "Doesn't mean I was following you. Only means we crossed paths at the same time, and your complaining happened to entertain me."

That didn't make sense. "You saw me, but you didn't let me know you were there? Why?"

"Why would I? I don't know you."

I didn't think I had ever had a more frustrating conversation in my whole life. "Are there any other people around? Have you seen anyone else?"

He shoved his hands into his front pockets and shrugged again. "Nope. You're the first person I've run across."

"And you didn't think letting me know someone else existed, was *alive*, would be important to me?"

He removed his hands from his pockets and held them up. "Like I said, I don't know you, and right now, I don't even think I *want* to know you."

Is he mental or something? "But there's no one else around?"

A huge grin spread over his whiskery face and his eyes brightened, enhancing a few wrinkles around the edges. "And ain't that perfect? The best thing that's happened to me in a long, long time."

I shook my head. *Unbelievable.* Of all the possible people to have run into, I had to find this guy! "What are you saying? This isn't perfect at all!"

He continued smiling at me as he squatted next to Callie and ran his fingers between her ears to calm her. "One man's hell is another man's heaven."

"You're insane!"

"That's debatable. I'm not the one shooting out glass doors, am I?"

I slipped the safety on my gun and shoved it into my waistband. "Stop touching my cat."

"But she likes it."

"Leave my cat alone and go away." I couldn't believe I'd actually said that. The only person I'd seen in nearly two months, and I'd had enough of him to last a lifetime.

He stood and brushed his hands off on his pants. "I'm not finished here. I still need a few things from inside."

"I need a few things too."

"Then by all means"—he waved his arm in front of him in a grand gesture—"after you."

I walked over the broken glass, grinding the pieces into the tile. I had come a long way to get here and refused to let him scare or annoy me into leaving. "I don't like you."

He gave his familiar chuckle. "Few people do."

We split ways, he heading to the personal hygiene aisle and I heading to the back corner of the store toward the pharmacy.

It wasn't supposed to be like this. Two people finding each other in the rubble of an apocalyptic aftermath should come together, lean on each other for support, and find a collective way to survive. I shouldn't be sick and he shouldn't be crazy. This whole thing was wrong.

A large security gate ran across the length of the counter. The door to the pharmacy was locked with some fancy contraption requiring a keycard plus punch code. Through the metal gate, bottles of medicine lined the shelves, untouched and waiting. So close, but nearly impossible to get.

I grabbed on to the gate and shook the heck out of it, pulling and tugging, using up what remained of my strength and causing my already aching arm to radiate pain. The gate wouldn't budge. I slumped forward, my forehead resting against the counter with my fingers still wrapped around the metal frame.

I needed tools. And getting tools required breaking into another store. The situation was beginning to feel a lot like the book *If You Give a Mouse a Cookie*—if you want prescription medications, you're going to need tools, and if you need tools, you're going to have to break into Home Depot, and to break into Home Depot you're going to need....

When would this ever end?

"Here, hold this. I'll be right back."

I lifted my head, and the insane stranger shoved several boxes of toothpaste, deodorant, and a stack of spiral notebooks into my arms before moving past me and down the hall toward the restrooms.

Really?

I was about to toss the whole lot on the ground, when he returned, winked at me, and produced a small black bag. He placed it on the counter, unzipped it, and removed several small tools.

"Better than bullets," he said, as he jammed them into the lock, twisting and turning them, until with a smile, he slid the gate open. "Ta-da."

Okay, that was impressive. "How'd you learn to do that?"

"Picking locks? My old man taught me when I was a kid. Thought it might come in handy someday."

"Really? What kind of dad teaches their kid how to pick locks?" Rude, I knew, especially when my own father taught me to shoot guns and build a bomb shelter. Who was I to judge?

He placed each tool back in the bag with precision, each one in its rightful place. "The kind of dad who happens to be a convicted criminal. Grand larceny."

I drew in my breath. *Jeez.*

He looked up at me and smiled. "Kidding. My dad was a locksmith. A real good one, too." He lifted his bag. "See? His lessons came in handy, didn't they? So what are you needing, and please tell me you're not after Oxycontin? It's not worth it. That stuff can really mess you up if you abuse it."

"No. Just antibiotics. I cut my arm and I think it's infected."

He nodded and let out his breath in an exaggerated way. "Show me."

"What?"

"Your arm. Show it to me."

I removed my jacket and rolled up my sleeve to expose the bandage. Blood and puss stained the gauze. It made me a little woozy, and I slid to the floor to sit.

"Yeah, that's going to need to be cleaned." He squatted in front on me, slipped a pocketknife from his jeans, and cut the bandage off without the blade touching my skin. He let out a low whistle. "That's a deep one, a'right." He stood and pointed down at me. "Stay there, I'll be right back."

I had no idea who he was, and I was pretty sure I didn't like him, but since I couldn't have my dad, the doomsday-loving lunatic would have to do.

CHAPTER 12

"Hope you like Berry Blast." He reached into the grocery basket, unscrewed the cap on a bottle of Gatorade, and handed it to me. He took my other hand and placed one large white pill and three smaller ones of various colors in my palm. "Take them all. You're going to need them."

"What are they?" I rolled the pills around.

"Does it matter?"

I glared at him. "Yeah, it kind of does."

He shook his head. "Fine. That one's an antibiotic. Those two are for your fever and that one"—he pointed to the smallest pill—"will liven you up a bit and make you nicer to be around."

"What?"

"It will take the edge off and make it easier for me to do what I've got to do." He started removing various items from the basket—needle, thread, rubbing alcohol, scissors, clean bandages, a bottle of Jack Daniels. *Great.* "That's mine, so don't touch it."

"I *am* a nice person." I held the tiny pill out to him. "I don't want it."

He pushed it back at me. "You're mildly pleasant, if that. Do yourself a favor and take it. Trust me. You're going to want it."

Trust him? He had a bottle of whiskey next to the supplies he planned to stitch me up with.

"Suit yourself." He poured the rubbing alcohol in the cap of the bottle then ran the needle and the entire pre-cut length of sewing thread through the liquid. With a sigh, he laid it all on a paper towel at his side, spreading it out like a medical scene from a television show. "I'm not the one about to have a needle shoved in and out of my arm, you are. Your choice." He held up the Jack Daniels and winked before taking a swig. "*My* choice." Letting out a low burp, he patted his chest. "Ahh, much better. You ready?"

I tossed all the pills onto my tongue and swallowed them down with a mouthful of warm Gatorade. Maybe I did need a little something to get through this. "Do you even know what you're doing?"

"We're about to find out, aren't we?" He smiled and rubbed the top of my head as if I were a dog. "Don't worry. I've sewn on buttons and mended socks several times. This ain't all that different."

I yanked my arm to my chest. *Oh, heck no!* "This is way different!"

"You know what?" He sat back on his haunches, tented his knees, and rested his arms on top. "Why don't we let that little pill kick in before we patch you up?" He took another drink from his bottle, screwed the lid back on, looked at it for a minute, and then launched it backward, high over his shoulders. It crashed in the next aisle over a few seconds later.

Jeez. "Are you drunk or something?"

"Nah, I'm no alcoholic. Addictions a bad thing." He wagged his finger at me. "Remember that. But I'm an adult and you're not, so it's okay if I need a swig or two to give me a helping hand. Adults get to have that distinct pleasure." He leaned forward. "You notice I tossed it away, right?"

He waited for me to answer, so I nodded.

"That's called restraint, something kids like yourself don't tend to have. Anything more than a sip or two and you're heading for a lifetime of pain and hurt. Remember that, too."

"I don't drink. I don't do drugs. Never have." I'd seen Toby hover over a toilet after a night of binge-drinking. I had witnessed him passed out, nearly naked, on our front porch, too tired or too high to open the front door. I had experienced enough of his anger, his wallowing, and his sappy love to know I didn't want any part of it. Besides, Dad had enough on his plate dealing with my brother. If I started any of those things, he may have given up completely and joined the both of us on the road to hell.

The odd stranger cocked his head and gave a quick nod. "Good. Don't start." He leaned back against a shelf full of drug and pregnancy tests. "So, what do you do for fun?"

"You mean when I'm not trying to survive the end of the world?" Warmness filled my belly and exuded from my core, creeping to the very ends of my body—my toes, my nose, my fingers. Light airiness surrounded my head and seemed to lift me up, making me feel feather-like. *Wow, that was fast.*

"Yeah, before all this. What kind of things were you into?" He stretched his legs out in front of him and crossed them at the ankles. "Sports? Music? Nah, I bet you were a book nerd. Am I right?"

How dare he? "I like books, but I wouldn't say I'm a book nerd. Just because someone likes to read doesn't mean they need labeling."

He smiled. "I totally called that one, didn't I?"

Idiot. "I bet the last time you read a book was when you were a toddler. ABCs and one, two, threes? Am *I* right?" I shifted my weight to become more comfortable, but the lightness of my head caused me to slowly fall to one side. *Weeeee....*

He caught me in his large hands and lowered me gently to the floor. "Ahh, it's kicking in. About time. How do you feel?"

"Awesome."

"Good." He took his jacket off, rolled it into a ball, and tucked it under my head. It smelled like a combination of Old Spice and Axe body spray.

So that was what he was doing when I had shot the door, making himself smell nice. The spray was actually quite lovely, and I took a deep breath, filling my lungs. Weird.

"Keep still so I can make sure to stitch your arm in a decent pattern. You move, you may end up with zig-zags and a puckered scar." He rolled my sleeve all the way up to my shoulder and leaned in close to my ear. "Just so you know, reading is a good thing. People should do more of it."

"What?" Nothing he said made sense—*ever*.

"Nothing. Here, hold this." He shoved a stuffed Santa into my arms, and proceeded to clean my wound.

What in the world? But when that first poke of the needle pierced my skin, I hugged Santa tight, almost squeezing the stuffing right out of him. *Holy* — "How many stitches?"

"Not sure yet. You're tough. Hang in there."

I was far from tough. Each pinch and poke caused my eyes to water. I closed them tight and hugged that stupid Santa as the thread weaved its way back and forth through my skin.

With more gentleness than I would have expected from him, he wiped the wetness away from my cheek with his thumb. He didn't say anything, just gave me a sympathetic look and went back to stitching me up.

I must have passed out, because one minute I was biting my bottom lip and fighting back tears and the next I was sleeping on top of a pile of Pillow Pets—unicorns, lady bugs, and brown floppy dogs—covered in a zebra-striped Snuggie. Strange, but definitely comfortable.

He sat across from me, his back against a shelf, a Pillow Pet of his own tucked behind his head, and Callie lying on her back in his lap. He rubbed her belly, and my kitten purred in delight.

"You're such a good girl. Yes, you are," he whispered.

Several cat toys littered the floor by his long legs along with a bowl of water and an opened can of cat food. I couldn't help but smile at the rugged man playing with the little orange and white ball of fur.

"How long was I out?"

He straightened. "I'd guess an hour or so. Not too long. How you feeling?" He placed Callie on a leopard-print dog bed with her leash tied to a bottle of fabric softener, and crawled toward me.

"I think I'm feeling okay." I took my time to sit up in case my head felt like floating away again.

He placed his palm on my forehead and nodded before removing it. "Fever's down. That's good." He picked up my partially drunk Gatorade and handed it to me. "You need to drink more. I'll get you another bottle and another antibiotic before I go."

He moved to stand, and I grabbed his arm, forcing him to remain squatting. "Go?"

"Yeah, there's a good hour of light left before the sun sets, and I thought I'd get a move-on."

My grip tightened. "You can't go."

He tipped his chin and smirked. "You can't stand me and I can barely tolerate you. Why in the world would I stay?"

True. He had a point. "Because we're the only people left," I argued. "It makes sense we should stick together." At least until I could find someone better, but I wouldn't tell him that part.

He shook his head. "Not a good enough reason."

"It's not safe to be on our own. We can work together." In every movie I'd ever watched the survivors stuck together. That was how it worked.

"Work together? What can you do? You have no skills."

True. He had *another* good point. "I've kept myself alive all this time. I must have *some* skills, otherwise I wouldn't be here."

"You've barely kept yourself alive—*barely*. I'm actually surprised you've lasted this long."

"That's not nice." I removed my hand from his arm.

"Maybe, but it's true. I'm doing just fine on my own, and adding a kid and her 'cat on a string' doesn't seem like the best move for me."

I bit the corner of my mouth to keep myself from crying and showing weakness in front of the jerk. "What about me? What's my best move?" I had hardly anything left to give, and if he walked out the storefront, leaving me on my own, I might curl up in a fetal position and call it quits. I hated him, but I needed him.

He didn't say anything, but kept his eyes on mine, unblinking and creepy.

"Tell me. What's my best move?"

He lowered his gaze and shook his head. "Damn it."

"What?"

"You're going to curl up and lie here in a ball if I leave, aren't ya?"

My shoulders stiffened. *How did he do that?* But who cared? He was softening. "Probably."

He sighed. "If I stay, you have to promise me one thing."

Heck, I'd promise him pretty much anything... well, almost anything. I nodded.

"Just promise me you won't suck all the fun out of being the last people around, okay?"

CHAPTER 13

He lit several candles and placed them around our staked-out corner in Rite Aid. Candles of all sizes and fragrances lined the pharmacy counter and nearby shelves, casting swaying shadows on the walls as the wicks flickered. Comforting, yet eerie at the same time.

"You okay?" he asked.

I nodded. The makeshift bed of stuffed animals, Snuggies, and packages of toilet paper cushioned my bottom and kept me off the cold linoleum floor. It sure beat the gas station, and happened to be more comfortable than I would have imagined.

He didn't make himself a similar bed, but spread out a blanket on the ground and used a couple stuffed animals of his own as pillows.

"I have a sleeping bag if you want it." I pointed at my packed duffle bag he'd dragged inside for me. "You're welcome to use it."

He tucked an arm behind his head. "I'm good. Besides, do you really want a smelly man sleeping in your bag? I haven't showered in days."

I hadn't thought about that. "When you put it that way, no, but you look uncomfortable."

"I'm good. I have all my stuff stashed at the motel on ninth and ninth. We'll grab it tomorrow when you're feeling better."

The motel on ninth and ninth wasn't far away, a few blocks at best. "I could've walked there."

He smirked. "Yeah, I don't think so. You're still a bit loopy in the head and even though my muscles are hard to ignore, carrying you while walking your cat doesn't seem all that joyous. There's only an hour of daylight left anyway. Best to camp here and then figure out what we're doing tomorrow."

I settled against a large teddy bear with my face against its belly. "Do you have a car?"

He laughed. "Of course I do. Several in fact. Don't you?"

"No, I was saving up for one."

"Saving up for one? What's with that?" He shook his head and continued to lie there all relaxed. "You're doing it all wrong, my naïve little friend." He waved his arm. "Just point at whichever car you like and say, 'mine' and it's yours. That's how I've been claiming things." He pointed to a vaporizer on the top shelf. "That's mine. See how it works?"

"Stop it, I'm serious. I need a car so I can charge my phone, call my dad, and get the heck out of here."

"I see." He dragged out his last word and turned to stare at the ceiling for quite some time before casting his gaze on me again. "Where have you been hiding for the past two months?"

My shoulders stiffened. "My dad installed a bomb shelter in our backyard."

"Bomb shelter... nice. Lucky you." He paused. "Here's the thing, and I hate to burst your pretty little bubble, but it's not going to be that easy. First, you're not going to get any reception. I've tried. Second, do you think I would be hoofing it if I could be driving instead?"

He lay back on his pillows and stared at the ceiling again. "I don't mean to knock your plans, I really don't, but you've got to be realistic. The satellite systems have all gone haywire and the roads are either so littered with junk and debris they're hard to maneuver, or giant craters have wiped out huge sections altogether." He rolled his head to the side to look at me. "So I assume you haven't seen I-15, have you?"

I shook my head. My chest grew heavier with each word he spoke.

"Between Natesville and Wilder, gone. There *is* no road, just a huge hole where those cities used to be. Viaducts have collapsed. Hundreds, if not thousands, of abandoned cars block good sections of road, and nearly every bridge between here and Madison has crumbled into the river. Those that do remain are hanging by a thread. I wouldn't cross 'em if you paid me. Well, maybe if you paid me."

Natesville and Wilder? That was over a hundred miles from here. And Madison? That was the next state over. *Another state.* How big was this thing? I straightened and drew my knees to my chest. "What do you think happened?"

He kept his eyes on me and took a minute before speaking. "I wish I knew. Meteors are my guess, though it doesn't explain the crazy weather patterns we tend to get now."

Crazy weather? I wrapped my arms around my legs, trying to ease my rising panic. "You didn't see it? Where were you?"

"I didn't say that I didn't see it, I just can't explain it is all. I'm not a scientist." He turned his gaze to the ceiling and tucked his arms under his head.

I waited for him to say more, but several minutes ticked by without a word. "You didn't tell me where you were?"

He took a large breath and released it through his nose. "I know."

What kind of answer was that? Now every worst-case possible scenario ran through my mind. Criminal? Mental patient? That was probably it. He'd escaped from a psych unit for the criminally insane. *Great.* "You're scaring me."

He glanced at me before looking back to the ceiling. "No need to be scared. I'm as gentle as a baby panda. Maybe even more so, but I'm not going back to my previous life, so the less you know about me the better. This is my opportunity to create a different, more improved life for myself."

"So basically, you're taking advantage of a pretty crappy situation?"

"I wouldn't say that. I'd say it's more like I'm trying to find the silver lining in all this mess."

"There is no silver lining."

He chuckled. "Potato potahto."

"But what about when everyone comes back?" This wasn't a game. At some point, people would return. They would, and... actually, I had no idea what would happen at that point. Not a clue, though I was certain anything this weirdo took and claimed as his, he'd have to return. I glanced down at my Doc Martens. *Shoot.*

"It's been two months, kid. If they were coming back, they would've done it by now."

"You're delusional!" I threw the teddy bear at him. "They will be back! All of this is temporary and you're crazy to think it isn't." I know I joked about it being the end of the world, but it wasn't. It wasn't! It couldn't be. "People don't disappear, you know? Especially this many people!"

He laid the teddy bear to the side and sat upright in the dim light, looking at me without a hint of anything but seriousness on his face. "Look around, because apparently they do."

Tears pushed against my blinking eyelids, and I swallowed hard. My lungs began to burn and my chest compressed, squeezing the little remaining air out through my nose. But no air came in, as though a handful of cotton balls had been shoved into my throat. My blood thrummed inside my ears and my heart pounded, smacking my ribcage like an angry fist against a door. He had to be wrong. No, he *was* wrong.

I stood quickly, but then fell to my hands and knees, holding the ground, staring at the dizzying tiles spinning around me. *I can't breathe. I can't breathe.*

He knelt in front of me, took my face between his hands, and forced me to look him in the eyes. "It's okay. You're okay. Small breaths. Like this." He took a breath in and released it. "Come on. Your turn."

My arms flailed at my sides, smacking the air as though I was drowning, but he refused to let go.

"Look at me." His eyes locked onto mine, and stayed with me even when I tried to remove myself from his hands. He mirrored my movements, turning his head as I turned mine. "Slow down. Relax. Everything's going to be okay. You're fine. Try a small breath now."

I gripped his upper arms, hanging on to him out of desperation and fear that if I let go of this person, this *one* other person, the earth would spin so fast I would be thrown off the planet and float away.

"That's it. One breath, now another."

Somehow, a squeak of air pushed past the invisible blockage in my throat and my lungs found a hint of relief. Another tiny breath managed to follow the first, until I gasped, taking in miniscule sips of oxygen, one right after another.

"That's a girl. Take your time. You've got it now."

A word here and there broke through my erratic sobs. "You're wrong."

He tugged me into his arms, holding me against his chest while his large hand held the back of my head. "For your sake, I hope I am."

"Here. You need to eat something." He placed a tray over my lap before setting a bottle of water and a couple of pills next to a paper bowl filled with something I couldn't distinguish, but which smelt an awful lot like canned dog food. "It's the best I could come up with, but you need to get something in you that's not all just sugary crap. So eat this. It's got meat and vegetables. Of course, it's all coated in fat sauce, but that's beside the point."

I lifted a spoonful and sniffed it, trying to make out the contents in the muted light. "What is it? It smells awful."

"Canned stew. Nothing fancy like I said, but much better than chips and soda, or whatever you've been eating lately. I even warmed it up as best I could over a pine-scented candle, so enjoy."

I hesitated, but with him sitting across from me, watching my every move, I managed to slip a bite of goo into my mouth and swallow it. It wasn't half bad. "Thanks."

He pointed his finger at me and winked. "You're welcome. Eat up and then get some rest. Looks like tomorrow is going to be a long day."

I let the spoon hover over the glop. "What *are* we going to do tomorrow?"

He plumped his stuffed animals and lay against them, seeming to settle in for the night. "Well, I had planned on pillaging the town and returning to my lair, but now that you and your cat have decided to come into the picture and make me a part of your gang and force some morals into me, I assume we're going hunting for humans."

Hunger left me, and I placed the spoon next to the bowl. "I thought you said there wasn't anybody left."

"I know what I said." He rolled onto his side with his back facing me. "Doesn't mean we can't look."

"I just want to find my dad, that's all."

"Then we'll do everything we can to find him, but for now, can you please eat your semi-nutritious dinner and go to sleep? All your girlie chit-chat is keeping me from getting my eight hours of beauty sleep."

I stared at his back and settled against the wall, slumping a little. He annoyed me, and I could hardly wait to be rid of him, but even though he might be a convicted serial killer or something equally terrifying, I was grateful I wasn't alone.

Callie curled up next to him, lying next to his messy head. Apparently, she was grateful too. It didn't even bother me that she chose him over me. I could live with that.

"Hey?" I fixed my blankets. "Can I ask you a question?"

"Seriously?" He rolled over and faced me, careful not to squish my cat. "You're not done talking? It's late, you know?"

"Sorry."

He positioned Callie near his chest and scratched her back while keeping his dark eyes on me. "So what's your question?"

I had almost forgotten what I had wanted to ask as I stared at him staring at me. "Umm, do you know that you never told me your name or asked me mine?" We'd been together for several hours now, and I had no idea what to call him beside the expletives that ran through my mind. But if we were going to be together for however long it may be, I should probably call him something other than "the crazy guy."

"You know, when a guy breaks into a pharmacy and steals drugs for you and then manages to stitch you up, feed you congealed canned stew, and make you a sweet bed out of toilet paper and Snuggie blankets, you'd think you'd ask his name." He smiled. "But you're not that kind of person, are you?"

"I'm not... *what*? That's not nice! I forgot to ask." *That kind of person? What did that even mean?*

"If you say so."

"You're impossible, you know?" So aggravating. I brought the blanket up to my chin and rolled over with *my* back facing *him*. "Forget it. I don't care what your name is anymore."

He laughed, which grated on my already thin nerves. "Well, it's Cole, and I would normally say it's a pleasure to meet you, but honestly, I'm not so sure that it is."

CHAPTER 14

I scanned the various MP3 Players, headphones, and gadgets on display, searching for the car charger that would work with my particular phone. Dad didn't have a lot of money, so I didn't own a smart phone like most of the kids at my school. Cheap. Useful. Portable. Dad didn't care about data plans, searching the web, or my desperate need to text my friends.

"Texting? Why do kids insist on finding ways to be less and less sociable? Call your friends and actually talk to them, or better yet, write them a note. That's what we used to do back when I was in high school when *nobody* owned cell phones. We wrote on a piece of paper, then folded it into a triangle and tossed it at our friends when we passed them in the hall. Somehow, even without phones, we managed to communicate and meet up at the right places at the right time."

He didn't get it. No one wrote notes anymore, and even though my phone had its limits, I made it work and tried not to complain—too much. One girl didn't even own a phone at all, not a cell phone, not even a landline, so I knew things could be far worse than not owning the latest gadget.

But as I looked at my phone, and the various *modern* chargers hanging there, I wished Dad hadn't been so antiquated.

"You ready to go?" Cole approached, snacking on a half-eaten candy bar. A few unopened candy bars stuck out of the breast pocket of his jacket.

"Almost. I'm trying to find the right charger for my cell phone."

He nodded, took a bite, and talked as he chewed. "Good, even if it is a little misguided. It shows you haven't completely given up. You're tougher than you thought." He held the candy bar out to me. "Want a bite?"

Really? "Gross. I'll pass."

He shrugged, slipped the last piece into his mouth, and then opened wide to show me the mushy, chocolaty, brown mess on his tongue.

"Eeww. You're disgusting!"

"Awesome." Then he did it again.

"You're worse than a child, I swear."

He smiled. "That's what I've been told."

I was about to look through the chargers once more, but stopped and turned around as he began to walk away. "What did you mean I'm misguided?"

He grabbed a package of green ear buds and looked them over before placing them back on the shelf and opting instead for the neon-pink ones which he slipped into his pocket next to the pilfered candy bars. "We already discussed this. Satellites are down, remember? But if you want to figure it out for yourself, then that's your right. Do what you gotta do."

"I'm looking at chargers because my dad left me a message, telling me where he and my brother were, but my battery died before I could hear the whole thing."

"Wow. Hate when that happens. The irony."

"Can you please be serious for one minute? *Please?*" The longer I spent with this guy the more appealing my idiot brother looked.

He cleared his voice, raised his chin, and held up his hand in the manner of Queen Elizabeth. "Of course. Please proceed."

I tipped my head and gave him an incredulous look. "Just be normal."

He dropped his arm to his side and shrugged. "Now you're confusing me. What do you want? Serious or normal? I can't do both."

"Forget it." I waved him off and turned to the display of chargers again. "I don't know why I even bother. You're impossible."

He came to stand at my side, our shoulders nearly touching, then grabbed a charger from the shelf, opened the package, and took my phone from my hands. He connected it at the base and smiled. "This should do the trick."

"Thanks." I tried to take my phone from him, but he held it outside my reach.

"Not so fast, short one. First, you need to tell me your name. It's only fair since you know mine."

I released an irritated breath. "My name's Tess, and my cat's name is Callie, in case you want to know that too." I reached for my phone again, and this time snagged it from his grasp.

He glanced over his shoulder toward the back of the store where we'd left my kitten. "Callie, huh? You do realize your cat isn't Calico but more like a Tabby, right?"

"I didn't name her Callie because of the color of her fur! I liked the name, okay?"

He raised both hands, palms out. "I was only pointing out the obvious. No need to be all defensive."

"I'm not being defensive—"

"Yeah, you kind of are." He took a step away from me, palms still raised. "Have you thought about checking out the women's personal hygiene area by any chance? I hear they make pills for this kind of thing."

"You're kidding me, right? You didn't just suggest my aggravation with you is due to PMS and *not* based on the fact you're freakishly *annoying*?"

He removed a candy bar from his pocket and tossed it at my feet. "Look, chocolate." Then he turned and took off down the aisle.

"You're going to need these." Cole knelt and placed several bottles of vitamins next to my already stuffed bag.

"I don't have room. I can barely fit everything in there as it is." My pile grew larger every time Cole left me and reappeared carrying more stuff—jerky, sunscreen, scarves, and gloves, packages of gum, knee-length socks, and now vitamins. "I won't be able to carry my bag."

"You make things more difficult than they need to be, I swear." He left me again and returned with an empty shopping cart. Why hadn't I thought of that before? Here I was, busting my back, when all along I could have used a cart like the homeless do—I *was* homeless after all.

I grabbed my bag to toss inside, but he pulled the cart away from me. "First things first—get in."

"Huh?"

"It'll be fun, I promise."

"Yeah, I don't think so, but thanks anyway." Trying to understand Cole was like trying to understand calculus—nearly impossible. For a guy who kept confessing his "adultness," he sure didn't act any more mature than a ten-year-old.

I reached for the cart again, but he yanked it away. "Get in."

"We don't have time for this—"

"Of course we do! There's always time for some fun, and right now we could use a little. *You* could use a little. Remember I said I'd only stay if you promised not to poop at my party?"

Poop at my party? "Do you mean be a party pooper?"

"Not much of a difference, really, but you promised, so get in or I'm walking out the bullet-riddled front door and not coming back." He stepped backward, taking the cart with him. He turned it one way and then the other, testing me by wiggling it back and forth.

I needed to find Dad, not goof around with stupid shopping carts. He was wasting time.

"Okay, suit yourself." He whipped the cart around. "See ya on the flipside, kid."

"Wait, Cole." I dropped my bag. *What am I doing?*

"Yesss?" He turned the cart toward me and raised a brow.

"Even though I think we should be doing other things like gathering bottled water and trying to find a way to charge my phone, I'll get in your stupid cart." Being with him had better be worth it, but the longer I was with him, the more unlikely it seemed.

"Sweet!" A huge smile swept over his face, and his expression of victory nearly caused me to change my mind. I could be stubborn too.

He gave the cart a shove in my direction, and I took hold of it, stopping it before it crashed into the shelves and knocked everything to the floor. *This is ridiculous. Sooo ridiculous.*

"Go on, get in."

"This is dumb." I slipped a leg over the side into the basket. "I haven't ridden in one of these since I was a little kid." When was the last time I rode in a grocery cart? Maybe when I was three or four years old? There was a reason for that—*carts weren't meant for grown people!*

"Really? I did this the other day." He maneuvered the cart in the direction of the front doors and steered without regard to its passenger—*me*—forcing me to grip the sides to keep upright.

"Yeah, I kind of figured this was something you did on a regular basis." I glanced over my shoulder. "You're not going to do something stupid that gets me injured or killed are you? I'm still recovering, remember?" I didn't want more stitches.

"Relax. You worry too much." He pushed us through the broken door. The shards of glass crunched beneath the wheels and the cart skidded a little, but he managed to get us outside without tipping the whole thing over.

"Hey, wait! What about my cat? Where are we going?" He was a crazy man. I had no idea what his intentions were or whether we'd even be back. We would be back, right? My cat and my things were there. Why had I agreed to this? *Because I'm a moron.*

"Shhhh... everything's going to be fine. Your cat has the best setup, toys, food, water, so she'll be okay until we return. We'll only be as long as it takes for you to liven up a bit."

He steered us past the cars in the parking lot to the four lane, normally busy, street out front. "Hang on tight!"

"Wait just—"

But he ignored me and began to run with the cart. The wheels fought against the momentum, twisting and turning, but they handled my weight and his persistence. The air whirled around me and whipped my hair across my eyes.

I brushed the wild strands away, and gripped the sides tighter as Cole pushed the cart even faster. I was certain shopping carts weren't meant for speeds higher than grocery store aisles allowed and Cole was going to get me killed. Stitches were the least of my problems.

He hopped on the back, adding his weight to the already burdened cart. He no longer steered the metal contraption on wheels down the precarious road, but threw his arms out to the side and coasted.

I gripped the cart as though my life depended on it, which at the moment, it did. This wasn't fun at all and I wished I'd never agreed to his stupid games.

"Close your eyes, Tess. Enjoy yourself."

"I can't! Jeez. You need to stop!"

He jumped off the cart, but instead of bringing the whole thing to an end as I had anticipated, he started running again, adding more speed to the already out-of-hand situation.

"Stop it!" The cart wiggled and the wheels strained to keep up. *I'm going to die. I'm going to die. Death by shopping cart.*

"Close your eyes."

"Heck no!" I yelled over the pounding of his feet on the pavement and the squeaking of the wheels. I needed my eyes to be open—*wide, wide* open.

"Close them."

"No!" My knuckles whitened.

"Trust me."

Trust you? Look what trusting him had gotten me into—careening down the street in a cart that threatened to collapse at any moment. "No!"

"I'm not stopping until you do." With that, he jerked the cart to the right, nearly tumbling the whole thing over as it balanced on two wheels to take the curve in the road.

A few choice words flew past my lips, words I had never, *ever*, uttered in all my life, but were more than appropriate for this situation.

He laughed. "Seriously, I've run marathons—several of them—so I can do this all day."

"Okay, okay!" *Father, which art in Heaven, hallowed be thy name...* I squeezed my eyes shut, prayed it would be over soon, and I wouldn't have to add a nasty road rash—or worse—to my list of bodily injuries. This was complete insanity, but being trapped in a metal basket with a crazy man steering didn't leave me with a lot of options.

He kept running, and the wind picked up around me, caressing my cheeks and messing my hair. Several times I felt myself floating, though the crisscross pattern of the cart never left my backside. The warmth of the sun bathed my face, and its light danced across my closed lids as we passed buildings and alleyways. It was almost like flying—almost.

Abandoned structures and the emptiness of my surroundings fell away, replaced only by the thumping of my heart, the sound of Cole's breathing, and the rickety whirl of the wheels as they turned. I should have been terrified, but somehow the act of closing my eyes had the reverse effect, though I never released my grip on the cart.

I wasn't that dumb.

I had no idea where we were headed or what dangers lay before us, but for a brief moment, it didn't matter. For two *very* long months, my life had consisted of wondering, worrying, and crying lots and lots of tears.

Now, with my eyes closed I could imagine people strolling along the sidewalk, crossing at the corner to visit the post office or to sit outside the ice cream parlor, enjoying a root beer freeze or crème soda. Cars obeyed the traffic lights, joggers enjoyed a mid-morning run, and kids played in the schoolyard—shooting hoops, playing foursquare or swinging from the monkey bars. Birds sang from tree branches overhead, a dog barked in the distance, a car horn honked, the school bell rang... with my eyes closed, nothing seemed wrong. I wasn't alone. Everything was normal.

And my family wasn't missing.

I didn't notice the slowing of the cart until it almost came to a complete standstill; I had been *weirdly* consumed by the moment. Cole stepped in front of me, his shadow falling over me, blocking the sun. I opened my eyes and the reality of my situation came into view—all too clearly. Closing my eyes, however briefly, wouldn't change anything.

Cole smiled and leaned against the cart, his face only a few inches from mine. "You enjoyed it, didn't you?"

Admitting my experience would give him power I wasn't sure I wanted him to have, but the smile on my face made denial impossible.

CHAPTER 15

"Okay, no more dilly-dallying. It's time to get real now." He waved a hand over his face, his happy-go-lucky expression changing to a sterner one. His effort to be more serious caused me to grin in spite of myself, and I wondered how long he could keep that up.

"We need water and supplies. Also, as much toilet paper and gum as we can handle." Cole pushed the empty cart to me. "Never underestimate the need for toilet paper and gum. Both, very handy. So pack up fast, kid. We need to hit the road, put our feet to the pavement, and soldier on." He gave me a salute, refusing to lower his arm or change his soldier-stance until I mimicked a salute—though I executed mine with exaggerated flare and I'd bent all my fingers except one.

Yep. His seriousness hadn't lasted long.

I grabbed the cart and steered it away from him. He might be aggravating and totally immature, but he was right; we did need to hurry. Arguing or pointing out the fact that *he* had wasted most of our morning wouldn't change anything, so I kept my mouth shut and my opinion to myself.

I packed everything I could—toilet paper and gum too—using my Tetris-like skills to jam the cart as tightly and efficiently as possible. Heavier items on the bottom, lighter things on top. Amazing how much could fit in such a small space.

If Callie had any inkling Cole and I had left her earlier, she either didn't care or had adjusted quickly. Like Cole had said, he'd set her up really nicely. A whole aisle was devoted to her with its array of pet toys. Not sure why he thought a rawhide bone would be appropriate, but he'd given her one. She had several dog beds to choose from, a litter box she'd taken full advantage of, and a bowl of wet cat food as well as a bowl of dry. In fact, he'd put together several leashes, giving her more area to roam, and she'd made her way to a middle shelf, pushed over items to make room for her fluffy body, and now slept peacefully on some dishtowels.

I hated to wake her and take her away from her kitty paradise, but it had to be done. Rite-Aid wasn't my stopping point even if Callie had made it hers.

I added her things to the cart, tied her leash to the handle, and then perched her on top. She protested by swiping a claw in my direction, but I jumped out of her way before she was able to land a nasty blow on my arm.

She soon settled down as she realized that attacking me meant she'd have to let go of her grip on my duffle bag. She held on for dear life, as I had done earlier with Cole.

"You ready to blow this Popsicle stand?"

"Yeah, I think so. How about you?" I spun around to see Cole had packed his cart in the most impressive way. It would have put mine to shame had he actually filled it with essentials like water and food, but his selections included things I couldn't fathom ever needing—not in a time like this anyhow. What was he planning on doing with a George Forman grill or a waffle iron? The guy was nuts. Again, I kept my mouth shut. I needed to charge my phone and starting an argument with him would only delay us further.

"Totally good to go." He pointed a finger at me and cocked it like a gun. *Why do people do that?* Having someone cock an imaginary gun in your direction, even with a wink, was still a bit disturbing. *You pretended to shoot me. How is that funny?*

"What do you think we should do first?" I ignored the fact he had fake murdered me.

He shrugged and smiled. "Since we're trying to find your dad, I think that puts you in charge. I'm only along for the ride, after all."

O-kay. "Well, then I think the first thing we should do is charge my phone. Once I know where my dad is, we can head that way." I dug into my duffle bag and held up the keys to the car back at the apartment building. "There's a car several miles back—"

He held up his hand. "Too far."

"But I have keys. Most of the cars around—"

"Really? I know I haven't checked every car in the area, have you?"

I released my breath. "No, but—"

"I'd think you'd want to take a moment and look around, just in case, but"—he held up both hands and bowed a little at the waist—"this is your mission after all. Do what you think is best."

"Fine!" I shoved the keys back in my bag. They would be plan B if all else failed. "I don't want to waste all day looking, so we'll look for half an hour and that's it."

He nodded. "But are you sure?"

"Damn it, Cole! I'm not sure about anything! All right?" *Argh!* He was so frustrating. "You tell me to be in charge and then you question everything I do!"

"That's because leaders should be challenged every now and again. That's how *great* leaders are born."

"Well, knock it off!"

"Aye, aye, captain."

I groaned under my breath, grabbed my cart, and pushed past him. And we'd only just begun. *Fantastic.*

The broken glass made it difficult to maneuver my heavy load out the door, but I shoved and forced the wheels over the shards, twisting and turning the cart, until I made it outside. The day before had been bright and sunny—a perfect spring day—but now the overcast sky looked as though rain could start falling at any given point. The last thing we needed.

Cole stopped his cart next to mine. "Do you know how to hotwire a car?" He glanced at me as he slipped on a pair of sunglasses, the UV tag still stuck to one of the upper lenses.

I shook my head. "Don't you? You have that cool tool bag of yours. Couldn't you use it to get a car started?"

"Just because I know how to pick a lock doesn't mean I'm mechanically inclined. I'm the son of a locksmith, not a criminal. I was kind of hoping you might be though."

"Excuse me?"

"Hmmm." He ignored me and looked up one side of the street and down the other. "I guess it's time for us to do a little Easter egg hunting. You take that side of the road and I'll hunt over here? If it pleases your majesty, of course."

I rolled my eyes but nodded. *Why not?*

"And to make it fun, because face it, this is kind of boring, how about the first one to find an open car with a set of keys is the winner and doesn't have to cook dinner or do dishes tonight?"

Everything was always a game with him. He had to be the most immature adult I had ever met. "Fine."

He lowered his glasses to the tip of his nose. "May the odds be ever in your favor."

His impression, though spot on, ruined my favorite book, but it did cause me to grin—just a little. I quickly removed the smile from my face. It would only encourage his insane behavior.

I gave him a head start as I parked Callie and the cart in the shade and gave her a quick pat. "Stay here," I said, though she didn't appear to care one way or the other. Cats, so cute and yet, so indifferent.

I cast a quick glance at Cole—he had his back to me, looking inside the open window of a truck left in the middle of the road. He was an awful lot like a cat.

Okay, that was weird.

Cars had been left everywhere—some in parking lots, others on the road, and others at the street light as if people had been there one minute and vanished the next. But why weren't there any keys? That part baffled me. Had people left their cars in the middle of the street, but taken their keys with them? As I peered inside vehicle after vehicle, I realized that, strange as it seemed, that's what people had done.

Perhaps they thought all of this was temporary and they'd be coming back soon.

I sighed. Being one of only two people left in the world, made the whole situation rather frustrating. I promised if the situation was ever reversed, *and* if I ever owned a car, I'd leave my keys behind in case someone needed them. I wouldn't be a selfish prick.

A car horn blared in the distance, and Cole waved at me. With one hand on the horn—so irritating—he used the other to cup his mouth. "Bingo!"

A smile spread across my face. I didn't care if I had to make dinner and clean up afterwards—Cole had found a suitable car, and now I could hear the rest of Dad's message and find out where he'd gone.

I could hear his voice. I could hear *all* their voices again.

The idea of listening to Dad, my friends, my grandmother, and yes, even my brother, created an emotional bubble in my throat. I swallowed it and ran toward Cole. I actually ran—something I never did unless there was some sort of edible reward at the end. But this was different.

I needed this.

"Does it work? Really?" I approached the old-looking station wagon with cautious optimism, though I had already let my emotions get ahead of me. If it didn't run or if Cole was only messing with me, I'd be devastated. *Really* devastated.

He didn't answer me, but reached inside and turned the key. The station wagon sputtered and kicked out a grey puff of smoke, probably from months of disuse, but eventually it roared to life.

I threw my arms around Cole in a moment of sheer excitement. "It works! It really works!" The hug lasted only a couple of seconds before I came to my senses and pushed past him to look at the gas gauge. A quarter of a tank. That would do.

"Turn it off, turn it off," I demanded. "We can't waste the gas." But as he reached in to turn the key, I slapped his hand. "Never mind. Don't. It might not start again. Leave it. Just leave it."

He backed away. "Wow, you're a whirlwind of craziness aren't you?"

"I'm excited, and yeah, maybe it does make me a little crazy, but this is huge!" I squeezed his arm. The crazy man had called *me* crazy, but who cared? "It's the difference between knowing what I'm supposed to do and not knowing anything and being alone forever."

"Alone, huh?" He motioned to himself and widened his eyes. "*Hello?*"

"You know what I mean." I glanced at my cart a block down the road. "I'll go grab my stuff while you wait here. Then you can go grab your things. "

"How about you stay put, and *I'll* go grab both our carts. It'll be quicker." He started off, then turned to me. "Not that I'm trying to step on your leadership toes, or anything."

I waved him on.

I got the feeling no one could lead Cole.

Cole sat in the driver's side and I sat in the passenger's seat. Callie roamed the interior of the car, climbing on the backs of the seats and hopping up on her back feet to peer out a side window.

"So far so good." He glanced at the battery icon on my phone. "It's at eighteen percent. You want to give it a listen now?"

I shook my head. I really wanted to listen, but I also wanted the battery to be fully charged; I had plans to listen to the messages over and over and over...

"So you heard the message from your dad the other day, right?"

Why was he giving me that strange look?

"Yeah, three days ago." Had it really been three days? Somehow, it felt so much longer.

Cole reached across me and opened the glove compartment. "Good. It means we're not too far behind him." He seemed too nonchalant. As if he was purposely tiptoeing around something. He removed several tape cassettes and held them up, smiling. "You don't even know what these are, do you?"

I didn't answer, though I knew exactly what they were. My mind whirled. *"We're not too far behind them."* But the message was only days old, not months.

I slumped in my seat and turned my face to the window as this realization settled over me like a suffocating plastic bag. Dad could be anywhere by now. He hadn't come for me in all this time, so why would he still be there now?

"You okay?"

"No." I bit my lower lip. "I heard my dad's message three days ago, but it's older than that."

He breathed out, like he was glad I'd figured out the bad news for myself. "Okay, so how old?"

I shifted on my seat so my back faced him. *No crying. Don't you dare start crying.* "I think he left it the day everything happened. I didn't have my phone with me until... until the other day."

Cole didn't say anything, but Callie leaped over the back of my seat and curled herself in my lap.

"Hmm... I can see where that could get you down, but honestly, does it change anything?"

I turned my head enough to see him without looking at him straight on. "It changes everything."

"Oh, really?" He yanked the charger from the cigarette lighter and let it dangle from his fingertips.

"What are you doing?" I snatched it from him, plugged it back in, and checked that the battery had begun charging once more. What was he thinking?

"Just what I thought. It doesn't change anything. Okay, sure, the message is older than either of us would like, but that's not going to stop you from checking it out, is it?"

I shook my head. "No."

He started thumbing through the cassettes once more until he found one he liked. "Oh, a mixed tape! This should be good." He slipped it in the player and turned up the volume.

A country singer sang about her cheating lover and slashing his truck tires.

I couldn't help but think I hadn't seen Dad or Toby in almost three months. I'd never been without them for longer than a day or two. Would I ever see them again?

"Hey, buck up." Cole tapped my chin lightly with his fist. "You've got a message to listen to, remember? That's nothing to pooh-pooh."

I glanced at Cole. "But he's probably not there anymore."

"Probably not." He kept his gaze on me and turned the volume up a little at a time. "But we definitely have a place to start."

# CHAPTER 16

Cole flew upright in his seat, and I straightened in my own.

"What's wrong?" I had no idea what had freaked him out, but his strange behavior had me on edge.

He raised his arm across me and pointed out the passenger window. "That's what's wrong."

My back had been pressed against the door while I waited for my phone to complete its charge, but when I turned around, I could see what had made Cole's eyes wide with fear. I was quite certain my own eyes held the same look — pure and utter horror.

In the distance, but growing closer with each passing second, a darkness, several miles wide and several miles high, rolled over homes and buildings, engulfing everything in its path.

Lightning zigzagged like a fourth of July fireworks display, highlighting shapes briefly before the giant black mass enveloped them.

Rumbling caused the car to tremble, and Callie disappeared under one of the back seats, tangling her leash in a spider-web pattern as she darted for safety.

My hair slowly rose, standing on end, touching the roof of the car. I reached up and tried to smooth it down to no avail.

Tornado? Electrical storm? How could that be? This wasn't Kansas! We didn't have those kinds of things around here.

"Cole, what's going on?" This couldn't possibly be happening, but the black mass continued toward us whether I believed it possible or not.

My words seemed to snap him out of his trance, and he threw open the car door without saying a word. *What? What is he doing?*

I opened my door, figuring I should follow his lead, and tugged on Callie's leash, but she'd dug her claws into the floor. "Where are you going?" I yanked on the leash again.

"Get back inside, Tess!" He started heaping items from the cart into the back seat. "Get inside now!"

What was he doing? The water, the toilet paper, the waffle iron — we wouldn't need any of those things if we died in the process!

I glanced over my shoulder at the darkness approaching. *Holy crap!*

Cole's hair began to stand upright too. I jumped back inside the car and slid to the floor with my face pressed against the seat, as if not looking would change the course of our fate.

Holy crap, holy crap! What is happening?

In all my seventeen years of life, I'd never seen or heard of a tornado or electrical storm in this part of the States. Lightning, sure, but it was regular old lightning — tame enough to be pretty — but this, this was of the devil. It had to be. Nothing else could explain it.

My ears began to buzz as the droning sound of the storm drew closer.

Cole threw open the driver's side door, and slid into his seat. It felt as though the air inside the car had been sucked out and replaced with something else entirely — breathable, but not air. He slammed the door shut, and looked down at me. "You better hold on. This is going to get interesting!"

Hold on to what?

He put the car in reverse and glanced over his shoulder as he pressed the accelerator. The car skidded backward, and I heard the crunch of metal carts as the station wagon plowed into them, scattering most of the things we had taken such effort to pack.

I clutched the seat as best as I could, and kept my eyes on Cole.

There was nothing confident about the way he stared out the front window, or how he glanced behind him every other second.

Was that thing gaining on us? Could we outrun it?

I tried to climb back up onto my seat, but the car bounced and swerved, and I was forced back to my spot on the floor. My back slammed against the passenger door when he took a sharp left turn, and the force caused the door to fly open and snap off the frame. It hit the ground with a metallic thud, shooting up yellow sparks, but lay there only an instant before it flew upward, spinning in a circle, and soared backward.

"Cole!" I grappled to find a handhold as my fingers slid over the plastic surface of the seat. Oh, to have claws like a cat! The storm sucked at my body, extracting me from the car inch by inch.

One of my feet slipped and dangled in the open, being whipped by the increasing wind. I felt as though I were riding an amusement park ride, as my stomach pressed tighter and the inertia pulled on me, stretching me like taffy.

I was going to fall out of the car!

Cole kept one arm on the steering wheel and used the other to clasp my wrist. "Hang on!"

Easy for him to say! He'd buckled himself in!

I positioned my good foot against the wall, and pushed myself forward enough to draw my dangling foot back inside the vehicle.

"Get in the backseat!" He tugged on my arm.

"I can't!" If I let go, for even a moment, I was certain I'd be sucked out of the car, and just like the door, I'd hit the ground before shooting upward and away.

"You're going to fall out!" He glanced over his shoulder once more.

"I know!" I couldn't keep doing what I was doing, I knew that, but I didn't want to hasten being sucked out of the car either.

"Get in the back!"

"I can't!" My toes ached as I pressed my feet against the floor.

"Well, I can't drive the car and hang on to you at the same time!"

"Don't you dare let go!"

"Get in the back or I will be forced to make a hard decision!"

I shook my head. *No, no, no.*

"On the count of three, Tess. You dive for the backseat. One, two—"

He didn't wait till three, but jerked my arm with such force, I had no choice but to follow his lead and shoot my body over the backseat or have my arm ripped out of its socket. His muscles strained and the veins of his upper arms bulged under his skin. He never let go, not even after I'd made it over.

He yelled at me to put on a seatbelt, and only when I was strapped in did he remove his hand from my arm. He shifted his entire focus to the mess of a road ahead of us. For the first time since I'd met him, he'd become serious—*very* serious.

He weaved in and out of cars, dodged fallen trees and random debris. Sometimes he would take a left turn or a right turn that not only left the wheels squealing but had me squealing too.

I glanced behind us, but quickly turned around in my seat once more, face forward, eyes wide. The monster of a cloud was catching up.

Holy crap, holy crap, holy crap.

"Cole?"

"Not now." He swerved the car down a side road to avoid the huge parked semi stretched across all four lanes, blocking our path.

I fell to my left, nearly floating, but the seatbelt kept me from hitting the roof. "It's gaining on us, isn't it?" I didn't want to look anymore. My heart couldn't handle it.

He didn't say anything, but glanced in the rearview mirror. He pressed the accelerator even more. My answer. If the cloud of death didn't get us, speeding at over eighty miles an hour down a littered residential street would.

Everything Cole had tossed inside the car—toilet paper, the George Foreman grill, the bottles of water—slammed against one side and then the other with every chaotic turn. All I could do was duck and throw as much as I could into the very, *very* back, praying none of it would come careening forward and smack me in the back of the head.

It didn't matter that electric-tornado-demon clouds shouldn't exist—because they shouldn't—all that mattered was that one now grew ever closer in the rearview mirror.

Cole bounced the car up over the cement gutter and through the parking lot, past car vacuum machines and the little store selling various tree car fresheners.

What in the —

He drove the car straight into the automatic car wash. The large brushes and hanging strips scraped and slapped against the metal frame, but Cole kept going, driving the car along the track, forcing the tires over the dividers.

A tire blew, then another, but Cole continued to drive the slowing car into the middle of the building. When the station wagon ground to a stop, he leapt into the back and shoved me down against the seat, covering me with his body.

The seatbelt cut into my shoulder, my chest, my waist, but I didn't say a word. The air around us seemed light, like helium. An intense roar filled my ears, echoing off the cement walls surrounding us, louder than anything I'd ever heard before.

The car vibrated and glass exploded, causing me to shake all over. Cole held me closer. Darkness cloaked us, covering us in black so thick I couldn't even see his face next to mine. No light shone, not even a sliver, but the incredible, deafening noise threatening to pop my ears made up for it.

A lion roaring at my left, a train horn blaring at my right— both within inches of my ears—would only be a fraction of the noise.

One sense replaced by a monster of another.

I coughed and choked on the dust and dirt swirling around us, sweeping in through the open car door. Cole drew his coat over our heads, tucking it in, which helped some, but didn't ease my rising panic. I wasn't good in these kind of situations, and in the past couple of months, I'd been dealt more than I thought was fair.

We were being engulfed by the dark mass, bit by suffocating bit, like everything around us.

I tried to focus on Cole's breathing to give my own a sense of direction. *Easy, no deep breaths, just simple and shallow.* Less dirt to scrape my throat as I swallowed.

Everything happened so fast. There hadn't been time to decide if driving a car right into a dry carwash was the best option, or if the building was even stable.

There had been no time at all.

All we could do now was wait.

CHAPTER 17

The storm now hovered directly over our building, tugging on our bodies with such suction and grip it threatened to rip us out of the shaking car. It popped my ears and filled my head with ringing. I could only assume Cole experienced the same.

The car moved, not much, but it jolted my senses, and I realized the car was inching backward toward the opening. A little here, a little there, bumping over the way we had come. Whenever I thought it had stopped moving, it would shift again. The brushes of the carwash scraped against the sides.

"Cole!" I could hardly hear my own voice—whether because of my buzzing ears or the loudness of everything around us, I had no idea. If he heard me or answered back, I couldn't hear...

Neither of us could stop the car from being sucked away into oblivion. Climbing from the car would prove deadly, even if staying in it might kill us. We could only hang on and hope.

I shoved the fingers of one hand into the crack of the seat, gripping it, and wrapped the fingers of my other hand around the metal frame under the front. Cole's hold on me tightened, as his body seemed to lift away. My seatbelt grounded us both.

Please, please, please. I pressed my feet against the front seat, fighting for leverage against the whirling darkness, and just when I didn't think I could hold on any longer... everything stopped.

It stopped.

The rain, the wind, the thunder, the lightning, the blaring noise, the hum of electrical currents, even the darkness, lifted, graying ever slowly. Shadows appeared through Cole's jacket, but even that little bit of light felt like a lighthouse beacon. Fantastic.

Cole's body fell heavily on mine, as though the beast had let go of its hold and he'd come crashing down with his full weight. He didn't move. Only his warm breath against my ear let me know he was alive. I didn't budge or push him off, but waited. We needed a moment to collect ourselves. Had we really lived through that? *Really?* It seemed surreal.

"You okay?" he whispered. The jacket still covered both our faces. His whiskered cheek rubbed against my forehead.

"I think so. And you?"

"I about crapped myself for a minute, but I'm good."

"Do you think it's over?"

He was silent.

"Cole?"

"I say we give it a moment before going to find out." He removed the dusty jacket from our heads, but continued to lie on top of me, listening.

I'd never seen his face so serious. He stared upward and tilted his head as if in complete concentration. I listened too. Deafening silence replaced all of the terrifying sounds from before. The light and lack of noise seemed like a good sign to me, but I had no idea if it was only temporary. We could be in the eye of the storm, for all I knew. I kept my fingers wrapped in place, gripping whatever I could.

I followed his lead and remained quiet, like him, but scanned the roof of the car, the dirty interior, and him. When my eyes fell on Callie's limp leash, I shoved him forcefully.

"Get off me!"

He didn't budge. "Not yet."

"Callie!" In all of the commotion and near death experience, I'd forgotten about her. I pushed against him again, and this time he rose to a sitting position.

I unhooked myself from the seatbelt and fell to the floor, squeezing myself between the sections of seats, not caring that the silence and calm may only have been a trick.

"Callie!" I grabbed on to her leash, drawing it toward me. When I held the long strap and the empty harness in my hands, I couldn't speak.

I couldn't do anything.

I pressed the harness to my chest, holding it. I was already on the floor of the car, but had I been able to sink lower, I would have.

"We'll find her." Cole placed a hand on my shoulder. "I'm sure she's here somewhere."

There was no way that could be true. Between racing down streets and taking sharp turns, not to mention the insanity of the suction power which held all of us in its grip, my kitten could be anywhere.

Anywhere.

"I... I should have held onto her. I should have —"

"You were doing everything just to hang on yourself. This isn't your fault." He squeezed my shoulder. "It's not."

Then whose was it? She was my cat, my responsibility. She was all I had had left, and now I had nothing. I'd failed.

"Hey, let me check if things are safe and then we'll go looking for her. Okay?"

I didn't answer.

He seemed to take my silence as acceptance and slipped out the side door.

I continued to sit on the floor and cradle the empty leash. I couldn't have grabbed her, a large part of me knew, but I should have at least tried. I hadn't even made any attempt. Not one. *So selfish.*

Some could argue she was only a cat—dispensable, replaceable, just an animal—but she held me together when the world seemed to fall apart. I placed my head against the back of the front seat, resting my forehead against the plastic. Tears rolled down my cheeks and I bit my lip to keep it from quivering. I could smell my stinky cat on the leash.

"Tess!"

Whatever Cole wanted, could wait.

"You've got to come see this," he called again. "Seriously."

I continued to hold the leash and the harness, and slid out through the open door. I pushed my way past vertical spin brushes and hanging strips and made my way toward the opening where Cole stood.

He glanced over his shoulder at me then looked outward again. "This is the damnedest thing I've ever seen."

It wasn't until I stepped outside myself that I realized what held him so captivated. I drew in my breath and without really thinking about it, I slipped my hand into his.

I needed to hold on to somebody.

Everything to the left of us lay flattened. Timber, bricks, and lots of glass. Homes. Stores. Buildings. All rubble. To the right, things looked pretty much the same. Hours before, the place had been left untouched—almost *perfectly* untouched. Spring blooms had poked through wet dirt. Grass had needed mowing. Wind chimes had hung from front porches and sales banners had clung from storefronts.

Now, nothing stood upright.

Only our carwash with its little store front remained intact. The windows were blown out, but the air fresheners still dangled from their hooks. Odd and improbable, but I wasn't complaining.

A double rainbow curved in the sky, stretching from the north to the south, and softball sized hail littered the ground for as far as I could see—thousands of balls like curled white rabbits. Had they not been so destructive, it would have been amazing—*all* of it would have been amazing—but right now, I was only horrified.

Cole bent, still holding my hand, and picked up a piece of hail, bouncing it up and down. "Yeah, this isn't normal." He held it out to me, but I didn't accept the ball of ice. I didn't want to hold it at all.

He tossed it and when it hit the ground, it shattered like fragile glass. A shiver ran up my spine.

He didn't mention Callie, and from the look of our surroundings, I knew exactly why.

We stood there, staring at the nothingness of it all. He didn't attempt to remove my hand from his as we stood side by side.

"Remember how I told you about the weird weather?" He kicked a ball of ice with the toe of his boot and it splintered and cracked, but didn't fall apart.

I nodded.

"Well, now you know what I'm talking about. Though this" — he waved his free arm — "was something unexpected." He looked up into the clearing sky and the hint of blue in the grayness. "Mother nature sure likes screwing with us, that's for sure."

After I'd looked around enough to know everything was a big fat mess, I let go of his hand and started back to the car. I needed to check on my phone, though chances were clearly against it being there, clinging to the charger. But maybe, just maybe....

"This is only a minor setback." Cole called to me. I didn't acknowledge him, but kept walking. "Tess?"

I didn't answer — didn't feel much like talking.

"*Tess?*"

The genuine concern in his voice forced me to stop, though it took me a few seconds to turn around.

"We've got this, you know?"

I stared at him. What was he saying?

"We're alive, and that's something." He gave a simple yet sincere smile. "Everything might look real bad right now, but we still have that."

Yeah, we still have that. I continued to the carwash.

A thick coat of dirt and grime covered the station wagon, and as I walked beside it, I dragged my finger over the paneling, clearing a thin wiggly line. A worm. I was about to wipe my finger on my pants but instead stepped closer to the car and wrote my name and the date on the back window. It wouldn't hurt, in case someone happened to see it.

After staring at it a moment, I decided to add Cole. I didn't know his last name, but maybe if Dad heard I was alive and with someone, it would ease his worry. A long chance, but something.

I wiped my hands on my pants, though the material was just as filthy and hardly cleaned the dirt from my fingers.

Meow.

I whipped around, and stumbled backward, searching.

Meow.

Clinging to the large horizontal brush above the car, almost lost in the bristles, Callie peered at me with large frightened eyes in dirt-encrusted fur.

A sob exploded past my lips as I scrambled to climb on top of the car, slipping and sliding over the slick surface. "Callie!" I lost my foothold and crashed down on my knees, but I ignored the pain, and climbed again. "Callie!"

On the roof, I reached for her, but inches separated us and prevented me from scooping my scared kitten into my arms. "It's okay!" I stood on my tiptoes, stretched upward, and wiggled my fingers. *Come on, come on.*

Hands grasped my ankles, steadying me, and I glanced down at Cole who grinned.

"It's okay now. It's okay. I've got you!" I stretched as much as possible, more than was safe, and when my fingers brushed over her matted leg, I took hold and yanked, freeing her.

She flew into my arms, digging her baby claws into my chest as she clambered to find safety against my neck.

I slid to my bottom, sitting on top of the car, holding my kitten against me as she wailed her high-pitched meows over and over against my ear.

Tears fell down my face. I couldn't stop crying.

Cole patted my leg and kept right on smiling. "One life down. Eight to go."

CHAPTER 18

It looked beat to hell—more so than when I actually dropped it on the roof of the apartment building and broke the screen—but the dirty cell phone still clung to the cigarette lighter. Barely. I'd never completely bought into miracles, but as I held my phone in one hand, my cat in the other, all while sitting in a car in the only intact building on the block, how could I not?

"Just do it already." Cole pointed to the phone. "What are you waiting for?"

What am I waiting for?

I pressed the on button and the backlight glowed. I checked to see if any new messages had come in, though I realized the nil probability. As I expected, the screen didn't blink. No new texts. Nothing. Still, I had hoped.

I played the saved messages, listening to each of the voices again. Tears nipped at my eyes and I wiped them with the back of my hand. How I missed all them, my family, my friends.

Cole watched me, saying nothing.

But when Dad's voice came on, I straightened, the tears flowed, and Cole leaned closer. I wished I could have put it on speaker for him, but the broken screen wouldn't allow it, so I leaned near him, our heads together, with the phone in between.

"Tess, it's me, Dad. I don't know if you have your phone or not or even if you can get cell service in the bunker, but honey, I'm not going to be able to get back to you as soon as I thought. I'm sending someone for you though. They don't know Morse Code, Tess, so open the door for them, okay baby. Just open the door. They will find me and your brother and bring you to us. Right now, we're staying at the lodge up Rockport Canyon. You know the one."

I did know it. I hated it. We'd spent every spring vacation and Labor Day hiking the mountainside or fly-fishing in the frigid rivers. Not my favorite location by a long shot, but it had become tradition and getting out of the excursions had become nearly impossible—except for Toby.

All he had to do was show up drunk, piss off Dad, and he'd be banned, which put me in the weird position of trying to make it all up to Dad and pretend I loved the great outdoors. I didn't mind the woods and the mountains, but when all my friends had glorious trips to Cancun or New York to brag about, saying I'd spent my spring break gutting trout didn't quite compare.

"It's better than being in the cities. Safer. They'll bring you here and then we'll head over the mountains and into Colorado. I wish I could come get you myself, but Toby's hurt. Nothing horrible, but I need to stay with him. I hope you understand, Tess. I love you. Get here quick, okay?"

That was it. That was everything. No more messages.

I lowered the phone to my lap and stared out the dirty window.

"Rockport Canyon, huh?" After we'd sat in silence for several moments, Cole sunk into his seat with his hands threaded behind his head. By the solemn look on his face, he had to be thinking the same thing I did: impossible, far, too difficult. *What was Dad thinking?*

"I guess I was kind of hoping your dad would have picked something closer, like a Hilton Inn near an interstate, but why make this easy, right? Where would be the fun in that?" Cole placed a hand on my knee, forcing me to look at him. "You a good hiker?"

I shook my head. "No, not really."

"Yeah, I didn't think so. But hey, this will be an adventure. You, me, the great outdoors! What could go wrong?"

I couldn't tell if he was being serious or sarcastic, but either way, I stared at him without replying.

He sat up, smiling—always smiling. So annoying. "We'll get a tent and some gear and some of those nasty, but good-for-you energy bars—nutrition in the shape of a brick—and we'll head to Rockport. Should only take like"—he counted his fingers, his mind seeming to calculate the length of the journey, but he stopped when he'd used up all ten fingers and simply waved his hand—"well, it's going to take a bit, but that doesn't mean it ain't doable. People do crazier stuff all the time. It isn't like we're backpacking across Europe or anything."

Rockport Canyon was a good two-hour drive north from here. The lodge was probably another hour up the winding canyon roads and through the dense forest. Yeah, it was definitely a safe place to be when all hell broke loose in the cities, but by foot? We may as well have been backpacking across Europe.

"Why is this happening?" I turned away from him to look out the window again, staring at nothing.

"I don't think your dad figured it would be that difficult for you to get to him when he left the message. A couple of hours at most."

"I don't mean that. I mean, why is *this* happening? Why aren't people back yet? Where is everyone?" I looked back at him. "Besides Callie, I haven't seen even one other animal. No birds. No stray dogs. Nothing. You can't evacuate this many people without someone or something being left behind."

He pointed at me then at himself. "We're the left-behinds."

He was right. *Very* right. Sort of. "*I've* been left behind. You... you're having a blast! You love all of this!"

"Hey now, I never said I *loved* this. I'm simply quite fond of this new way of living—a big difference—but that doesn't change anything, does it? We're still the only ones here."

I didn't say anything.

"And as for the animals and why no one's back yet, could be because the water's contaminated, so don't drink anything not bottled."

"Seriously? You're just telling me now?" *I could have died.*

"Figured you knew. Also, keep in mind with all the changes going on it's not safe for anyone. Not yet. It's like a war zone."

"And you *like* this? How can you possibly want to live this way?"

He shrugged as if it was no big deal. "It beats the alternative."

"The alternative?"

"You know, working my butt off for 'the man,' getting little to show for it. Right now, I'm free from all of that. The world is my oyster, so they say. Yeah, it's dangerous, but my other life was slowly killing me. This is an improvement."

I slid out the passenger side of the car, carrying my harnessed cat in one hand and my cell phone in the other. I didn't want to be anywhere near Cole, not now, not when he rejoiced in a situation that frightened, hurt, and depressed me.

I pushed past the carwash bristles and brushes and made my way out into the open. A thick haziness hung in the air even though the sky was clear of ominous clouds. It didn't seem safe, but sitting in a damaged car with a deranged person didn't seem much better.

I started walking, not really caring which direction I headed in this mess. I needed to get away and think. How in the world was I going to get to Dad, and was he even there, waiting? After all this time?

But what other option did I have? I wasn't like Cole. To me, this whole situation was totally unacceptable. I couldn't live like this even if he thought he could.

I needed my family. I needed my friends. I *needed* people and civilization.

This couldn't be it for me. It couldn't.

A few minutes later, I noticed Cole walking a safe distance behind me, carrying a few bottles of water and had his stupid George Foreman grill tucked under one arm. I closed my eyes and shook my head. *What an idiot.*

He didn't call to me or try to catch up, but followed without saying a word.

Crumbled buildings and the aftermath of the whirlwind tornado hindered much of my path and forced me to meander and take a more crooked course. The easiest path from point A to point B was a straight line, except when an apocalypse occurred. Then it became left, right, right again, maybe go in a circle, and head left until you can't head left no more. But since I had no idea where I was going, it didn't really matter.

I didn't look at much, but stared straight ahead, holding my still nervous, but wonderfully obedient, cat in my arms. Clothes would soon be important. Food and water for both me and Callie too, now that everything I owned happened to be clinging to my back. It would be foolish to walk to where we'd left the shopping carts and my things. I doubted my duffle bag had even survived. For the moment, I didn't really worry about any of that.

More important things dominated my thoughts—Dad, the impossible journey ahead, the fact that nothing would ever be the same again.

"Hey, Tess!"

I didn't answer. He viewed this all as a big joke, and I wasn't in the mood for his bizarre humor and lack of social grace.

"Tess, stop!"

"I don't want to talk to you, Cole. Leave me alone."

"Seriously, don't take another step."

Callie wiggled in my arms, and I had to change my hold on her. "Tess!"

I whipped around, "What? What do you want?"

His forehead creased and his lips drew into a line, and he waved me toward him—almost like a stalker trying to lure his victim into a white van. "Why don't you come back by me, okay?"

"I don't want to be anywhere *near* you right now."

"Okay, that's fine." He put his hands up. "But can you walk back this way? We'll take that side street a couple of blocks back and go around. It'll be better."

I shook my head. *What is wrong with him?* "You're free to go wherever you want." I turned away, managed a few short steps, then stopped.

My heart lurched. I couldn't breathe. For a brief minute, I was paralyzed.

The tornado had demolished the medical center, like everything else in its path, tearing it apart like a loose thread in a sweater, a semblance of what it once was. Bricks, beams, walls, and ceilings lay in a giant pile mixed with broken hospital beds, emergency equipment, and medical papers that now blew with the breeze.

In my mental haze, I hadn't noticed anything out of the ordinary before—I hadn't been looking at anything. Not really. Everything had simply blended together, becoming a backdrop to my sadness and anger.

Now, I put Callie down, secured her leash, and ran for the pile of rubble.

"Help me, Cole!" I knelt in the debris, not bothering to be careful of broken bottles, syringes, or anything else, and tugged at a large section of drywall then tossed brick and concrete aside. "Come on, Cole!"

"Tess—"

"We have to help them!"

I dug around the unmoving human leg peeking through the mess. I'd save this person and then move onto the next. An arm here. A leg there. Dozens of body parts poked out of the wreckage. I'd dig each of them out. All of them. It wasn't too late. It wasn't. Were they patients left behind? Doctors staying to help the injured?

"Cole!"

He shook his head, not coming closer as I wanted him too. "They're gone, Tess."

"No! Please!" Frantically, I pushed away garbage, maneuvered wires, metal, and dirt, and chucked what I could lift. Had they been taking shelter in the medical center? How many of them were there? Maybe we weren't the only ones left behind. Maybe there were others, somewhere else too.

"The tornado didn't do this to them." Cole maintained his distance. "Look."

I couldn't. Looking wasted time. I kept digging, becoming angrier at Cole and his unwillingness to even try.

"They've been dead a long time, Tess. Well before the tornado destroyed the building."

He didn't know anything—anything at all. He was all for himself, selfish and ridiculous. He hadn't even put down the George Foreman grill. Maybe he should live all alone away from humanity. It would be better for everyone, especially me.

I couldn't stop digging and trying to uncover the buried person, determined to save them. Throw away one more brick, lift one more section of wall, and they'd be free to breathe again.

It seemed so simple.

I wanted to make it work so badly.

But when I removed the last of the trash surrounding the leg, the limb fell away, tumbling down the small hill of discarded debris. A dark, discolored, rotting leg, severed at the thigh.

A piece of a person.

I froze, next to a crooked hand sticking out only a few feet away from me and the bloated human leg almost brushing against mine. Blood pounded in my ears like a kettledrum—*boom, boom, boom*. Everything spun in dizzying circles. Bile clawed its way up my throat, but I swallowed it back.

"Hey, it's going to be okay."

No, it wouldn't. None of this was okay.

"Tess?"

I was sitting on a pile of broken people.

"We'll go back the way we came and take that side road like I said. We'll get out of the city and into the open and avoid this, okay?" Cole set the grill next to my cat and carefully made his way to me, watching his step. He held his hand out.

Mr. Stanger and now this? I'd hoped that Mr. Stanger's dead body had been a fluke, a once in a lifetime kind of thing, but this... this was worse.

"Take my hand, Tess."

What else could I do? I reached out; he clasped my trembling hand in his, and drew me to him.

His hand, beside my own, was the only one attached to a living, breathing person.

CHAPTER 19

I had no idea where he was leading me, but since I had no suggestions of my own, I walked behind him and kept quiet. Even Callie toddled at my side as I held the end of her leash. The tornado must have put enough fear into her that the idea of a leash and collar no longer seemed to bother her. She didn't scratch or tug at it, but skipped along like an obedient pet—something cats weren't known to be.

Cole continued to carry his grill under his arm. Every once in a while, he'd turn around, smile, and encourage me to keep up.

"Where are we going?" My first question, my first words really, since witnessing the body parts. Yes, I wanted to escape the city and get away from the possibility of finding more dead bodies, but walking off into the unknown didn't seem like the best choice.

"Do you really think I'd lead you all the way out here without a plan?" Cole turned to face me, but kept moving backward so we didn't stop.

"Yes, that's exactly what I'm thinking."

Stores, homes, shelves, and pantries, all lay behind us—places to scavenge and find sustenance so we could keep living. Only dirt roads and sagebrush lay ahead—death in the form of barren landscape.

"You and me? We're a team, right?" He waited for me to answer.

I nodded. "Sure."

He pointed to himself. "Then let *this* part of the team lead us for a bit. I know I said this was your thing and that you were the leader, but sometimes a good leader needs to delegate. You can always go back to being in charge tomorrow."

I didn't know if I ever wanted to be in charge, but Cole annoyed me and didn't take things seriously, so of the two of us, I seemed like the better candidate to run this show. For now, I'd just follow him. "Yeah, you be in charge. I'm cool with that."

"Do people still say 'cool'?" He smirked. "Didn't that go away with the eighties?"

I was too tired and too drained from everything that had happened to defend my words. "I don't know, I wasn't born in the eighties. I used it. Whatever."

"See? Now 'whatever' seems more like something your generation would say." He looked over his shoulder and back to me while walking backward.

"My generation? You're not *that* much older than me."

"How old do you think I am?" He raised a brow.

"Mentally or physically?"

"Ha, ha. You're funny. Come on? Guess."

I tossed out a random number. "Twenty-three."

"Nope. Guess again." His grin widened.

"You're not older than twenty-five, are you?"

"Maybe. Maybe not." He sidestepped a divot along the dirt road without even turning around to see it. *Impressive.*

"Twenty-six."

He smiled huge and pointed at me, and for a moment, I thought I had guessed correctly. "So close, but nope."

"I give up. All I know is you're too old to do half the crap you do."

"Age is only a number, really. Why let a number define you? So maybe I'm twenty-four or maybe I'm not, but should that keep me from going roller skating if I wanted to?"

Roller skating? What in the world is he talking about?

"I say no. If an eighty-year-old wants to skydive, then so be it. If I want to blow soap bubbles in the park, then why not? Why is riding a tricycle good for a three-year-old but looks odd for a thirty-year-old?" He pointed at me, a little more sternly this time. "Don't let your number define you."

I smiled. "So, if I want to have a beer or a tall glass of wine, then I shouldn't let being seventeen stop me? Good to know."

My goading brought him to a complete halt. "No. Do what you want except for that. Your brain is still growing. Don't screw it up. Wait until you're older to mess around with the chemical makeup of your mind." He started walking backward again. "But feel free to jump rope or eat bubblegum when you're ninety. Don't let anyone tell you that you can't do it because you're old and shouldn't mess up your dentures."

What are we even talking about? "Let me get this right. While I'm a kid, I still have to obey rules like no smoking or drinking, but as an adult I can do whatever I want?"

"Pretty much."

"This has to be one of the weirdest conversations I've ever had."

"Maybe, but you're talking now, aren't you? And you're not thinking about everything happening back in the city either, right? Sometimes weird conversations are necessary." He flipped back around and walked forward, as normal people do. "We're almost there," he called over his shoulder.

"Wait? What? Almost where?" I looked around but couldn't see anything.

"There!" He raised his arm and pointed to the distance. The glare of the sun bounced off a metal surface, which I couldn't quite identify.

"What is it?"

He turned and winked. "I told you I had a lair."

Cole told me to wait outside as he slid open the large hanger doors only wide enough for himself to pass through. "Give me a sec. I want you to see it in all its glory." The door slid shut.

I looked down at Callie in my arms. "I know. This is totally weird."

A second later, Cole pushed the doors all the way open, stood back and swept his arm to the side. "Welcome to my humble abode."

Humble, my ass.

I took a tentative step forward, and my mouth dropped open as I took it all in. Intended to house airplanes, Cole had transformed the interior of the metal hanger into something else entirely, and I could hardly believe it.

Strands of white Christmas lights and decorative Chinese lanterns draped from one side to the other. The largest RV sat parked to one side with its canopy drawn and an indoor/outdoor rug thrown on the cement ground with a beautiful patio dining set on top—seating for ten. A little much, but with everything else going on, I guess having a dining table for ten didn't seem all that strange.

A movie screen with theater seating and a popcorn machine sat in one corner of the hanger. In another, a steaming hot tub with lounge furniture, robes and flip-flops, all under a gazebo. *A freaking hot tub!*

Another section of the hangar looked like a grocery store with shelves fully lined with canned goods, bottled water, and paper products.

Cole had thought of everything. He had a place to take a shower. He had a hammock, a putting green, and a small garden area—barley sprouting—all under artificial lighting. He'd even parked a red Ferrari, turned at an angle, to add to the madness.

"That's for show," he said, indicating the car. "But it's nice to sit in and pretend you're going somewhere. I'll let you sit in it as long as you promise not to scratch up the leather. There's a no cats allowed policy that goes along with my offer though."

"Where did you get all of this?" I shook my head. I knew exactly where he'd gotten it all. "Forget it, how did you get it all here and"—I waved my arm at the lights and everything—"how does any of this even work?"

"I used a truck and my muscles." He flexed. "Believe it or not, I'm stronger than I look, and as for the power, well, I pilfered enough generators and solar panels to keep everything going comfortably for a good while. Had to do a lot of rewiring and grounding of cables, and I'm always replacing a solar panel or two, but for now, it does a decent job. I've got candles and battery-operated lanterns, just in case." He smiled. "Do you like it?"

"Yeah, it's... it's great, but none of this is yours, right?" It looked awesome and everything, but I had to remember it had all been stolen, just like the grill he continued to hold. People would want their stuff back and we might end up in jail because of it.

"Possession is nine tenths of the law." He ushered me inside and slid the large doors into place. "So don't rain on my parade."

Always with the idioms, though he'd gotten this one right.

"Are you sure about this?" I stood there, a bit afraid to touch anything, but really kind of wanting to.

"Well, if the feds come, we'll tell them we found it this way and we were keeping an eye on it until everyone got back. We were being good citizens." He headed toward the RV and slipped his shoes off before entering the open door. "You coming?"

"If I put Callie down, she can't get out, can she?"

"No, it's locked up tight, but we're going to have to figure out her living arrangements. You know, where's she gonna poop and what's she gonna eat. For you and me, I've got all that covered, but I hadn't planned on taking care of animals, so we'll have to work something out."

I set my cat down but left the leash on in case I needed to grab her. She stretched her legs and arched her back, then started exploring and rubbing herself on everything.

"Great. Cat hair." He sighed. "Oh well, come on. Let me show you something."

When I got to the door of the RV, he yelled at me to take off my shoes. My Doc Martens were beat up and rather filthy. It took me a moment to remove them, and when I noticed my brown smelly socks, I took those off too. I hadn't showered in who knows how long and the stench was something awful.

"You coming?"

I grabbed the railing and climbed the few steps until I entered the biggest RV I'd ever seen–bigger than some apartments my friends lived in. Nicer too. The slide outs made it huge. *Wow.* "How did you get this?"

He looked at me with a blank expression. "Do you realize you ask the same questions over and over?" He let out his breath. "I went to the dealership, found the keys, and then drove the sucker over here. It was a pain in the ass, but I did it and I haven't moved it since. Anything else?"

"No, I guess that's it." The plush couch beckoned to me, but I didn't dare sit on it, not when I was covered in filth. The interior still had its "new car" smell and being surrounded by so many clean things, *new* things, my own awfulness shone from me like a neon sign.

"Okay, I've already claimed the queen bed in the back, which by all rights is mine since I was the one who drove this thing here. Did you know it took me three hours to drive twenty miles?"

I shook my head.

"It did. Like I said, the roads are a mess and this RV isn't easy to maneuver, but it was worth it. There's a set of bunk beds in the back, not big, but nice. Since you're a kid, you might like it. Or, there's a pullout bed in the front. It's bigger, sleeps two if you feel like you need a lot of room to move around at night. Totally up to you. *Mi casa es su casa.*"

"What about finding my dad?" He'd made a very nice home for himself here, but this wasn't *my* home, and I didn't want him to forget that.

"We're still going to find him. Nothing has changed, but we need rest and we need a plan, because climbing Rockport isn't going to be easy."

Hearing him say "we're going to find him" eased my worries. He still planned to come with me, even though after I'd seen this place, I figured he wouldn't want to leave.

"What was it you wanted to show me?" Unless the RV was the surprise.

"Oh, yeah!" He opened the door to the bathroom and when he returned, he told me to put out my hands.

I held them out, palms up, and he placed a trial sized bottle of shampoo and a new bar of soap in my hands. Not what I expected. "This is called soap. Use it. I don't mind sharing my abode with you, but Tess, you are smelling mighty ripe, my friend. You *and* that cat of yours. I'll show you how to use the shower then when you're done, we'll tackle bathing the cat." He smiled. "That should be some fun. I'm kind of looking forward to it."

"Cole?"

"Yeah?"

I swallowed hard. "Thank you, for everything. I know I wasn't being very nice to you before, but I just want to say I'm sorry. If I hadn't found you, I don't know what I'd be doing right now."

He smiled and patted my shoulder. "You're a good kid, a smart kid. I'm sure you would've managed. Sometimes we don't know how strong we are or what we're capable of doing until we're forced to find out."

Wow. He actually said something meaningful. "Thanks."

We stood there in awkward silence for a moment before he spoke. "This kind of feels like a hugging moment, but seriously, Tess, you reek."

CHAPTER 20

"Go on, get in." Cole drew the curtain aside. Steamy water ran from the makeshift showerhead, and he placed his hand in it. He then flicked the water droplets in my direction, wetting my face and forcing me to blink to keep the water from getting in my eyes. "It's ready for ya."

"Umm... I'm not going to get electrocuted or something, am I?" Even with everything he'd done to make the hanger homey — well, *rich* people homey — it didn't look safe. Cords covered in duct tape, keeping them in place, ran from one side of the hangar to the other, snaking about in a crazed and dangerous pattern. It was creative and ingenious on a certain level, but this was Cole. Ingenious and genius were two totally different things.

"The shower and hot tub aren't hooked up to anything that will kill ya." He shook his head. "Wait, that's technically not true. Don't touch the wood-burning stove or drown in the water and you should be fine."

He'd run an exhaust pipe out the side of the metal hanger, and amazingly, even though the miniature potbellied stove burned, heating up the copper coil carrying the water, I could hardly smell smoke. The scent was faint and actually quite pleasant.

"So it's safe?"

"Of course. What do you take me for?"

"You were able to do all this, but you can't hotwire a car?" The hanger with all its fancy, and somewhat unnecessary, gadgetry appeared a lot more daunting than twisting a couple of wires on a car.

He shrugged. "Who knows whether I can or can't. I've never tried before. Are you going to get in or what? You're wasting water."

Wasting water? He had run a drain and tube to a planter of dirt which sprouted green unidentifiable shoots. I wasn't going to eat any of that, but he seemed to have thought of everything, which had to be commended. All of this must have taken quite a bit of time to put together. But in an apocalypse, where the idea of being on your own sounded awesome, then his actions made total sense.

"There's a t-shirt and a pair of boxer shorts waiting for you." He pointed to a nearby table. "Sorry, they're the only underwear I have on hand, but no worries, they're brand new, never been used. I promise." He crossed his heart and held up several fingers, making a Boy Scout sign. "I have several packages. Next time we run into the city, you can grab all the feminine things you want. Until then, these will have to do."

He squeezed my shoulder and walked around the dividing screen that gave the bathing area privacy. After a moment, the sound of music filled the room, the base booming a little heavier than normal through the speakers and echoing off the metal sides of the hanger.

It almost seemed natural—a shower, music, Cole humming along. If I closed my eyes, I could almost forget about everything, and feel normal.

But I didn't close my eyes. Instead, I removed my dusty, sweaty clothes and dropped them in a pile at my feet.

The hot water on my back and shoulders burned a little, but soon I settled in and allowed it to flow over me completely. I enjoyed the music and the warmth on my skin, but quickly got to work. Cole was right, I didn't want to waste water, so I scrubbed and cleaned myself, wishing he'd given me a razor along with the soap and shampoo. Boy, the hair on my legs and underarms made me resemble a Sasquatch more than a teenage girl.

"Cole?" I yelled over the water and hoped the music didn't drown out my voice.

A few minutes later, his shadow appeared on the opposite side of the shower curtain. "Everything okay?"

"Yeah, it's wonderful, but you don't by any chance have a razor on you, do you?"

"Ahh...maybe. Give me a sec." He disappeared.

The next thing I knew, he'd thrust his hand into the shower, holding a disposable razor. I grabbed it from him and shielded myself, even though the curtain hid me. "Jeez, Cole! Boundaries!"

"Didn't see a thing." He disappeared once more.

I shook my head. *Holy crap, he is something else.*

I took only a couple of minutes to shave, then climbed from the shower and stood on the rubber floor mat to dry myself off before slipping on the large t-shirt and striped boxer shorts.

I felt amazing—clean, comfortable, and smelling like lemon verbena. I'd needed the shower for more reasons than simply washing the filth off. The water renewed me. But now, the heaviness of the day and everything we'd been though weighed down my eyelids and I couldn't wait to sink into one of the beds and disappear into unconsciousness.

I stepped around the screen, towel-drying my hair and saw Cole towel-drying Callie. He'd bathed her without me.

He looked up, but kept at his task. "You've got a weird cat."

His statement did not surprise me in the least. Callie was a strange cat for sure.

"She didn't even fight me when I poured water on her. I think this leash thing is messing with her head." He finished and sat her on the floor.

She took a few steps, shook herself, then plopped down and started licking her paws.

"I was expecting a whole lot of struggle, but the darn cat let me do what I needed to do. She seemed to really enjoy it." He tossed the wet towel to the side. "How was your shower?"

"It was fine. Thank you." I wound my towel on top of my head like a turban.

"Tired?"

I nodded. "Very."

"It's been a crazy day." He stood and started for the open door of the RV.

I followed, ready for the day to be over. "Yeah, it has."

"Have you figured out which bed you want?" He waved an arm toward the bunks and then the pullout couch.

The bunk beds reminded me too much of the bunker and my months below ground. "I'll take the couch."

He opened a storage bench and removed a couple of pillows, a blanket, and some silk sheets—nice—and placed them in my arms. "You should really get some sleep. We've got a lot of planning and a lot of decisions to make in the next day or two." He patted my towel- wrapped head. "I'll be outside if you need anything."

I made my bed, pulling out the couch until it lay wide open, and Callie climbed into the RV. She explored the space, checking out every nook, even climbing onto my bed, before going back outside again. I didn't worry about her too much; she needed to wander and feel free, and so I let her do just that. Soon, she would be back on the leash, trapped and bound.

I removed my towel and ran my fingers through my wet hair to untangle it. Jeez, I couldn't even remember the last time I'd run a brush threw it. Yeah, the world was a freakin' mess but it didn't mean I needed to look like crap. Tomorrow, I'd do better. I'd even ask Cole for some deodorant.

I climbed into the bed and tugged the blanket and glorious silk sheets around me, but as tired as I was, somehow sleep wouldn't come. I should be used to sleeping in strange places—

the bunker, the gas station, Rite-Aid—but what I really wanted, what I longed for, was my own bed back in my room in my destroyed house. Nothing else would *ever* match that feeling, or even come close.

I thought Cole had turned the music back on, but as I listened more carefully I heard that the loud music from before had been replaced by a lone guitar and one single voice, singing *Hallelujah*. I'd recognized the song, having heard it many different times on reality singing shows or even in major movie cartoons, but this version drew me to a sitting position.

The beauty of the words baffled and intrigued me all at once. So powerful. So rich. Goosebumps rose on my skin.

I slipped from my bed, carried by the music gracing my ears, and sat in the open doorway with my eyes on Cole.

His head was bent low, his eyes closed, his body curved over the acoustic guitar, becoming one with the instrument. His lean fingers plucked the strings in perfect rhythm, not once missing a note, and his voice—surprising and unexpected from such a juvenile man—held my full attention.

The beauty of his words, the rise and fall of his tenor, caused emotions to bubble in my chest and tears to wet my eyes. His talent, both in playing as well as singing, was beyond exceptional.

He'd made the song his own by changing a few things here and there, his voice falling where it normally would rise, or rising where it may have fallen in the original, but the effect was mesmerizing, making it better than any version I'd ever heard before.

He seemed to experience every one of the words he sang, drawing from some pain and loss in his past as his face reflected his feelings—something that couldn't be faked. He felt every bit of it, whatever it was, and in essence, I felt it too. The words were a part of him.

I didn't think I would have believed him capable of such beauty had I not witnessed it for myself, but sitting and watching him do something so natural—a gift—made me honored to be a part of it, even if my part was only to listen.

He hummed and continued to play the guitar with his eyes closed, and I leaned against the doorframe, not wanting this amazing experience to end. The music was more than beautiful; it was magical.

"Sing with me, Tess." His dark eyes locked onto mine as he thrummed the guitar. I hadn't noticed him watching me. When had he realized I was there, listening and watching him?

"No, I can't." I wasn't a singer, not even close.

"You know the words. Sing." He didn't turn his gaze away. "There's no one else here. Just you and me. So sing."

I did know the words, but how did he guess?

"Don't make me pluck this guitar until my fingers bleed, waiting on you." He stood, still holding the guitar and walked slowly toward me. "We'll start over at the first verse. You can do it. Open your mouth and sing."

He nodded at me, indicating it was time, and he began to sing, his voice deep and almost hypnotizing. Whatever insecurities I had felt before, whatever held me back, evaporated and my mouth opened. Something about the way he looked at me made it impossible to resist.

He had a way of making my amateur singing beautiful as he matched my pace and harmonized his words to my own. Perfect. Heavenly. By the time the song was over, and the guitar stilled, tears fell freely down my face.

I had never experienced anything like that before. *Ever.*

He smiled, placed one foot on the bottom step, and nodded. "You did good. Just like that little pig in the movie where he wanted to be a sheep dog, you know the one I'm talking about?"

I narrowed my gaze. "You mean *Babe*?"

"Yeah, that's the one." He rubbed my wet head. *"That'll do, pig. That'll do."*

I didn't think anything could have ruined the amazing moment we'd shared, but somehow, Cole had managed to do it.

CHAPTER 21

I lay on my side, my pillow tucked under my head, my kitten snuggled against me. A lone light above the sink remained on, and the glow from hanging Christmas lights peeked through the blinds, lighting the RV and making it difficult to completely fall asleep, no matter how much I wanted to. Sleep was cruel like that. It teased me, caused my eyelids to droop, and then flitter away just as I was about to succumb.

Cole opened the door, quietly. He stepped inside, a foot or so from where I lay wide awake in my bed, with only a towel draped low around his waist. My eyes widened. *O-kay.*

I should have closed my eyes right then, not looked, but I couldn't. Not that I was a pervert or anything, but dang. Tiny droplets of water clung to his chest and dripped from his dark hair. The water glistened on his toned skin in the dimmed light. *Jeez.*

He didn't notice me awake and watching, but turned his back to me as he headed toward his bedroom on the other side of the RV. I sat up, curious, as the strange but strikingly beautiful tattoo draping from one shoulder blade to the other drew my attention. *Angel wings.*

I had to stifle a chuckle. Okay, that was a bit too much, especially for Cole, even if the artistry of it was amazing. A dragon tattoo or even a portrait of himself, maybe, but I would have never expected angel wings. Not Cole. I'd seen wing tattoos before—mostly biker gangs in the area, or goofy teen girls getting one on their wrist or behind their ear—but those crude drawings in no way compared to the delicate and fine details of the tattoo on Cole's back. I'd never seen anything like it.

"Angel wings, really?" I smiled.

He whipped around, still clutching the towel. "Ahh... Tess! You scared me! I almost dropped my towel!"

Okay. That I did *not* want to see. Thank goodness for quick reflexes or I'd be scarred forever. "Sorry, I didn't mean to do that. I just find your tattoo... interesting." This time I did chuckle. I couldn't help it.

"Hey, don't judge me. I was going through some things at the time, and it seemed like a pretty good idea." He disappeared from view. "Let's just say some decisions should be slept on first."

"So you wouldn't pick wings if you had to do it all over again?" I scratched my sleepy kitty's belly.

He stepped back into view, pajama bottoms on and a t-shirt in his hand. He looked at me for a long moment. "Depends on the day."

"Can I see it a little closer?" I slipped from my bed, making sure not to wake Callie.

He seemed to contemplate my question for a while, but when he finally nodded, I closed the distance between us until I stood in front of him. With my finger, I drew a circle in the air. "Turn around."

He released an exaggerated breath, but did as I asked.

When the simple light in the RV highlighted his muscular back I took in my own breath, holding it. *Wow.* He was quite a specimen all right. I shook my head, forcing those thoughts away. He was old, for heaven's sake!

I turned my attention to the beauty of the tattoo and marveled at the fine lines and shadows that etched his skin. Toby had several tattoos, but since he was lacking in the money department, his tattoos looked shoddy in comparison. I think one of his buddies from high school even did one for him that ended up getting infected. What an idiot.

Cole's was far more professional and the eye for detail was incredible. Yes, they were angel wings on the back of a more than annoying kind of man, but still, I had to admire the artwork.

Maybe I shouldn't have touched it, but my fingers had a mind of their own. They traced the lines of one shoulder and then the other. Whoever had done this had a pretty incredible hand—steady and focused. On any other canvas, it would probably be considered a masterpiece in its own right.

He shivered and pulled away. "Okay, that's enough." He drew his shirt up and over his head. "Shouldn't you be sleeping or something?"

"I can't."

"It's late."

I nodded. "I know, and I'm exhausted."

"Do you want me to tell you a bedtime story, or something?"

At first, I thought he was kidding, but he stared at me with all seriousness and it took me a minute to respond. "I'm seventeen *not* seven. I don't need a story."

He shrugged. "You're a kid. I thought I'd offer."

"Well, I appreciate it, but I'm good."

I turned to go back to my bed and try the sleeping thing again, when thunder clapped overhead, rattling the metal frame of the hanger and shaking the RV. I grabbed on to the tiny kitchen counter to steady myself.

In my panic, I threw open the door, ran past the massive dining table and movie theater, and circled the hot tub only to come to a standstill in front of the RV again. Where was I going? If this place blew apart, whether I was in the RV or standing next to the popcorn machine wouldn't make a difference.

Nowhere was safe.

My breathing became labored, my heart raced, and when the thunder boomed again, I crouched on the ground and threw my hands over my head. *Not again. Not again.* Meteors? Tornado? I couldn't do this anymore.

"Hey." Cole knelt beside me and placed his hand on my shoulder. "It's only a thunder storm, Tess. That's all. We're okay."

My head snapped up. "How do you know? How do you know a tornado isn't barreling down on us right now or we're not going to be blown to pieces by falling rock from outer space?" I shook all over, waiting for the entire structure of the hanger to be ripped apart piece by piece.

"Outer space?" He shrugged. "I guess I don't."

Another boom exploded, and I found myself in Cole's arms with my face pressed against his chest. "We're gonna die!"

"Now you're being dramatic." He hugged me. "Listen."

I didn't move my head from his chest.

One more boom, but this time it sounded farther off in the distance. I still didn't release my grip on him.

"We'll probably be hearing rain right... about... now."

Sure enough, the pinging sound of raindrops hitting the metal building filled the hanger. It would be beautiful if I didn't imagine a large destructive cloud hovering nearby ready to suck us up into its vortex only to spit us out several miles away.

"Tess, I promise it's only a thunderstorm. That's all." He rubbed my back in small circular motions. "It's late. We should really go back inside and get some sleep. Tomorrow will be busy."

"Sleep? Yeah, I don't think so." My nerves were on edge. My tired brain worked overtime to scare the crap out of me by imagining all sorts of scenarios in which I would end up dead. Maybe it was only rain and thunder, but with everything going on this day alone, I couldn't rely on Cole's words to calm me. My stupid brain wouldn't let me.

He scooped me up in his arms, surprising me, and carried me toward the trailer. "You can worry just as much lying in your bed as you can crouching out here in a ball. What will happen will happen."

"Is that supposed to make me feel better?" I held on by wrapping my arms around his neck.

"It didn't? Hmmm... weird. Okay, well, what if I say *I'm* tired and you're going to sit in your bed really quiet-like so *I* can get some sleep?" He climbed the rickety steps into the RV without a problem, as though my weight didn't make a difference at all.

"Yeah, that's worse."

"Well, I tried. I can't help it if you're impossible."He placed me on my couch bed and tucked the blankets around me. "Stay there. You can sleep if you like or you can sit there and worry about everything, but you need to be quiet. Not a peep." He motioned to his lips and pretended to lock them. "Get it? Not a word."

The rain continued to fall on the hanger roof, but being inside the RV muffled the sound some. Still, I couldn't help if death and destruction plagued my mind. I'd watched a whole city get wiped away. I'd seen dead people, well, parts of dead people. We'd almost died ourselves. How in the world was I expected to fall asleep with all that running rampant in my brain?

Cole grabbed my bewildered cat from off the floor and placed her next to me. I loved Callie, but I needed something more than a crazy kitten to calm me down. I held her anyway and hoped.

He made the key locking motion by his mouth once more and then headed to his bed.

I followed his every movement and watched as he flopped himself down on the huge king- sized bed, sprawling out over the top, not even bothering to get inside the covers.

Within a few minutes, his snoring filled our living space. If only it were that easy for me.

I picked up Callie in one arm, gathered my blanket in the other, and tiptoed toward him. As quietly as I could, without disturbing him, I crawled onto his bed and made myself comfortable, leaving a good space between us.

Callie found a nice spot on the pillows, near Cole's head, and plumped them with her tiny claws until she found them suitable enough to lie down and fall asleep.

Thunder continued in the distance, moving on as he'd said it would, but the rain didn't let up, even growing more intense as time ticked by. He slept through it all, seemingly unbothered by it. *How does he do that?*

I knew my body couldn't go on like this. I would, at some point, fall asleep, but the very idea of closing my eyes and becoming vulnerable to *everything* scared me. How could I save myself if I was asleep?

Insane thinking, like running around the inside of a hanger had been, but where I once had wanted to close my eyes and sleep, now I fought against it. Someone should stand guard, right? Another insane thought. If a meteor fell on us or a tornado ripped through this area, I couldn't change it. What will happen will happen, just as Cole had said.

But that didn't mean I had to like it.

He slept with his mouth open, snoring so loudly that had I wanted to sleep, I wasn't so sure I could. There was a lot about Cole which irked me, but right now in that moment, I was grateful for his presence, which meant I wasn't completely alone.

I grabbed part of my comforter and draped it across him, sharing.

I didn't know if sleep would find me, but I did know I felt a lot safer lying next to him.

# CHAPTER 22

He bolted upright, startling me from my restless sleep. He didn't move, but his wide eyes stared straight ahead. Focused. Intent.

"Cole?" I sat up too, whipped my head around, listening for anything to indicate us having to make another run for it. My hands clutched the blanket, twisting it into a gnarled mess in my indecision. "You're scaring me."

His shoulders stiffened, but he didn't say a word. The veins in his neck throbbed and rose to the surface. He didn't blink. He didn't move. His stillness terrified me.

When Callie rose to all four feet, arched her back, and hissed in the same direction, the hairs on the back of my neck sprung to life. "What is it? Do you hear something?"

He didn't say a word.

Except for the rhythmic sound of the rain pelting the metal roof and the soft hum of the generators, nothing seemed out of the ordinary. I strained to see what he stared at, but the RV was empty except for the two of us and my bizarre cat. I might not have heard or seen anything, but it didn't mean I was going to go look either.

Fear kept me from crawling from the bed to investigate, like some people would. I knew better. People died investigating weird noises. I'd watched enough horror shows to know how it all played out. I also wore a t-shirt and underwear, which meant instant death. Horror movies were clear about that too.

I slid closer to him, our shoulders touching. "What's going on?" I leaned forward, trying to catch his eye, but he only looked through me. "Cole?" I whispered. *What do I do? What do I do?*

Not a word from my statuesque companion. Then I realized he wasn't even registering my presence.

How I wished I had my gun. Or a bat. *Anything* to make me a little braver. I had only my blanket, my near nakedness, and a paralyzed man at my side.

Gathering enough courage to kneel on the bed, I pushed the curtains aside only a fraction. The limited light in the hanger revealed nothing. The large doors remained closed and locked. Everything sat in its proper place. I looked out each of the RV side windows, crawling over Cole to do so, but found nothing strange there either. *What is going on?*

Braver people would go check things out, but since bravery wasn't my strong suit and I sucked at most things heroic, I hovered near Cole and waited. If I was going to die, I could easily do it sitting right there.

I kept my ears open and craned my neck from side to side as I listened for our impending death, then slipped my hand over his.

His eyes remained locked in his weird trance, but when I touched him, he gave one slow deliberate nod—*eerie*—before falling back against the mattress as if all the air had been sucked from him.

Callie stopped hissing almost instantly, jumped from the bed, and proceeded to use the litter box. Life as usual.

You have to be kidding me? What the hell?

I shoved him, but he only moaned in response.

"Cole." I shoved him again, this time a little more insistently. No way he was going back to sleep after scaring the crap out of me with his wacky dreams, or whatever had happened.

But if it was a dream, then how was I supposed to explain Callie and her hissing? I shook my head. *This is creepy and insane.*

"Cole."

He grunted.

"Cole! Seriously." I slapped his shoulder.

His eyes fluttered open, and he barely acknowledged me before rolling on to his side. "Hmmm...."

"What was that all about, huh?"

He kept his eyes closed, drew part of my blanket around himself, and settled into the pillows. "I don't know what you're talking about." He dragged out his words as sleep seemed to lure him away from me.

"The whole staring off into space thing and freaking me out. *That* thing."

"Tess, it's late." He used his foot to edge me from the bed but I caught myself before plummeting to the floor. The jerk. "Go away," he said. "I'm tired."

Ugh! I yanked my blanket from him and gathered it in my arms. "You're an ass."

He responded with a drawn out snore. Whether it was real or not, I didn't care. Of all the people in the world to end up with, why him? *Why?* He was just *so...* not normal!

Part of me wanted to storm out of the RV and go sleep somewhere else, but I still had no idea what had happened or if evils lurked in the darkness, so I made sure the RV door was locked, actually checking it a couple of times, and crawled into my own bed.

I had always felt like a tolerant person, giving people the benefit of the doubt, but now I wasn't so sure.

I didn't know how much more I could handle of Cole and his weirdness.

My poor body must have been completely exhausted and I succumbed to unconsciousness despite my brain reliving that night's experience, because I would have sworn I'd never sleep again. Not after *that*.

Somehow, I had fallen asleep, and when my eyes fluttered open, the RV was empty and the door stood wide open.

I sat up and looked around. "Cole?"

The echo of metallic sounds filtered in through the door, and I removed myself from the bed and stretched my arms above me, taking a moment for myself before investigating what Cole was up to.

Wow. I actually felt good. Amazing how sleep, even a little of it, could make a difference. My stomach growled its discontent, and I couldn't recall the last time I'd eaten—the stew back at Rite Aid, maybe—but knew before I remedied my hunger, I needed to find out what the heck last night had been all about.

He'd parked himself under the RV awning at the head of the mahogany dining table and spread out before him was the George Forman grill, or what was left of it. Tools littered the surface and he bent over the mechanical mess with a soldering tool. A strange place to do work. Anyone else would have treated the dining table with a soft hand and used it only for formal occasions. But not Cole.

Interesting. So, he wasn't planning to grill food after all. I felt a little better to know he wasn't completely nuts. He'd actually had a reason for the grill.

When I opened my mouth to quiz him on what he was up to and quiz him about last night, he looked up at me, set the soldering tool aside and lifted his safety glasses to the top of his head. "You can't do that anymore," he said.

"What are you talking about?" Hitting him? Waking him up? My brain had barely begun to function and his words confused me.

"Last night. You can't be sleeping in my bed anymore."

I scrunched up my face. "Don't you think that's the least of our problems?"

"Where I'm sitting, having you sleep in my bed is a pretty big problem. So don't do it anymore, okay?"

Oh. My. Gosh! "Wait... what are you... do you think there's something going on"—I motioned to him and then myself.—"That's not at all why I went and slept in your bed last night." *Eeew, eeew, eeew! Yuck.* "I was a little scared last night. Well, a *lot* scared last night, but that's it. I swear!"

"Because you're a kid and coming onto me, as flattering as it is, would be wrong—"

"You're grossing me out." I wasn't awake enough for this kind of thing. "Knock it off."

He stood and pointed to me. "You're cute and I'm magnificent, I get that, but even in an apocalyptic situation you can't let your hormones get the best of you. That would be wrong."

"You *think?*" I threw my hands up. "Why are we still talking about this? I can hardly stand you, so there's no worry about me having sex with you. Okay?"

He nodded and went back to his grill. "Good. I wanted to make sure we were both clear. No touchy stuff."

"Yeah, definitely." I shuddered. "Not even if you were the last guy on earth."

He glanced up, looked around, and smiled. "Touché."

I waved him off. "Are you going to tell me what last night was all about? The crazy trance thing, because it really scared me and you frightened my cat too, making her act all weird. I thought you might be seeing ghosts or something."

He shrugged, brushed the hair off his forehead, and placed his safety glasses back on. "I slept like a baby last night up until you hit me."

"Really? You don't remember anything?" Could he really have been *that* asleep? Even with his eyes open? I tried to play the whole thing back in my mind, but came back to the same conclusion each time—one of those paranormal freak of nature kinds of things. Definitely not normal.

"Nope." He bent over the pile that was once a grill and began tinkering again as though we'd reached the end of the conversation.

We *totally* hadn't.

"You're not the least bit curious?" I climbed down from the RV and came to stand at his side. I leaned closer and closer until I forced him to acknowledge me.

He let out his breath. "What are you doing?"

I rolled my eyes. "Isn't it obvious? I'm trying to talk to you about last night. It really, *really* scared me."

"Tess" — he adjusted his safety glasses — "*everything* scares you. Tell me something new for a change."

I grabbed those glasses from his face and tossed them to the side. "*You* scared me, Cole. *You.*"

He didn't say anything for a long moment, but took a deep breath and settled more comfortably into his chair. "Are you sure you weren't having a bad dream? Yesterday could do that to a person."

"I was wide awake! You sat up, stared intently at something not there, then you nodded, which was the creepiest thing I'd ever seen, before lying back down as though nothing happened. It was weird. Really weird."

Maybe he really didn't remember anything. People talked and walked in their sleep all the time and had no clue they even did it. I didn't know him well enough to decide if this was a fluke thing or something he did on a regular basis. Yet, I didn't feel right brushing it off.

"So you're telling me I sat up, stared at something, nodded and went back to sleep?" He held both hands in front of him shaking them for effect. "Oooo...that sounds horrifying. No wonder you were scared." He grabbed a screwdriver and waved it at me. "Have you always been like this? Frightened of your own shadow?"

"What? *Ugh*... you are so frustrating — "

"Believe me, the feeling is mutual, Tess." He gathered a couple of screws and an on/off switch in his hand, and started to walk away, leaving me standing there.

I threw my hands in the air. "Forget it, Cole! I give up. You win! Be a weirdo. Be a freak, I don't care anymore!"

"Good!" He turned and waved his arm around. "I'm free to be me! Now we need to work on fixing you."

CHAPTER 23

The damn rain continued to smack against the roof. In any other situation, I might have found it lulling and beautiful, but right now, it pissed me off. I had places to go and things to do, and being holed up in a giant hanger, as nice as it was, messed with my plans.

I needed to get going. I needed to be on my way, because so much time had already been wasted—*so much time.* I moved restlessly around the hanger from one thing to another, trying to keep myself occupied without talking to Cole. I was making a point of ignoring him, though it actually backfired. He didn't seem to mind, and kept right on adding overhead lights to his garden, rigging up a water supply and timer, and running tests to make sure everything worked. I kept silent. He kept silent. Everything was actually pleasant—for once.

But after a soak in the hot tub, a bowl of fresh popcorn and a round of putting golf balls into a hole, I soon found myself bored and irritated. Another day of this and I would be bouncing off the walls.

The hammock swayed slightly as I stared at the ceiling with my hands tucked behind my head. If only I could nap my time away, but for some reason, despite everything I'd been through since crawling out of the bunker, I wasn't tired. Lazy, but not tired.

Had Cole bothered to ask me for help, I may have, but he didn't. Instead, I rested in the hammock, rocking it with my bare foot that dangled over the side, and continuously blew and popped my bubble gum while staring at the ceiling.

"Can't find a way to entertain yourself, huh?" Cole stared down at me, blocking my view of the *oh so intriguing* corrugated roof.

"I'm bored."

"Only boring people get bored."

I didn't care if he had slighted me. It didn't matter. Maybe I was becoming used to his offhanded insults. I rolled my head to the side and decided to go back to ignoring him, so I gave the hammock a gentle push to get it swaying once more.

"You've been keeping up on your antibiotics, right?"

"Not sure how you would expect me to do that. The monster tornado sucked everything I owned away, remember?" I blew a large bubble, bigger than any of the previous ones, but it popped before I could pinch off the end and admire it.

"I think I might have more for you. I'll have to check. Also, I need to take a look at your stitches and make sure everything is good to go."

I didn't answer, going right on chewing my gum.

"Well, then. This hunting your dad down in complete silence should be *super* fun. So glad I signed on for this." He stopped the swinging of the hammock and waited for me to look at him. "I'll be back with your drugs in a second."

Besides the stitches itching every once in awhile, I hardly remembered they were there. Tornados, thunderstorms, angel wing tattoos, and wacky dreams—those things had me too busy to think about anything else.

When he returned, he handed me a bottle of water and two pills, and watched me swallow them both. "If we're gonna hike a friggin' mountain, you need to be in the best shape you can be."

He did have a point there.

"How's your arm?" He didn't wait for me to respond but raised the sleeve of my shirt. He peeled back the bandage and gave out a low whistle. "Yeah, we probably should have changed the dressing on this after your shower last night."

I tried to look at my arm, but couldn't quite angle my head to get a good peek. "What's wrong? Is it infected?"

He shook his head. "Nah, just needs to be taken better care of than what we've been doing." He removed the dirty bandage and replaced it with a clean one, taking his time to tape it in place. "You like playing video games?"

"Umm... sure. I'm not very good at them though." Toby played them all of the time, and I mostly watched. The stupid controllers always gave me problems, because there were too many buttons to push. My brother had no patience for my lack of gaming skills and usually sent me away after a few minutes.

Cole's face lit up like a kid on Christmas morning. "Perfect! Meet me at the movie theater in, say, ten minutes. I've got to shut most everything down to play, but you and me, we're taking on some ninjas!"

His excitement was contagious and I chuckled in spite of myself. "Sure. Why the heck not? What else do I have going on?"

He started walking away, a little pep in his step, but turned to face me. "Hey, Tess?"

"Yeah?"

"I get the whole bored thing. I actually feel ripped off that this apocalyptic mess isn't due to crazed zombies or an alien invasion. It would've given us something to do besides argue with one another all the time. No one can possibly get bored when they're busy fighting the undead or trying to keep from being probed."

As strange as his logic was, I couldn't help but nod. "Except, I'd be a zombie by now if we had to fight the walking dead." I hardly made a good survivor under my current circumstances; I couldn't imagine trying to fend off the undead too.

He tipped his head from side to side and raised his brows, thinking. "That's true. You'd be a walker, but in all fairness, you'd probably be a pretty damn good one because of how testy and mean you are."

Another backhanded compliment. I didn't say anything even though what he said was mostly right.

"You know I meant that as a good thing, right?"

I nodded.

"It's because of your feistiness that you'd be an amazing zombie, ripping off limbs and eating brains like a pro. I can picture the whole thing clearly. Total George A. Romero style."

"Okay, you can stop now."

He kept up with his cheesy grin. "Sorry. Meet me in ten?"

I blew a huge bubble, pushing its limits until it popped. "Sure. Ten it is."

"You weren't kidding when you said you sucked at playing video games." Cole kept his gaze on the oversized screen while maneuvering his hero through the ninja battlefield. His fingers pressed buttons quicker than any person could possibly blink.

I held up my controller—my hero had been sliced in half and I had to wait to regenerate. "I never said I sucked, just that I wasn't very good at it."

"Yeah, Tess. I hate to break it to you, but there is a difference between being no good at something and sucking at it, and you, my friend, suck worse than I could have imagined possible." He slid forward in his chair, becoming intensely focused on the game as though it were a real matter of life and death.

"Well, look at this thing!" I waved the controller at him. "There're too many buttons! One for jumping, another for swinging nun chucks, and I'm supposed to push these"—I held down the two buttons, moving my character forward while keeping him looking straight ahead—"all at the same time. It's impossible."

"Nothing's impossible. You need more practice, is all."

My character came back to life, and for a brief minute I thought I actually had a chance, but I was dead again within only a few seconds—stupid character staring up at the clouds while ghost ninjas pummeled him with blasts of powder balls.

I sank into the plush theater seating and drew my feet up and under myself. "I feel like I should be doing something other than playing video games, singing songs, and riding in shopping carts. Our situation is serious and all we seem to be doing is messing around."

Cole didn't look at me. "It's raining. When it stops, we'll be more serious. I promise."

"Do you even know *how* to be serious?" I tossed a handful of Skittles into my mouth.

"Of course, but being serious right now isn't going to change the fact that it's raining. Until it lets up, I'm going to enjoy myself." He glanced at me briefly, smiling, before turning his full attention to the large screen again. "Isn't that what life's all about?"

I gave a non-committal shrug. "I don't feel like I'm living right now. This is me being in limbo, waiting to live."

He paused the game even though his character had leveled up, becoming a master ninja slayer, and turned in his seat to face me. I'm not sure what I was expecting from him. Maybe a keep your chin up kind of thing, but he only leaned forward, coming closer to me than most people would find socially acceptable, and said, "You're ruining my gaming experience."

Instead of backing away, removing myself from the awkward situation, I leaned even closer into him, our noses only inches apart. "Good."

The goofy grin he wore faded and his dark eyes tracked mine, staring at me in a way that should have felt uncomfortable, but didn't.

I felt paralyzed and vulnerable, his gaze penetrating a part of me no one had ever been witness to, seeing something I wasn't sure I wanted to share. I couldn't blink. I couldn't move. His warm breath feathered over my slightly parted lips, natural and strange all at once. Tiny goose bumps rippled my skin in response, and my own breath lodged itself in my throat.

I didn't understand what was happening, but knew well enough that sharing this kind of intimate experience wasn't right—not between him and me. I barely liked him, so how could my body react in this way? The traitor. My mind whirled in confusion, never coming to rest on a single thought, but accepting the humility and realness his eyes reflected. The mystery of it all held me entranced, however wrong it was.

Then he blinked. Once.

Whatever had passed between us dissipated, and I fell against my seat like a ragdoll, but continued to watch him as my heart eased back into a normal rhythm.

He slumped in his seat as well, his eyes on the paused screen, his controller resting in his hands. Neither of us said anything, and I knew by the look on his face he had to be thinking the same thing: *What was that all about?*

I didn't want to know. I didn't want to understand, because there was no acceptable reason for that kind of behavior, especially after our lengthy talk earlier. *This is ridiculous.* I grabbed my open box of candy and distanced myself from him, trying to put some perspective on the whole thing. Weren't there dishes to be done? Maybe I should try washing my clothes? Another shower, maybe?

I headed toward the RV, leaving him sitting there to stare at the stilled screen.

"No touchy-feely, Tess," he called after me.

I glanced back at him, and planned to tell him no worries there, but he'd already leaned forward with his arms resting on his knees, engrossed in shooting flying ninjas from the air.

CHAPTER 24

Besides Cole telling me "no touchy-feely," we didn't talk about what had happened between us. A large part of me was relieved about it, too. *How embarrassing.* We'd slept in our own beds and said very little to one another when we'd woken up. A quick, "good morning," and even that'd had an awkward taste to it.

I had hoped facing a new day would have helped to put it all behind me, giving me something new to focus on, but the memory still nagged at my belly and teased my brain. Whatever had happened must have been due to our close proximity and the lack of other people existing in our tiny world. Being the last two people around would make anyone lose their minds momentarily.

The rain had stopped sometime during the night, and with the rising sun, the hanger started to grow warm so Cole slid the large doors all the way open. He stood there for a minute with his hands tucked into his pockets, and looked off into the distance before turning to me. "The cat's on a leash, right?"

I nodded. *Poor Callie.* She fought hard against me, wiggling and scratching in an effort to get away. She hated the harness, but it was for her own good. I couldn't keep her safe otherwise. I had the leash tied to a chair and she had plenty of room to explore, but she refused to walk around and continually howled at the top of her lungs.

"Looks as good a day as any to be on our way." He peered off in the distance again. "You ready for this?"

"Yes," I said, coming to stand near him, but not too close. "I have to be." I had no idea why everyone had disappeared or why no one had returned, but I did know I had to find out where they had all gone. I had to find my family, because living like this was killing me—existing in the unknown.

Was I strong and capable enough to hike a great distance and climb a mountain? No, definitely not. But what choice did I have? If there was any chance at all that Dad and Toby were waiting for me at Rockport Lodge, then I had to take it. I'd hike the world over if I had to; I *would* find them.

"Just so you know, we're probably not going to get very far today. We need supplies, enough to survive the great outdoors, but tomorrow will be better." He didn't look at me, and I didn't blame him. I tried my best to avoid staring at him, too. No way would I gaze into his eyes again.

"I'm kind of tired of always being told tomorrow will be better only to wake up and find out it's not." Not that I blamed him. I'd been telling myself that very thing for days. My words were more for me than for him. "But it's okay. Everything we do will be one step closer, right? How can I be upset by that?"

"Good attitude to have." He turned from the door but looked past me, over my head, and scanned all his stolen goodies. "I'm really going to miss this place. You have to admit I did a pretty good job here. Home sweet home to its finest."

Pretty awesome in a this-is-illegal-but-cool kind of way. "Yeah, it's great. Much better than anything I could have imagined, that's for sure."

He grinned, but still didn't look at me.

I mean, I had to give him props for doing all of this himself. His talent to rig together PVC pipe and electrical bits and pieces had to be admired. He was a much better disaster survivor than I'd ever be. "But if we find people"—I couldn't believe I'd said *if*—"I mean, *when* we find people, what are you going to do? Will you stay or are you planning on coming back here?"

There were people out there somewhere. There had to be. Cole always insisted this kind of life was perfect for him, and perhaps it was. He did have issues relating to people—to me— and he spoke a little more frankly than he probably should. Who knew what kind of life he'd had before all of this? Maybe he'd had a rough go of it before all hell broke loose, but I couldn't imagine him wanting to live alone, forever. Even weird people needed folks to bounce their craziness off of.

His eyes caught mine for a flicker of a second, somber and forlorn, but he turned away and gazed out the open door again before I could really translate the meaning of his look. "Ahh... society with all its rules and oppression." He chuckled. "How could a person not want to return to that? Working nine to five, barely getting by? No, when we find your family, I'll be coming back here. It's where I belong anyway."

"What? By yourself? How can you say that?"

He shook his head. "I've always been by myself, Tess. Way before any of this ever happened."

I stepped near him, but didn't force him to look at me. We didn't need that mess happening, not now, not ever. I wanted to touch his arm, but didn't, not daring. "Why? What happened?"

His shoulders rolled forward and his face carried a chiseled seriousness to it—something I hadn't witnessed before. It took me by surprise.

I swallowed, wondering what had happened to make him believe living alone, away from all civilization was an answer, *any* answer, to fix his life. "Who are you?"

He shrugged. "You wouldn't believe me if I told you."

I took another step, hesitant but curious. "Try me."

He looked at me for a moment, but when things started to become a little uncomfortable, he walked past me, his shoulder brushing against mine, and said, "We should really get going."

"Stand back." He waited for me to take several steps away from the large doors before he wound his arm like a baseball pitcher, even adding the drama of raising his front leg, and launched the rock at the glass pane.

Breaking and entering once again. What was this? My third or fourth break in? I'd lost count. "Couldn't you have picked the lock instead?" I should have known better, though. He had carried that rock for a good part of our ten mile journey, bouncing it from hand to hand with each step.

He kicked away the remaining shards of glass and knocked the frame clean to make passing through less dangerous. "Yeah, but where would be the fun in that?" He swept his arm to the side. "Ladies first."

I hesitated, not sure I wanted the benefits of being a lady in this moment. "I... ah... that's okay. You can go first."

"Worried about dead bodies, huh?"

Every empty building, every abandoned car, brought the potential for another horrific Mr. Stanger-like experience. "Yeah, sorry. I'm not up for any more dead people or scattered body parts."

"Understandable." He shifted the small backpack on his shoulder. "I'll go first, but stick to me, okay? I don't feel comfortable leaving you outside alone."

I agreed with him there.

"Be careful." He guided me through the broken door by taking my hand. "Watch your step."

Inside, he could have dropped my hand, but didn't, and I had no intention of letting go either. He led me farther into the interior of the building, past a toy store, a nail salon, and the specialty popcorn shop. The emptiness of the giant two-story mall became heavy, tangible, when we stepped into the center. My shoulders slumped forward as though my backpack had accumulated an extra hundred pounds.

I turned in a circle, still holding his hand, to take in the dusty Christmas sale signs, the Santa's village decorated to elicit the fantasies of every child, the dying trees and brown poinsettias in large pots, and all the closed shops. My breath seemed to echo along the tiled corridors; an intense silence.

The beautiful fountain, an attraction people flocked to see with its timed lights and music, held stagnant water after months of no use. Green algae lapped at the cement walls and large tufts of blackened leaves from dying plants littered the thick surface of the water. The silver and copper coins, tossed in to make wishes, had turned brown and slimy. The smell of tainted water wafted over me, and I pinched my nose to keep from breathing it in.

I hadn't expected people to be there, but it reminded me how alone we were. I'd never seen East End Mall like this before, devoid of everything that had once made it so popular, and it felt almost haunting.

"It's so sad," I whispered.

Cole gave a guttural laugh. "First off, why are you whispering? And second, it's only an empty mall. It's not sad." He held his hand up. "Oh, but wait. You're a teen and teens hang out in malls, so I guess somehow that should make sense. But seriously, think of it this way, all this can be yours. Remember? Just say mine and claim it. Except for Hot Topic, I kind of have a fondness for their shirts."

"I don't need all this stuff." I stared at the ceiling above us, taking in the vast loneliness of the mall. A couple of skylights were broken and the evening sun came pouring through. Dust particles danced in the rays of light, increasing the creepiness factor, and a slight breeze swirled some scattered leaves.

"Really? You've never shopped at Pacsun or Hot Topic then, because they've got some nice things. You don't make claim to them, I will." He released my hand, and the sense of safety I'd felt before seemed to leave with that simple disconnection.

"I'm only taking what I need to get me to Rockport." A free-for-all shopping spree did have its appeal, and would have been even more alluring if it weren't for the fact that it would be illegal. "If you want to carry several shopping bags of useless stuff up a mountain, go for it."

Callie wiggled in my arms, wanting down, so I released her, but held onto the leash as she explored. I followed her with tentative steps, eyeing everything. When she tried to walk too far away from Cole, I wrangled her back in. She might be brave, but I sure as heck wasn't. "I think there's a sporting goods store upstairs and another on the far end on the bottom floor."

"Good. You're staying focused. That's important." He took the lead and headed toward the stationary escalators, and even though we'd spent most of the day walking from the hanger back toward the city, he took the steps two at a time. *Criminy.*

I took my time, raising each foot to the next step to ease the muscle-burning sensation in my calves. A couple of blisters bulged on my toes and rubbed against my worn boots. Yeah, hiking the canyon road of a mountain would be *so* much fun. The ten miles spent walking to get here had almost done me in. I should have taken P.E. more seriously.

Callie toddled along beside me as the three of us walked by various clothing, jewelry, and electronic stores. Cole scanned each one and then smiled as he gave me a thumbs up.

Maybe I was being a bit foolish, but only a couple of days had passed since the whole medical center incident. The smells, the feel, were still quite clear. Not enough time had gone by yet to put those images from my mind, and I didn't know if I could handle any more.

Cole peered through the metal gate that locked the sporting goods store. "Yeah, this should do it." He glanced at me. "You camp a lot?"

"Umm... you mean in a tent and stuff?"

He cast me a look that read *"Duh?"*

"No, not really. We mostly stayed in cabins and lodges. You?"

He knelt and removed his lock-picking kit. "I've spent some time with nature, but probably nothing like what we're about to take on. How hard can it be, really?" He smiled as he slipped the small tools into the locking mechanism.

I didn't say anything. If it were easy, more people would be doing it. I didn't think any of my friends went camping in tents—RV's and trailers, sure, but would that really be considered camping? Especially when all the comforts of home were brought along?

He slid the large gate all the way open, like it would have been on a normal day, ready for business. He passed a mini Coke fridge near the checkout, opened it and removed a sports drink. "Here," he said as he tossed it to me. "You need to keep hydrated." He took out another, uncapped it, and guzzled half the blue liquid before I'd even lifted mine to my lips.

Warm artificial blueberry slid down my throat, but I kept drinking, not realizing how thirsty I'd been. "So... where do we begin?"

He tossed his empty bottle in a trash receptacle and took a moment to look around the store that sold everything from shotguns, fishing gear, and yoga mats to dart boards, athletic cups, and sport shoes. "*That* would be a very good question."

CHAPTER 25

During the small amount of time it took me to loop Callie's leash around a clothing rack, Cole managed to get distracted. A familiar dribbling and bouncing came from the back of the store, and I sighed in frustration. He was supposed to check out the sleeping bags, not play basketball.

"I need one of these!" he said when he spotted me watching him shoot hoops. He dribbled the ball to the painted free-throw line, turned, and made a fast break to the basket. One long stride into his run, he leapt into the air and slammed the ball through the hoop. The glass backboard trembled.

"Seriously, this is coming back with me to the hanger." He grabbed the ball and spun it around on his finger. "You ever play?"

"I've played a little." I knew more about basketball than I did camping. Having a dad and an older brother who were into sports gave me an advantage over other girls my age.

"Show me." He tossed the ball in my direction.

I barely had time to catch it—thank heavens for quick reflexes—or it would've hit me square in the chest. "It's been awhile. I might be rusty." A lie. I positioned my hands on the ball, just as Dad taught me, and arched it from my angled position near some golf clubs. With a *whoosh*, it went straight through without hitting the rim. All net, baby!

"Nice!" Cole ran after the ball before it knocked over a table stacked with discounted Nikes and water bottles. He tucked it under his arm and approached me. "You have officially earned my respect with that shot." He patted the top of my head.

I narrowed my eyes and moved away to get him to stop touching me like a pet. "You didn't respect me before?"

He shrugged. "No, not really."

"*Wow*, I had no idea. That's kind of hurtful."

"Hey, I didn't say I didn't like you, because I do, sort of, but respect has to be earned. Now, you've sunk a basketball. You have my respect."

"That's all it takes, huh?" I smiled, batted the ball out of his hands, and dribbled it past him. I went for a layup and he jumped to block it, but I curved my body and made the basket easy enough.

"You're good. I can honestly say I didn't expect that." He winked and placed the basketball back in the bin with the others. "Should we check out the tents? Start there?"

He could be so exasperating but I nodded. We needed to *start* somewhere, do something. "We'll need a light one, easy to carry, but also heavy duty in case of bad weather."

"True." He unzipped one of the large tents on display, getting distracted again before climbing inside. "So I guess this one is out of the question?" He poked his head out the door. "I like the built-in awning."

He had to be joking, but the look on his face kept me guessing. "It's nice." I treaded slowly in case he was actually serious. "But it's a lot bigger than we need and it will be way too heavy to carry." A three-room tent on a hiking trip? And I was hoping Cole would help me to get to Rockport Lodge alive? What was I thinking?

"I'm not an idiot, Tess. I was messing with you. It sure is nice though, isn't it?" He grabbed my hand before I could protest, and jerked me inside. The plastic bottom caught one of my boots and I tumbled forward. He reached out to catch me, but we fell over and ended up in a pile of tangled limbs.

There really wasn't anything too funny about the whole thing, just a stupid mishap, yet I started laughing, a little at first, but then it grew into something I couldn't stop, something that began to scare me. The look on Cole's face didn't help, and the more I tried to curb it, the worse my laughter became.

"You're really weird." He shifted out from under me, scooted a little ways off, and stared at me as though I'd lost my damn mind.

Maybe I had.

My laughter became maniacal and I rolled to my side, so he couldn't look at me while I tried to get myself under control. *What is going on?* Another panic attack? *Really?* But I was doing okay. Everything was fine! *I* was fine. We were making plans, moving forward, which was a good thing. So why this now?

My second panic attack in less than a week, two since meeting Cole — but only one of many since Mom died.

"Are you... okay?"

I couldn't talk and my attempt to nod looked like a seizure. I had never laughed so hard — and over nothing. *Nothing.* My stomach hurt so bad! My chest burned. My eyes blurred.

"You're kind of freaking me out here."

Yeah, well, I was kind of freaking myself out.

Another round of uncontrollable giggles took over my body, shaking my shoulders and squeezing my belly to the point I thought I might pee or throw-up. I pinched my inner thigh, trying to trick my mind into focusing on the pain, but it didn't seem to make a difference. I didn't understand what was happening or even *why* it was happening now. Nothing had triggered it. I pinched harder. *Stop it! Stop it!*

"Jeez, you're not okay, are you?" He placed his hand over mine, stopping me from inflicting more pain to myself. "It's okay. I've got you." He lifted my convulsing body into his arms and pressed my head against his shoulder. "It's been a rough couple of days, I get that."

A rough couple of days? It had been a rough couple of... years.

Yes, I had survived a catastrophic meteor shower and two months living underground. Yes, I had outlived a deathly tornado and bowling ball-sized hail that ripped everything apart in its path. And yes, I was planning to climb a freakin' huge mountain and live in a tent! *A tent!* But all of that, as crazy and huge as each of those things was, none of them compared to everything else I had survived to this point. All those memories came rushing over me, hitting me one right after another, unexpected.

The crazy apocalyptic disaster may have only been a few months old, but my life had been spiraling out of control long before the first meteor struck—ever since the police came to the door and told us they had found Mom's body.

There was nothing funny about remembering her death, or the fact that Dad took a shovel that same night and started digging a hole in the backyard, or Toby punching several holes in the walls, breaking multiple bones in his hand. Nothing at all, but I couldn't freakin' stop laughing! Only it wasn't laughter, not really.

"Tess"—he cupped my face and forced me to look at him—"we're gonna be fine. Yeah, we might have to eat bugs and wade through poison oak, but we can handle it. *We can.* We'll be together, slapping mosquitoes off each other's backs and hunting rabbit and picking wild berries."

Hunting rabbit?

"And we have all this awesome stuff to make it a whole lot easier." He waved his arm around to indicate the store, but cupped my face again as if my head might explode if he didn't. "Sure, it won't be like staying in a five-star hotel, but we'll make it work. They have thermal socks that keep feet dry. We'll have dry feet!" His eyes widened, showing his excitement. "Won't that be great?"

Was I supposed to stop my hysterical laughter over socks? His attempt to calm me had the opposite effect and I blubbered and chuckled until hiccups gripped my body. I had no idea what to make of myself, so how in the world was he supposed to understand that my laughter, my tears, my craziness, only had a small part to do with tackling a mountain and everything that went with it?

He held my face between his hands, and looked at me, *really* looked at me. "That's not what you're worried about is it?"

A little snort slipped through my lips despite my effort to force it back. It began to bud into more giggling and laughing. Could he see my pain in my eyes? Could he? *Help me.*

His mouth captured my own, colliding without warning, and my laughter and hiccups vanished as surprise and disbelief rushed in to take their place. My breath hitched in my throat, but I found I didn't mind. Not at all.

A wonderful unexpectedness.

Maybe I should have pushed him away, slapped him, stopped the very thing we'd told each other couldn't happen, but I didn't. I didn't want it to stop. My fingers weaved themselves through his dark curls, trying to take from him as much as he was trying to take from me.

His hands framed my face, held my neck, and the back of my head as our kiss heated and intensified—his hands always moving to hold me closer. His whiskers tickled the sensitive skin around my mouth, pleasurable and strange all at once, and the sensation of it held me captive as his hungry lips played with mine, teasing and commanding—straining, tugging, and drawing me closer and closer with his mouth, until my chest slumped against his, melding into him. Natural and effortless.

Sensations ignited my body, heightening my senses. The world faded away, and nothing else mattered, not empty malls or looming mountains or vanishing people or haunting memories. His heart thumping against mine and his breath giving air to my lungs became my only need. Yes, I wanted this. Yes, I needed this. Right now. Right here.

I didn't want to lose myself again.

But his hands slipped from my face and wrapped around mine, drawing them away from his hair. He brought our clasped hands between us, kissed my fingers, and then eased himself from me. My lips had never felt so light, as though they might float away like a single balloon released into the air.

When he let go of my hands, I knew it was over. Whatever it was we'd started had come to an end, and that frightened me more than knowing where it could have gone.

He avoided my eyes, and a crushing awareness crept through my veins and settled in my chest. A battle of morality wreaked havoc inside me, and as I watched him, the struggle was apparent on his sober face, too. We both felt it—a need, a want, a taboo.

If kissing was wrong, I didn't care. I didn't! But I had no idea how to explain that to him. He wasn't a bad person, if that's what he thought, for kissing me, and I wasn't some stupid teen girl for wanting it, but somehow it felt exactly like that.

He lifted me from his lap and sat me at his side. He bent his legs, rested his arms across his knees, and stared at the unzipped opening, his breathing labored but slowing with each intake and release. His face said it all—he wanted me, but knew he couldn't have me, and he was mentally beating himself up for it.

I kept my eyes on him, not breathing, as I struggled to find the right words to explain it was okay, but a small hiccup pressed through my lips instead, breaking the lengthy silence.

"Well"—he glanced in my direction, but didn't really look at me—"I knew I had to do something to get you to stop being so weird."

Huh?

"Glad it worked." He stood and pushed the tent opening wide. "I think I'm going to go check out the sleeping bags now. Maybe while I'm doing that, when you're up to it, you could look into getting us a camp stove and some water purifying tablets."

The tent flaps dropped into place as he disappeared from view.

What is going on? Shouldn't we talk or something?

I continued to sit there, staring after him, baffled and perplexed by his words.

Because there was no way, even if he wanted to pretend it didn't happen, that he hadn't felt it too.

CHAPTER 26

Cole dropped his pants in the middle of the aisle and stood there, wearing only his underwear while he flicked through a rack of athletic shorts. He grabbed one off a hanger, held it up, then tossed it to the side before looking again.

It took every ounce of will power not to ask what he was doing, though my eyes kept wandering to him, betraying my curiosity. I wanted to talk, to ease the tension between us, but if he wanted to act as though nothing had happened, pretend the kiss had been nothing more than a ploy to get me to calm down, what else could I do?

"Going for a run. Be back in a bit." He slipped a pair of black shorts over his hips, grabbed a pair of running shoes off the display, and headed out into the main part of the mall. After a few minutes, the sound of his feet hitting the floor echoed along the corridor, growing more intense with each lap.

"What am I going to do, Callie?" I held the kitten in my arms and rubbed her orange and white head. I debated whether to leave and go about finding my family on my own—it would be a lot less weird without Cole—but it would be terrifying to be alone. Not to mention a lot more dangerous.

The pros and cons of each choice equaled out. The best solution was to go back to how things had been before—but was that even possible?

My backpack stood ready—sleeping bag and pad, tent, synthetic clothing, water pump, camping stove, matches, first aid kit, rifle, knife, compass, map, ready-to-eat meals, flashlight, headlamp, coat, gloves, thermal underwear, and of course, socks to keep my feet dry. I had nothing left to do but wait until morning to be on my way.

It was too early to sleep, but too late to do much of anything else. Since I didn't relish meandering around a darkened building on my own, exploring the mall was out of the question, but sitting on my butt and listening to Cole run lap after lap around the place left much to be desired.

Ten metal darts poked out from a dartboard on display, beckoning to me, and after I left Callie with a bowl of water and food, I removed the darts and turned them over in my hands. I pressed one sharp point to my palm, drawing a bead of blood, satisfied that they would serve my purpose.

The intended target hung on the wall, round and waiting, but I had another target in mind. I chucked the darts, one at a time, at a stupid mannequin, aiming for its shiny faceless head. The bridge of the nose, between the eyes—perfect.

Several stuck and a few others missed the mark altogether, but the very act of throwing sharp pointy things at an inanimate object released a lot of pent-up frustration.

Take that!

The mannequin began to resemble a porcupine, and I couldn't have been happier. I'd finally found a way to deal with my feelings for Cole. Strange, but cathartic.

I picked up the scattered darts from the floor, yanked a few others free, leaving the mannequin dotted with my precision, and decided to increase the distance to test my skill. Several steps back, I reared my arm, but just before launching another round, I caught sight of a wide-eyed figure stared through the store window. I dropped the darts, barely missing my toes.

I stumbled backward, bumping into a table, but kept my eyes on the lanky boy, certain I had to be seeing things.

He inched closer to the store's opening, slowly and methodically, glancing down the mall corridor before returning his gaze to me. He didn't come inside, but remained at the edge.

Holy crap!

Tufts of black hair poked out from under the rim of the skater cap he wore. His clothes hung from his thin frame, loose and baggy. Deep-set circles encased the whites of his eyes, darkening his already mocha-colored complexion. He couldn't have been much older than I was, but he looked worn out enough to out-age me.

I wished I could speak, scream, move, *something*, but Cole's name barely passed through my lips at a whisper. *Cole, Cole, Cole!*

"I'm not going to hurt you." He peered down the breezeway in both directions as Cole's running grew louder, his return closer with each step. "I promise."

"Okay." I managed to answer.

He nodded toward our backpacks, leaning against the checkout counter. "Where are you going?"

"I... we're heading to Rockport Canyon in the morning." Why I revealed anything to him, I had no idea.

"Why?" Hope, more than curiosity, clung to his one word. He leaned forward, waiting my response.

"Because that's where my dad said he'd be." More answers I probably shouldn't have been offering, but I couldn't help myself. "I'm hoping he's still there anyway."

His face fell, his glance turned from me, and I knew I hadn't answered him in the way he'd hoped. "Oh."

"He's coming back," I said as Cole's steps hit the final stretch.

The boy glanced behind him before shifting and blending into the shadows, disappearing. My shoulders tensed and I took a small step. I couldn't see him, and almost wondered if he'd left, but when I made out his faint outline, relief enveloped me. He wasn't gone, and there was something rather comforting in knowing that.

He didn't say anything, and I didn't either, not even when a shirtless Cole flew past, running at an incredible speed. Cole's footsteps faded again, and I worried I'd made a mistake not calling after him. This boy said he wouldn't hurt me, but still...

His arrival was huge, and Cole should be involved, but for the moment, I wanted to keep this secret to myself. While he continued to stay hidden, I bent, grabbed a dart, and quickly returned to my regular stance with the mini-weapon tucked behind my back.

Several seconds ticked by before he eased into the dim light, scanning the area, and watching Cole's retreating back. "Are there any others?"

"People?"

He nodded.

"No, it's just the two of us. You?"

He hesitated. "No. I haven't seen anyone else."

"You're all alone?"

He pulled his cap a little lower on his head. "Yeah, it's just me."

"Do you... do want something to eat?" What do people say or do in these kinds of situations? Offering food seemed like a good place to start since he looked so thin and gangly. We were strangers, but we were also part of an even stranger dilemma— me, him, Cole. "We don't have much, but I could make you something."

He shook his head. "No, I'm not hungry. Thanks anyway." He snapped his head to the side. Cole's running grew louder. He looked at me, then back over his shoulder again.

"It's okay. He's nice, well, sometimes he is. Most of the time he's a jerk, but I—"

He didn't wait for me to finish, but sprinted toward our backpacks, snatched Cole's, swung it onto his shoulder, and took off, disappearing around the corner. His footsteps hopped the stairs several at a time, skipping whole sections.

I ran out of the store, the dart still in my hand, and leaned against the railing that looked over the first floor. The shadows swallowed him up, and I couldn't see him anywhere. "Don't go! Please!" *Why would he do that? Take Cole's bag and leave? Why leave at all?*

"Hey, I'm not going anywhere." Cole swiped a hand towel across his forehead before draping it over one shoulder. "I'm here."

"No, not you!" I pointed over the railing below us. "Him! The boy! He... he took your bag!"

"What?" Cole leaned over the railing too. "Where? Are you sure?"

I nodded. "I swear!"

"Which way?"

I waved my arm, and he sprinted to the stairs, chasing after the only other person I'd seen in several months. The railing pressed into my belly as I leaned over it and strained to see or hear anything happening below.

Come on, find him!

I couldn't make out anything in the dimness and tiny noises seemed to ricochet off the walls, sounding louder than they actually were. I had no idea what was happening.

When Cole returned a short while later—minus a boy and a bag—my stomach coiled and melancholy settled over me. *Shoot!*

He walked toward me with a look a parent gives a child caught in a lie.

I shook my head before he could say anything. "No, I'm not making this up! You've got to believe me! He was right here! I'm not kidding!"

"Tess—"

"He had baggy clothes and a skater hat. You know the ones? They wear them all the time, even in the summer, though they look like winter hats? He seemed tired and hungry. We talked!"

This time Cole shook his head. "Did he look like that?" He pointed to a life-sized poster of a teen boy modeling the latest rue21 clothing line. The model wore a knitted hat and baggy pants, and looked a lot like my description, except for the fact the teen on the poster was Caucasian!

"I know the difference between a poster and a real person, *Cole!* Give me some credit here."

"I didn't see anyone, Tess. Not a soul. It's lonely and scary, living like this, and I can see where you might mistake a picture as a real person. The mind can be a tricky bastard sometimes, especially after the giggling fit you had. You may be experiencing some sort of residual effect here, and that's okay. I'm not judging you."

No. Way. "For the last time, I saw a *real* person! He stood right here!" I marched over to the exact spot the boy had been standing when we spoke, and I used both hands to indicate the floor and make my point. "He took your bag. Go check for yourself!" How would he explain that? *Residual effect, my behind!*

I followed him inside all the while getting the feeling he was only humoring me. Sure enough, only one bag leaned against the checkout counter.

"There! See? I told you! No poster could've made that happen."

He took a deep breath and let it out slowly before giving me a stern look which reminded me a bit like my father. *Yikes!* "This isn't a game, Tess. What did you do with my things?"

My eyes widened. "What? I didn't... are you accusing me?" I threw my hands in the air. "I didn't do this!"

"And I suppose you didn't do that either, right?" He nodded toward the mannequin with a few darts still lodged in its head.

"*That* I admit to, yes, but I didn't take your bag!" I exaggerated each word as though he were hard of hearing, because apparently he was!

"Okay, I get it. I get you're mad at me, but now you're being childish, and I don't appreciate it."

"Childish?"

"Yeah." He stepped closer to me. "You're a *kid* and you're acting an awful lot like one. And that is why, this" — he moved his hand between us —"can never happen. You get it?"

So he *had* felt it? But I didn't have time to think about it, because he had everything wrong. I didn't take his bag. I wasn't a crazy person who talked to posters!

"I'm going to go get ready for bed, because this has been a *very* weird day and I'm tired. While I'm doing that, you're going to get my bag and put it back next to yours." He started walking toward the clothing racks, but turned and looked at me as he shrugged. "Unless you don't want me helping you anymore. Just let me know, because I'm good either way."

CHAPTER 27

Screw this! Screw *him!*

If I hadn't run into Cole several days before—*Has it really only been several days? It feels so much longer*—I would have been on my own anyway, surviving and searching for Dad and Toby myself. Did I need him?

No.

No, I didn't.

I kept feeding myself that big lie, hoping to embody the bravery I lacked and desperately needed, especially for what I intended to do.

I slipped the straps of my backpack over my shoulder, grabbed Callie's leash, and walked straight out of the store. Yeah, the sun was setting, and yeah, I didn't have much of a plan beyond getting away from Cole and leaving his jack-assery behind, but it didn't matter. I was *so* over this.

Survival was mostly about winging it anyway, right? I took a deep breath and released it. I sure hoped so.

"That's it, huh? No goodbye?" He stood nonchalantly near the door, his hands tucked into the front pockets of his camouflage cargo pants. His shoulders rolled forward and relaxed, as if a burden had been lifted from them. Maybe it had.

"Yeah, I guess so." I kept walking, heading for the same set of stairs the mysterious boy had used earlier. Cole had never really wanted to help me—I'd coerced him into it with my tears—so now I released him of his obligation. He was free.

He followed me but kept his distance, moving slowly, and taking one step for my eager two. "You going to be okay on your own?"

"Yep." I avoided his eyes as I bent and scooped Callie into my arms, deciding that letting her walk would hinder my quick escape. She had a habit of stopping to lick her paws every few feet, and I didn't need that. No more distractions. No more dawdling. I wanted a clean break from him before I changed my mind.

"Do you have everything you need?" He leaned against the railing, his hands dangling over the side, and watched me descend the stairs.

"Yep."

"Tess?"

"Yeah?" I shifted the irritated cat to my other arm and fixed the backpack strap that kept slipping down my shoulder. Hiking with a bulging backpack that didn't want to stay put and a feisty cat would be interesting.

He didn't say anything for a moment, forcing me to glance up at him. "I'm sorry... about everything."

He looked sincere, but that didn't mean I planned to forget this whole thing or that I wanted to deal with him any longer. From the moment we'd met, our relationship had been nothing but aggravation and annoyance. He wanted to be on his own, live without people, and the more I had gotten to know him, the more I agreed he probably should. His people skills sucked.

"I'm sorry, too." I turned away and took the rest of the steps to the bottom floor. Yes, this was for the best. We were the least compatible people I had ever met—always fighting and getting on each other's nerves. We definitely did not belong together, regardless of the disastrous situation. An apocalypse wasn't an excuse for two people to stay together anyway—though, what better excuse was there? I shook my head. *Whatever.*

"Good luck," he called.

"Thanks." I kept walking toward the broken doors, stepping over the shattered glass, and made my way outside.

I stood there for several minutes, breathing in the cool evening air, and gathering courage. *Don't think about dead people or tornados or climbing mountains on your own. Don't think at all.* Thinking would only get me into trouble.

The street lights would normally have started to turn on about this time, but of course the few upright lampposts remained unlit. Papers and dried leaves tumbled with the warm breeze across the partially empty parking lot. Adjacent buildings fell into thick shadows. I wasn't brave and I had no idea what to do next except place one foot in front of the other.

I began walking.

I left the mall and Cole, and refused to look back.

And as for luck, I would probably need as much of it as I could get.

Nowhere was safe. Not really. Anything could happen—I'd been witness to it—but with darkness creeping in and sounds starting to play tricks on my ears, I needed to find a place to sleep for the night before going full-out crazy. Perhaps I should have stayed at the mall until morning, but I hadn't trusted myself to still have the courage to leave once the sun rose.

Impulsive? Smart? I wasn't sure.

At this point, I couldn't go back. Okay, I could, but I refused. My impulsive decision must have been more than an act of stupidity.

Callie snuggled against my shoulder and tucked herself under my chin. Her sleepy purrs and warm fur weighed my eyes down, and though I hadn't walked more than a handful of miles from East End Mall, and the surrounding area appeared to have been hit by a bomb—tornado, meteor, who could tell anymore?—I couldn't go on.

Most of the homes in the area looked as though they'd topple to the ground if I sneezed funny. Quite a few others had already met their demise and lay in heaps of rubble mixed with personal belongings—a shirt, a doll, family pictures in broken frames, and a pair of kid's shoes.

A modular home didn't look half-bad, weird it was still intact, but the simple act of pushing the door open started a domino effect of destruction. The back portion of the roof caved in, the walls collapsed, and I barely had enough time to jump off the porch before the entire thing imploded, sending up a cloud of dust and debris.

Jeez. Way too close. And *way* too visual.

I lay sprawled on the dying lawn and couldn't help but glance over my shoulders. The roads and side streets remained empty. No Cole.

Good, I convinced myself and sighed. That settled things. If there had ever been a time for him to show himself, come to my rescue, this would have been it. Only, he hadn't. My stomach hurt a little, knowing Cole hadn't bothered to stop me from leaving and hadn't even followed me, but I forced myself to take it as a sign I had done the right thing by leaving.

I brushed myself off and made sure Callie was fine before moving on. The farther I walked, circling blocks and meandering through ruined subdivisions, the heavier my decision felt. Being on my own had never seemed so hard, especially when I couldn't find a safe place to rest.

Another mile of walking in a sleepy daze didn't prove much better. Whole areas had been decimated, several miles wide, and that many more miles long, as though a giant hand had swiped civilization clean.

I had almost resigned myself to sleeping in a shed, better than nothing, when I spotted a garage door to a tiny brick home across the street. The door had come disengaged and hung at a lopsided angle. After checking out the circumference and determining the house sat securely on its foundation, I figured the garage would do.

I gave the locked back door a firm jiggle and waited. Nothing tumbled over or crashed in on itself. The roof stayed put, and I breathed a sigh of relief. The crooked garage door left a gap big enough for me to crawl through, but before doing anything, I dropped to my knees and removed a tiny flashlight from my bag.

I knelt next to the hole and carefully aimed the yellow beam into the darkness. At this moment, I felt extremely grateful we weren't fighting the undead or creatures from outer space. For the most part, this apocalypse was boring, but that suited me fine. To be safe, I refused to put my hand in the hole, but kept it where I could snatch it back if I had to.

No car. Not much of anything, really. Just the usual garage stuff — push lawnmower, tires, shovels, ice coolers, and tools.

"Okay, Callie." I took a deep breath, calming my rising nerves and doing my best to keep my anxiety in check. No more panic attacks. I could do this. "Let's check it out."

I lay flat on my belly and army-crawled through the space while dragging Callie along on her leash. She tugged back, not wanting to follow, but I gave her no choice. I reached back through the gap and hauled my backpack inside too. I'd be needing it.

A few tools lined the workbench, all orderly and organized. A dark oil mark in the middle seeped into the wood, but a tiny bit still pooled on top. *Odd.* I touched it and rubbed it between my thumb and forefinger before wiping it off on my pants.

I pushed open the side door leading into the kitchen, but waited a minute before going in just in case the house decided to try and kill me. Nothing happened. The house was one of the precious few in the area continuing to hold itself together and stand upright, but I remained cautious anyway.

Everything looked normal. Even the pictures on the walls hung straight on their hooks. *Strange.* The surrounding area had pretty much been demolished, but except for the broken garage door, this particular house appeared untouched.

Callie wanted down, so I set her on her feet but continued to hold on to her leash. Past experience told me to leave the fridge alone, but I carefully opened each cabinet and pantry door in hopes of finding a little something to appease the gnawing in my belly.

I stood in the middle of the linoleum floor with each door wide open, my bottom jaw nearly hit my chest as I took in the bounty. *The mother lode.* I swore I heard angels singing.

Each shelf was lined and stocked to overflowing. Cans of all shapes and sizes, with their labels facing outward, beckoned to me. Jars of tomatoes, various fruits, green beans, and pickles almost had me drooling. A dozen jars of peanut butter. That much more of jam—all flavors. Bags of chips, pretzels, Hostess pastries jam-packed on several shelves with one whole shelf dedicated to jar after jar of Nutella. *Nutella.*

I blinked several times. *No freakin' way.*

The temptation was too much, and I reached for a jar of Nutella, cracked open the lid and peeled back the safety seal. I dipped my fingers inside, but hesitated before slipping the chocolaty goodness into my mouth.

Something wasn't right here.

Not a hint of dust covered the kitchen table or counters. A back window, missing its glass, had a board nailed over it. Every piece of furniture sat upright. Books lined the tall shelves. Only a porcelain figurine, perched on top of the television, showed any visual damage. Its tiny arm lay next to it, waiting to be fixed, along with a tube of super glue.

I slipped my chocolaty fingers into my mouth and sucked at them, not wanting to waste it, and took in my surroundings, noticing for the first time how "clean" and orderly everything really was. Carefully, I sat the jar of Nutella on the counter without making a sound, and reached into the side pocket of my pack to remove my gun.

I bent and tied Callie's leash to a kitchen chair, turned off my flashlight, and started down the hall, placing each footstep without a creek. It took a moment for my eyes to adapt to the dim light, but doing so was better than walking around with a spotlight on my head—X marks the spot.

The bathroom, though empty, revealed more signs of living— a toothbrush, comb, a folded towel on the counter and a partially used bar of soap. Practically brand new.

Angling my body just so, I gently pushed open the bedroom door while staying hidden. I waited and listened, in case the person I suspected of claiming this place had plans to blow my head off.

"Hello?" I waited.

No sounds, no shuffling. Nothing.

"I'm friendly, I swear." I added bonus cheer to my voice, sounding extra non-threatening. Then I worried I sounded *too* friendly, like someone they could easily take down should the situation come to that. *Shoot.* "I don't want any problems. I only want to talk. I promise."

No response. Whether I should be grateful or disappointed, I wasn't quite sure.

I waited a little more and then peeked inside briefly before returning to the safety of the hall. -The small glimpse had revealed just an empty, well-made bed, a stack of folded clothes on the dresser, and a coat draped over a chair.

But one thing had caught my eye, and as I stood there in the hall, trying to steady my breathing, as I realized what it meant. *No way.*

I lowered my gun and leaned my head against the wall, thinking—something I told myself not to do.

After a few minutes, I stepped into the darkened room and approached the double bed.

Sure enough, Cole's stolen backpack leaned against the footboard.

CHAPTER 28

How was this even possible? Sure, the house was practically the only upright building in the area, but really? Come on.

Though, I had to admit, knowing the occupant was the mysterious boy from the mall and not some end-of-days weirdo seemed a blessing. At least the boy and I had already developed some rapport. Still, the whole coincidence seemed rather odd.

I could have grabbed the stolen backpack, headed to the mall, and presented Cole with it. *Ah-ha, I told you so!* But I didn't. I had cut ties with him and decided it best to keep them severed. Knowing Cole, he'd find a way to twist it all around and make me look like a lying fool again.

Nope, I would not be going back. Good riddance.

Besides, I was curious about the skater boy, who he was and what he knew. And more importantly, why was he still here?

I understood Cole's reasoning—he was a giant jerk, after all and liked stealing everyone's left-behind belongings—but a boy, not much older than me? Why hadn't he left, searched for others?

The kid wasn't here, not now, but at some point he would return — he had a shelf full of Nutella, *hello?* — so I decided to take advantage of the situation and help myself to some goodies. I ate most of one jar, and then cracked open a can of chicken noodle soup and a bag of potato chips.

The kid had stolen Cole's bag, so he had no right to complain that I'd eaten some of his food. All was fair play. If he happened to get mad, so be it. I still had a belly full of food I couldn't return. Well, at least not in the most pleasant of ways.

I was determined to stay awake, regardless of the exhaustion clamping down on me, but after several hours slipped by without any sign of him, I crawled onto the sagging couch and adjusted the decorative pillows under my head. I placed my gun under the cushions for quick access, but trusted I wouldn't need it. The boy had told me that when we first met he had no plans to hurt me, and I'd believed him.

I still believed him.

Maybe I should have been more afraid, been more prepared for his return, but when Callie lay in the crook of my arm, and her warm little body purred against mine, my eyes drooped shut.

The instant my eyes opened, shaking off sleep, I knew I wasn't alone.

I rolled my head to the side and sure enough, he sat across from me on a chair with his long legs stretched out in front of him and his dark eyes locked on mine. Tightness grew along my shoulder blades and my breath became stilted. I pushed myself upward, trying to cram my body into the far corner of the couch, but the plastic bands looped around my wrists and ankles hindered my efforts. I nearly tumbled face-first to the floor. *What the — ?*

No, no, no!

I twisted my hands and kicked my legs, fighting against the zip-tie restraints, but the hard plastic held tight, not budging an inch. My struggling pulled them tighter, pinching my skin and digging into my tender flesh. Even trying to bite them didn't work.

"I'm not going to hurt you." He leaned forward in the chair, his eyes still on mine. "I promise."

The exact same words he'd spoken the day before. Somehow, with my hands and ankles bound, I didn't quite believe him like the first time. I lifted my hands. "Then why do this?"

"Because I don't know if you're going to hurt me." He cocked a brow and lifted my small gun.

My gun! Holy crap! I must have really been out of it for him to bind me and take my gun from the couch cushions. I should have prepared better. So dumb. Now here I was, practically hog-tied and at his mercy.

"I'm not going to hurt you either," I said, hoping to fix this situation, and quick. "I'm a really, *really* nice person." Not a smart person, but nice and trusting, sure.

He looked at the gun for several minutes then turned his attention to me. "Why the gun?"

I shifted on the couch with my bound feet on the floor and my tied hands in my lap. "I don't know. It makes me feel safer, I suppose. Also, I'm a girl. I'm on my own. Everything is really crazy in the world right now, if you haven't noticed."

He seemed to think about that for a moment before putting the gun down on a side table. "But you followed me."

"No!" I shook my head. "I didn't. I swear! This happened to be the only decent house in the area, but I had no idea you'd staked claim to it. Honest." This looked bad. Really bad.

His eyes narrowed and he raised his chin.

"I know, I know! I'd be skeptical too, but I'm telling the truth. I had no idea which way you went after you left the mall. This is all a giant misunderstanding, a fluke really, and believe me I'm just as surprised as you are."

"Where's your friend?"

I shrugged. "I don't know. I kind of left him at the mall."

He leaned back in the chair. "Why would you do that?"

I brushed away a loose strand of hair falling over my eyes and tickling my nose. Not an easy thing to do with bound hands. "Because he's a bit of an ass, that's why." I waved my hands around for effect. "What is it with you guys? Here we are, stuck in the middle of a natural disaster of epic proportions and the only two people I've come across so far have turned out to be slightly... mean."

Maybe calling him mean wasn't the best approach, but it flew out of my mouth before I really thought about it. "What I meant was shouldn't we all come together to figure out what is going on instead of doing this?" I waved my arms again before dropping my aching hands back in my lap. "Oh, and for the record, the guy you saw at the mall isn't my friend."

He crossed the room, and pushed aside the curtains to peer out.

"He's not with me anymore. I promise."

"I believe you." He continued to look out the dirty window.

O-kay. Apparently, I'd exchanged one crazy person for another. *Good job, Tess. You really know how to do this whole survival thing, don't you?*

He stood watching out the window and saying nothing. What he was looking for, I had no idea. If someone or something was out there, it wouldn't take much to get inside. Besides, the only other person I knew hadn't followed me. He had probably returned to his "lair" with a basketball and hoop in his possession. The immature jerk.

"Why did you steal the backpack? We would've put together one for you, you know?" I really wanted to know, so I tossed the question out there, breaking the silence. Ever since he'd taken it and run off, I'd tried to make sense of it, coming up with nothing remotely sensible.

He shook his head and adjusted his knitted beanie. "I don't know."

"What?" I angled myself on the couch to get a better view of him. "You don't know? I'm sorry, but that's not a good answer. You *had* to have had a reason." I was losing feeling in my toes. *Darn zip-tie.*

He turned from the window to look at me. "I needed stuff and I got nervous. Is that better for you?"

I wiggled my feet. "A little better, but not by much. See? This goes back to my original question as to why we don't all work together to get out of this mess instead of doing weird stuff like stealing each other's supplies or tying up people."

He didn't answer me and we both fell back into silence. I lifted my bound wrists to my mouth again, but unless I wanted to lose a few teeth in the process, biting the strap off wouldn't work.

I was about to settle against the couch, give in to being captive, but I sat straight up instead. Crap! Where was Callie? Jeez! I shifted around on the couch, searching for her, but didn't see any sign of my kitten anywhere.

"Callie?" Oh, he'd better not have hurt her. Bound hands or not, I'd kill him! "Callie!"

"I'm allergic to cats, so I put her in the bathroom. Don't worry, she's fine." He kept his back to me.

A tiny *meow* flittered down the hall, supporting his statement. I let out my breath and sank against the couch cushions, satisfied Callie was okay for the moment.

"You know," he said, turning from the window and letting the drapes fall into place, "your cat is the first animal I've seen in a long time. Where did you find her?"

Shouldn't we be talking about other things, like the fact that I was still tied up, and what he planned to do with me? "I got her from the local animal shelter."

"Really?" He seemed surprised and stepped closer to me. "Was she the only one alive or were there others?"

Alive? Others? "Oh, wait. That's not what you meant, is it? No, I adopted her from the animal shelter *long* before all this happened, and she's been with me ever since."

His face fell, looking very similar to when I told him I was heading to Rockport Canyon to find Dad. He flopped down in the chair, laid his head back and closed his eyes.

I noticed the lack of animals in the beginning, but hadn't paid much attention since then. I had bigger things to think of, like trying to *not die* for one, but no animals was pretty strange for sure. "Cole, the guy I used to..." — *what do I call it?* — "be with, he thought it had to do something with the weather and the water being contaminated. That's why the animals are either dead or have left."

"Yeah, you're...I mean, he's probably right." He didn't open his eyes. "I guess I kind of hoped when I saw your cat things were getting better." He looked up then, startling me a bit. "You know, a sign?"

What do I say to that? "I'm... sorry." I couldn't think of a better response.

He shook his head. "Not your fault. It's mine, actually. I keep expecting things to get better, but it doesn't look like it's going to happen anytime soon, does it?"

"Maybe it's not going to get better *here*, not for a while anyway, but somewhere it's better than this. That's where the animals are. That's where the people are. And that's where *we* should be."

A smile broke out on his face, but it wasn't sincere — sad, really. "You still planning to go to Rockport? Look for your dad?"

I sensed a trap, but nodded anyway. "Yeah, I am."

"What happens if he's not there? What are you going to do then?"

I scooted forward on the couch with my butt on the edge. "Why does everyone assume he's not going to be there? Why does everyone have to be so negative?" Everyone meaning him and Cole.

He mimicked my movements and sat on the edge of his chair. "Did you get a phone call or a message? Something that told you to meet him there?"

Where is he going with this? I nodded.

"How long ago was that?"

"A couple of months."

"And you're just going to check it out now?"

I owed him nothing, least of all an explanation. "I couldn't before."

He got up from the chair, crossed the room, and knelt in front of me. He grabbed my ankles in his hands. "I'm from Denver."

Denver? Jeez. That was like... what? I didn't know, but Denver was a long, *long* way away. Lots of miles.

"My granddad left a message on my phone, too." He slipped a small knife from his pocket and flicked it open, then positioned it under the plastic strap around my ankles and cut me free. "He told me they'd wait—him, my uncles, my aunt, and two of my cousins. No matter how long it took. They were safe, and they'd wait for me. As long as we were together, we'd be fine, he'd said."

"That's great." I moved my ankles in a circular motion, to work out the kinks. "Where are you supposed to meet them?"

He took my wrists, his dark hands holding my pale ones, but he didn't cut the band as I expected. His eyes focused on mine. "You're looking at it."

CHAPTER 29

"You were supposed to meet them *here?*" The family pictures strung on the walls adopted a more ominous feel than ever before, and I searched for him in the frames amid the strangers and the smiling faces. The house evolved and became dreadfully real—a painful possibility.

A sense of heaviness weighed me down, more mental than physical, though I sank deeper into the cushions of the couch.

He sliced through the plastic band around my wrists, but instead of releasing me, he ran his thumbs over the indents in my skin. "Next door, actually, but..." He shook his head. "You saw what it looks like out there."

Of course I did. The barrenness, the emptiness, the destruction—I'd seen it all. A sigh pressed through my lips as I tried to process what his revelation meant, and what he expected me to do exactly. Give up looking for Dad and Toby? Never. "I'm sorry your family isn't here, but it doesn't mean my family is gone too. They might still be waiting for me."

He nodded. "If I had a clue to where my family might be, or even a hint they might still be alive, I'd probably be chasing after it too. I get that, but I have to warn you, it hurts like hell to get to your destination only to wind up no better than when you first started out. Believe me, I know."

Of course those thoughts had plagued my mind—I wasn't naïve or stupid. It had been over two months after all, and of course I'd wondered why Dad hadn't come back for me in all that time, but his message to me was all I had to cling to. Thinking anything different, expecting the worst, would crush me into nothingness.

"What's your plan if you get there and they're gone?" He continued to massage my wrists while bruising my confidence.

I shrugged. "I don't have one."

He studied me for a moment. "Yeah, I kind of figured you didn't. You should probably have one though. You need to stay at least one step ahead of this. Two or three is even better."

I jerked my hands away from him. "I don't want a plan B! If I allow myself to give into doubts I may never attempt plan A! I'm not good at this survivor stuff, I'm not, but this is all I have. This is it for me. So, stop it, okay? Just stop."

He stared at the floor while turning the broken plastic band around in his hand. "Okay."

I didn't care whether the whole idea was foolish or not; I would climb that damn mountain. I would! "What's your plan now, huh? What are you going to do since your family isn't here? What's *your* plan B?" Tough questions could go both ways.

He turned the piece of plastic over and over in his hand, increasing the speed before finally dropping it at my feet. "My plan B changed." He stood, brushed off his dirty pants, and looked down at me. "You're my plan B."

"Oh, no, no, no!" I clambered from the creaky couch and positioned myself in front of him. "No way. I don't want to be your plan B. I don't want to be *anyone's* plan B! Go and do whatever you were planning to do before I showed up, okay?" I couldn't believe I'd actually said that, but I'd said a lot in the last couple of days I wouldn't have thought possible. Logical? Heck no! But I no longer cared. Cole had ruined that for me.

"If I hadn't shown up, what were you going to do? Where were you going to go?" He'd drilled me on having a second and third plan in the back of my mind. Now I wanted to know his plans.

"It no longer matters."

He tried to walk past me, but I grabbed his arm and stopped him. "No, really, tell me. What were you going to do?"

"I said it doesn't matter, okay?"

I refused to release his arm. I wasn't sure what to expect from him, what words of wisdom he might hold, but if he knew something I didn't, then he needed to spill it here and now. He had to tell me. Cole had taught me something important during my time with him—that I could be stubborn too.

He glanced at my hand clasped on his forearm and then back to me. "My plans seem to change every day." He gave a noncommittal shrug. "That's what I'm trying to tell you. Be prepared for anything and everything, because two weeks ago, I had decided to hole up here, make this place work for me, gather supplies, and wait this thing out. See if my family or *anyone* would come back. A week later when nothing changed, I tried fixing up an old motorcycle, thinking I would ride until I couldn't ride anymore, but then this happened." He paused as he reached up, his fingers hesitating for a moment as if rethinking his decision, before finally removing his worn beanie. He stared at the floor then squeezed his eyes shut.

My hand slipped from his arm. *Jeez.*

Patches of dark hair dotted his scalp, thin and wiry. Long pieces and short pieces mixed together, looking as though a toddler had gotten hold of a pair of scissors and decided to play barber. His smooth scalp peeked through the fine strands, and as he ran his hand lightly over his head, several clumps fell away like dandelion fluff, hardly attached at all. But that wasn't the worst part—the healing scabs and open sores were.

He grabbed the discarded hat, and with shaking fingers, shoved it back on, drawing it down over the tops of his ears.

"Are... are you sick?"

"I have to be, right?" The circles I'd noticed under his eyes the day before—something I had attributed to exhaustion—stood out as another unhealthy sign. He shook his head. "I don't know what's going on, but before all of this happened I was fine. I have a military physical to prove it, but whatever this is I do know it's getting worse. Much worse."

What does that mean? "You need to get to a hospital and be looked at." The suggestion came out of my mouth before I realized how impossible that might be.

He must have realized it too and gave a soft laugh. "I'll be sure to do that."

"See? This is another reason why I can't be your plan B, and why you need to stick to jumping on your motorcycle and trying to find a doctor." He wanted to follow me and climb a mountain when he might be dying? No way. He needed help, and by the looks of it, he needed it sooner than later.

"Finding help was several plan Bs ago. Besides, whatever is happening to me is getting worse. I gave up on the idea when my vision went a little haywire and I crashed my bike. It's ruined."

"Then walk there if you have to."

His shoulders rolled forward. "Walk where? Look around us."

"You have to try."

"No, actually, I don't."

I stood my ground, forcing him to look at me. "That's it then? You're not going to search for your family or try and get any help for yourself? You're just going to follow me and maybe die in the process?"

He let his breath out slowly and gave a single nod. "Yeah, I'll probably die one way or the other, so I may as well do it trying to help you."

"Help me? Why? Why would you do that?" Maybe his sickness had affected his brain too, because nothing he said made any sense whatsoever.

I felt fine. He didn't.

His eyes watered, but the tears didn't spill over. "Until yesterday, I didn't know anyone else existed, from Denver to here, not a living soul. You're the first person I've talked to in months, and that gave me hope. Before that..."

I waited for him to finish his sentence but after several seconds ticked by in silence, I nudged him on. "Before that, what?"

His eyes held a sadness I'd only seen one other time in my life—my father's face after he was told my mother had been killed. "You said you weren't a good survivor." He shook his head. "Well, I'm not either."

His words told me very little, but his hunched shoulders, the tears rimming his eyes, the small tremor of his bottom lip— something he fought to hide by biting it—and his overall defeated appearance told me exactly what his plan B had been. He didn't have to say the words for me to know.

"Then why did you run away from us?" Understanding his motives was almost as complicated as trying to figure Cole out. "Why did you leave? We could've all worked together and tried to find some help."

"Maybe, but I couldn't be sure. I didn't know what kind of games you were playing with me, so I planned to follow you to find out, except you ended up following me first."

"What are you talking about? I didn't follow you, and I'm not playing any games." Who the heck had time for mind games and weirdness at a time like this? Okay, bad question, because apparently Cole had, and this guy wasn't turning out to be much better, but still.

"The guy you keep talking about? The one you said you were traveling with?"

I nodded. "Cole? Yeah, what about him?"

"I watched you... for a long time before I talked to you. At first, I thought I was seeing things, confusing you for a store mannequin or something. I thought my eyes were playing tricks on me again."

I wanted to tell him me too, and that Cole had actually accused me of the same thing about seeing him—confusing a real person with a store advertisement—but the way he stared at me, the intensity and emotion in his eyes, kept me from opening my mouth. It wasn't the time to speak.

"You kept saying 'us' and 'him' and 'we'," he continued, "and even now you keep saying it, but the only person I ever saw at the mall, the entire time I was there, was you."

He can't be serious? I tipped my head to the side, incredulous. Who was playing games now? "Cole was running around the mall, maybe you didn't see him"—*how could he not have?*—"but you definitely heard him? He's a big guy and he was pounding the floor pretty hard."

He kept his eyes on me, unfazed. "I know you were on your own, which is scary, and you didn't know what I might do or if you could trust me, but now you know. If I had wanted to hurt you, I would've done it already. So, you can stop pretending with me. No more games, okay?"

"I... what... I don't." I pushed his shoulder. He might be deathly sick, but that wasn't an excuse for him to mess with me. "You stop pretending. You stop playing games!"

He raised his hand to stop me. "How long were you with him?"

"A few days."

"And before that?"

"I was in a bomb shelter in my backyard."

"Was he there with you, in the bomb shelter?"

"Of course not, it was just me and my cat. Why all the questions? This is getting really weird."

His eyes narrowed and his brow pinched together. He stepped away from me, moving with calculated steps, until the plush chair brushed against the back of his legs, and he sank into it. "You really think someone was there with you at the mall, don't you?"

No, not this again. What is it with these guys?

"I don't *think* anything. Cole *was* there! He's real! You can't make up that kind of crazy, and I'm not losing my mind, if that's what you're suggesting. You may not have seen him and he didn't see you, but that doesn't mean anything. Maybe your sickness is starting to affect more than just your hair."

Mean words, but this was going too far. He didn't say anything, but stared at me in such a way it forced me to take a small step backward.

I raised my hands. "What? Why are you looking at me like that? Are you planning to tell me I don't own a cat either or that all of this is a figment of my imagination? One big fat lie, a glitch in my brain?"

"No, I'm not. All of this is real, too real." His eyes remained on mine, and he leaned forward. "But I do think you're starting to get sick like me."

CHAPTER 30

"Nope! I'm not doing this. Cole told me you didn't exist. Now you're telling me he doesn't, and I'm telling you you're both nuts. This is the most bizarre experience I've ever had. I'm done. I'm done!" I knelt next to my bag and shoved my loose belongings inside. "I'm fine, by the way. I feel great, so I don't need your help."

He scooted to the edge of his seat. The faux leather crinkled with his movement. "I'm sorry. I didn't mean to scare you."

"Oh, really? Telling me the person who stitched my arm, saved me from a beastly tornado, and who kissed me isn't real, that I'm probably losing my mind and will end up with no hair on my head wasn't meant to scare me? Then let *me* apologize. I'm *so* sorry for reacting in a way you hadn't expected."

I swung my bag over one shoulder, and as I marched through the kitchen on the way to bathroom to fetch Callie, I pilfered two bottles of Nutella from the open cabinet. "I'm taking these. I think I've earned them." I shoved them into my bag.

He followed and did nothing to stop me. "Take whatever you want. I won't be needing any of it after today."

I spun around to face him. "Don't you dare try guilting me into letting you come along."

"I'm not."

"Yeah, you are. I want to make it clear, whatever you do from this point on is on you, not me. Do you understand?" I didn't want to think what he planned to do once I left. I refused to carry that responsibility.

"Of course."

I inched the bathroom door open, squatted down, and caught Callie's leash as she shot through the crack, trying to zip through my legs. She jerked backward, coming up short when the leash tightened. I gave her furry head a quick pat as a way of apologizing for knocking her on her behind. "I'm leaving, and I don't want you following me." I scooped her into my arms. "I mean it."

"I won't." He shifted and made room for me to pass him in the tight space of the hall.

I stopped mid-movement, trapping him against the wall, my chest against his. "I'm doing this on my own."

"Okay."

"I just want to find my dad and my brother, and for all of this to be over."

He offered a single nod. "I know."

"We're clear?"

"Yeah," he said. "We're clear."

He followed me into the balmy garage, watching me in the same way Cole had when I'd left him. Why couldn't I have found another female survivor? It would have been so much easier. No mind-games and nonsense, just hair braiding and drama—something I knew how to deal with.

I knelt next to the gap in the garage door, hardly believing I was about to leave another person in the span of two days. At one point, the idea of being alone would have put me in a panicked state. Now, I couldn't wait to be on my own and away from these guys and their insanity. Last people or not, I couldn't stand them.

But before crawling through the space, I stopped, turned around and looked at him again. "You said no one was at the mall, and I'm probably getting sick and that creating another person is my mind playing tricks on me. A symptom of being ill?"

He tugged on his beanie and leaned against the wall for support. "I'm only telling you what I saw and what I think might be happening to you."

I waved him off. "Yeah, yeah, okay, but then by that logic, maybe you're the one who's not real. Maybe you're the figment of my imagination. It's possible my sick brain created you."

I didn't really think any of those things. Both he and Cole were real, *very* real. I had felt Cole's lips on mine, and this boy touched and caressed the indents in my skin left by the plastic band. Minds could be tricky, but not that tricky.

I wasn't delusional or sick—well, not anymore. My fever was gone and the antibiotics had cleared my infection. For the past several days, I'd felt physically fine. Yeah, I had suffered a mini-meltdown the day before—a panic attack—but I'd suffered them long before the world started to fall apart. Nothing new.

I *was* fine.

He shrugged. "Then by that logic, maybe I am."

Great. His response didn't help me at all. "You're not going to try and convince me you're a real person?"

"What would be the point? Anything I do or say can be taken as real or not, depending on what you want to believe. I guess it's up to you to decide."

I let out a frustrated breath and shifted my anxious cat in my arms. "Forget it. It doesn't matter." I moved toward the gap, but stopped again. "Please go get some help. I'm not giving up, and I make a horrible survivor, but if I can do it, I know you can. So don't do anything crazy, okay?"

He sighed. "I'll try."

"No, like Yoda advised, 'Do. Or do not. There is no try', except don't do the 'do not' part, okay?" *Just shut up already.* I didn't know what I was saying anymore. Maybe I *was* losing my mind. I shook the thought off before it took root.

His lips curled in a semi-grin, then he coughed into his hand and wiped the spit off on his pants. The grin disappeared. "Okay."

I tried to shove Callie through the gap first, but she meowed and clawed her way backward, getting as far away from the hole as possible. "Stop it!" I jerked on her leash, but she arched her back, thwarting my efforts. "Fine, I'll go first." I'd drag her out if she gave me no other choice.

I pushed my backpack through the hole, doing my best to get it out of the way so I could crawl though without being hindered. Early afternoon sunlight swallowed my backpack and part of my arm, but in those few seconds the light touched my exposed skin, an intense heat branched out from the tips of my fingers all the way to my shoulder.

I screamed and yanked my arm inside. A hand to a hot burner, steam raising from a teakettle, touching the metal surface of an iron—none of it compared to the sensation that pricked my skin and heightened my nerves.

And I hadn't done anything, but reach outside.

He knelt next to me and moved to take my hand, but I jerked it away and cradled my seared limb to my chest. "No, don't touch it!"

"What did you do?" He tried again to touch my arm, but I shot him a look and he backed off, raising his hands like a white flag.

"Nothing! Ahh... it hurts!"

"I won't touch you, but you've got to show me what's going on so I can help." He inched closer, but kept his hands up. "I promise. I won't touch."

I eased my arm from the safety of my chest and balanced it in the air, not wanting to bump it against anything. If he touched it, I would kill him, but he didn't even attempt to grab my shaking arm.

After a moment, he released his breath and ran into the house. Callie's leash slipped through my fingers and she took off after him, using my injury to her benefit, but I didn't care. Good for her. No wonder she didn't want to go first through the gap in the garage door. She'd be a fried cat right now, if she had.

The burning pain continued to throb. I tried to replay the scene over in my head: Did I touch the metal garage door? Did the sun reflect off something, intensifying its rays? My mind ran wild searching for logical explanations but ended up settling on "this is impossible," and "this makes no sense." No one gets sunburned in seconds. No one. And if the sun was that hot, then the house and everything surrounding it should have gone up in flames, spontaneously combust — but it didn't. *Thank heavens.*

But we didn't get tornados or electrical storms or bowling ball sized hail either.

He skipped the two garage steps, jumping over them, and skidded to my side. "Put your arm out."

Heck no! "What are you going to do?"

"It'll help, I promise." He held his hand out in front of him, palm up as if waiting for a gift to be placed in it. "Come on, trust me."

I took a deep breath, held it, and then laid my arm in his outstretched hand. I bit my lip when my sensitive skin made contact with his, but didn't yank my arm away. If he had an answer to end my suffering, then I'd play along.

"This should help." He used his teeth to unscrew the cap to a bottle of water before pouring the cool liquid over my burns. "How's that feel?"

"Better." Not by much, but it did help some. The fiery feeling seemed to dissipate a little.

"It's only a mild burn, no blisters or anything, so that's good news."

"Good news?" My eyes about popped out of my head. "Maybe it is, but how did this even happen in the first place? I got sunburned in less than ten seconds! That's the opposite of good. It's bad, *very* bad."

He took a second bottle of water from where he'd tucked it into his waistband and poured its contents over my burn as well. "I gave up trying to make sense of all this weeks ago. Why does the sky sometimes turn green? I have no idea. Why does the temperature drop to near freezing one day and then boiling hot the next? Not a clue. I don't think we're supposed to make sense of it. We're only supposed to try and live through it, somehow."

For a minute, I forgot about my arm. He'd said, *"We're only supposed to try and live through it."* I took it as a good sign. Maybe he'd given up on following through with his plan B.

"So, it's not hard enough being the only people left, but now Mother Nature is setting out to try and kill us too? That's not even fair." I didn't even care if my statement resembled a toddler's. None of this was fair.

What was next, huh? Hurricanes and volcanic eruptions in our land-locked city in the West? This was the kind of thing people wrote best-selling books about, or made millions of dollars on by producing action-packed movies, starring Tom Cruise. This was far-fetched, not real!

"I agree it's not fair, but we have to deal with Mother Nature's tricks anyway. There's no getting around it." He poured the last of the water over my arm. "How does it feel now?"

"Still hurts, but better."

"I know you wanted to get away from me and everything, but you're stuck here for a while. At least until the sun goes down. You can leave later tonight or try again tomorrow. Everything tends to be better the next day, if you think you can wait that long."

"I don't have much of a choice, do I?"

He stood, held out his hand to me, and helped me to my feet. "I guess not."

"What did you mean by the sky turning green? What's that about?" I followed him back into the house, careful to avoid any specks of sunshine coming through the cracks in the wood or sneaking in through the partially covered windows.

He shrugged as he went about closing the drapes and twisting the blinds to block the sun. "I haven't a clue. I've only seen it twice so far. Something to add to the ever-growing list of weird things. Nothing surprises me anymore."

"But the sun? Have you seen that happen before? And what would I have done if I were outside when it got this hot?" I grabbed a kitchen towel from where it hung over a cabinet door, drenched it with a bottle of water, and wrapped it around my arm. The cool wetness eased the sting of the burn. "I'd end up with third degree burns, or worse." A minute in the direct sunlight, and I'd have blisters. Ten minutes or more, my skin would be falling from my bones. Or at least, those were the images my mind created. Vivid and frightening.

"No, I haven't seen that before. It's something new." He leaned against the counter, watching me. "Whatever is happening out there seems to be getting worse too."

CHAPTER 31

"Hungry?" He placed a small pot on top of the kerosene camping stove and proceeded to light it. "I've got a can of stew if you're—"

"No, no stew." The waxy essence still clung to my mouth from the first time I'd eaten canned stew—Cole's offering when he'd found me at Rite Aid. Thinking about canned stew brought the tinged taste to memory. Strange this boy would offer me the same thing. "Anything else would be fine though."

He nodded, removed a different can from the cupboard, and began the task of heating the small meal over the tiny flame. "If you're thirsty, there's soda in the fridge, warm of course, but you can help yourself."

"The fridge?" I hadn't dared open it due to my past experiences. Meat, eggs, and cheese did not keep for more than a few days without cooling temps to hold mold and rot at bay. Remembering caused a shiver to snake across my shoulder blades. *So nasty.* But soda? I'd risk it for that.

"Yeah, it seemed like a perfect place to store it. Go on. It's all good." He stirred the pot with a spoon, clanking it against the sides with each rotation; a small metallic noise to fill the silence.

I continued to hug my burned arm to my chest, and used my good arm to open the fridge door. No light came on, like it would have under normal circumstances, but the light from candles and lanterns shone on the treasure of flavored goodness inside. I settled on a orange Fanta, hoping that even though the soda was warm it still might live up to the memories of my past—pizza, orange soda, breadsticks, and salad with vinegar-and-oil dressing.

My stomach growled. *Oh, how I miss Tony's Pizza Pie!*

Would I ever experience normalcy again? Pizza? Cold soda? A simple fridge light?

"It's ready." He motioned to the table, and I squashed my memories, and sat my bottled soda on the flat surface. He waited for me to scoot out one of the chairs before he approached with two steaming bowls, placing one in front of me and the other on the opposite side of the table.

Instead of sitting down, he went to a cabinet, took down a box of crackers, and grabbed a warm soda for himself from the fridge. Orange, just like mine.

The hot tomato soup wasn't pizza, not by a long shot, but it hit the spot and settled the ache of my belly. "Thanks," I said. "It's good."

"It isn't much, but it'll do." He lifted his spoon to his lips and blew across the surface before placing it in his mouth. His face pinched together, for only a flicker of a moment, and he lowered the spoon.

"You okay?" He kind of looked like he might throw up.

He nodded. "Yeah, I'm fine. Just give me a second." True to his words, it seemed to pass and he smiled at me to ease my worry. "Go on, eat. You're too skinny."

Me, skinny? Maybe, but he obviously hadn't looked in a mirror lately. I had a good twenty or more pounds on him. He was the one needing to eat.

"Please." He motioned to the bowl.

I slurped my soup from the spoon and drank the warm bubbly soda as though nothing had happened. "What I wouldn't give for an apple or a piece of bacon right now." I dipped a cracker into my bowl. "Something fresh and not processed."

Normal conversation in an abnormal situation.

"Everything fresh is dead." He showed no emotion, a straight-faced fact giver, and took a small sip from his bottle. "All of it."

"Yes, I'm totally aware, that's why I said it, but wouldn't it be nice if something fresh *wasn't*? I could go for a thick piece of homemade bread about now. What about you? What do you miss most?"

He shrugged. "I don't miss any one thing over anything else. I pretty much miss it all."

I nodded. Now that I thought about it, I pretty much missed it all too. Food. People. Even standing in really long lines or being shoved around on over-crowded school buses. I missed lettuce, peaches, warm showers, indoor plumbing, traffic jams, and barking dogs. All of it. The noise and taste of living. We weren't living right now. Not really.

He reached across the table and held out his hand to me. "I'm Dylan."

If Cole were here, he'd have pointed out my social foibles with some smartass remark about rudeness and my lack of grace, but since he wasn't, I took Dylan's hand and shook it. "Tess."

"I wish we could've met under better circumstances, Tess," he said as he released my hand. "But I'm not sure our paths would have crossed any other way."

"Yeah, probably not. I've never been to Denver."

He smiled. "I haven't been back here since I was a kid. Maybe twelve years ago, I think?"

I leaned forward. "So, what does it look like between here and Denver?"

He placed his spoon down next to his bowl. "Looks about the same as it does here, though some places are worse than others."

"What did you see?" I scooted forward even more. "Before everything went crazy, I mean?" We had several hours to kill, until the stupid sun and its death rays disappeared from the sky. I might as well try to use the time to cipher useful information from the guy.

His eyes lowered and the fingers of his right hand traced the checkered pattern of the Formica tabletop. "Everything happened really fast. Probably a lot like what you saw here. It was as if pieces of the sky caught on fire and then came crashing to the ground, destroying everything."

Orange and white streaks had tarnished the otherwise clear sky and the ground shook below my feet as Dad rushed me to the bunker. I'd had only moments, seconds really, to take in what was happening—my demolished house, the mushroom clouds of smoke, and the neighbors' cries. Not enough time to come to any conclusion, but enough to know all hell had broken loose.

"It seemed to go on forever," he continued, still tracing the lines in the table, not looking at me at all. "But maybe it only lasted ten or fifteen minutes. I can't be sure. Most everyone at my college campus panicked and took off running through the snow—some to the dorms, others to the art building or library, but a whole lot more stood in the square, transfixed by the flecks of fire in the sky."

He glanced at me, quiet for a moment. "Nowhere was safe, not really, and I think somewhere in my shocked mind that knowledge kept me from standing there. I started running, away from everything and everyone, not sure why exactly. I tossed my backpack on the ground and ran—my track scholarship kicking in, I guess."

He shook his head. "Good thing too, because I'd only made it a few miles away when another round hit the campus. The impact knocked me off my feet and sent me flying. Kind of what you'd see in the movies, only it felt like slow motion. Had I stayed with the others, I wouldn't be here now. Most of the campus disappeared into a crater."

Jeez.

I slipped another cracker into my mouth, chewing slowly, but kept my eyes on him. Dylan's account held me spellbound. He knew way more than I did.

"After awhile, things settled down some, no more rocks from the sky, but people were terrified, coming out to the streets or what was left of them, wandering around as if in a daze, unsure what to do or where to even begin. Parents cried and screamed over the tops of everyone else because the elementary school had collapsed. Most houses had crumbled in on themselves and people began digging through the rubble for survivors, but I just climbed to my feet and ran past them all." His fingers stilled. "I ran. I should have stopped and helped, but the thought didn't even occur to me."

"Maybe you'd suffered a concussion when you fell?" A concussion was possible. He had to have been in shock too. Nobody could think normally in those kinds of situations.

He shrugged. "Maybe. Still doesn't make me feel any better about it."

"But there were people, right? You saw them? Heard them?"

He removed the cap from his bottle of soda, placed it on the table but didn't drink from it. He spun the cap around in circles. "Yeah."

"Okay, that's good. Where did they go? Those people who survived all this *have* to be somewhere." I don't think I could have leaned forward any further. This wasn't the end of the world — only a temporary setback. People were out there, somewhere. He'd seen them!

"I have no idea."

I slapped the table, rattling the bottles of soda and surprising myself. "You have no idea? How's that even possible? Where were you?"

His gaze narrowed, focusing on me. "Where were *you*?"

"I was stuck in an underground bunker for the past couple of months, and didn't get to see anything. Five minutes, maybe, was all I had before my dad shoved me down there. If you feel as though I'm drilling you, I am, because I have a lot of questions and so far I have very few answers."

"Consider yourself lucky then, because I saw more than I'd ever want to, and I still don't know what happened or where

everyone went. Not really. Believe it or not, I have questions too."
He ran a quick hand over the top of his beanie. "Only, I don't
think I'll make it long enough to get any answers."

I slumped down in my seat, and sighed. "Don't say that."

"It's the truth." He picked up his spoon and attempted a
couple of bites, but never placed the spoon in his mouth.

I contemplated what to do or say. Nothing came to mind that
wouldn't make me look like a real jerk.

"Stop staring at me like that." He kept his gaze down while
he moved the spoon around in the bowl, so I had no idea how he
knew I was watching him.

"I'm sorry." I didn't feel much like eating anymore, but
turned my spoon around in my bowl like he did and tried my
best not to look at him.

"I don't know everything. I wish I did, for you, but I feel like I
have a handful of pieces to a puzzle—not nearly enough to make
a full picture."

"Well, that's more than I have." I rested my elbows on the
table. "Anything is better than nothing, believe me, so if you have
any idea where everyone went, any idea at all, you need to tell
me."

"But you want hope, right?"

I dropped my hands in my lap. "Yeah, I do. What's so wrong
with that? Hope is all we have."

"So what happens when I can't give you any?" His dark eyes
followed mine, scaring me a little with his intensity.

"You've already given me some by telling me there are
people who survived all of this."

He shook his head slowly. "Not *are*, Tess. *Were*. There *were*
people."

Were? What did that even mean? That didn't even make any
sense. "That's not—"

He straightened in his chair, leaning slightly toward me, his
eyes on mine. "The military swooped in—jeeps, tanks, trucks,
hazmat suits—blasting sirens and yelling at everyone to evacuate.
At first, I thought them being there was a blessing because of all

the looting and fighting going on, but it didn't take long to realize they weren't there to bring order." His Adam's apple bobbed and fell as he swallowed hard.

"They were forcing people to leave and they weren't kind about it either, yanking them from vehicles and their homes at gunpoint, and giving them no time at all to gather their belongings. They weren't helping; they were herding. That's what it seemed like anyway."

Military people always seemed rather rough. They have to be. "But they took them away from here?"

"Yes... and no."

He was impossible. "See? That doesn't help me. Either they did or they didn't. Tell me which way they went. Did everyone head north to Canada or east toward New York? South maybe? That's what I need to know."

He smirked. "No one left Colorado, Tess. That's what I'm trying to say."

"You're confusing me."

"I'm not meaning to."

"Then where *is* everyone? No one is here either! That's too many people to not be *anywhere*." We were going around in circles, and it was driving me crazy.

He slumped back in his chair, glanced at the floor and took a deep breath. His eyes returned to mine, and he finally released the breath he held. "They're here, Tess. If you look hard enough, you'll see the graves."

CHAPTER 32

"They killed everyone?" A load of invisible bricks dangled around my neck and pressed against my chest, heavy and painful. My fingers trembled, and I forced myself to take several deep breathes. *Don't lose it, Tess. Don't freak out. Not now.* Dylan had to be wrong.

"The best way to get everyone out of the area would be by plane, right?" He'd answered my question with a question and waited for me to nod before going on.

Of course, a quick flight to somewhere safe would be the best option since the roads were a tangled mess of rubble, buckled pavement, and debris. It would be the difference between a flight taking a couple of hours versus driving for weeks along a mish-mash of broken highways and back roads.

"Planes came in, Tess. Dozens of them. They dotted the sky like an impressive flock of birds, and for a moment, I wondered if I'd made the wrong decision. Maybe I should have followed the group instead of dodging them." He sat up straight in the chair and rested his arms on the table. "But when they swooped through the area, over and over, hovering a few miles above everyone, never landing, I knew something wasn't right."

"Maybe they couldn't land." My brain ran wild, trying to make sense of the insensible. "The roads were a mess, so it's safe to assume the runways weren't any better."

He shook his head "I thought that too, until they started to spray something from the tail of the planes. One plane would fly overhead, drop its load, like crop-dusting a field, and then a second would follow doing the same. One right after another, so quick, dumping it on people, houses, buildings."

"And you saw this? For real?" I didn't want to believe what he was saying. How could I? This was nothing but science fiction bullshit. It had to be.

He pushed his chair away from the table, grabbing both his bowl and mine. "You think I'm making this up? Why would I do that?" He strode into the kitchen and dropped both bowls in the sink.

"No, I just... I don't...." I couldn't speak clearly because I couldn't *think* clearly. "If this is true, then why would they do that?"

"It *is* true, and I have no idea." He rested against the counter as if needing a break and stared at me. "The government trying to find an easy solution to a pretty big problem, maybe?"

"And killing everyone is the easiest solution? How's that a solution at all?"

"Look around us. Look at me!" He motioned to his hat. "I'm sick and dying, so whatever fell from space did more than destroy buildings and wipe out populations of people. It set off some sort of toxic weather-transforming chaos. We're either breathing it in or it's seeping in through our skin. Either way, it's killing us."

"Toxic?" I shook my head. "Do you mean radiation?"

He shrugged. "If it was radiation, we'd all be dead right now, but something else, something just as harmful, yes."

I leaned forward. "But I feel fine."

"You haven't been exposed as long as I have. For your sake, I hope I'm wrong about all of this."

For my sake, I hoped he was wrong too, but I didn't say so.

"Can you imagine if the government had had to care for millions of sick people like me? How would they explain that? How would they even physically *do* that?"

I shifted sideways in my chair to look at him. "That's just it, millions of people! We're not talking about a few thousand, but millions. You can't kill millions of people and hide that very well."

"They don't have to hide it. They evacuated those who weren't killed in the initial blasts, and then wiped them out. The bodies are there, Tess—all over the west desert."

"You saw this?"

"Yeah, I did." He swallowed hard and took in a deep breath. "And I can't unsee it."

I didn't want to believe him, but I did. My stomach tightened, and I leaned back against my chair with my hand pressed against my stomach. This was too much to take in. "What about the rest of the world? Why aren't they here helping or stopping our government from doing this?"

"I'm sure the rest of the world is too busy handling the fallout in their own way to care what's happening here or how it's being dealt with."

"How big is this?" It was hard to think about other parts of the world going through this same thing. I thought it had only happened here.

"I don't know, but we can't have been the only country hit by this, and even if we were, everyone will be looking for a fast way to fix it, even if it's only to put a Band-Aid over the top."

I pushed away from the table and stood. "This is completely nuts! I don't know what you saw, but you're losing it." This wasn't how the government worked, not at all. Okay, maybe a little bit, but not to this extent. Yes, some officials might be shady and corrupt, but murdering people, *lots* of people, to fix the situation with no one stepping in to stop it? No, not possible.

He shrugged. "Maybe I am, but let me ask you a question?" I didn't indicate one way or the other, so he must have taken my heated silence as an okay to go on. "Where is the government now?"

I had wondered the same thing for a while, but there was no way I would tell him and feed into his delusions.

"No one is here fixing anything. Doesn't that seem the least bit weird to you?" He ignored the fact that I hadn't answered his first question. "I mean, it would be hard to fix this mess, but no one's doing *anything*. Remember the Katrina disaster?"

I nodded.

"The government was slow to come to the rescue then, but they did come. We're talking months now and still there's no one here attempting to fix anything. No Red Cross. No National Guard. No rescue volunteers. No one. It's pretty apparent to me they don't plan to come either, because it's too dangerous for anyone to be here."

"But they did come once. You saw them. The planes—"

"And look what they did." He threw his hands up. "Believe what you want, but I know what I saw."

"If they were spraying everyone, how did you walk away? How did you end up so lucky?" There were too many loopholes, too much that didn't fit. Besides, he didn't think Cole existed, so how much could I really trust anything he said anyway? He wasn't reliable.

He opened his mouth to answer, but stopped. A puzzled expression creased his forehead and pinched his brows together. He reached up and touched the space below his nose. When he drew his hand back, blood coated his fingertips.

"Lucky?" He shook his head, his eyes widening. His hands quivered. "I'm far from being lucky."

By the time I crossed the small room to help, two tiny streams of blood ran from both his nostrils, flowed over his lips, and dripped from his chin. So much blood. So fast.

I caught him before he hit the floor.

"Dylan!"

His eyes rolled back, and I held his limp head in my lap.

"Don't do this." *What do I do? What do I do?*

With shaking hands, I grabbed a dirty dishtowel from a hook and pressed it to his face, pushing harder than perhaps I should have. Blood soaked through the material, wetting my fingers, as though the barrier didn't exist. The cloth wasn't working and seemed to absorb the blood like a sponge instead of staunching the flow.

I tossed the towel aside—*useless thing*—and pinched his nostrils closed, trying to remember how Dad used to stop my nose bleeds as a kid. *Don't tip your head back, Tess. Lean forward.*

Gurgles rose in the back of his throat, and I rolled him to his side, lifting him slightly, worried he'd choke to death before the bleeding stopped. He coughed several times, splattering blood over the kitchen cabinet and sides of the fridge, but his eyes remained closed and his body heavy in my arms.

"Come on!" My fingers were slick with his blood which made gripping his nostrils difficult, so I switched hands, nearly dropping him on the floor. It seemed like no matter what I tried— pinching his nose, raising his head, rolling him to the side— nothing worked.

A trickle of blood slipped from his ear, oozing from the dark cavern and down over his lobe. A sob shot through my closed lips. *No, no, no!* This couldn't be happening.

"Wake up!" I wiped my blood-covered hand on my jeans and pinched his nose with a better grip. Several times, I struggled to get him to sit up. His head flopped backward and his limp body resisted. "You were going to try and get help, remember? No giving up. Please!" Callie meowed from her safe place on the back of the couch, adding to my pleas for Dylan to open his eyes.

Blood ran down his face, his shirt growing thick with it, and both my hands were covered in red nearly to my elbow. "I'll let you come with me. You can climb a stupid mountain at my side. I changed my mind. We'll do this together." *Stop bleeding. Come on.*

I lowered his head to my lap again, unable to hold his heaviness upright. "Please, Dylan."

His body shuddered, quaking against mine, mini-seizers, twisting and contorting his features. Then he fell still, his breathing labored.

"We'll find my dad. He'll know what to do. I know you think you'll never find the answers, but we will. We'll do it together." My fingers shook as I pinched his nostrils tighter, and rolled his head to the side to allow thick globs to slip from his mouth. "Don't do this."

His eyes flew open, but he looked through me. "Go." One simple word, strained and barely audible. The stream of blood from his ear grew more intense, and the whites of his eyes swirled a deep red as I stared down at him.

I shook my head. "No, we can—"

"Go."

"I'm not leaving you!"

He coughed and choked up more blood. Crimson tears trickled from the corners of his eyes. "Get out of here, Tess." His hands trembled.

"I can't—"

"Now!" He frightened me with his outburst, something I hadn't expected from him in his weakened state, and my hand fell away from his face. I reached to clasp his nose again, but he batted away my efforts. "Run from here!"

He could hardly move, but he managed to slide to the floor, out of my lap, and squeezed his eyes shut as he whispered, "Go before you can't."

I didn't move.

"Please."

I scooted backward, away from him, but his blood on the linoleum made getting to my feet difficult, and I struggled to stand. My heart raced, my breath burned in my lungs as I held onto it, afraid to breathe, while I looked at Dylan's crumpled frame on the floor.

He shook all over; several violent tremors racked his body, before leaving him silent and unmoving.

"Dylan?"

He didn't respond, but lay face down in his own blood.

I ran from the room, my boots slipping and leaving red streaks in my wake across the linoleum and shag carpet.

Callie shrieked and hissed when I scooped her into my arms, coating her fur in blood. I pressed her to my chest and sprinted for the garage, refusing to glance at Dylan lying there. I couldn't.

The sun hadn't quite set, but hung low enough that dark shadows came to life where the light couldn't reach. Though gambling my own safety, risking a massive sunburn, I couldn't stay there any longer.

Dylan had told me to run from here, and I had every intention of doing so.

I shoved Callie inside my blood-covered jacket, knelt next to the gap in the garage door, and thrust my hand through the hole.

Only a second.

I yanked it back inside.

No searing pain.

I did it again, leaving it longer, and when nothing happened — the shade saving me — I rolled to my back, and shifted through the opening feet-first.

My backpack remained in the exact spot where I'd left it earlier, though it sat upright instead of on its side as I remembered. But what did it matter? I grabbed it by the straps, threw it over my shoulders, and glanced from side to side. *We've got to get out of here.*

Callie clawed her way up my chest and poked her head out through the opening of my jacket. Her head rested below my chin. She seemed content to stay right there, looking around, and I was grateful I didn't have to fight her.

Streaks of sunlight danced across the ground, peeking between bent trees and damaged homes. I stuck to the shadows, moving from one dark spot to another, not daring to test out the sun's strength. Not yet. My arm ached, but in the scheme of things, it meant nothing. It actually felt good to focus on the physical pain, because my mental pain threatened to tear me apart.

I picked up the pace, skipping between buildings, dodging the light.

The very moment the sun slipped beyond the horizon, casting everything in darkness, I held onto the straps of my backpack and started running down the middle of the road. My feet hit the cracked pavement, beating out a painful rhythm that matched my heart. Warm air whipped my hair around my face, and loose strands hung in my eyes.

Tears screwed with my vision, but it didn't matter. I didn't know where I was going, but that didn't matter either. Not now.

After miles of intense sprinting, carrying a heavy backpack on my aching shoulders and with a cat clinging to my shirt for dear life, I dropped to my knees under an elm tree. Lightning had split the large trunk in two and the branches fell in the shape of an M, touching the ground on either side.

Sobs tangled with my jagged breath, and I hit the dead trunk with my fists before pressing my face against the rough surface. *Damn it!* I wiped at my tears, but only succeeded in smearing Dylan's blood across my cheeks.

I'd only known of his existence for a little more than a day, and yet, his impact had been huge. His words, his illness... left me reeling.

I allowed the bag to fall from my shoulders, and leaned my back against the trunk of the tree, hugging Callie's warm little body to me. She didn't fight me, and I rubbed my wet cheeks against her furry head while I continued to cry. Maybe she'd sensed my need. Whatever caused her to allow my affection, I appreciated it.

Had she rebuked me, I wasn't sure I could have handled it.

Being alone and afraid really *really* sucked.

CHAPTER 33

I shuffled along, putting one foot in front of the other. My thoughts rolled around inside my head without latching onto anything for more than a few seconds at a time, which might have been a good thing. The moon lit my way for most of the night, but when it disappeared completely behind dark clouds, I took my first break in hours, and searched through the pockets of my backpack. I knew I'd put a flashlight in there somewhere, but I couldn't find it. I could have sworn I'd packed it in the same spot as my first-aid kit and knife.

My fingers wrapped around a thick elastic band, something unrecognizable, and I removed the odd item—a headlamp. *Ok-ay.* I switched the buttons on top and the bright LED lights came to life, forcing me to blink and look away to let my eyes adjust. *I don't remember packing this.*

Cole had insisted a headlamp would be the way to go, freeing my hands, but I'd wanted the mini-flashlight instead because the headlamp squeezed my skull. I turned it over several times. No, I hadn't packed it, but I slipped it on my head anyway and tweaked the beams. Light was light.

The six-foot area around me brightened as I turned my head from one side to the other, taking in my surroundings. Everything looked a lot better in the dark—less depressing. I sighed, but kept the lamp on, the desire to see outweighing the desire to hide from the destruction around me. I'd have to keep in mind the battery life, because this sucker had to get me to Rockport Lodge, and I didn't know if Cole had packed fresh batteries in his haste to steal my flashlight and replace it with the headlamp.

The tiny beam of light fell on my backpack, hitting it just right, and a brown bottle in the mesh side-pocket gave me pause. *What the heck?* I knew for a fact I hadn't put it there. First the headlamp, now this?

Cole had administered the antibiotics for my infection since I had a canny way of forgetting to take my medications. Even though I felt better, he insisted I needed to finish out the regimen to be safe. For once, he'd actually taken the adult approach.

Several pills rattled inside the plastic container, and I whipped my head around, casting light into the darkness.

The reflection made it impossible to see too far into the distance, so I reached up and switched the light off. A few bushes down the block swayed, and my breath caught in my throat. "Cole?"

Both my heart and expectations fell when the light breeze stopped and the bushes stilled. They only moved when the wind blew. *Damn.*

I wasn't nuts. He had to have followed me, at least part of the time, because the headlamp and the bottle of antibiotics weren't in my bag when I'd left him back at the mall. I'd been in such a hurry to get away from him, I hadn't thought far enough ahead to realize we had split the heavier items—he had the tent, I carried the camp stove; he had the ax, I had the tarp in my pack; he had my antibiotics, I carried his gum. We'd planned to hike to Rockport together, a team, but I'd ruined that by being a stupid teenage girl, determined to prove how right I was.

I wasn't right and knew it now.

Nothing good had come from leaving him. Nothing at all.

I slipped my leg through the loop of Callie's leash, giving her a bit of freedom, then turned the headlamp back on and decided to take a closer look at my backpack. Each unzipped pocket produced something new—a cigarette lighter, a package of M&Ms, a bag of granola, and a piece of paper folded into a tiny square—none of which I had placed there.

He must have shoved stuff into my pack when it sat outside the garage door, but how? The sun had fried me; it would have blistered and boiled him. Despite the logistics of it being impossible, I was grateful to know he'd been close by.

It also saddened me. Had we been together, we might have been able to help Dylan.

No more crying.

I pinched the bridge of my nose and closed my eyes for a moment, pushing aside thoughts of my reckless decisions leading to reckless results. Knowing there might have been a chance, however slim, would always haunt me.

I hadn't eaten anything since my meal with Dylan, but didn't feel like stomaching any of the snacks Cole had snuck into my bag. I shoved the food items and cigarette lighter back in my pack, but held onto the folded piece of paper. It drew my interest more than any of the other things he'd given me.

I carefully opened it, making sure not to rip the paper, and aimed the beams on the headlamp to make out his scrawled handwriting.

> *Tess,*
> *I'm sorry.*
> *I'm nearby if you need anything. I'm nearby if you don't.*
> *I'll leave it up to you to let me know.*
> *-Cole*

I undid Callie's leash from my ankle, hooked her to my backpack, and scrambled to my feet. White light from my headlamp swiveled as I turned in a circle, searching the darkness for any signs of him. What did he mean by nearby? How nearby was he? *Please be really nearby.*

He could say insensitive stuff to me. He could call me a kid, and do dumb things like push me around in a cart and throw chocolate bars in my direction. I no longer cared. I just wanted him here with me.

"Cole!" My voice carried in the cool air. I waited and listened for his response, expecting him to clamber from the shadows at any moment. Bushes and trash rattled around with the breeze, and I turned my head with each movement, ready to have him back... wanting him back.

But every noise left me disappointed.

I snapped off the headlamp and strained to catch any sound indicating he had heard me. "This is me letting you know!"

Still nothing.

Where is he?

Callie meowed and rubbed against my ankles, but I ignored her. I held the letter in my tight fist and called his name again. He'd given me a lifeline I didn't deserve—childish behavior he had every right to ignore—and I wouldn't abuse it this time. *Please don't ignore me.*

I thought I could leave him, leave Dylan, and do this all on my own. How had I ever thought I could find Dad without anyone's help? Dylan's death had destroyed my resolve, and shattered my false bravado. At one time, I may have been able to do it all—climb the mountain, save Dad and Toby—but now, I doubted it.

My anger and ego seemed to get me into unnecessary trouble.

I waited and watched. Seconds turned into minutes and minutes started piling on top of one another, ticking by. Callie scratched at my leg, demanding attention. She meowed and clawed at me until I gave in.

I sighed. "He's not coming back, is he?"

She stood on her back legs and stretched up. I scooped her into my arms, dug a piece of dried meat out of my pack, and then tucked her and the treat inside my jacket.

I'd stood there long enough, knowing I should go, but still looked around one final time. "Please, Cole," I whispered. Tears rimmed my eyes, but I bit my lip and refused to cry.

I'd made this stupid choice, leaving him behind. Now I had to live with it.

I grabbed my pack and slipped my arms through the straps. It felt so much heavier than when I had carried it before, but I shifted it to a more comfortable spot on my shoulders, and started walking.

The sun would rise soon, and I needed to find a place to stay until I knew the rays wouldn't burn me like before.

Callie snuggled inside my coat, my backpack hung from my shoulders, and Cole's note remained crumbled in my hand.

I couldn't let go of it.

Over half the derailed train lay toppled on its side. A large portion of the connected cars slid down the hill and the first few in line disappeared into the ravine below—a domino effect that only seemed to end when the engine hit the river's bottom. Maybe broken train cars wasn't the safest place to hole up, but given my options—which were none—I chose to call it home for the day.

A few cars remained upright on the tracks, and I refused to think about how little it would take for the boxcars below to shift and tug the others off the rail. Yeah, I tried not to think about that at all.

The sun revealed itself over the top of the distant mountains, and its rays highlighted everything to the west, crawling toward me as it grew higher in the sky. The rickety train would have to shelter me, so I removed my pack and tossed it in through one of the open doors before gripping the ladder.

Callie screeched from inside my jacket, the lucky feline riding in comfort as I walked all night, and I shushed her. "It's okay. I've got you." I gave her a reassuring pat.

My shoulders ached from carrying the backpack, and when I reached from one ladder rung to another, a burning sensation rocketed across my shoulder blades. In shape people, who worked out in gyms lifting weights and drinking protein shakes, should be the doomsday survivors. They had it going on. Not people like me, who enjoyed TV marathons and used sweatpants for pajamas. Somehow this was all backward, but despite the pain, I managed to work my tired body into the empty train car.

The left side doors slid closed easy enough, but the ones on the right side wouldn't budge, which was probably for the best since it allowed some light to enter, instead of casting me into stifling darkness. I dragged my bag to one end, as far from the doors as possible, and flopped down with my back against the wall. I'd never been so tired.

Callie poked her head out through the top of my jacket, meowed, and then licked my chin. *So sweet.* I kissed the top of her furry head. "As long as we've got each other, we'll be okay."

I had to believe that.

"You're not sleepy anymore, are you?" I unzipped my jacket and placed Callie on her feet. She arched her back and stretched out the kinks in her limbs, then took a few tentative steps, exploring the confines of the train car. "I know you want to play, but I've got to get some sleep." As if on cue, I yawned, proving the depths of my exhaustion.

I kicked off the boots from my aching feet and set them to the side. Marin Peterson wouldn't want them back, not in this shape, but she'd be impressed with how well they'd held together. My feet were thankful for the release, and I wiggled my toes inside my dirty socks. I removed those as well, made a ball with them, and tossed it to my cat. She attacked it and batted it around. A sad smile curved my lips. She'd be fine.

Sleep pulled at my eyelids, so I rummaged through my pack, yanked out my sleeping bag, a bottle of water, and a packet of cat food. After setting Callie up with the essentials, I tied her leash to the pack good and tight and placed some newspaper in the corner.

"Sorry, girl, but if I don't get some sleep, I won't be any good for either of us." I shook out the sleeping bag and crawled inside. No matter that the wooden floor wasn't comfortable at all, because the very act of stretching out my body and being off my feet drew a contented sigh from my lips and I closed my eyes.

I hoped for dreams to come and carry me away from reality, but didn't fully expect them to.

I hadn't dreamt in a long time, and began to wonder if I remembered how.

CHAPTER 34

Time, the realm of minutes and hours, no longer applied—only light and darkness and the space in between. When I opened my eyes, I had no idea whether the time was nine at night or three in the morning. It didn't really matter, though I hoped I hadn't wasted too many hours that should have been used to find my family.

My body and mind had needed the extended sleep so much that I'd experienced one of the best nights—or I should say days—of sleep in a long time despite the hard boxcar floor. But as I rolled to my side, my neck, back, and hips protested my sudden movement. *Not good.* I took it easy, sat up in the darkness, and stretched each of my limbs in turn to work out the knots in my muscles. It felt like I had literally not moved a muscle the entire time I'd slept.

Moonlight flittered through the open door, splashing over the wooden floorboards, but not enough to pierce the dark corners. I reached for my backpack to find the headlamp I'd discarded earlier, but my fingers brushed over Callie's leash, reminding me of what was really important. *The poor girl, forced to watch me sleep for hours.* I planned to make it up to her with lots of love and a few extra treats. She'd been so good to not bug me, and deserved a showering of kitty-loving attention.

I whistled low and tugged the leash to draw her to me, but it didn't resist as I'd expected and snapped toward me, empty of one cat and her harness. *What? No!*

I fought against my sleeping bag, struggling to maneuver my body from the tight confines, and felt around in the darkness until my fingers found the much-needed headlamp. "Callie? Hey, girl!" I clicked the small buttons, bringing it to life, and brightening the interior of the train car.

She'd disappeared.

I was all alone.

My heart plummeted to my stomach. How in the world had she managed to get the harness unlatched from the leash? Impossible, but obviously hours left unsupervised had given her time to figure it out. *Damn it.*

"Callie!" I scrambled to my feet, forgoing socks and shoes, and ran to the opening of the train car. I aimed the small light into the darkness, knowing she could be anywhere, but hoping her escape had been a recent one and she hadn't gone too far. "Callie! Here, kitty!"

I climbed down the ladder, skipping rungs. My toes touched the cool earth, and I stood there unsure where to look first. "Come on, Callie. Don't do this to me." *Please be here, please.*

Not knowing quite what to do, I skipped from one upright car to another, casting light in the open doors and under each box car, but no cat meowed or stared back at me. Such a little thing, the vast darkness could easily swallow her up. I might walk right by her and never know it.

I berated myself for sleeping so long, for not paying attention to her, and not being a better cat owner during an apocalyptic situation. A harness! What a dumb thing to put on a cat! I should have bought a pet crate or carrier to keep her safe when not watching her. They had been right there too, on the shelf of the pet store back at the very beginning! What was I thinking? *Dumb, dumb, dumb.*

She'd been at my side the entire time, and to lose her now... "Callie!" I couldn't let my mind go there, especially after everything with Dylan and ruining my relationship with Cole. I needed my cat. Hadn't I told her as long as we were together everything would be okay? Where was she?

The train cars revealed no trace of her, and I attempted meowing, calling to her in her own language, desperate. I sounded nothing like a kitten—more like a screeching bat caught in death's grip—but I did it several more times anyway, cupping my mouth to extend my calling farther. *Please, please.*

"Your impression of a cat is seriously killing me. Please make it stop."

I whipped around and stumbled, barely keeping myself from tumbling down the hillside and ending up in the ravine next to the sunken wreckage. The unexpected voice in the dark stopped my heart and held me captive all at once. I couldn't move, but I was okay with that—I didn't need or want to.

He stepped around a fallen boxcar, out of the shadows, and my heart burst to life, beating beyond containment. The moon accentuated his features, his long wild hair in need of brushing, the smile in his eyes, and the curve of his lips. "That was the most pathetic sounding cat impersonation I think I've ever heard. I wasn't sure whether to point and laugh or put you out of your misery."

I barely heard a word he said—mumbled, foreign, unrecognizable. His presence, something I thought I'd never see again, kept me mesmerized, and I couldn't move. I couldn't blink, but the grin on my face couldn't have expanded any further.

"Your cat needed a break from watching your comatose body, so I took her out for a walk." He held up a thin-coiled rope and I followed its length to find Callie attached to the opposite end. She rolled around in the dirt, content, kicking up dust. "I'd have taken the leash, but you tied it to your backpack like... jeez, not even sure what. A boy scout earning a merit badge maybe?"

One step.

Then two more.

Soon I was running, flying past broken train cars and skipping over rubble. My teary eyes focused on him. *He's here! He's here, and he has my cat!* The beam from my headlamp bounced around and he raised a hand to block it. He held the other out in front of him and his eyes widened. "Tess, wait a—"

"Cole!" I collided with him, knocking him off balance. He took a step backward but remained upright and wrapped an arm around my waist to steady the both of us. My arms wound around his warm neck, clinging to him like a baby monkey clinging to its mother. I stood on tiptoes so I could hang on to him even tighter, pressed my face into his shoulder and allowed the past couple of days' events to burst from me in a torrent of tears and sobs.

I'm not ever letting go of you. Not ever.

"I... missed... you... too." He sounded surprised, but I refused to be petty or picky. He'd come and that was all that mattered. Maybe his words didn't provide the comfort and reassurance I longed for, but he held me—one hand around my waist and the other pressed against my upper back—hugging me to him and letting me know he *had* missed me, even if he couldn't voice it without being an ass.

He allowed me to hang on and cry into his chest, taking turns patting and rubbing my shoulders and cupping the back of my head. His lips brushed against my ear and he whispered, "Are you okay?"

I couldn't answer him. The answer would have to be no and yes. No, I wasn't okay at all. Everything was a giant mess and I happened to be stuck right in the middle without a single clue how to fix any of it. And yes, I was better than ever—he was here now. No matter what else happened, he was here and that changed everything.

He smoothed my hair away from my face. "Looks like you've had a rough couple of days."

That was putting it mildly.

"I have to say, I was hoping we might be able put our differences aside, but this is quite unexpected." His arms tightened around me. "By the way, a guy could get used to this... even if he shouldn't."

I ignored the last part. Whatever this was between us — good, bad, or otherwise — didn't matter. Right now, I wanted him to keep holding me and telling me everything would be okay.

"It's going to be okay, Tess. You're going to be fine."

Wow. Did he just say that? I hugged him more, melding into him, feeling his heartbeat against my chest and his breath against my cheek. "You followed me." I managed the three words, even though numerous questions begged to be asked.

"Of course." He thumbed away a few of my tears.

"Why?"

He shrugged. "Does it matter?"

No, it really didn't, so I let it drop. Any explanation he gave would probably lessen the impact of having him here. He had a way of ruining moments by telling me what a dumb kid I was or saying something equally mean. I'd already had that conversation with myself earlier, and didn't need him reiterating it.

"Sorry about freaking you out about your cat. I was going to put her back before you woke up."

"It's okay, I'm just glad you're here."

He squeezed me tighter. "Really?"

"Yeah, really."

"I thought you hated me."

I pressed the palms of my hands to his back. "I thought I did too."

"But now you don't?"

"Well, maybe a little, but I'll work on it."

He kissed the top of my head, his lips lingered for a moment, and I closed my eyes, listening to his heart thrum against my ear. "I'm okay with that," he said.

Not much had changed, not really. The world was still a mess, and I still had a long ways to go to find out why. But even though there was nothing safe about living amid the unknown and the dangers coming along with it, I felt protected wrapped in his arms, and for now that measure of security would have to do.

Still, I worried. "Do you...." Did I really want to know? Would it even change my decision to be with him if he said yes? Could I handle it?

"Do I what?"

Not knowing might be worse, so I asked and braced myself for the answer. "Do you feel okay?"

His shoulders rose and fell, lifting me along with his shrug. "I feel great. Why?"

I stepped back, but didn't release him. My quick scan of him revealed nothing out of the ordinary. If he had been exposed to the elements as long as Dylan had, he'd be experiencing the same effects. "You don't feel sick to your stomach? How's your eyesight? Any bloody noses or hair loss?"

"Umm...No, great, and no." His eyebrows pinched together. "What's going on?"

"You feel fine? Are you sure?"

He nodded. "I'm pretty certain. Granola isn't all that filling, and I could go for an apple or a slice of bacon right now, but otherwise, I'm good. Why the twenty questions?"

"I want to make sure you're fine, that's all." I could have delved into it, told him everything about Dylan, but for some reason, I didn't want to. Dylan's illness might have been a fluke, and as long as I didn't push matters, I still had that hope. "How did you get this"—I pointed to the headlamp—"and the other stuff in my bag without being burned?"

"Burned? You sure are asking a lot of bizarre questions, and now I'm starting to wonder if *you're* okay." He held me at a distance with his hands on my upper arms. "Physically you look fine but mentally you're starting to scare the crap out of me."

"I'm fine. Here, let me show you." I maneuvered myself from his grip and rolled up my sleeve to show him the severe sunburn I'd received that afternoon. The light from the headlamp illuminated my pale skin. *Pale skin? What in the world?*

"Okay, I have no idea what's going on here, but when you make it back to civilization, you may want to get that mole looked at." He pointed to a brown mark near my elbow, something I'd had since birth.

"No, that's not...." I couldn't finish my thought. My arm that couldn't be touched earlier that day, without bringing tears to my eyes, no longer hurt. The redness was completely gone, wiped away as though nothing had happened.

"You okay, Tess?" He tipped my chin, forcing my eyes away from my arm.

I shook my head several times. "No, I'm not. I think something is really *really* wrong with me."

# CHAPTER 35

"What are you talking about? You look fine to me." Cole took my outstretched arm in his hand and turned it over several times. "I don't see anything."

"That's just it!" *How is this possible? No freakin' way!* "I... I don't understand this. I don't understand any of this." I ran my opposite hand over my skin and splayed my fingers, searching for any hint of the burn, but finding no signs at all. "This isn't right."

"If being okay isn't right, then I'm struggling to understand your logic."

I had ceased to hear him as worries piled on top of one another and pinpricked my brain. *How am I to trust anything anymore? What is real and what isn't?*

I touched Cole's whiskered face, needing to feel him, and dragged my fingers along his jaw line, hoping it would ease my worry, but it didn't. My hand fell to my side, and I shook my head. I didn't even know if he was real. Not really.

What is happening to me?

"Tess?"

Am I losing my mind? Am I sick?

"Come on, talk to me."

I dropped to my knees as realization sank in. I had to be sick, because nothing else made any sense. I combed a quick hand through my dark hair, but no strands fell away. That had to be good news, but I ran my hands through my hair again, this time feeling my scalp for signs of sores. Nothing.

Just because it wasn't happening now didn't mean it wouldn't.

Cole crouched in front of me. "What are you doing?" The inflections in his voice hinted at my craziness. "You're filthy, but I think you're a few days out before you need to check for bugs and little critters."

I jumped to my feet, glanced down at my clothing, and then looked at him. "Shine the light on my pants!"

He cocked a brow and slowly rose, standing in front of me with his head tilted to the side. "You're freaking me out a little."

"Do it! Shine the light on my pants."

He released his breath, but aimed the headlamp at my jeans. "You're the strangest girl I have ever met, and I'm not talking by a little bit either. If there was a crown for this kind of thing, you'd be wearing it."

"There! Look!" I grabbed at my pants, tugging the material tight. A smear of dried blood. "And here, look at this!" I pointed to the blood splattering on my jacket and smiled. Dylan's blood. "Do you see it?"

"Jeez, Tess! What did you do to yourself?" He stepped forward and reached for me, but didn't quite follow through. His hand hung in the air. "Why are you smiling like that?"

"Don't you see? This isn't my blood." I shouldn't be smiling. This wasn't a smiling type of situation, but a grin curved my lips anyway. "The boy I told you about, Dylan? The one who stole your backpack? This is his blood."

Cole's hand dropped and he took a half a step backward. "You didn't kill him did you?"

I shot him an incredulous look. "Really?" I shook my head, even though his question didn't deserve an answer. "I don't know what's going on here. I know you told me he didn't exist, and then he told me you didn't. He said I made you up. He told me I was sick and getting worse. And this—" I raised my arm and waved it around— "with the whole sunburn thing, I thought I was going crazy. But his blood is on me. *His* blood!"

"And you're happy about this?" His face squished together like he smelled something bad.

"Yes!" I waved my hand around. "But not like you think. I feel like I'm losing it."

"You think?"

"Knock it off, please."

He placed his hands out in front of him, palms forward. "Sorry, go on."

I was going to sound insane, I knew it, but started talking anyway. "You don't understand. Ever since Dylan showed up, I've been questioning everything—you, him, myself—*everything*. He was really sick, Cole. He lost his hair, he lost weight, and then he bled to death in front of me. He told me about planes coming in and killing everyone, and how no one is coming to help. He said I was sick too."

"And this makes you smile, why?"

"Because he was real! Don't you get it? At least he was real. Everything else sucks big time, especially the part about possibly being sick too, but at least I have this!" Knowing Dylan had been real was only a small victory, but it *was* a victory, as bizarre as that seemed. I'd take what I could.

"Okay, then what about me?" He stepped closer, holding the headlamp in his hand, aimed upward, highlighting the both of us. "What am I?"

His eyes searched mine, and I couldn't turn away. After a few minutes, I answered, "I don't know."

"You don't know?"

"No."

"I don't feel real to you?" He grabbed my hand and placed it on his thumping heart. "And now?"

"You feel very real."

"But you're still unsure?"

"I *know* I had a major sunburn on my arm this afternoon, but now it's gone. How do I explain that?" My fingers lingered, enjoying his hand on mine and each breath he took beneath my palm.

He shrugged. "Quick healing or maybe your sunburn wasn't as major as you thought?"

"Maybe."

"You didn't answer my question."

I crinkled my brow. "What question?"

"What am I? Real or not?"

"I don't know. Dylan didn't see or hear you running around the mall. He said he watched for a long time before deciding to talk to me, and never saw anyone else, just me." *Why am I doing this?*

"He was a stupid teenage boy, and a sick one at that. What do you believe?"

I kept my eyes locked on his. "What should I believe?"

He held my gaze for a long time then turned away from me and whispered, "Would it make a difference if I was real or not?"

"Yes," I was quick to answer. Of course it would matter. It would mean the difference between sanity and going out of my mind. "And no," I added, leaving me no better off than before we'd got into this discussion. If he was a figment of my imagination—a damn fine one at that—I didn't want to know. Figments of the imagination would only lead to disappointment, and I couldn't handle that right now.

"What do you want me to be?" He continued to hold my hand against his chest and stepped closer.

The back of my hand, still touching him, pressed into my own chest—the space between us disappeared. "I want you to be what you are, whatever it is."

He grinned. "You're a strange girl, Tess."

"I know, you've already told me."

He cupped my face, turning it toward him, our mouths only inches apart. He stared at me and smiled softly.

He's going to kiss me. I steeled myself for his lips on my mine even though I knew it would complicate everything. Somehow, it just seemed right. To hell with age differences! It was an apocalypse, for heaven's sake!

"Tess?"

"Yeah?"

"We should really get going." His lips brushed my forehead and he tapped my nose with his finger. "I'll help you grab your things." He patted his leg and gave the rope a small tug, enticing Callie to follow after him

What the –? That didn't just happen, did it? "Are you serious?" I called after him.

"Yeah." He smiled at me over his shoulder. "I'm not tired and you slept like the dead, so I figure we can get ten miles in before the sun comes up."

"That's not what I'm talking about."

"What are you talking about?" He scooped Callie into his arms and scratched between her ears, avoiding looking at me.

"This" —I pointed to him and then back to me. "What was that about? I thought..." What did I think? That Cole would be any different than he'd been several days ago? That we could be something more than traveling buddies? I knew something was there—the whole hand on the chest thing, what was he thinking by doing that? "You're screwing with me, aren't you?"

Seriousness replaced his smile. "If anything, that's the one thing I'm trying to avoid."

Did he say what I thought he said? My breath caught in my throat. Oh, my heck! I was right! He did like me. I knew it!

"I told you I'll help you find your dad, and that's what I'm going to do. I'm taking you to him all in one piece" —he waved an arm around—"exactly as I found you."

"Exactly as you found me?" I paused as the meaning of his words settled over me. "Wait, do you think I'm a virgin?"

He stopped petting Callie mid-pet and stared at me. "Aren't you?"

"Would it make a difference if I was or wasn't?" I threw back at him the same question he'd asked me earlier.

He kept his eyes on me for a long time then shook his head. "Nope. Not at all." He cleared his throat. "Now go grab your bag. We need to get going."

 # CHAPTER 36

"What if you're wrong?" I pressed my back against one of the bridge's wooden trusses as shadows outside my safe zone started to disappear. The rising sun swallowed them inch by inch. *Please don't be wrong, Cole. Please.*

He released the buckle of his backpack and let it fall to the ground with a thump, causing the bridge to vibrate, then stepped fully into the morning light. He closed his eyes, turned his face toward the sun, and held his arms outstretched at his side. "Is my skin sloughing off?"

"Please don't joke around."

"Am I starting to smoke? Do you see any flames shooting out from my head?"

"You didn't get sunburned before, so standing out there now doesn't prove anything." I glanced up at the roof of the old covered bridge—weather-beaten and broken in several areas, it wouldn't take long for the light to creep in and take over, leaving me with only a foot or two of possible shade.

I was pretty much screwed regardless if I stepped into the sun or remained here. "We should have stayed at the motel we passed several miles ago, and walked tonight after the sun went down."

Cole dropped his arms and opened his eyes. "You want to climb a mountain in the dark? In pitch blackness? Yeah, that sounds like a much better plan to me, way more reasonable."

"And if I burn, what are you going to do? By the time you can pick me up and run from here to there"—I pointed to a small thicket of trees—"you'll be carrying my fleshless skeleton in your arms."

"Wow, you're dramatic and incredibly visual with your words." He held his hand out toward me. "Come on. It's going to be fine, I promise."

I looked at Callie cradled in the crook of my arm. "What about her?"

"What about her? Did she get burned by the sun too?"

"No, but she went crazy right before I reached my arm outside the garage. She knew something wasn't right long before I did."

He pointed a lazy hand at her. "She looks pretty darn peaceful to me. Come on."

I knew what happened to me, even if I couldn't understand how I'd healed so quickly. Whatever had happened, I didn't want to experience it again, especially if I could avoid it. "What if you're wrong?"

"I'm not." He wiggled his fingers.

I swallowed and hugged Callie closer. "I don't think I can."

"Well, the sun's going to get you one way of the other." He indicated the decreasing shadows near my feet. "You can waste time by standing there, or you can trust me. The choice is yours."

"How fast is your running ability?"

He shook his head. "Not too good."

Great. "I'm supposed to step into the sun likes it's no big deal?"

"Yeah, because that's exactly what it is—no big deal. If I believed you'd be hurt, I wouldn't make you do this."

"And if something bad does happen?"

He threw his hands into the air. "Then I'll let you set me on fire so we're even, okay?"

I took a couple of deep breaths and looked at him. "You better be right."

"I am." He wiggled his fingers again, this time with a little less patience.

I braved sticking the toe of my boot into the light. Normal warmth heated my foot. No human combustion, but that didn't mean anything—my foot was covered. My arm hadn't been.

Please, please, please.

I reached into the light with my free hand, sticking it out for a millisecond and drawing it quickly back in. Again, normal warmth. Okay, not bad.

"Do it again," he said.

The shade around me shrank several more inches. "I really hate this."

"I know." Cole made himself comfortable in the middle of the dirt road, his legs straight in front of him and crossed at the ankle. He leaned back on his arms and tipped his face to the sun. "Ahhh... it feels wonderful."

"You're a huge jerk."

He smiled, but didn't look at me. "I know."

Light trickled over both my boots, and pierced the broken beams overhead, though not quite touching me—not yet anyway. Either I would die a horrible death or this experience would turn out to be something funny to look back on.

Please be funny. Please be freakin' hilarious!

I wrapped Callie's leash around my hand and took one final deep breath. All or nothing. No going back. *Do it.* I kept my eyes on the stand of trees and took off running across the open space between them and the bridge, not giving myself an opportunity to change my mind.

Dust kicked up around my boots. Callie screeched, coming awake, and dug her baby claws into my arm. *To the trees, to the trees!* I zipped past a relaxed Cole, hardly noticing him as I ran for the shade and instant safety.

Mr. Wanket, my P.E. teacher would have been so proud at my sprinting ability. Yeah, his name was Wanket, and yeah, the jokes were plentiful, but in that moment, I couldn't remember even one. My focus was that intense.

When I got to the trees, huffing and panting, I realized the only pain I suffered came from the scratches inflicted by my surprised cat. I glanced at my exposed arms then reached up and patted my face.

"I'm okay!" *Thank heavens!*

Cole stood, brushed off his pants, and smiled. "That's debatable, but you *are* still as pale as ever, so that's a good thing." He seemed to think for a moment, then waved a hand at me, pointing from my head to my feet. "Now that I think about it, you should probably put some sunscreen on."

A small fire crackled in the makeshift pit. Occasionally, a few embers would float into the sky, but die a quick death in the cool air. A breeze swayed the branches high above our heads, but otherwise, a thick eeriness permeated everything. Where normally an owl would hoot or a wolf would bay at the moon, only silence filled the night. No crickets chirping. No bullfrogs croaking. No life at all. It should have felt more comforting—no threat of being eaten by a bear or attacked by a moose—but the deadly silence was almost worse.

I adjusted the blanket around my shoulders and petted Callie as she slept belly-up in my lap. The fire warmed us, though the night was cool and pleasant.

Cole knelt near the fire, keeping an eye on a pot of water. "The altitude must be screwing with the boiling process. This is taking forever."

"You filtered the water, right?"

He'd spent a good deal of time before the sun went down pumping water from the small creek next to our camp. The process was slow, but necessary.

"Yeah, but I want to take every precaution possible. The last thing we need is stomach cramps and the turkey trots." He used a large stick to shift the hot coals. "Hate being frank like that, but we're out in the woods with only a couple rolls of toilet paper between us. Those rolls are worth their weight in gold, and I won't easily share mine."

He thrived on having no decorum. I only smiled—a different response to his uncouth words. He must have worn on me or I had decided correcting his behavior wasn't worth the effort.

"Did you get enough to eat?" He looked across the flames. "I'm pretty sure you're getting skinnier with each passing day."

Really? I hadn't noticed. My pants hung a little loose, and I'd had to tighten my belt, but in a world where fresh proteins and veggies were scarce, this would be expected. A person could only live on "add water and stir" meals for so long without it affecting their physique. "Remember how you tried to stop me from laughing and having a panic attack? You told me we'd pick wild berries and hunt rabbits on this camping trip?"

He made himself comfortable on a fallen log and poked the flames with the stick—a giant dangerous kid. "Nope."

Go figure. "Well, you did, and now I'm telling you I could go for either one of those."

"Sorry, kid. I shouldn't have said it then. The most I can offer you is a peanut butter granola bar."

I sighed. "Yeah, I figured."

"You want a granola bar?"

"Heck no. If I eat any more granola, I'm going to turn into a vegan nature-loving hippie. It starts with granola and the next thing you know you're wearing your hair in dreadlocks and forgetting to shower." I hadn't set out to be funny or curt, but he laughed, and I realized he had worn on me in more ways than one. Maybe that was a good thing. Maybe not.

"Well, you've got the granola and no showering parts down, so I guess the next logical step is dreadlocks."

I shook my head. "Not happening."

"I know a few vegan hippies and they're some of the nicest people I've ever met. They make the best natural soaps and grow some of the best organic wee... wheatgrass." He cleared his voice, stopped poking the fire, and looked at me. "Forget it. You're not a vegan-hippie kind of person."

"I don't want to be a vegan or a hippie, remember?" *Why are we arguing?*

"That's good. You'd make a terrible one." He leaned over the pot and smiled. "About time." He used the stick to swing the pot away from the flames. "As soon as it cools, we'll fill our water bottles."

"Okay." I stood, holding a sleepy cat. "I think I'm going to go to bed now. It's been a long day and I'm exhausted. You coming?"

"I'll get some sleep in a bit. I've got to string up my hammock and make sure the fire is out first."

"Hammock? The tent is all ready to go. There's plenty of room for your stuff and mine."

"I think the hammock will be much better for the both of us, don't you think?"

I shrugged. "Do whatever you want, Cole. I'm too tired to argue with you let alone try to molest you while you're sleeping, if that's what you're thinking. If you want to sleep in a hammock, go for it. You might want to rig up a tarp while you're at it, too. Looks like it might rain tonight."

He glanced at the dark clouds circling the tops of the trees, making them appear larger and taller than they actually were. Precisely at that moment, a drop of rain landed on his cheek. It couldn't have been timed better.

He turned his gaze from the sky to the pup tent and then to me. "I'll take my chances."

CHAPTER 37

Rain drizzled from low-lying clouds, carrying right on into the following afternoon without a break. What had once sounded beautiful and lulling against the tent walls soon began to annoy me outside. Wetness curdled my toes and water logged my fingertips. Even with a raincoat thrown over my clothes and backpack, water still managed to work its way inside, drip down my neck, and soak my socks, making the very act of walking miserable.

The trails became muddy encumbering pathways, and both Cole and I slipped our way along them. We would have stuck to the paved roads, the easiest routes through the mountains, but when we'd come to the mouth of the canyon, we'd found it blocked by a massive impassable landslide.

"That doesn't look natural," Cole had said. "Look there." He'd pointed to the smooth canyon walls. "That didn't happen on its own."

"What do you mean?"

"There and there." He pointed once again, this time to several different spots. "Someone blasted the mountain and forced a road closure. If the weather did this, there would be more of an angle to it. This looks chiseled and deliberate to me."

"You're saying someone did this on purpose? Why?" *What did this mean?*

He shifted the pack on his shoulders. "I don't know, but an awful lot of trouble went into this decision, so whatever the reason, it must have been a good one."

Even now, as we traversed the dangerous mountainside, weaving between trees and boulders, my mind couldn't shake the vision of someone purposely exploding a mountain.

The reason must have been a good one. Cole's words thumped at my brain, and with the rain making it too miserable to do much of anything but place one foot in front of the other, talking gave way to silence and I was left alone inside my head.

Callie had it good, riding in the front pocket of my backpack. She didn't even complain when I shoved her inside, but curled up and fell asleep, probably realizing it was better to be dry and uncomfortable.

Every time it seemed as though the rain would let up, giving us a reprieve, the clouds would slam back together and rain once again. Too many disappointments taught me to stop hoping when I saw a hint of blue in the sky.

Cole didn't grumble or voice his discontent, but trudged through the soggy mud sucking at his boots, and tightened his rain jacket around his neck. He had to be just as tired and wet as me, but never said so.

We climbed steep paths and made our way through thick trees, following the downward flowing river. Cole didn't want to venture too far away from our only source of water; besides, it kept us from walking around in circles. Even with a compass to direct us—something I couldn't quite figure out and left up to Cole to interpret—it wouldn't take much to become lost.

Each step, however wet and awful, got me closer to Dad. I kept my mouth shut, my head down, and trudged along.

We rounded a bend and our path opened wide, revealing a beautiful grove of tall grasses and multi-colored wildflowers bordering the large crystal-clear lake. Jagged mountain cliffs walled it in, and pines and junipers grew in clumps, giving the entire area a tranquil mystical feel.

Mirror Lake. I'd been here before with Dad and Toby. We'd camped under a blanket of trees off to the south and fished the inlet of the river to the north. Years had passed since I'd last set foot here, but the memories rushed back as though only a few days had gone by.

I smiled—*we're getting closer*—but my grin slipped away as I was overcome by dread and fear. The beautiful flowers and trees faded and the gruesome scene before us came into full view.

From a distance, the lake appeared to be circled by large rocks and boulders, almost like sandbags used to keep the water from overflowing and flooding the exquisite space, but as we drew closer, it became quite apparent the mounds weren't rocks at all.

The bodies of hundreds of dead animals, bloated and decaying, lay on their sides along the lake's edge, the carcasses wrapped around the entire length of the lake, ten to twenty animals deep. Smaller animals lay on top of the larger ones like Russian stacking dolls, with their milky eyes wide and their mouths gapping. Tongues hung from open jaws. Stiff legs jutted at awkward angles. Bears, deer, birds, horses, domestic dogs and cats, mice, bobcats, chipmunks, rabbits, beavers—the predator and the prey—all asleep in death; all sharing the massive unnatural gravesite.

Worse yet, dozens of animals floated in the clear blue water, some just below the surface, while others lingered and swayed on top. Creepy and unreal. Rain rippled the water and rolled over the dead animals bobbing along the edges, washing away the smell that would've accompanied the scene.

I couldn't move or look away, even though I wanted to run. This solved part of the mystery of where all the animals had gone, though I couldn't understand what it meant. Had some of the animals run straight into the lake? None of them would have been able to swim across the expanse. Had they known they were sentencing themselves to death? But most importantly, what were they running from?

Cole came to stand at my side. Rain dripped from the brim of his hat. "Now you know why filtering the water isn't good enough."

We've been drinking this water? I bent at the waist and vomited into the wet grass until I had nothing left to throw up. Cole didn't try to comfort me, but stood quietly at my side until I had finished. I swiped a wet hand over my mouth. "We need to get out of here."

"Agreed." He shook his shoulders, spraying rain like a wet dog. "Be careful where you step."

"You have got to be kidding me." Cole bent down, picked up a handful of thick snow from the pile wrapping around our legs, and held it out to me. "We're not prepared for this kind of thing."

My body shivered and my teeth chattered. I agreed with Cole without having to voice it. In the space of a week, we had seemed to experience all four seasons—extreme heat, torrential rains, and now a snowstorm. He was right: we weren't prepared for winter conditions. A snowstorm this time of year, especially in the higher elevations, wasn't unheard of, and packing a winter coat among our supplies would have been a smart thing to do, but neither of us had.

I'd already put on every piece of dry clothing available. With the way the weather seemed to change every few hours, it seemed we just needed to wait out the storm. Eventually, it would get better. I had to believe that.

"How're your feet?" Cole brushed the snow from his gloved hand.

"Frozen."

"Can you feel your toes?"

"No, not really." The Doc Marten boots, though stylish, didn't do much to keep my feet warm or dry. The souls were cracked and my toes threatened to poke through the leather at any moment. They made horrible hiking boots, but they'd gotten me this far and I hoped they'd hang in there long enough to take me the rest of the way. "But that's normal, right?

"Normal if you like walking on stumps instead of feet. No, not feeling your toes is never considered normal. It's pretty bad, actually."

"I'll be fine. If we keep moving, I'll warm up." I didn't want to waste time on a standard part of being out in the cold. We were so close to finding Dad, and I didn't want to get sidetracked. True, I hadn't experienced this kind of snow and cold before—most of our winters consisted of a few inches of light snow mixed with icy rain, not sub-zero temperatures like this. My wimpy, summer-loving body needed to adjust.

I took off my gloves and blew on my hands, trying to instill some warmth back into my numb fingers. My breath turned into white puffs that hung in the air, and my nostrils began to freeze. I instantly regretted the removal of my gloves. Breathing on my fingers hadn't helped at all.

Cole grabbed my hands right as I tried slipping my frozen digits back into my gloves. "How long have they looked like this?"

I hadn't noticed the redness creeping over my fingers or the pasty-white patches covering their tips. "I don't know. This was the first time I've taken my gloves off." The cold air bit into my flesh.

He pinched each finger in turn. "Do you feel that?"

I nodded.

He helped me put on my gloves, but kept turning his head, looking around. For what exactly, I had no idea. "We need to get you out of this cold."

"Should we pitch the tent?" We didn't have many options as far as shelter went, and I wouldn't mind slipping into my sleeping bag for a minute or two.

"No." He held both my hands between his, rubbing warmth into them. "The snow is too heavy. It'll collapse. We can't even start a fire, because the falling snow will smother it." The look on his face told me if he could have punched something, he probably would have.

"Then let's keep walking," I suggested. "Standing here is making it worse." Cold seeped through my boots and crept up my spine. Each intake of breath chilled my lungs, and every release meant I was forced to take another. The longer we stood there, the colder I became, and the more the pile of snow around us deepened.

"This isn't good, Tess." His eyes held a sense of seriousness that should have scared me, but didn't. "I'm getting worried about you."

"We'll be fine. It's not far now, just over the hill there."

Cole's eyes narrowed. "No, it isn't. That's not even the right way." He pointed in the opposite direction. "We have to head for that ridge, you know that."

I smiled. *Why is he getting all worked up?* "Yeah, I'm sorry. I guess I got a little turned around."

He swore under his breath as he removed the crinkled map from his pocket, stared at it for a long time, and then scanned the area around us. "There's got to be a cabin or a hunting shack around here somewhere."

"We haven't seen any so far."

Cole kept glancing around. "Doesn't mean they aren't there. This is serious, Tess. We've got to get out of the cold before you lose your fingers and toes."

I'd thought he'd been joking before about the stump thing. "How are your hands? Are you freezing?"

He shook his head. "I'm fine."

"Let me see." I grabbed one of his hands, and even though he didn't make it easy, I managed to remove his gloves. *What the heck?* I snatched his other hand, took off that glove too, and held both his hands in mine. "They're not cold."

"I told you I was fine."

His hands gave off warmth right through the gloves covering my own. A normal flesh- colored tone proved his words true. He was fine. No sickly white spots or bright-pink areas. His fingers didn't look anything like mine though we both wore the same gloves. In fact, he probably didn't even need gloves at all.

"You're not shivering." I hadn't noticed it before now, too focused on my own cold and discomfort. My body hadn't stopped shaking for at least a good hour. I didn't think I could stop, or ever would, and I assumed he was suffering like me. "Why aren't you shivering?"

He snatched his hands away and worked his gloves back over them. "I have more endurance than you, I guess." He pointed to the west of the ridge. "We should head for that section, because if I had a cabin, I'd build one there."

Beautiful majestic mountains rose up behind where he pointed—a perfect Ansel Adams backdrop for a cabin.

"Okay," I said, wrapping my arms around myself, "we'll head there if you think that's the way to go."

"I don't know if we'll find anything, but it's worth a shot. Otherwise, we're in a whole lot of trouble."

I let him take the lead. He stomped out the path—an arduous task of lifting one leg, putting it down on top of the snow, and then sinking nearly up to his thigh. Walking in the snow was hard and time consuming.

I kept my eyes on him as I trudged behind, but my mind kept going back to his warm hands. *Why didn't he shiver?* "Are you okay?" I called to him.

He glanced over his shoulder at me. "Yeah, I'm fine. How you holding up?"

"I'm hanging in there." I managed a few more steps, but walking was getting harder and harder. "Are you cold?"

"I'm fine.

"You're not even a little cold?" *How could he not be?*

"Oh, I'm cold," he said. "I just seem to handle it better than you." He zipped his jacket a little higher around his neck, rubbed his hands together, and shivered once. "You need to stop thinking about it so much."

My teeth chattered non-stop. My body shook. I couldn't feel my feet or hands, and my nose had turned into a giant ice-cube on my face. The only thing missing was an icicle dangling from my nostrils—a real possibility. How could I *not* think about being cold?

Because I knew how miserable I was, I couldn't buy into Cole's act one bit.

CHAPTER 38

Cole flicked my nose. "Stay awake."

My eyes snapped open, and I blinked several times, breaking the crystals forming on my eyelashes. I'd fallen asleep standing against the cabin's porch railing, and it took a moment for me to remember where we were. I hadn't meant to fall asleep, for however short a time, but the cold made it increasingly difficult to stay awake. "Are we here?"

"Yeah." He tapped both of my cheeks. "Don't close your eyes, okay?"

I bobbed my head and my eyelids fluttered, fighting to stay open.

"Step back," he said. When I didn't move, he took hold of my shoulders and positioned me away from the cabin door. "Don't move and don't fall asleep on me again."

"Okay." The word pressed through my frozen lips.

He took a step back, lifted his leg, and kicked the wooden door. The frame splintered, but continued to hold. He kicked it again and the door gave away a little more, but instead of kicking it a third time, he let out a tribal yell and rammed it with his shoulder, over and over, until the wood finally split under the pressure.

Cole slipped through the tight space, entering the cabin sideways.

He didn't open the broken door, but pressed his face through the crack in the middle of the wood. "Heeere's Johnny!"

Cole's antics were funny, but all I could manage was a tightlipped, teeth-chattering grin.

"You don't even know what that's from, do you?" He opened what was left of the door, half-hanging on hinges, and half-falling apart, then came to me, took my arm, slipped it over his shoulder, and helped me inside. "I'll give you the chocolate candy bar I've got hidden in my bag if you can name the movie."

He didn't have a candy bar. He didn't have the will-power to keep one on him this long, but I played along anyway. "Stephen King's, *The Shining*."

His laugh echoed off the cabin walls. "No way! How did you know that?" He removed my backpack, set it carefully on the floor, then lowered my frozen and tired body on the nineteen-seventy plaid style couch. "That's way before your time."

"Who doesn't love Stephen King? Dad had it in the bomb shelter. I think I watched it half a dozen times."

He grabbed an old quilt off the back of the couch, shook off the dust, and draped it around me. "Have you seen *Misery* with James Caan and Kathy Bates?"

I shook my head and hugged the blanket tighter. "No, but I've read the book." I tried to lie down, but he grabbed me by the shoulders and righted me.

"Keep talking to me, Tess. Stay with me okay?"

I nodded. "I'm really tired."

"I know, and I promise you can sleep in a minute, but not yet. I need you to keep me company while I get a fire going."

He propped the broken door mostly in place, though large cracks on either side let in a few swirling snowflakes. They gathered on the floor in a soft pile. It was too cold, even inside the old cabin, for them to melt. "What other Stephen King movies have you seen?"

Cold nipped at my brain, and I struggled to think. "*Cujo*, but the book was way better."

"I heard the ending in the book was sad, where the movie ended a little more optimistically." He unzipped the pocket of my bag, and Callie popped out of the opening. She let out a high-pitched meow and shook her head; her fur stood upright.

"Like I said, the book was better. Books are always better."

He scooped Callie into his large hands and brought her over to me. "Here you go." He placed her on my lap and tucked the blanket around the both of us. "Hold on to her."

My fingers were too numb to really feel her. Pinprick sensations ran from the tips of my fingers toward my palms, but I placed my hands on top of her warm little body anyway.

"What else do you like reading? Romance? Sci-fi? Mystery?" Cole knelt in front of the rock fireplace and stacked old newspapers, kindling, and a few logs inside. The cabin's owners had a nice pile of wood next to the door. Good people.

"Pretty much anything, as long as it's good. How about you?"

He shook his head. "I don't like reading."

"Then you're doing it wrong."

"You're probably right." He stood and searched a few shelves, pushing nick-knacks and other random items aside before he dug into his backpack and removed a lighter. "I'll have a fire going before you know it."

"I can't wait." I couldn't remember what feeling warm was like anymore.

"Let's just hope I don't accidently burn this place down." He clicked the lighter and a small flame came to life. It didn't take much for the newspaper to catch fire, or for the flames to engulf the kindling and wood. "Let me get it going a little better, and then I'll move you closer."

"Okay."

He placed a couple more logs in the fireplace. "That should do it." He crossed the room, slipped his arms under my legs, and lifted me from the couch. "I'll go see what blankets I can round up." Callie enjoyed the ride, purring while he carried us. He placed the two of us on the woven rug in front of the fire. "I'll be right back."

The dancing yellow and orange flames intrigued me, almost hypnotizing, emitting a gradual warmth—kissing at my face then at my hands as I held them out in front of me. The pinpricks worsened, and I snatched my hands back and hid them in the blankets.

"Here we go. Look at this." Cole stepped out of a side room with a large pile of blankets and comforters in his arms. "We're going to be nice and cozy."

I didn't answer. My eyelids had already started to close.

He gave my shoulders a gentle shake. "Not yet, Tess."

"I'm still freezing." I knew the warmth of the fire wouldn't heat me instantly, but I couldn't help wishing it would hurry and do its job.

He took Callie, removed her from the sock, and sat her to the side. She took a few timid steps, but overall stayed close to the fireplace, which was good since I didn't think I had it in me to chase her down. If she wanted to take off, I'd probably let her. *Be free, little kitty!*

Cole slipped the quilt from my shoulders, and as I tried to grab it back, he pushed my hands away. "We've got to get you out of those wet clothes. They're probably stuck to your body." He removed my gloves and cursed at my hands.

"What?" I tried to look, but he maneuvered himself so I couldn't.

He picked up one foot at a time, and gently removed each of my battered boots and threadbare socks. He didn't swear this time, but the look on his face said it all.

"It's that bad, huh?"

He reached forward to unzip my pants.

"Am I going to lose my fingers and toes?"

He shook his head as he maneuvered my stiff jeans from my frozen legs. "Not if I can help it." Tiny pieces of my flesh peeled away with the material, as he said it might. The small sores bled, but stopped after a few seconds. Even so, they appeared raised and angry looking. Not pretty at all.

"Sorry," he said. "They had to come off." He removed my jacket, unbuttoned my shirt, and cast them aside.

The cold kept me from caring I sat there in only my bra and panties. Being ogled was the last thing on my mind. "Hurry. Please." Goosebumps rippled my skin and my shivering increased tenfold, even though I couldn't have imagined either of those things being worse than they already were. "I'm going to die here."

He removed an old woman's flannel housedress from the pile of blankets—a dark blue and pink flowered print my grandmother might have worn—and slipped it over my head, lastly helping to work my arms through the holes. He eased me into a resting position and placed a pillow under my head.

"I can sleep now?"

"Almost." He covered me in one after another of the various blankets he had gathered earlier. "How does that feel?"

I continued to shake without reprieve, but could feel a slight difference. "It's great." I would say almost anything so he'd leave me alone and let me sleep.

He slipped a knitted cap over the top of my head and tucked the blankets tightly around me. I closed my eyes, but heard him moving around the cabin—placing more logs on the fire, boiling water, and feeding Callie. He opened and closed closets and drawers, but I wasn't curious enough to open my eyes to see why.

The fire crackled and a hint of smoke hung in the air. It warmed my nose—the first time I could breathe without my nostrils sticking together or my lungs filling with icy air. Yeah, I could totally go to sleep.

"Here you go." Cole lifted the edge of the blankets and slid the most amazing bag of heat next to my body. *A hot water bottle.* My new best friend. "How are you doing?"

I smiled with my eyes still closed. "Better. How about you?"

"Don't worry about me, okay? Concentrate on getting yourself warm." He reached under the blankets and touched my hands, then each of my feet. "Damn."

"I'm getting warmer." I tried to stop his worrying. I *did* feel warmer.

"You're still shaking."

"I am?"

"Yeah," he said. "You are."

"I'll be fine."

He sighed, long and hard. "I'm going to make sure you are."

He was quiet, and I couldn't hear him moving or doing anything, but could sense his presence kneeling next to me. *Is he praying?*

I cracked open an eye, then the other eye quickly followed suit. He wasn't praying at all. I tried to sit up. "What are you doing?"

He had removed his shoes, pants, and shirt. He knelt next to me in wearing only his boxer shorts. "Move over."

"What?"

"Just do it."

I shifted a little, and he lifted the blankets and quickly slid inside next to me. "Jeez, it's cold."

He didn't shiver. No goose bumps attacked his skin. In fact, as he curled his body against mine—his stomach pressed against my back—heat radiated from him. He wrapped his arms around me, and he laid his head next to mine. "You can go to sleep now, Tess. I've got you."

"You're not a real person are you?" *How else could he be this warm?*

"Shush," he whispered against my ear. "Close your eyes. We'll talk more tomorrow."

CHAPTER 39

Warm breath escaped Cole's partially closed lips and swept over my eyes, my cheeks, and my mouth. Our faces had turned toward one another sometime during the night. And now, as he continued to sleep, I watched him by the light of the fire with only one question on my mind: *What are you?*

I kept still, breathing in rhythm with Cole's. His chest rose and fell against mine. His eyes, deep in sleep, danced behind his lids. His nearly naked body exuded warmth I'd never experienced before, but wholly appreciated even though I questioned its probability.

Alien. Imaginary. False. Unnatural.

All the facts I played over in my mind pointed to him being one, if not all of those things. Dylan not seeing him; his overall heath; his bizarre warmth and lack of shivering in below-freezing temperatures—but his unshaven face, no matter how much I stared, revealed nothing. If anything, the mole below his ear, the small scar above his left eyebrow, and the scattering of faded freckles on his bare shoulders—signs of realness—caused me to question myself again.

His eyes opened and he caught me staring. "Hey, there."

"Hey."

"How long have you been awake?"

"Only a few minutes," I lied.

"You should've woken me."

"I didn't want to. You looked peaceful."

He grinned. "I was going for handsome and rugged, but I guess peaceful will have to do. Are you feeling any warmer?"

"Yeah. I am."

"That's great." He sat up, slid the blankets to the side, and took one of my hands in his. He turned it over, examined my palm and then each of my fingers before doing the same thing to my other hand. He moved to my feet, studied them, and then looked at me and smiled. "Everything's looking good. No stumps or pirate hooks for you."

I lifted each of my hands and glanced at them, then wiggled my toes, surprised to find I could. The whiteness and waxy look were gone. No more redness on my hands. No more pinpricks stabbed my fingertips and toes. He was right, everything did look and feel good; they appeared almost normal.

"How's that possible?" I asked him. I had witnessed the horrified look on his face the day before and didn't need to be told how bad my hands and feet had been; I had known by his grimace how dangerously close I'd been to losing them. "How did you fix this? What did you do to me?"

His forehead wrinkled. "Do?"

"Yeah, how did you make me better?" I grabbed the blankets and tucked them around me again. A chill still hung in there air, though nothing like the day before, and I needed the blankets.

Cole sat in his underwear, seemingly unbothered by the cold. "I started a fire. I put blankets on you, wrapped my body around yours, and hoped for the best. But you already know all that."

"No, what did you do, *really*?"

He cocked his head to the side. "Umm...I'm not sure what you're asking."

I matched his posture by sitting up, and placed my hands on top of the blankets for effect. "My hands and feet were in bad shape yesterday, now they're not. I crawled into a train car with a severe sunburn on my arm, but when I woke up, you were there and the sunburn was gone. What have you been doing to fix me?"

He eyed me as if I'd sprouted another head. "I don't know what you're talking about."

"Come on, Cole. You can't tell me all of this was a coincidence. Tell me what you did. I'm open-minded, and I can handle it." He could shoot white light from his eyes and spit fire at that very moment, and I was fairly certain I'd be okay with it.

"Wait a minute." He smiled. "You don't think I'm a miracle healer like Jesus, do you? Because as flattering as it is for me, I'm fairly certain the Son of God would take offense to the comparison."

I leaned forward. "I'm being totally serious."

"*Okay*, I see that now." He put his hands up, palms facing me. "Just to be clear, I'm not Jesus. The guy fed like ten thousand people with a loaf of bread and a couple of fish. I can barely keep us alive with a can of soup. While we're at it, you are *not* open-minded and you can't handle much of anything."

I ignored his humorous crap and insults. "Are you an alien or something?"

He smirked. "Now, you're being cruel. First, I was like Jesus, and now you're comparing me to one of those bald-headed, big-eyed creatures from space? Please, stop talking before I really get my feelings hurt."

"How did you know where this cabin was?"

"I didn't. We got lucky."

"When the tornado was chasing us, you drove the car straight into a carwash that ended up being the only building in the area not destroyed. Are you saying we got lucky then too?"

"I would have to say yeah, we got damn lucky."

"What about these?" I reached forward and ran my fingers over the angel wing tattoos on his back. "There's something more to these isn't there? Are you like my guardian angel or something?"

He turned his head sideways and squinted at me. "Ahhh... I was demoted from Jesus to an alien and now I'm promoted to guardian angel. Nice. You're buttering me up again. I like it. But honestly, Tess, does every good thing I do have to have a deeper meaning behind it? Because that's a lot of pressure for a guy like me. I don't think I can keep up these so-called 'miracles' you believe I'm capable of performing."

I scooted closer to him. "Please, if there is something unearthly going on, or if I'm going crazy, tell me. I need to know, because I'm not sure of anything anymore... and I hate feeling like I'm going out of my mind."

Cole released his breath and moved toward me, our knees touching. "You want to know the truth, huh?"

I nodded. "Yes, I do."

He took both of my hands. "Then here it is." He looked away briefly, cleared his throat, and brought his eyes back to mine. "I want to tell you I'm just a boy, standing in front of a girl, asking her to love me."

What the – ? I ripped my hands from his. "Did you quote *Notting Hill* at me?"

"Well, yes and no. Technically, Julia Roberts quoted this to Hugh Grant's character, so it was a girl standing in front of a boy thing. Literally, they were standing in a bookstore where as we're sitting on the ground, but that is beside the point. The message is still the same. I'm an ordinary guy, who happens to have had some pretty amazing luck lately. That's all. Please, can't that be enough for you? Why do you have to make this more complicated?"

"You're not going to tell me anything, are you?"

Cole reached for his pants and slipped each leg inside before standing and hiking his jeans over his hips. "There's nothing to tell."

"Fine. Whatever." I sank back against the pillows and jerked the blankets around me. I'd let him get the fire roaring before getting up and attempting to get dressed in something that didn't come from my grandmother's generation.

"Besides," he said as he grabbed his shirt and pulled it over his head, "if I was an angel, do you really think I'd admit it? There are rules about that kind of thing, you know? The whole mortal versus immortal aspect needs to be in balance. Rules that angels, vampires, and elves alike must abide by."

Of course there are.

"Now, witches and warlocks are different. Also fairies. Those nasty little bastards love to brag about their pixie dust. You can't shut them up."

"You're annoying."

"But adorable, right?"

I shook my head. "Well, if you're an angel, then God must have been pretty desperate."

Cole smiled as he knelt next to the fire and placed more kindling and timber on top. "If I was an angel, then God probably was."

"Tess, come here! You've got to see this." Cole poked his head over the edge of the cabin loft. "Seriously, it's amazing."

"What is it?" I wasn't in the mood to climb a rickety ladder to only be shown a dead mouse or something equally non-amazing. With Cole, I could never be sure. Our definitions rarely lined up.

"I can't explain it. You've got to come up here and see it for yourself." His head disappeared. He cursed out of awe, and said, "Incredible."

Fine. He had me intrigued. I climbed the ladder, taking my time, so I didn't lose my grip or footing and end up falling backward. My hands and feet were doing great, but still felt a little awkward from being frozen stiff for so long. "What is it?"

He lay belly down on a huge king-sized mattress with Callie curled at his side, grooming herself. He had to have carried her up with him, and I found it a little sweet.

With the pitch of the roof, the mattress had to be placed straight on the floor without a box spring beneath. Heat rose and warmed the small area, so even with the window wide open, I didn't feel cold.

He patted the mattress next to him. "You're going to like this."

I crawled across the floor and climbed on beside him. "So what am I supposed to be looking..." I couldn't finish my sentence. He didn't need to explain anything. *Wow.*

Splashes of color—deep greens, reds, and purples—rolled across the early morning sky and formed waves shifting and blended above us for as far as I could see. The snow reflected the colors, making the experience twice as fantastic. The lights went on and on, dancing and swaying, encompassing the entire sky for miles. I'd never seen anything like it. Magical and mesmerizing all at once.

"What is it?" I whispered, too amazed to be frightened by something so beautiful and unnatural.

"I believe we're witnessing the great Aurora Borealis."

"What? You mean the northern lights?" I glanced at him and then stared outside again, unsure. *Impossible.* The northern lights were seen in places like Norway, Sweden, and Alaska. Not Utah. Cole had to be wrong. "That can't be right."

"Well, I'm pretty sure that's what it is, but if you want to believe it's my mother ship signaling me to come home, you're welcome to that theory too."

The lights hypnotized me, and I watched them until the sun rose completely and they faded away. It saddened me to see them go, even though they shouldn't have been there in the first place.

"That was the best thing I've seen since leaving my TV back at the hanger." Cole wiggled off the mattress, picked up Callie, and started down the ladder. "I'm going to see what goodies they have in the cupboards and whip us up some breakfast. You should start searching the closets for a decent pair of boots, and hope they've got something that will fit you."

Yep, the Doc Martens had to go, but I worried that this cabin, as great as it was, wouldn't have anything worthwhile. If there were boots, they would most assuredly be hideous.

I waited until Cole reached the bottom before starting my decent. Part way down, an itch behind my ear aggravated me to the point that I stopped midway to scratch the heck out of it. A mosquito bite this time of year? Bed bugs, maybe? Scratching only made it worse. I struggled to stop and find some sense of self-control. *Seriously?*

"You need some help getting down?" Cole called from the kitchen.

"No, I've got it."

"You sure you're okay?"

I forced myself to stop scratching—*knock it off for goodness' sake*—and when I finally removed my hand from my head, a thick clump of brown hair dangled from my fingertips.

"Tess?"

I stared at it, unmoving. It had come out so easily. Not a few strands, but a nice-sized chunk.

"You sure you're okay?" he called again.

I could hear his footsteps in the kitchen, coming closer, so I quickly tossed the section of long hair into the loft, and climbed the rest of the way down. "Yeah," I answered. "I'm fine."

CHAPTER 40

I had wanted to leave the cabin and get on our way as soon as possible, but Cole insisted on taking one more day to rest and make sure my limbs thawed before venturing into the cold again. Actually, he'd wanted to take a few days, but after one day of restlessness — the longest day of my life — I said we needed to go.

Cole had put his ingenuity to work during our stay at the cabin. He managed to make the two of us a set of snowshoes by breaking two kitchen chairs apart, then pulling the fur off the old bear hide and ripping the rug into strips. I doubted they would work or stay together for long, but they held together much better than I had expected, keeping us on top of the surface instead of sinking into the thick layers of snow: an improvement I greatly appreciated.

Before leaving, we'd ransacked the place, gathering anything useful to take with us on the remainder of our journey. I'd found a pair of decent boots to replace the Doc Martens — I hated parting with those awesome boots. They had carried me a long way. The new boots were a little big, but with two pairs of thick socks, they worked out just fine. We took the bulky winter coats from the bedroom closet and rolled two wool blankets into our bags.

While we scoured the place, Cole took my hand in his, stopping our pillaging, and attached a knotted bracelet to my wrist. "I thought you might like this."

The bracelet wasn't much really — a stamped out metal plate with the words *"Where there is a will there is a way"* and two leather straps that tied it together — but I loved the gesture. He had told me nothing was impossible if I wanted it hard enough. All I had to do was look at the bracelet and remember.

Now, with miles and miles of snow-covered trees, hills, and ridges breaking through the terrain, making our climb steeper and more difficult, I found myself removing one glove, and slipping my fingers under the sleeve of my coat to touch the engraved words, reminding myself I could do this.

"You're being a dork, get in here!" I knelt inside the tent, holding the flap open, and watched Cole struggle to find two conducive trees to jerry-rig his hammock. The pine branches hung way too low to the ground, and the other trees in the area were too scattered for the hammock to stretch between any of them. He kept walking from tree to tree, moving farther away from our makeshift campsite and small fire in what appeared to be a desperate attempt to avoid sharing a tiny tent with me.

What an idiot.

The whole thing seemed silly. Hadn't we spent a night together with his mostly naked body wrapped around mine? At this point, he'd already crossed that figurative line in the dirt. If something was going to happen, it could have happened then, but it didn't. *Nothing* happened. We were capable of sleeping in close quarters together without fear of things getting out of hand. Besides, he'd made it abundantly clear that this particular relationship was never going to be *that* kind of a relationship.

"I'll find something to make this work," he called to me. "Go to bed, I'll be fine."

If he wanted to be stubborn about this, then who was I to stop him? I zipped the tent closed and sat back on my sleeping bag to remove my boots, careful not to squish Callie who had curled up inside the bottom.

My feet ached, but climbing a mountain seemed to get easier with each passing day. Okay, maybe not easier, but my body had become more accustomed to the strenuous walking. I had fewer blisters and didn't collapse into bed each night completely exhausted. My leg muscles didn't burn and feel like jelly anymore. I hailed all those things as small victories.

"Watch out, kitty. Here I come." I slid my feet into the sleeping bag, and sighed at finding Callie's body had warmed the bottom for me. *So lovely.* I rolled onto my side and placed my backpack under my head, trying to find a soft spot to settle into.

Callie shifted and crawled up the inside of the bag to curl against my stomach—her favorite place to sleep. I scratched between her ears and her soft purr vibrated against me. Oh, to be a cat! She was carried everywhere we went, fed when put down, petted and loved, oblivious to the state of the world. Many times, throughout the course of the day, I envied her.

The tent zipper slid open in one quick swoop and Cole tossed his backpack to the side of me. He poked his head inside. "Fine, you win."

I wiggled over, making room for him. "I wasn't trying to win anything. We have a tent made for two, and since I'm one and you're two, it makes sense for the both of us to use it. Aren't you tired of waking up with a frozen beard every morning?"

He stroked his furry face several times. "It is starting to fill out nicely, isn't it?"

I smiled. "If you think that's impressive, you should check out the hair on my legs."

"Thanks, Tess." He spread out his sleeping bag next to mine and groaned. "Just the image I want to take with me to bed."

I chuckled. "I thought you'd enjoy it."

He kicked off his boots, crawled into his bag, and rolled onto his side to face me. "Tomorrow's the big day. If everything goes well, we should reach Rockport Lodge sometime before night fall. You ready for this?"

I had been trying not to think about it: strange, but true. Tomorrow would mean the end of my journey, and it excited and terrified me all at once. Either I'd see my Dad and Toby again. Or I wouldn't. Those were the only two options.

"Tess? You okay?"

I'd never answered him. "Yeah, I'm fine."

"You don't sound fine to me." He tucked a bent arm under his head. "What's going on? I thought you'd be overjoyed to have come this far."

I petted Callie, taking comfort from her before giving voice to my biggest fear. "What if all of this has been nothing but a waste of time? What if no one's there?"

He shrugged. "Then no one's there. At least you'll know. That doesn't make it a waste of time. It only means we keep going until we figure out where your dad and everyone else went. It will be a setback, that's all."

Maybe he was right. I had to know—good or bad. "You'll help me keep looking?"

He nodded. "I told you we'd find your dad, and I have every intention of sticking this out to the bitter end."

"Cole?"

"Yeah?"

"Are you still planning to go back after you hand me off to my dad?"

He was quiet for a moment, but kept his eyes on mine. He took a deep breath and released it. "I know you want me to say no, I'll stay, but Tess, I can't do that. You need people. Me, well, I do a lot better without them."

He'd told me from the very beginning he planned to go back, but I'd hoped after all this time he would've changed his mind. Knowing he hadn't, that he still wanted to leave once this was over, almost brought me to tears. I blinked several times to keep from crying. I didn't like him at first, but now, I couldn't imagine life without him. "What if I begged you to stay, would you?"

He reached across the small space separating us and cupped my face.

I turned into it.

"Tess, if I stayed, you'd never be truly happy. Maybe at first you'd feel like you were, but after a while, you'd come to realize how wrong I am for you. We're from two different worlds—you're a kid with your whole life ahead of you. Me? Not so much." He brushed his thumb over my cheek. "We're only together now because circumstances forced us to be. Had none of this happened, you would have walked right past me on the street without looking my way. I'd just be some old dude you'd never glance twice at."

Blinking no longer helped. The tears fell, and I couldn't stop them. He was right. Had none of this happened, I would be hanging out with my friends, doing stupid teenage things: things seeming so important at the time—planning for prom, posting selfies to my social networks, and trying to figure out how to stay out past curfew without getting caught. Homework, dating, makeup, boys—that was my life.

I would have never thought to say hi to someone like Cole. It embarrassed me to think how shallow my life before all of this had been—how shallow *I* had been. I prayed I was a better person now. I really wanted to believe I had changed.

"Worse yet," he continued. "You'd always wonder if I was happy being with you and living like everyone else lives. I'd say yes, I was very happy, but that nagging voice in the back of your head would never let you fully believe I told the truth."

"So you really think you'd be better off without me and without other people?"

He shook his head. "Other people? Yes. I'll be fine. Without you? No, I won't, but I know *you* would be better off without me, and that's why I can't stay."

"I don't want you to go."

"I know." He went to remove his hand from my face, but I covered his hand with my own, keeping it in place.

"I don't think I'll be better off without you," I said.

He smiled, his eyes watering. "You will be."

"Cole?"

"Yeah?"

"Promise me before you go, you'll say goodbye first. Don't just disappear like some douchebag vampires in teenage books tend to do, thinking it's best for everybody. I'd hate it if you did."

He leaned toward me and kissed my forehead. ""I promise. I'll make sure you receive a proper goodbye before I go."

CHAPTER 41

Cole stood at my side, our shoulders touching, our chests heaving from the climb, and neither of us moving. "What are you waiting for?"

A very good question. What *was* I waiting for?

The lodge's peaked roof rose above the flock of pine trees and aspens surrounding the log structure. Glimpses of the wrap-around deck danced between branches that the wind tossed from side to side. Beautiful, just like I remembered it.

The distance between us and the lodge was less than the size of a football field, but I couldn't take another step. Not yet.

"It's going to be okay." He took my hand in his and gave it a gentle squeeze. *"You're* going to be okay."

I wasn't so sure.

I reached up with my free hand and adjusted the knitted cap covering my head, pulling it lower. A few loose strands of hair threatened to fall away, and I tucked them back inside my hat, trying to ignore what was happening to me—a hard thing to do—

since every day it seemed to get worse. "I don't think anyone's there," I said.

"How can you tell?" He glanced from me to the lodge. "We're too far away to see much of anything."

I pointed to the rock chimney. "There's no smoke. Don't you think there would be smoke?"

"Come on, Tess. That doesn't mean anything, and you know it, so stop making excuses." He released my hand and started walking. "You can stand there if you want," he called over his shoulder, "but I've hiked an entire mountain to get here, and I'm not stopping now. I would've thought you'd be sprinting the last few yards to get to your family."

I thought I would have too. "It's not that easy."

He quit walking and turned to face me. "No, what we've done to get here wasn't easy. It was damn hard, but this"—he swung his arm between us and the lodge—"*this* is the easy part.

"You're wrong. This part is really hard."

Cole retraced his steps to come stand in front of me. "What's going on, Tess?"

"What if..." I shook my head. I couldn't finish.

"What if *what?* We've already been over this. If they're there, we'll celebrate. If they're not, we'll figure out where they went. Standing here isn't going to change anything."

"Maybe not, but for right now, standing here keeps them alive, inside, waiting for me." I bit my lip to stop it from quivering. Living in the unknown was painful, but facing certainty head-on might kill me. They could be dead in there.

He came closer and placed his hand on my forearm. "You and I both know whatever happened to your friend—what's his name, Dylan, was it?—doesn't mean anything. His sickness was a fluke. I'm fine. You're fine. You're dad and brother are probably fine, too. Shouldn't we go find out?"

I could've pulled off my hat and shown him what was going on. I could've told him no, Dylan wasn't a fluke, but I didn't. That would mean admitting something was wrong with me, and I wasn't ready.

What could he do about it anyway?

A sunburned arm and frozen limbs were one thing; Dylan's type of illness couldn't be mended—not by mortal, angel, or alien, whatever he happened to be. This was beyond fixable.

"Tess." He reached out and took my hand, shaking me from my thoughts. "You can't avoid this. Whatever we find in there is going to be the same today, tomorrow, and the day after that."

I weaved my fingers between his and held on tight. "That's what I'm afraid of."

It seemed surreal to stand in the middle of the floor, looking up at the massive chandelier created from dozens of elk antlers. The first time I saw it, I cried. I had to have been six or seven at the time, and thought someone had hurt a lot of poor animals simply to make a complicated light fixture.

Dad had knelt next to me, wiped my tears, and explained how each antler had been collected through elk shedding. He promised no animals were hurt; he pinky-swore. From that point on, every time we visited the lodge, I'd stand below it and stare. It fascinated me, because I couldn't understand how an animal could grow something so magnificent only to have it fall off later. It didn't seem right.

When lit, the chandelier bounced light across the walls in scattered patterns, but now, in the darkened dirty foyer, the hanging relic only gathered dust. There was nothing special about it anymore.

The river-rock fireplace had the same feel. With a fire roaring in its monstrous cavern, the entire hall glowed in oranges and yellows, its warmth like a comforter. Without the dancing flames, it became hollow and depressing. An inch of undisturbed dirt lay across the cushions of the leather couches, with their gold decorative studs along the edges. The smell of mildew and faded smoke rimmed my nostrils.

Outside the A-framed windows, the ski-lift remained still. Only a few chairs, clinging to the cables above, rocked when the wind moved them—eerie and ghostlike. Leaves and pine needles gathered in the corners and along edges of the once majestic room.

For the most part, I kept my eyes on the dead chandelier. I couldn't look anywhere else.

Cole's footsteps resounded along the second-story balcony as he ran from one room to another, flinging open the guest bedroom doors. I'd flinch when each door smacked the wall—the boom painful to my ears—and Callie meowed in response from her tethered place at the bar.

He searched the lodge because I couldn't.

Knowing we were all alone grounded me to that one spot in the middle of the foyer, numbing me to everything else. I had expected to find the lodge empty, but I wasn't prepared for it.

"They're not here." Cole, panting, stood at the top of the winding stairs and looked down at me. "There're no bodies."

I didn't answer. Of course, I was grateful to hear their bodies weren't lying on beds upstairs, but they may as well have been.

Alone was still alone.

Dad had left; he'd never come back, and worse than either of those things: he hadn't waited for me either. He'd written me off, cut his ties, and left me behind.

"I know what you're thinking." He leaned against the railing. "And you need to stop it."

He couldn't possibly imagine what I was thinking. I turned in a slow circle, still staring at the chandelier that used to bring me so much joy.

"Your dad loves you, Tess. Don't doubt it. Whatever reason he has for not being here must have been a good one."

I'm sure it was.

"We'll find him and we'll find your brother."

No, we wouldn't. I continued to turn around and around.

"Where there's a will, there's a way, remember?"

I stopped moving, undid the leather strap from my wrist, and flung it above me. The bracelet snagged on the sharp point of an antler and dangled from the tip, too high to reach.

Stupid bracelet. Stupid memories. Stupid expectations.

My will was broken. *I* was broken.

Cole crossed the room and came to my side, staring up at the discarded bracelet. "Remind me never to give you a gift again."

The moment it had left my fingers, I regretted it. He didn't deserve that, especially since he wasn't the target of my anger, but I couldn't do anything about it now. "We should go." I didn't know where to exactly, back to the hanger maybe, but I knew we needed to leave. I couldn't stay any longer. No point.

I started toward Callie, but Cole grabbed my hand and drew me back. "What's that?" He pointed above us. "Right there. Do you see it?"

He wasn't pointing at the bracelet hanging from the outside edge, but to the middle of the tangled antlers. He grabbed my shoulders and twisted me so I could see what he was seeing.

A dingy white sock.

It blended in with the whiteness and drooped over several sharp points. Unless we stood directly below it, like we were now, we would never have seen it.

"Just a second." He left me standing there and took off across the room then threw open the glass doors to the pool hall and disappeared from view. A few seconds later he returned carrying three pool cues. "There's a roll of duct tape in the front pocket of my bag. Go grab it for me, will you?"

I did as he asked, bringing the silver roll of tape back to him where he'd stretched out the pool sticks on the floor in a long line. "It's a sock, Cole."

"Yeah, it is, but *why?*" His eyes widened and he bobbed his head. "Ask yourself that." If he expected a response, he didn't get one. He knelt next to the poles, tore off long pieces of tape, and began fastening them together. "Aren't you the least bit curious?"

Maybe a little. "Please don't do this to me."

He wound more tape around the sticks without looking at me. "Do what?"

"I don't want to be disappointed again."

"I hate to break it you, but life is brimming with disappointments. There's no getting around it." This time he looked at me and cocked a brow. "Would you rather I leave that sock where it is? I can, you know."

I glanced up at the hidden thing, curious. Someone had a reason to throw it up there. But a sock? Really?

"Fine."

It took several tries to manipulate the extra long stick into place. Cole got close, but the upper pole slipped and didn't want to stay together. He lowered the whole thing back to the floor and started redoing the tape again.

I folded my arms across my chest. "Why don't you use your magical abilities and fly up there and get it?"

"Ha, ha, you're funny." He glared at me. "Stop being a pain in the ass and give me a hand with this."

I knelt beside him and tore off the long pieces of tape he needed, though I couldn't imagine the wobbly contraption actually working. The whole thing looked awkward, and he looked awkward trying to work it.

"This should do it." He positioned himself below the antlers again, balancing on his toes to get enough height and leverage, and poked the sock, trying to dislodge it from its hammock-style position. After a few more jabs, and with a bit of nudging and probing, the sock fluttered to the ground.

Cole dropped the poles and they clattered on the tiled floor. He nodded to me. "Go ahead."

If it was just a sock, and nothing else, I didn't know what I'd do. Yes, disappointment was part of life, but hadn't I already suffered more than my fair share of it?

"Do it already. If nothing else, we now have a new sock for your cat to play with." His attempt at a positive spin didn't help me any.

"It is what it is, right?" I looked at him for encouragement.

He gave an impatient nod. "I'm going to grab it if you don't."

I bent over and snatched the sock into my hand, trying my best to keep my expectations low. It crinkled like paper.

What? I squeezed it again, unsure I had actually felt something inside the old sock.

It crinkled like before.

I took a deep breath and let it out slowly as I slipped my hand inside the dingy thing. My fingers wrapped around a tiny piece of paper, folded into fourths. I removed the worn and wrinkly paper and allowed the sock to fall to the ground.

"Tess, you're killing me here!" Cole motioned to the paper.

I carefully unfolded it, read it, and then read it again. I looked up at him with tears glistening in my eyes. "It's from my dad." I recognized the handwriting, even if he hadn't used my name to address it to me or signed his own. *He left me a note.*

"Sweet! What did he say?"

I shook my head. "I'm not sure."

Cole took the paper from me and angled it so the natural light fell on it. He read it, flipped it over, saw nothing on the backside, and then flipped it over and read once more. "He's a man of few words isn't he?"

"Why this?" I tapped the paper he still held. "Why not leave a complete note on the door or place it on the bar so I could see it? A cryptic note shoved into a sock way up high in an antler chandelier? What was he thinking?"

Cole shrugged. "Maybe this was his way of protecting you in case someone else found it."

"Someone else? There is no one else!"

"We don't know that. We don't know much of anything, if you think about it."

He had a point, but really? "Okay, so what does this mean? *'Follow the arrows. Wait by the window. 2:37 a.m. Watch for me.'* That doesn't make any sense. What arrows? What window?" Could he have made this any harder?

"I don't know, but I suggest we start looking. We only have a few more hours of light before this scavenger hunt becomes a lot more difficult."

I tucked the strange little note into my pocket and followed Cole's lead. He moved around the room and ran his hands over the log walls, feeling them like he was reading Braille, so I explored the guest check-in counter, the bar, and each piece of furniture, doing the same. Nothing.

Arrows, arrows, arrows... where are you?

I examined each large window, thinking maybe I could skip the first step, but none of the windows were marked with anything other than a layer of grime. "I don't know what I'm looking for. I might have already run across an arrow and didn't know it."

"Then we keep looking until it becomes clear." Cole crept along the dusty floor boards on his hands and knees. "You want to find your dad then you need to start looking harder."

"Harder? I am looking hard! This is impossible."

He sat back, smiled, and pointed to my bracelet hanging from an antler. "Where there is a will, there is a way. You'd know that if you still had your bracelet."

I narrowed my eyes. "Yeah, thanks for reminding me. Except, that's not always...."

No friggin' way!

My fingers brushed across a notched-out emblem along the edge of the bottom stair. A tiny carved arrow pointed upward. My breath hitched in my throat and I blinked several times. I ran my finger over and over it.

Hotcakes on a burner! I found it!

"Except it's not always what?" He stared at me, waiting for me to continue. "If you can't finish your thought, then there is no exception and I win."

I couldn't speak, but waved frantically for Cole to come see.

"What? You found it?" He jumped to his feet and ran across the room to where I knelt next to the stairs. I pointed to the tiny arrow, and his face broke out in a huge grin. "All righty, then. Now we know what to look for."

Each consecutive arrow became easier to spot: one along the balcony railing; another along the edge of the carpet; a third notched into the picture frame hanging on the wall. Ten total arrows led to a small room on the far end of the lodge—maids' quarters.

I would never have guessed the window, the size of a book, was the one mentioned in the note, but a small arrow had been carved into the frame. It overlooked the lake and part of the valley, and even though the window was small, a whole lot of land was packed into that space. Miles and miles of it.

Cole had gathered Callie from downstairs, and now the three of us sat on the edge of the twin bed, staring out the box-sized window as the sun faded to darkness. We had no way of knowing the correct time, not really, but it didn't matter; the blackness outside captivated us like a movie screen. If there was something to see, we would see it.

Time ticked by, and we sat in silence, watching, each of us lost in our own thoughts. Cole wrapped his hand around mine, and we sat together, waiting.

At first, I thought I might have been seeing things, so I scooted forward on the edge of the bed and blinked my blurry eyes. "Do you see that?"

A white light, steady and constant amid the blackness. A light where there shouldn't be any.

"I do." Cole released my hand and jumped up from the bed. He looked out the window several minutes before running to the side table and circling a section on his worn map with a Rockport Lodge complimentary pen. "I think that's where it's coming from. I don't know how far it is, I can only guess, but I'm estimating maybe five or six miles. Ten at the most. We can be there tomorrow if we get going first thing in the morning." He went back to the window and fiddled with his map by the light of his fading headlamp, double-checking his markings. "What do you think? Leave here by dawn?"

He swung his head in my direction, and the light from the small headlamp illuminated the slick dark substance coating my shaking hands and running from both my nostrils. The coppery taste of blood dripped down my throat, choking me.

I couldn't speak, but at the rate the blood flowed, picking up pace as it raced over my fingers and soaked the front of my t-shirt, waiting until dawn wasn't an option.

Trees zipped past as though caught in a spinning vortex. Their shapes and sizes blended together becoming blurred lines in my peripheral vision. The crunch of snow beneath Cole's feet developed into a soft hum—solid, consistent, and without pause.

"I wish you'd told me." He kept repeating the words. "You should have told me, Tess."

Maybe, I should have, but honestly, I thought I had more time than this. And if I was even more honest, I'd hoped this wouldn't happen at all.

It didn't hurt, not really. Only when the blood oozed down my throat, making it difficult to breathe, did I panic at all. The rest of the time, I lay in Cole's arms and stared at the swirling stars above me and the flash of dizzying trees around us.

It felt like flying, and I really hoped we were.

Because there was no way we were going to make it in time.

And I really wanted to see Dad.

# CHAPTER
42

Large industrial fans whirled over head and their giant blades moved without sound. Florescent light bulbs faded in and out, popping and hissing in my ear, and the corrugated walls reminded me of Dad's underground bunker. Similar, but different.

Wherever we were, we moved quickly. Multiple footsteps slapped the cement and echoed down the long corridor. Indistinct faces hovered around me, coming into view and then receding. A steel gurney pressed into my back, cold and uncomfortable, its creaky wheels carrying me away.

"Where did you find her?"

"By the entrance."

"Alone?"

"Yes."

That wasn't true. Cole was with me. Where was he? *Cole?*

"That's impossible. She shouldn't be alive, not after all this time."

"I'd have to agree, but impossible or not, she's here. She made it."

I made it.

"Jon insisted she'd find a way."

"I can't believe that fool turned out to be right."

Dad? Where is he?

The table rolled on and bumped over the divots in the floor. I'm not sure how I didn't slide off, we moved so quickly. My eyes began to tear, and I blinked several times, but blinking only made the tears fall faster, though I wasn't crying. The tears distorted my vision, giving everything a crimson hue.

Where's Dad? Why isn't he here? I needed to see him.

Blood gurgled in my mouth. I coughed and left a splattered mess on the passing wall. I couldn't catch my breath. My lungs filled with my own blood, drowning me, and I pounded the table. *Help me, please!*

"Hold her down!"

Hands gripped my body from all angles, pressing down on my shoulders, hips, and ankles. The gurney didn't stop moving.

I struggled to sit up, to fight them off, to force a breath, but an unfamiliar face bent near mine. "This will hurt, but it will help."

The front of my shirt was ripped away and cool air chilled my bare skin. Before I could understand why, a man climbed on top of me, and straddled my waist, though not putting his entire weight on me. He raised my left arm above my head, and someone held it, keeping me from lowering it back to my side.

What are you doing?

He nodded to the others, then leaned forward and without warning, stabbed me between the ribs. I screamed and couldn't stop.

At least I think I screamed.

The man continued to ride on the gurney with me, sliding a plastic tube into the incision he'd made between my ribs, while the others pushed us along. Blood ran down my side, and I could breathe—not deep breaths, but I no longer struggled. The more he inserted the tubing, the more my head swirled with pain, and I wished I'd pass out. That luxury hung out of reach, and instead, I felt everything.

"Tess!"

Dad?

I tried to lift my head, to search for him, but the hands on my body held me in place.

"Get out of the way, Jon!"

"That's my daughter!"

I turned my head toward his voice, and smiled as my father forced his way toward me. He ignored those who yelled at him to stay back and pushed through them. He ran along the side of the moving gurney, holding on to it with one hand while tentatively touching my face with his other. His fingers quivered against my skin and tears rolled down his cheeks.

"Oh, Tess. Oh, my sweet girl."

I wanted him to pick me up and carry me away, but he only cried and smoothed the hair from my eyes. *I want to go home, Dad.*

"You can fix this, right?" He glanced to the others, but continued to stroke my face. "Right?"

"That's what we're trying to do here, but she's lost a lot of blood, Jon, and it's not showing signs of stopping."

"Take mine then! Do what you have to do!" Dad cursed. "Give her my blood!"

"If we can't get her stable right now, your blood won't help."

Dad looked at the man who sat on top of me for a long moment and neither of them spoke. Finally, Dad glanced to me and forced a smile. "He doesn't know you like I do. He doesn't know what you're capable of, so you fight this, okay? You fought to get this far, so now that you're here, I expect you to stay."

My eyes drooped, feeling heavy. *I want to stay too. I'm not going anywhere.*

"Where is she?" Toby's voice echoed down the corridor. He sounded so far away. "Where's my sister? Tess! *Tess!*"

I'm here, Toby. I'm here!

I couldn't see him, but heard him running toward me and despite the differences we'd had the past few years, I *needed* to see my brother. The gurney turned down a smaller corridor heading for a set of large doors faster than he could catch up.

They told Dad he could go no farther, something about isolation and contamination, so he released my face and slipped away from view. "You'll be okay," he called to me. "You'll be okay."

Dad? I had just found him, and now I had to leave him? They planned to isolate me? *No.* I tried to reach my hand out to stop him from going, to stop them from taking me away, but couldn't muster the strength to lift my hand from the table. *Don't leave me.*

This wasn't fair. A handful of minutes with my family wasn't enough. *I just got here!*

I turned my head in time to see Dad standing next to Toby — the two of them side by side, both looking defeated.

"We love you, Tess!" Toby's voice cracked as he hollered after me. "We love you!" He hadn't said those words to me in years.

I love you, too.

The double doors swung closed behind me.

"Tess, can you hear me?"

Grogginess held me captive in its powerful grasp. I couldn't quite open my eyes or turn my head, but I answered, "Yeah." The oxygen mask muffled my words.

"Sweetheart, I need you to wake up now. Can you do that for me?"

Dad? Why does his voice sound so weird?

A crackling, buzzing sound filled the room. "Open your eyes, honey."

I really didn't want to, but I forced one eye open and then the other.

He smiled at me through the glass and pressed a button on the wall. The crackling sounded again and his voice came through the intercom imbedded in the ceiling. "How are you feeling?"

I slipped the mask off. "Not so good."

"I know, baby. I know."

"Then why did you wake me up?"

He didn't say anything, and I wondered if the intercom had stopped working, but I could see his finger on the button. "Toby's here, too." He motioned to my brother and Toby stepped into view, his face grim.

"Hey, Tess."

"Hey."

Toby glanced to Dad, and Dad nodded at him. "It's okay," he whispered, and the emotion in his voice carried through the intercom, something I didn't think I was supposed to hear.

"Dad, what's going on?" I glanced around, taking in the sterile room, the IV bag hanging above my head, and sensors attached to my chest. A large tube ran from my side to a machine next to the bed; other machines displayed my inner workings. They beeped and hummed, filling the room with their droning. "What's happening?"

Dad looked at Toby but neither of them said anything for a long time. He turned away, his back to me, his shoulders rising and falling. My big, strong dad was crying.

"Dad?"

My brother moved closer to the intercom and held the button. "It doesn't look good, Tess. They're trying, but nothing seems to be helping. You keep getting sicker."

Behind Dad and Toby, two men sat at a table with computers. They seemed intent on the screens in front of them rather than listening to our conversation. It gave our family reunion a clinical feel. Not at all how I imagined this moment to be.

I tried to shift on the bed, raise myself, but couldn't. I gave up and sank back against the pillows. "What's wrong with me?"

Toby took a minute to speak. "Toxins in your blood are attacking your immune system and shutting your organs down." He paused, glanced to Dad, but Dad kept his back to the both of us. Toby turned to me again and his eyes met mine. "Your case is pretty severe, Tess. They're doing everything they can, but the things that have normally worked for others... aren't working for you."

I lifted my hand and pointed at the men sitting at the table behind my brother. "They say this? Are they the ones saying they can't fix me?"

Toby nodded.

"Are they even doctors? Do they even know what they're doing?" I peered around the sterile room, taking in my full surroundings. The machines beeped louder. "Where are we?"

"Tess, don't... don't get worked up, please." He peered over his shoulder at the two men. One of them made a sign with his hand, and Toby turned back to me. "I'll answer your questions, but take it easy, okay?"

"Take it easy? How exactly am I supposed to do that?" A machine went nuts at my side and let out a high pitched beep that wouldn't stop. One of the men got up from the table, put on a surgical gown, hat, mask, and gloves, and then stood inside an adjoining room the size of a closet. Air whirled around him for thirty seconds, before he punched in a code and came into my room.

"Are they doctors?" Toby didn't answer me and I rolled my head to the side and faced the masked man. "Are you a doctor?"

He adjusted a machine. "No, I'm not, but I'm the closest thing you've got."

I recognized his voice. "You stabbed me in the chest, and you're not a doctor?"

"You're alive and breathing because I did."

"But not for long, right?"

He lifted my oxygen mask and held it close to my face. "You've been given a chance to say goodbye to your family. I suggest you do it. A lot of people never had that opportunity."

Say goodbye? I turned to face my brother again. "Who is this guy? I don't understand. Please, tell me what's going on."

Toby brushed his dark hair off his forehead. "You've seen the mess outside," he said. "Once those meteorites hit the ground, all hell broke loose. Radiation levels are higher than normal. We can hardly breathe the air because of all the crap in it and the water is so contaminated it's impossible to drink. You've been out there in it longer than everyone else, so you've seen how crazy it is. What more can I explain?"

I had seen every miserable aspect of it, but I still didn't understand anything. "Why isn't anyone fixing it?"

"Sometimes things are too catastrophic to be fixed. And sometimes instead of fixing anything, people in charge make things worse. Those of us stuck in the middle are doing what we can to survive—pulling together, gathering resources, and doing what we can to keep from being more exposed than we already were."

"Is that why the government killed everyone?"

Dad turned around, approached the window, and shouldered Toby out of the way. "How do you know that? What did you see?"

I shrugged. "I didn't see anything. A friend, before he died, told me about the planes."

The lights above my head flickered and the alarms on the machines sounded. My chest tightened and one of my arms began to twitch. The "doctor" inserted something into my IV, and heaviness fell over me. He left my room in a hurry. The mask, gown, and gloves were tossed into garbage cans, and the gust of air sprayed him again.

The lights stopped their flickering, the machines whirled, and my chest rose in relief.

I could see them talking through my heavy lids, but couldn't hear a thing. Dad seemed to disagree with the two men, but when his shoulders slumped forward, I could tell that whatever argument they were having, Dad had come out the loser.

After a few minutes he approached the glass window, defeated. "I know you have a lot of questions. Hell, we all do, and I want to answer every one of them, tell you what I know, but honey," his lips quivered, "I don't want to waste what little time we have left together."

Little time left together? I dropped the oxygen mask on the bed and blinked over and over again. "How much time are we talking about?"

Dad placed a hand on the glass and let it slide down the smooth surface. He lowered his head and kept it there as he spoke. "Tomorrow morning, if you're not showing improvement"—his voice wavered—"we'll be turning off the machines." He looked up at me and tears ran down his face. "You won't feel a thing, honey. I promise. I'll make sure."

"No, don't turn them off. I'll fight this, please." I just got here. This wasn't right.

"The generators are struggling to keep up. I'm afraid we don't have a choice."

"I don't want to die."

"I don't want you to either." He hung his head, and his sobbing brought reality crashing down on me.

This was really happening.

Toby placed a hand on Dad's shoulder.

I didn't speak. I didn't cry. Numbness took over and I didn't feel much of anything. A day? They were only giving me one day?

"We'll be by your side the whole time. You won't be alone."

I was no longer listening. "Where's Cole?"

They exchanged a look.

"Where is he? Why isn't he here? Let him in, please. I need to see him."

Toby leaned close to the intercom, taking Dad's place. "Tess, what are you talking about?"

"The guy who brought me here? Where is he?" He promised he wouldn't be a douchebag and leave me without saying goodbye.

"There's nobody —"

I waved my hand, stopping my brother. "Never mind." *Cole, you asshole.* I shouldn't have been surprised that he'd take off.

"Tess, I'm sorry. I wish...." Toby choked. "If I could trade places with you, I would."

The tears came then, running silently over my cheeks and down my neck. I adjusted the oxygen mask over my face, rolled away from both of them, and squeezed my eyes shut.

I wouldn't want anyone to take my place.

I didn't want anyone to hurt as bad as I did.

CHAPTER 43

"Do you remember when you were a little girl and used to carry around Mr. Pickles everywhere you went? Do you remember that?" Dad smiled.

I nodded, but kept my eyes closed. I loved that darn stuffed bunny. One of the ears had fallen off and most of its whiskers, all except for one clear plastic strand that stuck straight out and snagged on everything. That stuffed animal slept with me every night until I was almost ten. I'd always wondered what happened, because it seemed like one day I had it and then the next day I didn't. It just vanished.

"Why did you bring that up?"

Toby shifted in his chair and gave Dad quite a look. "Thanks a lot."

He knew something! I lifted the oxygen mask and watched them both through the glass. "What did you do to Mr. Pickles?"

He raised both his hands. "Before I admit anything, I want you to know I'm really sorry, I swear."

"What did you do?" My eyes fluttered open.

"You've got to admit that thing was getting pretty gross and was on its last legs."

"Tell me, Toby. What did you do?"

"Okay, okay. You know that BB gun I got for my birthday?"

I nodded, not liking where this was going.

"And remember how Mom told me I couldn't shoot real animals?"

I lifted the mask, but held it within a few inches of my face. "You shot Mr. Pickles."

"By accident. I shot your rabbit by accident, and then I buried him in the backyard."

"That doesn't sound like an accident. That sounds pretty deliberate to me."

Toby smiled. "Maybe a little."

"I forgive you, you big jerk. I guess while we're admitting things, I should tell you about that Dale Murphy autographed baseball you loved?"

Toby sat forward and smacked the window. "I knew you did it! What did you do with my ball?"

I smiled through my sleepy haze. "I gave it to Robby Grindstaff in exchange for five bucks."

"No!" He slumped back. "Do you know how much that thing was worth?"

"I'd have to say five bucks."

"I can't believe you did that. Please tell me you at least spent the money on something good."

"Not really. I think I spent it on packages of Pop Rocks candy." Medicine swirled through my body, causing sleep to tug on my eyelids. "I'm feeling kind of tired, why don't you and Dad go get something to eat? I won't even notice you're gone. I promise I'll be here when you get back."

Dad placed a hand on Toby's arm. "Go. I'll be there in a minute."

"Are you sure?" Toby looked from Dad to me. "I don't know."

I nodded. "We still have until morning, right? No one's pulling the plug on me before then, so go, please. Don't make me worry about you guys."

Toby stood and placed the palm of his hand against the glass. "I'll be back."

They'd moved my bed closer to the window, and I touched the glass where his hand was. "I'll be here."

He left and Dad scooted his chair closer to the glass. "I wish I could touch you."

I smiled sadly. "Me too."

"I'm sorry. I should never have left you in the bunker. I should've brought you with me to go find your brother..." He shook his head, his eyes closed. "There were a lot of things I should have done differently."

"Dad, don't. You did what you thought was right. I don't blame you."

His eyes met mine. "I blame myself."

"Please don't."

"I should have gone back for you. I broke my promise to you."

I shook my head a little. "Toby needed you. You had to stay with him. Besides, if you'd come for me, we'd both be in the room and Toby would have nobody. I don't want him to be alone."

Dad hung his head, crying. "I love you, Tess." His hand mirrored mine on the window. Only a few inches of glass separated us.

"I love you, too." I blinked away sleep, trying to hold on for a moment longer. My hand dropped from the glass. "Are you and Toby going to be okay? I mean, with everything going on? Are you safe here?"

He sighed. "As safe as we can be, but as far as being okay? I'll never be okay. Not without you. Not without your mom."

I didn't want to think about any of that. "What are your plans? You can't live underground forever, can you?" The facility, an abandoned military base, though providing most of the necessities, could never be a permanent solution.

"I don't know, honey. We're taking it one step at a time. Radiation levels outside are dropping. The air is getting better, but we still have a long way to go before it's livable. You saw what the government's solution was, so for now, hiding is the best option, but we hope that will change soon. That's all we can do."

"I'm really tired." Hanging on to consciousness became harder with each passing minute. "I'm going to sleep for a little bit, okay? Just a little while."

"You do that, sweetheart. You do that." He patted the glass.

My eyes drooped closed. "Don't turn off anything yet, okay?"

"We won't. We're still hoping for a miracle."

"Me too, Dad. Me too."

"Hey, sleepy-head."

Cole?

I forced my eyelids to shake off the heaviness holding them closed. He sat on the foot of the bed, grinning like he always seemed to do, and he patted my leg before giving it a gentle squeeze.

I eased myself into a sitting position, careful not to disturb any of the dozens of tubes and wires attached to various parts of my body. I skimmed the room, saw we were alone, and slipped the oxygen mask from my face. I wasn't supposed to, but wearing it made talking difficult.

"I thought you'd left. I even called you an asshole."

"Sounds about right. We have this up and down kind of relationship, don't we?"

"I hated you."

His smile faded. "I told you if I hadn't said goodbye, then I hadn't left."

I pulled the sheets up over my chest, covering my near-nakedness. "What are you doing in here?"

"What? You're not happy to see me?" He squeezed my leg again. "I thought you'd like a visitor."

"Of course, I just..." I glanced at the large window separating me from everyone else, making me feel like a goldfish in a bowl.

Those monitoring me, watching my vitals, checking on me for improvement, weren't there. Neither was Dad or Toby. Strange to see the little room completely empty. "Are you even supposed to be in here, and aren't you supposed to be wearing all the precautionary stuff?" Anybody who entered the room wore masks, gloves, and hazmat-like suits.

"First," he said. "I don't believe what you have is contagious. I'd already be sick right now if you were, but I'm not. We spent a lot of time together, right?"

I nodded slowly.

"They're being a little excessive. Second, I've been living out there in the elements a lot longer than you, and I'm fine. I'm not worried, so don't you be. And thirdly, no one is keeping me from seeing you. I needed to see for myself that you were fine. I brought you here, and I wanted to make sure they were treating you right."

"They're treating me well, but it doesn't matter. I'm not getting any better." I indicated to the machines wrapped around my bed. "They're turning those off in the morning."

He didn't say anything, but stared at the beeping and humming equipment.

"It's okay," I said. "At least I got to see my dad and brother again. I didn't think I would. You gave me that. Thank you."

"That's not right." He shook his head. "That's not supposed to happen."

"I know."

"No, that's not supposed to happen." He took my hand in his. His fingers trembled against mine. "Are you certain?"

I nodded.

Neither of us spoke for a moment. I relished his hand in mine as he traced his thumb over my palm—the only place not covered in wires.

"I *am* glad you're here," I said. "I really am."

"Me too."

"Where did you go?"

He tipped his head and leaned in a little closer toward me. "I brought you something."

"Really?" I didn't think I was supposed to have anything in the room—not even him—but I was dying, so what did it matter?

He released my hand, held up a finger to tell me to wait, then reached in to his thick jacket and produced the ever-growing ball of fluff.

Callie meowed when he placed her into my arms.

I hugged her to me, pressing my face against her, and my tears fell, wetting her fur. "I didn't think I'd ever see her again. Oh, my gosh, Cole! You went back for her." I couldn't believe it. "Thank you, thank you!"

Cole half-smiled. He scratched Callie's head. "Did you really think I wouldn't go back for her? She's worn on me almost as much as you have."

Tears poured down my face. "With everything going on, and leaving her behind, I thought—"

He put his hand up, stopping me. "I wasn't going to let anything happen to either of you." Tears rimmed his eyes. "I'm *not* going to let anything happen to you. We've been through too much to let this happen." He pointed to the machines. "Don't give up."

I held on to Callie with one hand, holding her against me, and reached for him with my other, needing to touch him. "I don't think I have a choice."

He shook his head and took my hand in his, holding on as though if by letting it go I would drift away. Maybe I would. He slipped his hands into his front pocket and removed something else.

Silent tears ran down my cheeks as he tied the familiar bracelet around my wrist. He lifted my hand to his lips and he kissed my fingers, but said nothing.

"I don't know that I have any will left," I said. I appreciated the gesture, but I could feel my body fighting me. Each breath became harder than the previous. "But thank you."

"Are you in any pain?"

"No, not really."

"This is ridiculous." He smacked the bed. "What can I do, Tess? Tell me what to do and I'll do it."

"There's nothing you can do."

"There has to be something!"

I blinked a few times and smiled. "The only thing I want is for you to stay. Just stay."

He didn't say anything, seeming to contemplate my request. "Okay," he said. "Okay."

"Really?" I didn't expect it to be that easy.

"Yeah, I'll stay as long as I can."

I couldn't have asked for more than that. I made room for him beside me, and he hesitated for only a minute before lying down and curving his body around mine. Callie purred and stretched on the opposite side with her body against my belly and her furry head below my chin.

"I'm scared," I said. "Not for me, but for my dad and brother. For you."

"Don't be scared," he whispered against my ear. "Don't worry about any of us."

"You know, I didn't really like you in the beginning."

He chuckled. "Yeah, I could tell, but to be fair, I didn't much care for you either."

"Now, the funny thing is that I can't imagine being in a place where you're not."

He kissed the back of my head. "Don't give up yet," he said. "It's not quite morning."

I could see them panicking behind the glass, but couldn't hear a word they said. Dad finally pressed the intercom, asking the same question that had already been asked and answered a dozen times. I didn't understand the fuss. Callie wasn't hurting anything.

"Tess, tell me again how the cat got in there?"

Callie curled at my side, sleeping, and I ran my hand over her fur. "Cole brought her. I already told you. He went back for her and brought her to me." I held up my wrist. "He brought me this too."

The intercom remained on, an accident I suppose, as Dad, Toby, and several men argued back and forth.

"She's been monitored the whole time. No one has gone in there. Not today."

"Are you positive?"

"Yes."

"You didn't leave your position, not even for a moment?"

"I was gone for only a few minutes. Ten at the most, but there is no way someone came and left in that short a time."

"Then how do you explain the cat? It's a cat, for crying out loud! A cat!"

"Maybe it wandered in somehow. I don't know."

"Through the decontamination chamber and into her room? When did cats start entering security codes?"

"Maybe my sister picked out the smartest kitten of the bunch."

"Toby, you're not helping."

"And you're sure that's her cat?"

Dad nodded. "Yes, that's the kitten she picked out at the shelter."

"Does anyone else think this is complete insanity or is it just me?"

"Toby, seriously. You're not helping."

"Did anyone check her bag?" one of the men asked. "Maybe the cat was inside it and we missed it."

"She didn't have a bag. She came in with only the clothes on her back, and we took all those. She didn't have the bracelet on either. We would have seen it if she had. Neither of those things was there this morning."

"Your daughter is keeping something from us, because there is no way a cat should even be alive let alone *here* in that room with her."

"My daughter's not a liar."

"I'm not saying she is, but if someone came in here with a cat, we need to figure out how they got in and how they got out without anyone seeing them."

"Well," Toby said. "I don't care how the cat got here. All I know is that ever since it showed up, my sister has started getting better."

The other men argued some more, but Dad held his hand up, stopping them. "You guys go figure out how the cat got here," he said. "As for me and my son, we're taking a bowl of food and water in for her. Then we're sitting by Tess's side until she's well enough to come out of there. Until then, I'm going to touch her and hold her hand, and there is nothing anyone can do to stop me."

I knew Cole had come to see me. I had proof. I also knew he'd left, like he'd always said he would, having stayed until I fell asleep. I accepted his leaving, because he told me that as long as he didn't say goodbye, he wasn't really gone, and since he'd never uttered those words, they could argue all they wanted— Dad, Toby, the others—I didn't care.

I already knew everything I needed to know.

| THE END |

ACKNOWLEDGEMENTS

Wow! I can't actually believe I'm writing the acknowledgement section, since this book took me *forever* to write. This is a glorious feeling. I'm going to pretend I'm holding a gold statue while I write this, so just know I am typing this with one hand while the other is at an awkward angle in the air.

A lot of people have helped me to get to the point of actually completing this novel. I'm going to list their names, in no particular order (okay, in a bit of an order, but don't think their contribution is lessened if they're at the bottom). They know what they've done, and they know how much I love and appreciate them for having done it.

Here goes:

Scott Cornford, Caden Cornford, Calder Cornford, Callie Cornford, Trudy and Larry Helton, Diana Tracy, Mallory Rock, Stevie Mikayne, Lane Diamond, Merlaine Waldron, Dottie Taylor, Kimberly Kinrade, Amber Armstrong, Kathleen Allen, Ari Evans, Merlin and Zoey (my two furry/feathered writing companions), friends, family, strangers, and most importantly, above all—my fans who kept asking when the new book would be ready and encouraged me to write faster.

ABOUT THE AUTHOR

Angela Scott hears voices. Tiny fictional people sit on her shoulders and whisper their stories in her ear. Instead of medicating herself, she decided to pick up a pen, write down everything those voices tell me, and turn it into a book. She's not crazy. She's an author. For the most part, she writes contemporary Young Adult novels. However, through a writing exercise that spiraled out of control, she found herself writing about zombies terrorizing the Wild Wild West--and loving it. Her zombies don't sparkle, and they definitely don't cuddle. At least, she wouldn't suggest it. She lives on the benches of the beautiful Wasatch Mountains with two lovely children, one teenager, and a very patient husband. She graduated from Utah State University with a B.A. degree in English, not because of her love for the written word, but because it was the only major that didn't require math. She can't spell, and grammar is her arch nemesis. But they gave her the degree, and there are no take backs.

WHAT'S NEXT?

ZIA THE TEENAGE ZOMBIE &
THE UNDEAD DIARIES
WATCH FOR THIS YOUNG ADULT ZOMBIE ADVENTURE,
COMING IN THE SUMMER OF 2015.

CHAPTER 1

Dear Diary,

I wish I'd been given the whole casket and burial plot kind of death. I even know the type of headstone I'd like. Not the ones that lie flat on the ground; no one sees those. They get mowed over and stepped on. I'd want an upright one in the shape of a heart. It would have a built-in vase for a nice flower or two. Preferably a daisy. My favorite.

My headstone would say my name, AnnaZia Evans, and my birth date — the day I actually came into the world and not my "rebirth" as many call it: April 16, 1998. And of course, the day I died, July 3, 2014.

Sing a song. Cry a little. Let me go to the great beyond. But no. None of that for me.

Today is November 6, 2014.

The day I died has come and gone and isn't recorded anywhere. I still walk the earth and do everything I used to do but with a "handicap" — as I call it — and no one cares when I died anymore.

I remember though.

Because the day I died was also the day I became a part of the walking dead.

And also the day my life totally began to suck.

***

I run the brush through my stringy hair and pull it back from my face with a head band. Except, of course, for a long strand that I leave intentionally hanging down over what is left of my right ear and discolored cheek. The only problem: a strand of hair can't hide the fact that I'm ugly. I used to be pretty, but not anymore.

Death has a way of doing that to a person.

"Will you hurry? I need to get in there too!" My stepsister pounds on the bathroom door and rattles the doorknob as if that might make me quicker. It doesn't. In fact, I slow everything down....

"I'll be out when I'm out. Go away!" I hate her. Ever since my dad married her mom and they moved into *my* house I've hated her. I've never wanted to eat a person's brain more than I want to eat hers.

I look down at the metal band wrapped around my neck and give it a flick with my index finger. *Stupid compliance band.* I hate it too. I'm a teenager; I'm supposed to hate things. But above everything, even my stepsister Isabelle, I hate the band the worst. I'm hungry *all* the time and the stupid compliance band won't let me do a thing about it.

"*Mom!*" she yells. "Zia won't let me in the bathroom!"

I take a quick peek at myself in the mirror and release a frustrated breath. There's not much I can do to fix what I see, but I try anyway. I dab a bit of foundation over my gray skin and place a bit of red lipstick on my lips.

The red is too dark and looks like blood. I quickly grab a tissue and wipe it off. Kids at school would freak, but a part of me wants to wear it anyway. If I didn't know they'd turn up the voltage on my neckband, I totally would.

"Zia, darling?" My stepmother Judy coos at the door. "I'm giving you two more minutes and then its Isabelle's turn, okay?"

I have to give it to my stepmom. She tries. She tries a little too hard sometimes to keep the peace between Isabelle and me, but she's not so bad. She makes Dad happy and for that I'm grateful. After my mother left us when I was two years old, Dad deserved to find some happiness. And it just so happens that Judy is the gal for him. Too bad Isabelle was part of the package

"Sure," I call back. I'm actually done getting ready for school, but she's giving me two more minutes to make Isabelle wait, so I'm taking it. Anything to make her suffer.

Even though I don't like what I see in the mirror I know it could be a lot worse. I'm missing an ear and my left foot doesn't work like it used to, causing me to have to wear a brace and shuffle a little. Other zombies—yes, I know the politically-correct term is "living impaired" but I just call it what it is—have it far worse than I do. Some don't even have a leg at all and have to wear specially designed prosthetics. So my brace is just fine. I shouldn't complain.

But no matter what I do, brace, makeup, I'm still the girl who was killed in a freak boating accident and whose dad had a witch raise her from the dead with a bit of voodoo magic. I'm the girl everyone fears, even though I've never really eaten a brain before or bitten anyone for that matter. I'm rather harmless, especially with my neck cuff. Maybe without it I would be a crazy lunatic—could be interesting—but with it, I'm just like everyone else. Except I'm dead, in an undead kind of way.

"Time's up!" Isabelle jiggles the doorknob again. "My turn."

This time I unlock it and step aside. She pushes past me and wrinkles her nose. "Jeez, Zia. You smell."

I get that all the time. It comes with the territory of being dead. I still rot. I still decay. No one has quite figured out how to stop that process. I fear someday I will be nothing but a walking skeleton wearing a neck band. It sucks being me.

"I showered," I say.

"Did you use the special soap?" Isabelle runs the tap and dips her toothbrush into the cold stream of water.

"Of course."

"Well, you still stink. Maybe you should wear a car freshener around your neck." She sticks the toothbrush in her mouth.

I really don't like her, but I don't say anything. I grab a bottle of body spray from the top shelf and give myself a good squirt of its fruity freshness.

"Ahh! Now you just smell like rotting apples. You made it worse!"

I don't know what else to do. I can't cover the smell and I can't eat her either, so I do what I normally do and just walk away.

"The bus will be here any minute, girls! You need to hurry!" Judy calls from downstairs.

Yippee. I can't wait. I'm totally being sarcastic here.

I grab my backpack off my bed and slip it onto my shoulder. My shoulder cracks as it pops out of socket, but I don't feel a thing. The noise and the fact that I can't move my arm clue me in that something is wrong. Perhaps that's one good thing about being a zombie: I no longer feel pain, physical anyway. Emotional is a whole other matter that I try to suppress.

"Judy!" I yell. "I did it again."

Isabelle walks past my room and scowls at me while shaking her head. She doesn't stop to assist me. Heaven forbid she'd ever come to my rescue. She avoids me like the plague. She pretends I don't exist at school and has even gone so far as to tell me not to talk to her in public, ever. That's okay. She's not very interesting to talk to. Besides, I didn't talk to her before I died, so why in the world would I start now?

"Oh, goodness!" Judy steps beside me, removes my overstuffed backpack, and gives my arm a good tug and push. My shoulder snaps into place no worse than it was before. "There you are. Good as new." My ste-mother smiles and gives me a gentle hug.

I would have argued with her that my being "good as new" wasn't all that great, but I didn't. "Thanks. I appreciate it."

She pushes the hair from my face; she doesn't like the hanging strand, but I quickly rearrange it back into place. I have to hide the ear. Even I know a missing ear is disturbing.

"I want you have a wonderful day," she says. "Make some real friends. Smile at people. You have a beautiful smile and I'm sure if everyone can see how friendly you are, they'll climb all over one another to be your friend."

She gives me this same pep-talk at least once a week. I tried smiling. But there is a fine line between a zombie smile and a zombie who wants to eat your face. Most of my classmates don't like my smile. They cringe and move to other side of the hall — the usual reaction.

The bus sounds its horn and Judy gives me a gentle pat on my arm. "Your thermos is on the table by the door. Don't forget it."

How can I?

My raw ground-up animal meat, fresh fish guts, coagulated human blood, and "special vitamins made especially for zombies" all blended together in a nice thick warm shake. It's what I have for breakfast, lunch, and dinner. It's not all that bad, really. It at least staves off the hunger somewhat, though it never truly satisfies.

Judy makes it for me every day, changing up the meats for variety. Never once has she complained, but Isabelle and Dad did. They said the smell was awful and so now Judy makes it for me in the garage. And if I sip it through a straw in a hole in the top of the thermos, no one else can really smell it so I'm allowed to eat it at school and at family meals. But I have to make sure I brush my teeth right after. It makes for some gnarly bad breath. Worse than the normal undead breath.

I slip my backpack on once more using my other arm, and lumber down the stairs to catch the bus. I grab the thermos and follow after Isabelle, staying several feet behind her — her rule — which seems silly since everyone on the bus know we live in the same house and are related by marriage.

I'm not sure who she's trying to kid. I'm a zombie, for crying out loud. People tend to notice me.

I struggle to climb up the steps of the bus, which annoys the driver, but he never says anything. He just shakes his head and makes a face. It's a wonderful way to start off my school day.

No one says hi as I pass down the tight aisle to the back of the bus. This is usual and so it doesn't faze me anymore. I find my normal spot and sit down. Even though it's November I crack the window next to me—another rule.

I slump in my seat with my backpack on my lap and stare out the half-opened window. The next few bus stops are uneventful, but the third one, the one I look forward to, Gunner climbs aboard and makes his way down the aisle toward me.

Someone howls—such an old joke—and several other guys join in. Gunner is a lot better at this stuff than me and so he turns to the guys making fun of him. "You call that a howl? Maybe for a Chihuahua, but you have a long way to go to be a big dog. Who knows? Maybe with a little practice you can become a big dog someday, too."

Corbin, one of the football jocks, stands up. "You threatening me? Because you know what happens when you threaten a human, right?" Corbin pretends to be electrocuted and shakes all over as if that is the funniest thing ever. His cronies join in and shake all over too.

If it bothers Gunner, he doesn't show it. He watches their antics play out and when Corbin stops moving, Gunner just shrugs. "When I threaten you, you'll know it."

Before Corbin can say anything else, the bus driver yells to Gunner to move it to the back. He waves at the driver and continues down the aisle and slides in the seat beside me. Supposedly he smells too—like a wet dog, that's why he's banished to the back—but I don't smell a thing.

"How's it going?" he asks.

"It's going okay, I guess." I nod toward the jocks. "Doesn't that bother you?"

He shakes his head. "Nah, I've dealt with worse. A few idiots howling at me is no big deal. Try having someone come after you with a pitchfork or a torch. That tends to put things in perspective."

I nod. I guess it would. Besides being teased, no one has tried to destroy me, so I should consider myself lucky.

I notice the bands on his wrists. They're very similar to my neck band. Gunner has been a werewolf longer than I've been a zombie so it's understandable that his bands are worn and the silver tarnished. He told me that as long as he wears them, a full moon doesn't affect him like it used to. My band is made from the toughest titanium and is screwed right into the base of my neck, attaching to my brain stem. His are made from silver—for apparent reasons.

I'm pretty jealous of him, not to the point it has ruined our friendship, but jealous non-the-less. He's a pretty handsome guy, rugged and muscular, though I'd never think of him as anything more than a friend—we living impaired, or L.I.'s or short, don't mix, so we have been instructed. I'm jealous because he can still walk among the humans without being detected. If you didn't know him, or notice his bands, you'd mistake him for human.

I will never be mistaken for anything other than what I am. I can't hide the fact I'm undead.

We have one more stop before we reach the school, and this is my least favorite stop. This is where Willow gets on.

Sure enough, she climbs aboard, all dressed in her usual black garb. Today she even makes her presence worse by wearing dark sunglasses that cover her eyes and she's dyed her once golden hair completely black. Even her lips are painted the same dark color. There is no hint of anything but black on her anywhere, which only emphasizes her already pale features.

Even though she hides behind the black, she's still beautiful. Extremely so. I'm pretty jealous of her, too.

We used to be best friends, back before she changed and way before my accident. But now, she won't even look at me. I suppose that is my fault. When she was fifteen and was bit and changed to a blood sucker, my father did what parents who are afraid for their children tend to do: he prohibited me from ever hanging around with her again. He didn't even give me a chance to explain my sudden disappearance from her life. I was just forced to stop taking her calls.

Karma has a real funny way of making you pay for being unkind. Look at me. I'm a zombie. The lowliest monster of them all. My own friends—Becky, Amy, and Danielle—no longer have anything to do with me. Just thinking of them turns my attention to the front of the bus. Becky is hanging all over Tyler. He looks like he's enjoying the attention and my own non-beating heart breaks a little more. Rumor has it that my ex-best friend and my ex-boyfriend are going steady. But as I watch them together, it looks as though the rumors aren't rumors at all.

I look back to Willow. No one teases her. She's lucky that way. I think a lot of it has to do with her striking beauty. Everyone can see it despite her attempts to hide it under all that black.

She's trying to hide her beauty; I'm trying to hide my ugly.

We have a lot in common. If only she'd acknowledge me, but she never does. She walks to the back of the bus, not because she smells, which she doesn't, but because that's where all the L.I.'s have to sit, and she slides onto a bench opposite of mine. She doesn't say anything, not to anybody, and she pulls her dark hood up over her head and stares out the window.

Her bands are different from mine and Gunner's. Her bands are decorated with little crosses all the way around. I can see that her pale wrists are red and raw because of them. They burn her skin, much how the silver bands affect Gunner. Besides being a pain in the butt, mine only annoys me. But then again, maybe mine does cause a similar reaction and I just can't feel it.

I feel sorry for the both of them because I can't imagine wearing something that always hurts. But I'd rather wear a cuff that hurt me than be me. That's for sure.

I'd be a vampire or a werewolf over being a zombie any day.

I just wish someone had thought to ask me before dooming me to this kind of existence.

MORE FROM EVOLVED PUBLISHING

CHILDREN'S PICTURE BOOKS

THE BIRD BRAIN BOOKS by Emlyn Chand:
Courtney Saves Christmas
Davey the Detective
Honey the Hero
Izzy the Inventor
Larry the Lonely
Poppy the Proud
Ricky the Runt
Sammy Steals the Show
Tommy Goes Trick-or-Treating
Vicky Finds a Valentine

Silent Words by Chantal Fournier

Thomas and the Tiger-Turtle by Jonathan Gould

EMLYN AND THE GREMLIN by Steff F. Kneff:
Emlyn and the Gremlin
Emlyn and the Gremlin and the Barbeque Disaster
Emlyn and the Gremlin and the Mean Old Cat

I'd Rather Be Riding My Bike by Eric Pinder

VALENTINA'S SPOOKY ADVENTURES by Majanka Verstraete:
Valentina and the Haunted Mansion
Valentina and the Masked Mummy
Valentina and the Whackadoodle Witch

HISTORICAL FICTION

Circles by Ruby Standing Deer
Spirals by Ruby Standing Deer
Stones by Ruby Standing Deer

LITERARY FICTION

Torn Together by Emlyn Chand
Carry Me Away by Robb Grindstaff
Hannah's Voice by Robb Grindstaff
Turning Trixie by Robb Grindstaff
The Daughter of the Sea and the Sky by David Litwack
The Lone Wolf by E.D. Martin
Jellicle Girl by Stevie Mikayne
Weight of Earth by Stevie Mikayne
Desert Flower by Angela Scott
Desert Rice by Angela Scott
White Chalk by Pavarti K. Tyler

LOWER GRADE (Chapter Books)

TALES FROM UPON A. TIME by Falcon Storm
Natalie the Not-So-Nasty
The Perils of Petunia
The Persnickety Princess

WEIRDVILLE by Majanka Verstraete
Drowning in Fear
Fright Train
Grave Error
House of Horrors
The Clumsy Magician
The Doll Maker

MEMOIR

And Then It Rained: Lessons for Life by Megan Morrison

MIDDLE GRADE

NOAH ZARC by D. Robert Pease:
Cataclysm (Book 2)
Declaration (Book 3)
Mammoth Trouble (Book 1)
Omnibus (Special 3-in-1 Edition)

MYSTERY / CRIME / DETECTIVE

Hot Sinatra by Axel Howerton

SCI-FI / FANTASY

Eulogy by D.T. Conklin
Shadow Swarm by D. Robert Pease
Two Moons of Sera by Pavarti K. Tyler

SHORT STORY ANTHOLOGIES

FROM THE EDITORS AT EVOLVED PUBLISHING:
Evolution: Vol. 1 (A Short Story Collection)
Evolution: Vol. 2 (A Short Story Collection)

All Tolkien No Action: Swords, Sorcery & Sci-Fi by Eric Pinder

SUSPENSE / THRILLER

Forgive Me, Alex by Lane Diamond
The Devil's Bane by Lane Diamond
Whispers of the Dead by C.L. Roberts-Huth
Whispers of the Serpent by C.L. Roberts-Huth

YOUNG ADULT

Farsighted by Emlyn Chand
Open Heart by Emlyn Chand
The Silver Sphere by Michael Dadich
The Sinister Kin by Michael Dadich
THE DARLA DECKER DIARIES by Jessica McHugh
Darla Decker Hates to Wait (Book 1)
Darla Decker Shakes the State (Book 3)
Darla Decker Takes the Cake (Book 2)

JOEY COLA by D. Robert Pease:
Cleopatra Rising (Book 2)
Dream Warriors (Book 1)
Third Reality (Book 3)
Anyone? by Angela Scott

THE ZOMBIE WEST TRILOGY by Angela Scott
Dead Plains (Zombie West #3)
Survivor Roundup (Zombie West #2)
The Zombie West Trilogy – Special Omnibus Edition
Wanted: Dead or Undead (Zombie West #1)

CPSIA information can be obtained
at www.ICGtesting.com
Printed in the USA
FSOW02n1511300717
36833FS